MIDSUMMER NIGHT

Books by Freda Warrington

AETHERIAL TALES
*Elfland**
*Midsummer Night**
*Grail of the Summer Stars** *(forthcoming)*

THE BLACKBIRD SERIES
Book 1: *A Blackbird in Silver*
Book 2: *A Blackbird in Darkness*
Book 3: *A Blackbird in Amber*
Book 4: *A Blackbird in Twilight*

THE BLOOD WINE SEQUENCE
Book 1: *A Taste of Blood Wine*
Book 2: *A Dance in Blood Velvet*
Book 3: *The Dark Blood of Poppies*

Sorrow's Light
Dark Cathedral
Pagan Moon
Dracula the Undead
The Rainbow Gate
Darker Than the Storm
The Court of the Midnight King

THE JEWELFIRE TRILOGY
Book 1: *The Amber Citadel*
Book 2: *The Sapphire Throne*
Book 3: *The Obsidian Tower*

*A Tor Book

Freda Warrington

MIDJUMMER
NIGHT

TOR®

A Tom Doherty Associates Book
New York

MIDSUMMER NIGHT

Copyright © 2010 by Freda Warrington

Edited by James Frenkel

A Tor Book
Published by Tom Doherty Associates, LLC
175 Fifth Avenue
New York, NY 10010

www.tor-forge.com

3 9547 00350 4896

Tor® is a registered trademark of Tom Doherty Associates, LLC.

ISBN 978-0-7653-1870-1

First Edition: November 2010

Printed in the United States of America

0 9 8 7 6 5 4 3 2 1

For Mike

MIDSUMMER NIGHT

Prelude

The Night of the Dunkelmen

It was all I could do to stifle my laughter. The forest at night was frightening, but the longer we hid in delicious terror, the funnier it seemed. I was sixteen, not too old for lying in wait to play a prank. My sister Melody shot me a glance from beneath her hood. She and Adam were almost invisible in the darkness but for their shining eyes. The trees around us were full of rustling secrets.

Uncle John was some yards away, adjusting the big, unwieldy plate camera on its tripod. Although he'd turned the lantern low and tried to make a screen of branches around him, he blundered like a carthorse in the undergrowth. We could hear his fast, anxious breathing. When he lifted the lamp to make a last check, it swung wildly, throwing ghostly shadows between the trunks. Surely if the Faerie Folk, the Dubh Sidhe, *were real, they would have fled from his clumsiness.*

I clamped a hand over my mouth, laughter almost spilling out. Melody put a fingertip to her lips, but I saw the mischief in her eyes. For all she'd resisted this enterprise, behind her prim mask of disapproval lay excitement, a streak of nastiness. I thrilled to see it.

And Adam, my beloved brother—his shoulders shook, his eyes sparkled. For those moments, he was a boy again. I saw the gleam of his teeth. It was the first time I had seen him smile since he came home from the War. Oh, the sheer silliness of the prank was worth it, then, just to see him smile.

Uncle John waited beside his camera. He became feverishly quiet, betraying himself by the occasional crackle of leaf mould beneath his boot.

"Now," I whispered.

Adam breathed a hollow whistle between his thumbs. An owl's call.

I brought a little string of Indian bells from my sleeve and gave them the faintest shiver.

Uncle John's head jerked up. We heard him gasp.

"Now," I repeated, giving Melody a push. She uncovered the lantern she was carrying, just enough that its light glimmered through green glass and lace to slide in elusive dapples over the forest floor.

This was it. Our game was in motion. We began to spread out, taking care to stay beyond the reach of Uncle John's dim lamp. Adam pulled his hooded cloak (made of curtains) around him and it occurred to me that we resembled medieval monks more than faeries; but the effect, in the flickering darkness, was eerie.

"I know you're there," said John. His voice was strained and breathy with excitement. I nearly wept with the effort of swallowing giggles. Our uncle's face, lit from below, became a map of fear and hope. "Please, show yourselves. I—I won't harm you."

I let the bells shiver again, echoing the sound with a faint laugh. Uncle John was now in a fair ecstasy of panic, fumbling with equipment—but he had too much, for he was trying to wield a hand-held box camera, too, and of course he would capture nothing until he could ignite the magnesium flash.

I heard Adam's delighted whisper, "I can't believe the old fool's falling for it!"

Emboldened, we circled him. We were everywhere at once. A spark of light here, a shiver of bells there. John's head whipped this way and that, trying to catch us out, not knowing which way to point a lens. This is wonderful, I thought. Let the silly devil have his photograph. Let him develop it, and find his nephew and nieces grinning back at him! What a perfect lark!

John was intent on the two shadowy forms before him—Adam and Melody—while I circled behind him and now began to creep forward until I was almost at my uncle's shoulder. I couldn't resist it.

He was murmuring to himself, as if to a skittish animal, "That's it . . . my fair ones, don't go yet. There's nothing to fear. Just a bright light for a second . . . oh my god, oh my god, yes, just another few moments . . . it's only a light, it won't harm you . . . let me have this one little proof that you are real. Now . . ."

"You know we're real," I said into his ear, and clutched his shoulder.

Uncle John jerked and yelled in shock. The magnesium flash ignited, bleaching night into day; and in that split second I saw, not only Adam and Melody, but a dozen other figures between the trees.

At the same instant, my uncle spun to face me, his face horrible, eyes white-ringed. Then I was blinded. There were lights and shadows everywhere, images on my shocked retinas. The joke was over. We entered a nightmare.

John was gasping, "The Dunkelmen. *Oh no, no," and then my sight cleared enough to see that he was staring straight past me, transfixed by something that loomed behind Adam . . .*

Adam turned, and saw it too. An enveloping cloak, as inky as the shadows around it. The hint of a face, a cheekbone, a glaring eye . . . ghostly, reptilian. Not human. Not human.

"Run, Adam, you fool," John wheezed.

I heard Melody scream. The ground seemed to tilt; Uncle John fell away from me like a stage prop; the whole forest thrashed and trembled with the thunder of hooves, the gleam of dark horns. That was all I could see in the darkness. I was running to help Adam, staggering between the entangling trees, deafened by the sea-roar of the wind, by Adam's hoarse, despairing cries.

    I couldn't find him. We were lost in a storm of whirling shadows . . . I shudder still to think that that was the last Adam knew, that no matter how hard he ran, the Dunkelmen *were there behind him—pursuing him as they pursued us all—reaching out cold fingers to tangle in his hair.*

—from Corah's scrapbook

1

Cairndonan

Arrival. Stumbling out of a taxi, catching her balance on her painful leg, looking up at a gatehouse: a neat structure of mushroom stone with pointed gables and black window frames. A long driveway curved away beyond wrought-iron gates, but Gill could see nothing of the great house itself, only a wisp of smoke drifting up behind a green haze of conifers. The estate was fringed by woodland and softened by drizzle misting from a bleak grey sky. Inland stood the sweeping shapes of mountains, all in slate hues in the chilly gloom of the day. She could smell the sea. It was May, but felt like winter. The highland landscape looked barren, wild, hostile; nothing had prepared her for the physical rawness of it.

Gill wondered what she was doing here.

"Rotten weather for you, miss," said the taxi driver, a Sikh with a broad Glaswegian accent. He dumped her case beside her. "Sure you don't want me to take you up to the house?"

"No, it's fine," she said, startled out of her blank moment. "They said I'd be met at the gatehouse."

She paid her fare. It was a sum that might have made the locals blanch, but she was used to London prices and thought nothing of it. As she fumbled in her purse, a small shock whipped across her stomach. Nothing waited for her in London.

With a cheery salute he drove away, leaving Gill alone on the drive. She spotted a distant church spire, but there was no other hint of habitation, only woods, heather and forest, and a silver rim of ocean to her left. That seaweed scent, mixed with the tang of gorse on a sharp breeze, was exhilarating. Several hundred miles from London on the northwest coast of Scotland—and not a soul knew where she'd gone.

I made it, I've escaped, she thought. Her hand convulsed on the handle of her case as the wind took her breath away.

The door of the gatehouse opened and a tall, thirtyish man with scruffy blond hair came strolling out to her. He had stubble and ripped jeans, a lazy, confident swagger, and a shrewd, unfriendly gaze. He wasn't local, she realized as he spoke; his voice had an antipodean twang.

"Hello, there. I hope you're not from the tax office. No one goes in without an appointment and you lot are really pushing your luck."

She frowned. "I've rented a cottage."

"Oh yeah? Think you can trick your way in? That's new."

"No, really." She pulled her booking confirmation from the front pocket of her suitcase. "I'm here on holiday. Gill Sharma."

He glanced at it, gave a quirky, one-sided smile. "Oh. Miss Sharma. Robin Cottage. Right. Sorry, just checking. You look like you're on a mission, and that case could have been full of documents, you know?" The blue eyes came to life and his voice became friendly and teasing—or was it mocking? Her judgment on such nuances had never been great. Because she'd traveled first-class on the train, she'd dressed appropriately, as if for work; a charcoal-grey suit with pencil skirt, black tights, no-nonsense shoes with a medium heel. Her outdoor jacket was stuffed inside the wheeled case. Her hair was tied back and her narrow, black-framed glasses were businesslike. She felt exhausted and rumpled but, apparently, still looked smart enough to be mistaken for a tax inspector.

"Am I in the right place?"

"You certainly are, Miss Sharma. Hi, I'm Colin, apprentice genius and general dogsbody. You've booked Robin Cottage for six weeks. So, no car."

She shook her head, opening one hand to emphasise the self-evident fact that she was on foot. Colin raised an eyebrow. "Come on, jump on the buggy and I'll take you over there. Welcome to Cairndonan."

He let her through a side gate beside the wrought-iron main gates and flung her bag onto a golf cart that was parked just inside. As she climbed up beside him, her hip joint zinged with pain and she gasped. It would sometimes catch her like that, a stab of fire, so sharp that she couldn't hide her reaction.

"You all right?" Colin asked cheerily.

"Fine," she said through her teeth. "I'm getting over an accident. It seizes up sometimes."

"Wow, that's not good."

Stiffening her face to a mask of calm, Gill pretended the heavy throb of her leg belonged to someone else. She watched the landscape sliding past; deer grazing the rough parkland, distant hills reaching steep arms towards the sea. She waited for a glimpse of Cairndonan House but it remained hidden behind folds of land and forest.

Colin swung onto an unexpected right fork. The buggy began shuddering its way along a narrow track with a meadow on the right and thickly tangled woodland on the left. Gill swallowed a twinge of unease. "Don't I need to check in at reception, or something?"

He smirked. "We don't have anything as grand as reception. Just an office and three slaves; me, Flora and Ned Badger. You can drop into the office later. Get settled in first, eh?"

They were descending a slope, steep enough to make her hang on to her seat. She heard the music of running water. As they passed into the damp shadows of a wood, she saw a stream ahead, running between the rugged sides of a gorge. Trees grew out of the rock itself to form a lacy tunnel above the flow. This was as isolated as she could have dreamed.

"And where's the office?"

"Up in the big house. There's a footpath up through the woods, about half a mile. Hope you brought your walking boots."

"I did," she said. The smell of the stream reached her, a fresh scent of wet rock and leaf mold. In response to all the damp and cold, her leg began to ache fiercely. 'Not that walking is my strong point at the moment."

"So, you're not booked on the course, then?" he asked.

Puzzled, she hesitated. "No. There's a course?"

"Oh, yeah." He inclined his head over his shoulder, as if to indicate the unseen mansion. "Annual art school. Three weeks. Starts today, goes until the fourteenth of June. You know who the owner of Cairndonan Estate is, don't you?"

Gill felt a twinge of dismay. An art course meant people, when all she wanted was solitude. She should have realized, or at least read the website more carefully. "Dame Juliana Flagg," she answered quietly. "I didn't see anything about it when I made the booking."

"Well, you wouldn't. She doesn't need to advertise. You know she's mega-famous, don't you? She's a living bloody legend!"

"So I gather, but I'm not really into art."

"That's a shame." He sounded disappointed that she wasn't more impressed. "That's a bit like visiting Buckingham Palace and saying you can take or leave the Queen."

Gill bit her lip, annoyed but forcing herself to smile. "I'm sure Dame Juliana would rather not rent cottages to gawping fans."

"Fair point," he said, drumming his fingers on the steering wheel. "Have to admit, I'm a fan. I'm her student. I work for her—odd jobs, estate maintenance, studio help—and in return, I get a few precious hours of tuition. That's the deal."

"Sounds like a tough apprenticeship."

"She doesn't take any prisoners," said Colin, with a grimace.

"You don't look like an artist."

"Well, what's an artist supposed to look like? I'm a sculptor, big-scale. You need a bit of muscle for that. Never had a chance to go to art school; what you see is raw talent." He grinned; she rolled her eyes at the way he managed to be self-mocking yet full of himself at the same time. "Bet you can't guess where I'm from."

"New Zealand?" she said.

Colin looked impressed. "Spot on. People usually say South Africa, or Australia."

"And I suppose they ask if you got the muscles from sheep-shearing?"

"Always. That gets a bit old. So what's your story, then? Up from London, aren't you? Long journey."

"Endless," she sighed. "My story is that I'm knackered, and dying for some peace and quiet."

"Sure. Don't mind me, I'm just nosy." The path meandered downhill until it reached a stone bridge. The golf cart negotiated the span, the torrent swirling over rocks beneath. Turning left, fifty yards along a gravel track that ran along the far bank they came to a tiny cottage. A tall rock face rose behind it, seeming to shelter and cup the building. All over the rocks and around the cottage itself grew gnarled trees, briars and ivy.

Gill took this in only superficially because she saw someone there; a skinny man, wearing faded black trousers and jacket, who seemed to be fixing something on the front door. She tensed. "Who's that?"

"No worries," Colin said dismissively. "That's Ned Badger."

"What's he doing?"

"Lord knows. Nothing I couldn't have done, I'm sure. Here we are, Robin Cottage. Mobile phone reception is poor to nonexistent, by the way."

As he pulled up, the man turned to them, holding a screwdriver in one hand. He had thick black hair streaked with grey and a pallid, expressionless face. It seemed he'd been attaching a horseshoe to the door; then she realized the horseshoe was actually a door knocker.

"Here's our guest," said Colin, helping her down before hefting her case. "Miss Sharma, this is Ned; one or the other of us will come if you have any problems."

"Problems?" she said stiffly. She wanted them both to go. Colin made her uneasy, and Ned Badger's Dickensian seediness gave her chills.

"Yeah, with plumbing, electric, anything at all."

"There will be no problems," Ned said impassively. "I've checked everything and made repairs where needed."

"Great, well I can take over from here. You want a lift back, mate?"

The friction between the two men was tangible. "No," said Ned. "I'll walk."

"All set, then," said Colin to Gill. "Here's the key; if you need another, you can get it from the house."

"One key is fine," she said, and then felt a flash of panic. Great, the staff knew she was on her own, and they had other keys. She pushed the fear back into its box.

She willed Colin to leave, but he insisted on letting her in, taking her case upstairs, then striding around jovially showing her light switches, kettle, teabags, all things she could have found without help. "Flora will pop in to vacuum, dust, change bed linen and that. But if you need anything at all, just come up to the house and we'll help you out, okay? In fact, if you're lonely, you can come up of an evening for a glass of wine with the students. Dame Juliana won't mind."

His easy friendliness was sandpaper on her nerves. She was shooing him out of the cottage now, almost physically pushing him with the front door. Ned Badger had already gone, disturbingly, as if he'd simply melted into the air. "Thanks, Colin, but I wouldn't want to presume on her hospitality."

"She can be a diva," he said confidingly, "but underneath, she's sound."

"Just worried about tax inspectors?" she said dryly.

He grimaced. "That was a joke."

"Oh. Thanks, but I'll be fine."

"See you tomorrow, then," Colin said cheerfully, and she closed the door behind him, locked it, rested back against it with a long sigh. Alone at last.

Robin Cottage was tiny and old-fashioned. There was a small parlor with a flowery sofa, a fireplace fitted with a glass-fronted log-burning stove, a television. At the back was a small, basic kitchen with a back door leading to a yard. There was no garden, just few flagstones, a brick outhouse, and then the sheer wall of rock rising up until it was lost in a cloud of greenery.

The rock barrier gave her a sense of security, and the doors were sturdy, with big solid bolts. Gill stood in the center of the small front room, imagined herself truly safe and hidden within the stone walls. She allowed herself to test her feelings.

Safe. No one knew where she was. No one could torment her anymore.

All that was over now.

She looked out of the front window at a veil of tall ashes, poplars and sycamores on the far bank of the stream. They swayed, the spring green of their leaves vivid against the rainy sky. This moment was all she'd thought of for weeks but she had never considered the reality of how she would get through the minutes of the hours of the days with absolutely nothing to do, no goals, nothing but a receding tunnel of images that she couldn't escape.

The idea that Ned Badger had been inside, "checking things" just before she arrived, made her feel unaccountably violated. He had a key, he could let himself in any time he liked . . .

Suddenly she began to quake. The feeling came up from deep inside her, like an earth tremor. She felt no emotion, no fear, no anger, nothing, just a wide-open numb shock that seemed to shake the world.

No sooner here, than she wanted to leave. Really, to fling open the front door and run as fast as her legs could carry her—at that thought, she grinned sourly. And flee to where, exactly? The panic had no possible resolution. It would come with her wherever she went, like a cloud of angry wasps.

From long practise, she ignored the impulse. Instead she climbed the narrow twist of stairs. The first step made her thigh zing with pain, but she kept going. It was going to be even more fun coming down.

There was one bedroom, almost filled by a double bed with a puffy white duvet. An old oak wardrobe and dresser leaned towards each other on uneven floorboards. What must once have been a second bedroom had been converted to a bathroom with a white suite. It was plain but clean, with blue towels and a selection of soaps and shower gels in a flowery china dish. It was all she needed. It was fine.

I'm safe and I'm staying, Gill told herself.

The first thing she unpacked was her toiletries bag, stacking bottles into a mirrored cabinet. As she closed the cabinet door, her reflection slid into view and she grimaced. The tracery of worry lines and the black-framed glasses made her look severe. She didn't actually need the glasses; they were camouflage she'd worn for work, to affect a demeanor of unapproachable efficiency. They, and the charcoal suit, had been a sort of armor she'd gotten into the habit of wearing, but—strange to realize it—she didn't need them anymore.

As an office worker, she'd always felt a fraud. Her true self was an athlete—but she wasn't even that anymore.

With the glasses off, her face looked naked and vulnerable. Her dark brown eyes were haunted, and her skin had more the look of tepid coffee than the dusky glow on which she'd sometimes been complimented. Her complexion came from her Indian father, as did her good bone structure and kohl-lashed dark eyes. Since the accident, though, all she could see was the pale and harassed English half of herself.

Gill pulled the ponytail band out of her hair, letting the blue-black waves slide over her shoulders as she leaned down to turn on the bath taps. Steam rose around her as she discarded her clothes. The body underneath, which once had been honed and athletic, was now merely thin; wasted from long weeks in the hospital, tracked with scars. She tried not to look, tried to ignore the familiar feeling of disappointment.

Suddenly she felt like someone who'd been dropped onto a strange planet, or who'd crawled up a deserted beach with amnesia. The past was a mangled mess that she'd left behind. Present and future were a clean, clear blank.

She ran water into a tooth mug and took her medication; one anti-depressant, two painkillers.

Juliana Flagg released the catches and let the bulky, oblong lid of the kiln rise from the sand bed below. It was a serious piece of equipment, designed to heat a huge slab of glass to the consistency of soft toffee until it slumped over a pre-made form. Residual warmth radiated from the interior. Even in her mid-sixties—*my immense age*, she thought wryly—she loved the hard physical work of sculpture, the heavy stuff that really made the muscles ache, the furnace heat, the fountains of light from her arc-welding torch or the scream of a chainsaw on seasoned oak.

At this stage, the raw glass looked a mess, like an amorphous mass spewed from a volcano. She rubbed sand away from one rounded edge and saw the greenish translucence beneath, rough and cloudy with bubbles. Promising . . .

"Hey, don't even try to take that out on your own, Dame J," said Colin, slipping in through the big double doors of the foundry. "That's what I'm here for."

Ned Badger followed him, a slip of darkness. Their antagonism, their competition for her attention, amused her; but it was their own affair. She let them get on with it.

"I'm not taking it out," she said crisply. "It's annealing. Did that woman arrive for Robin Cottage?"

"Yes," Ned began. His slightly husky local accent was drowned by Colin speaking over him.

"She sure did. I nearly sent her packing. I thought she was from the bloody tax office!"

"Colin, for heaven's sake. You didn't say that to her, did you?"

"No, no. Just had to double check before I let her in."

"Thanks for the loyalty, but I hope you weren't too rude. You sorted her out, I take it?"

"Yeah, no problems, Dame J, but you know, she got me wondering."

Juliana didn't respond, to indicate her lack of interest in gossipy details.

"Mm, almost like she was in disguise, you know? I reckon I know who she is, though."

"Really," Ned said under his breath. He frequently managed to dismiss Colin with all the exquisite subtlety of a royal butler; too subtle for Colin to notice, unfortunately. He was too pleased with his own detective work.

"Yeah. She was wearing a seriously sexy pair of glasses, but behind them she was the spitting image of a long-distance runner—remember, that Brit who won silver at the last Commonwealth Games? What was her name?"

"I don't follow athletics." Juliana was only half-listening to Colin's chatter. Her attention was still taken by the raw glass. No two pieces were ever the same. Each had its own personality, its own power. And did this have any merit? It had a one in three chance; it might have the right feel, or it might have a dark, skewed energy, or it might have nothing at all. Once doubt set in about a piece, she was ruthless.

"Gillian Shaw, that's it. This woman's name is Gill Sharma. Too close to be coincidence, I reckon."

Juliana turned her gaze to Colin, silencing with the frigid light of her eyes. "So? Your point is?"

"Nothing." He shrugged, deflated. "Just be interesting if it was her, that's all."

"No, it wouldn't. It would be an idle scrap of gossip. Cease."

"Sorry, Dame J." Colin came to inspect the cooling mass. "Looking good."

He gave a sort of wink as he said it, so it wasn't clear whether he meant the glass slab, or her. She ran a sweaty hand over her hair and gave an imperious sniff, dismissing the notion. "No, it isn't. Destroy it."

Colin stared at her in despair. "Oh, come on. Not another one."

Ned, too, gave her a narrow look, but said quietly, "If Dame Juliana is not happy, her judgment is all that matters."

"It's not good enough," she said.

"It looks bloody fine to me."

A dark impulse seized her, woken by Colin's witless remarks, by the prospect of eager students thirsty for her wisdom when she hardly trusted her own gifts anymore, by—everything. She grabbed the slab and dragged it to the edge of the bed until it tipped and fell, cracking into three neat pieces on the concrete floor. Colin flailed in a comical panic, jumping back as he failed to stop her. "Christ, Dame J! After all that work!"

She exhaled, gathering herself as the dark mood subsided. Ned Badger watched her with a narrow, calculating gaze; Colin stared, shaking his head. At least he wasn't afraid to stand up to her. For all his cheek infuriated her at times, she liked him for that.

"You know, Colin," she said coolly, "until you stop being afraid to scrap any work that isn't absolutely perfect, you will never be an artist. You will only ever be a technician."

"That's below the belt," he murmured, leaning down to lift the first broken piece. "Maybe you're the one who needs to loosen up and let a bit of imperfection through."

He doesn't understand, she thought grimly.

As Colin carried the pieces away and Ned swept up glass splinters, Juliana walked into the great shadowy space beyond the furnace room, a bigger workroom that contained her unfinished masterwork, *Midsummer Night*. Shapes loomed in semidarkness, lightly brushed by red furnace-fire. She wondered if she should destroy them, too. These pieces were all part of a large group that had consumed all her energy for fifteen years and still she dared not exhibit, let alone sell the work.

At the heart of the group was a single statue, some seven feet in height. In snow-white marble it portrayed the life-size torso and head of a woodland god, emerging from the twisting grip of a tree trunk. Its title was *Winter Came to the Wood*; she thought of it simply as *Winter*. Its face gazed down benignly on her as she raised a hand to trace the marble cheekbone. Strange, the way it had seemed to emerge fully formed from the block, as if she'd not so much created as discovered it. Beautiful young gods were not her normal style.

"When are you going to come to life, *Winter*, like in the stories?" she said dryly. "If only you could speak, what would you tell me about all this?"

Gill opened her eyes to a silver dawn. She had survived the night. She felt limp, sweaty, relieved. The pills had knocked her out and she'd woken only once with the nightmare that had haunted her in hospital. That familiar, horrible panic of not knowing where she was, but finding herself aware of a *presence* waiting in the shadows, breathing, watching her . . . And the second stage, dreaming she was awake and running through a series of strange rooms, securing dozens of doors and windows but always finding another that was open, or unlocked.

A dart of fear compelled her to get up and reassure herself for real. The floorboards were rough under her bare feet and the cold made her leg ache. Gill pulled on her dressing gown and slippers, carefully eased herself downstairs. There she found the cottage secure, serene, ordinary; no one had broken in. Of course they hadn't.

There was a term for it. Post-traumatic stress disorder. She knew that, but it made her night terrors no less real. In the kitchen, she boiled the kettle and soothed her dry mouth with tea.

I'm fine. I'm safe, she told herself. Cradling her mug, she looked out of the front window at the swaying trees and the stream, all the soft shades of green and muddy brown. *No one can find me and why would they want to? I'm old news. It's over. Over. Now what the hell am I going to do? Why did I come here? I feel like Alice falling down the rabbit hole. No, I don't, I'm fine.*

Go for a run; that was what she used to do first thing, whether she was in training for a race or not. Knowing she couldn't partake of that most natural activity was unbearable.

"At least I can still walk," she said out loud. "Even if it hurts like hell. It could've been so much worse." She had to keep telling herself that. "Food, that's what I need." The basics had been left in the kitchen for her, bread, butter and milk, but Gill knew she would need to shop. Finding a local store would give her a something to do. A goal.

A shower, toast and more tea. Feeling calmer, dressed now in jeans, sweatshirt and walking boots, she stepped outside. Late spring was capricious this far north, and the day was cool enough for a mist to have risen from the ground. Gill breathed fresh air that was saturated with damp scents of earth and vegetation, and wondered which way to go. Left would lead to the bridge and the track along which Colin had brought her. So she turned right, hoping to find a path to Cairndonan village.

The issue of keys niggled at her as she walked along the high stream bank, the water below rushing over tilted rock masses on its way to the sea. Her hip caught with every step, making her gasp until she schooled herself to ignore it. The wooded glen around her was beautifully lush and green but eerily deserted. Why had she expected isolation to make her feel safe? Anything could happen here . . . she pushed the thoughts away.

Farther along, the path turned onto a wooden footbridge across the stream. On the far side it meandered up a wooded slope. Gill followed it, noticing the silence—no, not silence, since the air swelled with birdsong. Lack of traffic noise, that was it; strange and startling after her journey. And the eerie cries of seabirds.

Something came surging through the trees. Shock froze her in an unreal, parallel world for a moment; then she recognized the crashing shadow as a red deer stag, as startled by her as she was by him. He veered and went on his way, leaving her to laugh shakily at her own shredded nerves.

Gill pushed up through the trees for ten minutes until they gave onto a semi-wild garden. Suddenly the house loomed in the cloudy atmosphere. It was a construction of grey stone with pointed gables, the walls softened in places by clouds of roses and vines. Saturated in eighteenth-century wealth and ostentation, Cairndonan House was worthy of being called a mansion. Softened by mist, it appeared to wander indefinitely into the tangled gardens around it.

Feeling self-conscious, Gill followed the path across a lawn and along the front of the house. She walked past bay windows veiling grand, dark rooms, caught glimpses of paintings and statues inside. With a start she realized there were people in there too, who must clearly be able to see her staring in at them.

A woman turned to stare back, her face a small white heart looking out of the shadows. Gill quickly looked away.

The entrance had a broad porch, with a set of wooden double doors standing open and another set of glass-paneled doors inside. So this was it; Cairndonan House, the seat of Dame Juliana Flagg. Gill steeled herself, and went in.

The first thing she saw, on a half-landing at the turn of a double flight of stairs, was a wall entirely filled by a massive stained-glass window. The flood of color arrested her. The image was of a beautiful young man with dark red hair, standing over a fallen figure as if in grief. The young man's hair hung down in heavy skeins, so textured and detailed it was almost sculptural. There was a quiver of arrows on his shoulder, a bow limp in his hand; so it appeared he had shot his fallen friend, who lay in a pool of ink-black hair and red blood. The colors were mostly ivory, russet and blood red. The scene held her for several seconds before she looked around.

The hallway was otherwise somber, with dark paneling and a black and white chequered marble floor. There were various doors, and a couple of corridors leading off the rear of the hallway. She heard soft voices, but no one came out to her.

She took the nearest passageway, which ran past a couple of bright, empty art studios, until she found herself at the rear of the house, looking through a glass door into an enormous conservatory. She'd read a little about Cairndonan Estate and realized that this was the famed Camellia House, built in seventeen-something to house exotic plant species from all over the world.

Amid ferns and palms, she saw a dozen students of various ages, sketching at easels. They all looked rapt, busy and contented, except for one pair of women who were deep in conversation beside an easel. Gill chewed her lip, feeling strange. Almost envious. How would it feel to be part of such a group, to *want* to be part of it?

She saw from the easels nearest to her that they were sketching a nude male. Her eye was drawn to the center, to a naked young man lying on a couch, languishing on a carefully rumpled white sheet. He was facing towards her. Suddenly he caught her eye and in the same moment she realized it was Colin. He grinned, entirely unembarrassed. She dropped her gaze, not before she'd seen far too much and noticed that he was quite hairy, arms and legs fuzzed with pale ginger-blond hairs.

"Can I help you?" said a voice behind her.

Her heart nearly stopped. She turned to see a short, upright, fiftyish woman, with tawny hair swept up on her head in a lacquered wedge shape. She wore a grey suit with a knee-length skirt and fitted jacket, making her look not unlike a small sergeant major in dress uniform.

"I was looking for the office. I'm staying in Robin Cottage."

"You've overshot the office by miles. I'm Flora, Dame Juliana's assistant." The woman gave a tight smile and firmly shepherded her along the corridor back to the entrance hall. Her Scottish accent was soft and precise. "How can I help you? Is everything all right?"

"It's fine." Gill smiled, finding that she still remembered how to be friendly and civil. "Only I wondered how many keys there are."

"I can let you have a spare," Flora said grudgingly.

Gill nodded and smiled even more. "Thank you, but I'd like them all, if you don't mind."

Flora drew back her head until her small chin almost vanished into her neck. Her features were delicate, rosy-pale; a once-pretty face made severe by stress lines. "What for? I don't think I can lay hands on them all. How are we going to get in?"

"What do you want to get in for?" Gill gasped.

Flora looked puzzled. "Housekeeping, of course. It will be either me or Ned."

"No. There's no need. I'll clean it myself. I thought self-catering meant exactly that! I'd rather not have people able to come freely in and out while I'm staying there."

"But we're providing your clean towels and linen, and what about maintenance, or even emergencies?" The more Flora huffed and argued, the more murderous Gill began to feel behind her cheerful mask.

Behind them, there were voices and footsteps in the passage and two sixtyish women appeared in full sail, their argument immediately drowning Gill's exchange with Flora. If Gill had already claimed her keys, she would have seized the chance to sneak out. As it was, she refused to leave empty-handed and so she stood her ground, while Flora hovered, tight-lipped.

"Did you read the curriculum?" one woman was saying. "Or did you stick a pin in a list of activity holidays?" The one who spoke, the taller of the two, was slim and elegant in a dark blue kaftan. She had a long, full silvery mane of hair, and she simply commanded the attention, as if surrounded by a glowing pool of light, like an actress on a red carpet. Like a goddess.

There she is, thought Gill. *Dame Juliana Flagg.*

The victim of Dame Juliana's sarcasm was of similar age but rather less stylish, enveloped in hippie-ish blue and white cottons, her grey hair short and messy. "Of course I read it," she said indignantly.

Juliana's tone was calm but unbending. "Then you should have understood that this is not a course for beginners. I have postgraduate students and professional artists, stretching their skills. Also dedicated amateurs, yes, but ones who've been studying with me for years. Not those who barely know which way up to hold a sketching pencil."

The woman trembled, her face reddening and eyes flooding. Gill felt a pang of sympathy. "I'm not a beginner! I've been drawing and painting all my life!"

"I'm sure you have, but many people plug away at things for which they have no natural aptitude. A nice watercolor course in the Lake District would have suited you. And I'm not here to indulge people whose ambitions are far in advance of their talent. Look, I'll ask Peta to take you in her class instead."

"I paid good money to be taught by the master!" the woman exploded. "Not by her—monkey!"

"You've paid good money. Exactly," Juliana said icily. "The reason my course is so expensive is that *it is a master class*. Since you've come all this way, Peta will help you with the basics, I'm sure. However, if you stayed with me, you'd be far out of your depth, wasting both my time and your own."

"You're wrong, Dame Juliana. This isn't fair. I've done nothing to deserve this—humiliation. I will not be demoted to another class!"

"Fine," Juliana snapped. "Pack your bags. Flora will issue a full refund and call a taxi for you."

The rejected student jerked as if she'd hit a wall. She stood quivering, red-faced. "You are my idol, Dame Juliana. I have saved and saved for this chance to study with you. Now you stand there and say I'm not up to it? Well—well—*fuck* you!" she finished, and came barging past Gill, almost knocking her over in a flurry of fabric as she stormed up the stairs.

"Oh dear," said Juliana in a small voice. Shaking her head, she turned to Flora and Gill with an expression of wry regret. In the photographs Gill had seen she always looked stern; in the flesh she had a radiance that the camera didn't capture, a hint of humor in the lines around her eyes. "I take it you heard that?" Flora nodded. "Give her the refund if she wants it, but offer her a cup of tea first; I expect she'll calm down within the hour."

"I'll do whatever's necessary, Dame J."

"Thanks," Juliana sighed. "These self-deluded people! I have to take new students on trust and there's always one . . . And who have we here? Is this Miss Sharma?"

"It is," answered Flora, with a warm deference she hadn't shown Gill. "I was just explaining, with regard to Robin Cottage, that we can't give her all the keys because of housekeeping . . ."

Flora continued explaining until Juliana cut her off with a tired wave of her hand. "Oh, if she wants the keys, just give them to her. Are you a half-decent artist?" she flung at Gill. "An unexpected vacancy has just occurred."

"Er, no. Thank you." Gill grinned to show she knew it was a joke, albeit a dark one. "I'm just here for a rest, not for public humiliation."

"Don't worry, you only get the public humiliation if you've paid for it," Juliana said in a dry tone. "Good, well, enjoy your stay." And she swept back the way she'd come.

Flora stepped into her office for a moment, returned and pressed four keys into Gill's palm with disapproving emphasis. "When you want fresh linen and toiletries, you'll have to collect them yourself," she said briskly.

"That's fine. No one needs to come to the cottage. Not Colin, and not Mr. Badger."

"If that's what you wish."

"I do." Gill felt a wave of relief, followed instantly by gnawing doubt. "Are you sure these are all the keys?"

"Yes," Flora hissed over her shoulder. "If I find any more, I'll be sure to let you know."

Gill headed for the doors and pushed into the fresh air, feeling riled by the exchange and by her own paranoia. Immediately she heard the doors open again behind her and felt a trace of panicky annoyance at being followed.

"Hello?" called a female voice behind her. "Were you looking for me?"

It was the woman with the pale, heart-shaped face she'd glimpsed through the bay windows. Slender and bohemian in dark red and purple, she couldn't be anything but an artist.

"Why would I be looking for you?"

"I'm waiting for my last couple of students. I'm Peta Lyon."

"I'm not here for art classes," said Gill, again trying to sound more friendly than she felt. "Perhaps you ought to be chasing after that poor woman who was in a flood of tears just now."

"Oh dear." Peta winced. "You heard that? Juliana speaks her mind, I'm afraid."

"Obviously. I'm glad it's nothing to do with me."

"Are you okay?" asked Peta, showing concern that Gill did not want. "You seem a bit wound up."

"No, it just seems rather a lunatic asylum here." Gill's smile thinned. "I'll be fine, once I locate the 'peace and quiet of the idyllic coastal setting' I was hoping for." With that she walked away, severing the insistent tug of the woman's attention. Her retreat was spoiled by the fact that even a fairly short walk had made her thigh seize up, so it was impossible to walk without an obvious limp. As she crossed the lawns and dived into the cover of trees, she sensed Peta's gaze on her back.

By the time she reached the door of Robin Cottage, the pain was like a spear driven through her hip. Gill staggered into the kitchen, swallowed pills, then collapsed on the sofa to gasp and swear until the fiery ache subsided.

Were these *really* all the keys?

"Stop it, you idiot!" she told herself. It took nothing, these days, to leave her shaking with anger, the fight-or-flight impulse. What had made her think she could escape from herself, just by getting on a train to Scotland? And why on earth had she chosen to come here, of all places? What was supposed to happen if Dame Juliana had recognized her?

"But she didn't," Gill murmured. "Juliana Flagg does not recognize me."

2

Mask-maker

Why should she recognize me? Gill asked herself. *What could it be, except awkward and pointless? I doubt she even knows my name.*

She was out on the cliff tops, picking her way along a track with a rough breeze fighting her and the ocean tumbling and shining below. A night's rest had eased yesterday's pain to a dull throb. Walking in moderation was supposed to benefit healing, but she wasn't good at moderation when it came to exercise. She refused to indulge the injury; she wanted to walk until pain made her eyes stream, as if to walk the wretched limb off altogether. It was her against the Leg.

She went to the very edge and looked out at the pearly sweep of sky and sea. Far out across the waves rose the misty bulk of islands. This was Cairndonan Point, according to the map; the highest outthrust of the cliffs that edged the estate. Beyond it, the coastline curved inwards, tilting down to the small fishing harbor of the village. The mouth of a small river flowed out there.

Beneath the carpet of tough vegetation on which she stood, the rock face dropped sheer to the ledges of tumbled rock at its base. Gill wondered how high and fierce the waves came; just now the tide was out, revealing a perfect crescent of sand. The sword cut of the wind pierced her. It took her breath, stripped her to the bone.

North and south there stretched miles of coastline: great reddish cliffs, thatched with greenery, dropping towards the ocean like the edge of the world, tilted up and jigsawed to this savage beauty by the immense pressures of the Earth. A tall stack of rock stood some way out to sea, severed from the mainland by relentless waves. Gill stretched out her arms and leaned into the wind. Here was the wild isolation she needed. At last.

She tried to ignore the thoughts that niggled at her. *I wanted to flee where no one knows me—so why come here, risking Juliana's attention? I don't know. Why should I know what I'm doing? I'm a mess!*

The hard, pure stretch of beach below looked tempting. Gill imagined running, feet pounding, the sand giving back her reflection to the sky . . . A short distance to her left, she found a steep, fearsome path with steps roughly carved into the worst sections. It proved a challenge to climb down there. By the time she reached the bottom—as much on her backside as on her feet—she was so cold and windblown that she could barely feel her painful hip against the background ache of her whole body.

She felt battered but exhilarated. It was almost warm in the shelter of the cliffs. They soared above her in tilted, crumbling layers, pushed up and eroded over billions of years. A stench of seaweed rose around her, a nostalgic childhood smell. Out in the shallows, she saw black dots bobbing on the water: seals, she realized. Gritting her teeth against discomfort, she set out northwards with the sea on her left, bands of shingle and shells crunching under her boots.

The beach narrowed where Cairndonan Point thrust out in a headland. She slithered on rocks to get around it and, reaching the next bay, walked straight into a scattered group of artists. She must not have been at the right angle to see them from above. There were a dozen of them, seated on folding stools, bent over sketchbooks. She recognized the blood-red hair of Peta Lyon. Dismay pricked her; it seemed she couldn't escape Juliana's mob wherever she went.

Peta saw her and waved. Gill nodded back with a curtness meant to discourage attention. Unless she made an obvious detour, she had no choice but to thread her way between the students. Peta, however, wouldn't take the hint.

"Hello again," she called, turning as Gill passed behind her. "You can't escape us wherever you go, can you? The lunatics are out of the asylum for the morning."

She spoke with impish sarcasm. Gill felt slightly ashamed, her instinct to be polite warring against her need for privacy. "I take it back," she said. "I was frazzled from the journey, not to mention dealing with Mrs. Danvers."

Peta gave a gulp of laughter. "Oh, I knew Flora made me think of someone! I'll call her that from now on."

Gill stopped to watch Peta work over her shoulder. Her sketch was unlike the earnest seascapes of her students taking shape around her. Instead, she was drawing a stylised semi-human mask in greens and blues, the face of some aquatic god emerging from the sea. Beneath, she'd written in tiny blue letters, *Marcus Talovaros*.

"How d'you like Robin Cottage?" asked Peta.

"Oh, it's fine." Gill realized she'd lost the art of small talk. She could think of nothing to say that didn't sound completely asinine. Why must everyone know where she was staying? "Perfect."

"Really? Dame J has a job to rent it out most years, she says, since it's tiny and stuck down a ravine. So you're here for the scenery, not the arty ambience?"

"It's not my thing," Gill said quietly. "I didn't even know the school was on."

"You do know Dame Juliana's massively famous, don't you? Her sculptures are legendary. She was awarded the dame-hood for services to the art world."

"So I gathered. I'm suitably impressed. Just not interested."

Peta grinned. Her coppery hair blew about, escaping a loose ponytail. "Great artists are supposed to be monstrous, you know. It's part of the job description."

"Is she that bad?"

"She has her moments. The summer school, it's like a queen presiding over her court, I swear. Or a rock star with groupies. They worship her. She loves it."

"I'll keep out of it." Gill hunched her shoulders, pushing her hands deep into her jacket pockets. "I'm not in the mood for worshipping anything." *Apart from oxycontin*, she added grimly to herself.

Without a pause, Peta flicked over the page of her sketchbook, secured it with a clamp, and began a new drawing; this time a long, featureless face with black holes for eyes. "You're Gillian, aren't you?"

"Just Gill."

"Gill, sorry. You wouldn't do me a huge favor, would you? I'm running a 3-D workshop tomorrow. I desperately need a model. How do you fancy it?" She looked over her shoulder and caught Gill's expression of panic. "I don't mean modeling in the totally naked Colin sense!" She grinned. "I only need your face to make a mold. It's a mask-making tutorial. Would you? All you have to do is lie there while I slap gunk on you."

There was something about Peta that was impossible to resist. The sketched face became clearer, staring at Gill from the page as she hesitated. *No, I'm sorry, I'd rather not*, she thought—only to hear her voice saying, "Yes, all right. What time?"

Having said yes, she couldn't back out.

She barely slept that night. Her bones shrieked in revenge for the punishing walk; she took extra painkillers, but swam through turbulent hours of darkness, medication pulling her just beneath the skin of consciousness. Every thought and sensation became part of a ghastly dream. A dozen times she woke gasping for breath, fighting off creatures in black hoods who weren't there.

Next morning, she could hardly move. Having to feed the fire with logs to get the boiler going; that was a novelty, after her life in London. A hot bath, more pills, some gentle flexing; then she was able to hobble up the footpath to the house. She refused to use a walking stick. *All you have to do is lie there*, Peta had said. Handy, since it was all she could manage.

Juliana's students were ghosting around the Camellia House, preparing to work on their life-drawings of Colin, although the man himself was absent. No sign of Juliana, either. Looking in through the glass doors, Gill thought how content they looked; individuals united by a *glow*, the creative excitement of working with their idol. It was almost self-satisfaction, the smug pride of being one of the elite. *Oh, aren't we all so special*, thought Gill.

She sneered, yet she felt a pang of envy. What was it like, to be part of such a clique? Dangerous, maybe. You could find yourself suddenly rejected by the pack, alone and broken.

She found Peta's workshop in one of the smaller studios. Bright natural light fell through floor-to-ceiling windows. Rows of workbenches were covered in the messy paraphernalia of sculpture. Scrunched chicken wire, toolboxes, clay, wood, plaster of paris. Those materials gave off a rich, raw smell of creation that reminded her of new houses. Black and white photographs formed a frieze high around the walls, showing a series of extraordinary shapes; Dame Juliana's work, she assumed. Massed photos of her disciples' work had been pinned haphazardly below.

Peta's students greeted her with polite hellos. There was a mix of male and female, from twenties to sixties, including the rejected woman who'd told Juliana where to stick her master class; apparently she'd decided to humble herself and stay after all. Again, it struck Gill how excited they all seemed, positively shining with it. Their pleasure warmed her, even as it made her feel an outsider. Peta was in conversation with a couple of them, so Gill went to look out of the windows.

Outside there was a garden with gravel paths running between formal beds of roses, lavender, herbs. Dominated by the tall glass majesty of the Camellia House, the rear of the house was joined by two rambling wings to enclose the garden on three sides. The fourth side was open, shrubs beyond the manicured area tumbling into semi-wildness. Natural ridges of rock, mostly overgrown, ran from somewhere beyond the house and out towards the cliffs. There was a profusion of stunted, hardy trees and gorse bushes. The lie of the land gave a view of Cairndonan Point over to the right, a rough green expanse of cliff tops. Some distance to the left and south—directly behind the house, near the coastal path—Gill could see the top half of an odd building; an old smithy, perhaps, with great double doors and smoke drifting from an industrial-style chimney.

"That's where Juliana does her serious work," said Peta over her shoulder. "No one goes in there without invitation. We call it the Fiery Furnace. The Gates of Hades. Wayland's Smithy."

"To her face?" asked Gill.

"Oh yes," Peta whispered. "It all adds to her mystique, you see; she likes that. But she really will kill anyone who sneaks in."

"Precious about her unfinished work?"

"Partly, but it's the equipment, you see. Furnaces, kilns, welding, molten glass and metal flying around." Peta's left cheek dimpled. "Health and safety."

Peta was wearing a white apron over a long, narrow purple skirt and a crimson top. Her looks were strikingly gothic, with deep colors in place of black; powder-pale complexion, her eyes smoky violet and inquisitive, her mouth a dark red rosebud. Her hair, long and tied back, was blood-colored, with wavy kinks all through it in the style of a 1920s film star.

She handed Gill a plastic bib and a shower cap. "To protect your clothes and hair. It can get messy, but I'll try not to splatter you. You don't mind, do you? It takes less than an hour. Is it okay if I cover your eyes and mouth? I'll keep your nostrils clear, and pop a straw between your lips just in case, so don't worry."

"Do whatever you need to," said Gill.

Peta invited her to recline in what appeared to be an old dentist's chair in the center of the studio. It sent a pang of nerves through her, like surrendering to the unknown, although she knew logically that she was safe. Beside the chair was a table with strips of gauze, a bowl of water, scissors. The students gathered expectantly.

"Gill's kindly volunteered to let me demonstrate," Peta began. "You can practice on each other later. This is a basic technique of mask-making, with plaster bandages soaked in water, then laid over the contours of the face. The first thing is to apply plenty of Vaseline, so the mask will come away cleanly and not take her eyebrows with it."

There was a subdued ripple of laughter. Gill tucked stray strands of hair under the cap, and closed her eyes in nervous anticipation. The touch of Peta's fingertips made her jump. They were cold, and the unfamiliar touch sent a tingling shock through her. The fingers warmed as they pushed petroleum jelly over her face, the stiff globs softening and becoming oily from the heat of her skin. The massaging pressure became sensual, hypnotic.

"This is like having a facial," Gill remarked, drawing another laugh from the class. Peta's fingers traveled tenderly over her nose and cheekbones, around her eye sockets, over chin and jaw, oiling every surface. Her voice murmured, telling the class about trimming the mask, about gesso and acrylics, materials and techniques. Gill felt slips of plastic placed over her eyes. Then there came the cold slap of the first bandage on her fore-head.

As one strip after another was molded wetly to her, her breathing became stifled under the weight of layers. Her eyes were sealed shut. The material was turning hot as it reacted; she hadn't expected that. She felt sweat oozing from her face, forming a slick with nowhere to go. The plaster began to stiffen.

Peta's voice murmured on, but Gill lost the meaning and went downwards in a strange kind of panic attack, one that paralyzed her and left her unable to make a sound. She was deep underwater, struggling to breathe through the thin tube that connected her to the surface. Flashbacks to the hospital, the anesthetic mask descending on her, the same feeling of falling backwards and drowning . . . endless nights of pain and morphine, floating under the thick rippling surface of awareness . . . someone pushing her down, down, with a huge hand covering her face . . .

She was quite certain that she was going to die. She had no will to fight. Instead, calm resignation came over her and she let the weight take her down into limbo . . .

The crack of the mold coming off her face made her start awake. She was disorientated. Her face felt cold and raw.

"All done," said Peta, handing her paper towels to clean her face. "Are you okay?"

"I think I fell asleep," Gill said, dazed. Although shaken, she was adept at keeping her nightmares private.

"You look like you needed it," Peta murmured. She helped Gill off with the protective clothing. "Come on, we're taking a break now. You've earned it. I'll show you where the cloakrooms are, so you can tidy up."

Gill wasn't vain. In the cloakroom mirror, she saw that the procedure had left her face a shiny mess, but once she'd blotted off the Vaseline and combed her hair, it wasn't too bad. She felt weird. Peta had pushed inside her somehow, and she'd been powerless to stop her; but perhaps all these disturbing feelings were nothing more than side effects of her medication.

Gill pulled her fake, black-framed glasses from a pocket and put them on. Her *Don't mess with me!* shield.

The dining room, along the front of the house, was where Gill had first glimpsed Peta's face inside the big bay windows. In contrast to the modern studio, it was paneled in dark oak, unashamedly old-fashioned. There were big silver urns on a side table where the others were helping themselves to tea or coffee. Peta was already at a small window table, waiting for her with two coffees and a plate of biscuits. Gill sat down opposite. It looked as if she'd deliberately chosen a table for two so no one else could join them.

"Wasn't too awful, was it?" Peta said with a quirky smile.

"No, it was . . . different. Sorry I nodded off. I'm really tired today."

"So I noticed. You do seem a bit out of sorts. So come on, what's your story?"

Gill tensed. She hated being put on the spot; most people were either too polite to ask, or too dense to realize they were being grotesquely intrusive. Peta was different. Her eyes held a knowing look. Her slight, enigmatic smile seemed to convey that she knew Gill didn't want to answer and didn't care; she was going to drag it out of her anyway.

"Oh, nothing." Gill shrugged. "I smashed my hip in a car accident and also lost my job. Needed to get away for a while."

"Colin thinks you're a famous athlete," said Peta, deadpan.

From anyone else, this bluntness would have been crass. The way Peta spoke, though, was gently challenging, and empathetic, as if to say, *You don't need to hide anything from me,* in the kindest way.

It was still bloody annoying. "Oh, does he?"

"He thinks you're Gillian Shaw. Silver medal at the Commonwealth Games, big hope for the Olympics. Ten thousand meters, he says? I don't follow sport, although it's educational for an artist to study those highly trained bodies . . ." She paused, hoping for a response. Gill was stony. "Then you dropped out of sight."

Gill exhaled slowly between her teeth. She looked away. "Bloody hell. I wasn't famous. And obviously, no hope for the Olympics now."

Peta blinked. "Sorry, I didn't mean to embarrass you."

"Tell Colin he made a mistake," Gill said stiffly. "In fact, tell Colin to mind his own effing business!"

"Absolutely." Peta's eyes were wide with innocence as she sipped her coffee. "And you can tell me to eff off, too. I'm thick-skinned."

"Look, I don't mean to be rude, but I'm here to rest, not to rake over dead ground." Gill was shaking, but she pushed the anger down inside herself. It felt old. Her emotions were dotted around in the distance; the only thing she felt sharply was hunger. She took a stack of biscuits and began to work her way through them. "What about you, then? What's the mask-making about?"

Touché. She saw a glint in Peta's eyes that gave her away; it was fine for her to interrogate other people, but the other way around, she didn't like it. "It's always fascinated me. Mostly I make them for theatrical or ceremonial dos, and parties. It's used to disguise the identity, of course, which is fun, but I like to go further than that. Sometimes I use masks to make the inner essence visible."

"What does that mean?" Gill asked mulishly. "You can tell I have a low tolerance for arty mysteries."

"Well, a good portrait tells you things about the sitter that you might not see in the flesh. I put the truth straight onto people's faces. My interpretation of it, anyway. Like putting the inner spirit on the outside. For example, there might be an animal that encapsulates the person's character."

"So for someone with buck teeth, you'd make a rabbit? If they were small and timid, you'd make them a mouse-face?"

"And you'd be a panther, dear." Peta half-closed her eyes, amused. "It's rather more subtle than that. It can be to do with elemental affiliations."

"You've lost me." Gill looked into the bottom of her empty cup.

"An intellectual could be seen as affiliated to the element of Air, so her mask might be a hawk or eagle. If you live through your emotions, a fish or a mermaid to show you are drawn to Water . . . like in the Tarot?"

"Oh my god." Gill looked out the window, but Peta only laughed.

"My masks are in great demand, I tell you. If a person hates what I've made, I make them one they like instead, even if it's not the truth about them. But then it's still revealing, because their truth is that they're pretending to be what they're not." She shrugged. "Really, I just like messing with glue, gold leaf and gems."

Gill smiled at that. "Does Juliana approve of classroom crafts in her great art world? How long have you worked for her?"

"Only for a couple of weeks," Peta answered. "It's just a summer school job, so I hardly know her at all, yet." She rose from her chair. "Anyway, time to get on; do you want to watch the rest of the workshop?"

"No—thanks. But if you could point me in the direction of the village, I need to buy food . . ."

"No problem." Peta touched her elbow, leaning towards her. "Thanks so much for your help, Gill. See you again soon?"

Not if I can help it, thought Gill. *How did I let her talk me into that?*

Peta was nice enough, but there was a sort of osmotic quality to her, as if her friendliness seeped inside and seduced you before you realized what was happening. It was not in Gill's plan to socialize, nor explain herself to anyone.

On many grueling cross-country runs in the past, she'd never had a problem orienteering. Today, though, the unfamiliar landscape got the better of her. Peta's directions made no sense; the church spire kept shifting position but never came closer. She walked one muddy path after another up and down endless wooded glens, until she had to admit she was lost. The pain in her hip was searing. She was starting to panic. What if she collapsed here, lost in the woods?

She had a sudden, unwelcome picture of meeting Ned Badger on the path. The thought horrified her. She'd only met him once, had no reason to dread the man . . . but he'd stirred something visceral connected to the accident, the nightmares . . . the dark figure that sometimes stood in the corner of her room . . . *I just don't want to bump into strangers,* she told herself angrily. *Is that so unreasonable?*

The familiar sound of water rushing over rocks suggested she wasn't far from Robin Cottage. All she had to do was to reach the stream, then follow its course. Shopping would have to wait. There'd be enough soup and toast for a couple of days, survival rations. A few more steps . . .

The loud, jarring rasp of a chainsaw wrecked the silence. A few yards on, the path brought her into a clearing, where she saw a pile of cut tree trunks and the cloud of blue smoke from the chainsaw's noisy motor. Gill paused, leaning against an oak tree to rest. What she'd expected to see was someone like Colin doing the work. Instead there was a woman with an unmistakable hank of silver hair hanging down the back of an olive-drab jacket. It was Juliana Flagg manhandling the machine, going at an eight-foot-high section of tree trunk set in the ground. Gill felt compelled to watch. Juliana was not cutting the wood but carving it, using the chainsaw like a giant, unwieldy chisel.

Juliana had no idea she was being watched. She appeared as impregnable as a knight in armor under a visor and earmuffs. Sawdust showered around the totem, filling the air with a glorious sappy scent.

Eventually, Juliana killed the chainsaw and stepped back, in a kind of triumphant exhaustion, to study what she'd created. Gill withdrew behind the tree, hoping Juliana wouldn't turn and see her; suspecting that if she did, she'd receive a barrage of insults, like that poor woman before her.

The figure was crude but recognizable. It looked like a small human figure, trying to fight its way out of the wood. A child. Its eyes were closed, the mouth open in an oval of pain, hands pushing up in supplication as if the very fabric of the wood were elastic. Rough as it was, it was incredibly powerful. It was the first time Gill had seen her work in the flesh. She'd seen photographs and glanced at reviews; never really knew what the critics were rhapsodizing or carping about, but now she began to *see*. Juliana's work was all about isolation, they'd said—figures locked outside, figures confined, imprisoned. Controversial, for showing children in pain, even mutilated—some had called it pornographic.

This figure simply looked desperate and disturbing, like some tribal god. To create that, with a saw! Breathtaking, to think it had come out of nowhere, and so fast. Gill cursed the fact that she had no camera.

After a minute or so, Juliana hefted the chainsaw again and brought it back to noisy life. With steady strokes, she began methodically to destroy the carving. She cut through it, a slice at a time, gradually reducing it to a pile of logs.

Gill watched in numb shock. Juliana was destroying something that might have been worth—god knows—several thousand pounds? To create art out of nothing and destroy it again, just like that! What a strange power.

It seemed inappropriate to approach her, perhaps cowardly to slip away, but Gill chose the latter. The racket of the motor covered her movements as she crept away through the trees, eventually rejoining the path on the far side of the clearing, well out of Juliana's view.

That was when the pain really hit.

She got back to the cottage—somehow. For two days after, she was laid up in agony. No one came by, not even nosy Colin; she'd been so very insistent on her privacy. There was no telephone, so calling for help would have been a problem; but she told herself she didn't need help. It was only pain. She had to cope.

Battling up and down stairs took minutes, with much swearing and many tears. The rest of the time she lay on the sofa, trying to find a comfortable position and a TV channel that was not snowed out by poor reception; or dozing, hallucinating that her pelvis was an anvil being repeatedly struck by an evil dwarf with a sledgehammer.

It was her own stupid fault, Gill knew. Trying too hard, pretending she knew better than her physical therapist. Finally, on the second afternoon, the ache subsided. By then she was too exhausted to do anything but lie on the sofa in simple relief that the pain had sunk to a bearable level.

About five, there was a knock at her door. Gill jerked upright in alarm. She was in a tracksuit with her hair unwashed, feeling and looking wretched. Jaw set, she opened the door and found Peta Lyon there, framed by the stream bank and the rising slope of trees behind her. She was carrying two plastic shopping bags and her rosebud mouth was curved in a conspiratorial smile. "Hi, Gill. Oh god, you look awful! Are you ill?"

"I'm fine." She gave a short sigh. "I still get pain from the injury and it's kind of tiring. The worst has eased off now."

"Are you sure? Did you find the village store? Have you eaten?"

"Are you my carer, or something?" Gill frowned and stood looking down at the doorstep, arms loosely folded, waiting for her to go. "I'm all right."

"Good, well, I just dropped by to show you the finished mask."

"Finished . . . sorry? I thought I was just a demo model."

"Oh no, I never start a mask without completing it." She held up one of the bags. "I brought food and a bottle of wine, too. As a thank-you. If it's inconvenient, tell me and I'll go."

"Food?" The word was a spell, changing Gill's mind instantly. She stood back and beckoned her in. "Well, you can see I'm in this big social whirl of watching children's TV until it's time for more oxycontin. Come in."

Peta was dressed in something purple and Victorian-looking, with huge black lace-up boots. She took the bags into the kitchen, saying as she did so, "I'm going to feed you first. Plates?"

She'd brought curry and rice in foil containers. Gill devoured it, so hungry that the unexceptional chicken madras became a symphony of exquisite flavors, turmeric and cardamom and coriander. She didn't speak at all until it was gone, then asked, "How on earth did you turn up with a hot Indian takeaway? Are you a sorceress, or something?"

Peta, still picking at her meal, smiled. "Hardly. It's from the restaurant in Cairndonan village. And I know a place to park on the edge of the estate that's only five minutes' walk from here. Not magic, just planning."

Gill sipped at a glass of red wine while her companion finished her meal. She wasn't meant to drink with her medication, but she wasn't good at doing anything right lately. She asked, "So, what's it like up at the house?"

Peta swallowed a mouthful, and smirked. "The court of Queen Juliana? A bit odd, really. The couple who run the house, Ned and Flora, are so devoted to her it's scary."

"They're a couple? I didn't realize."

"Mm. They're like a pair of waxworks. Souls of discretion, bowing to Juliana's every word, guarding her like the secret police. A little eccentric, to put it mildly. You get the impression, if anyone threatened her, they'd turn into a pair of ninja assassins. Then there's Colin."

"The apprentice." Gill noted how ready Peta was to share gossip with someone she barely knew.

"He's the opposite. Oh, he *adores* Juliana, but Ned and Flora can't stand him. He's like me, doesn't know when to keep his mouth shut."

"Sounds like a bit of rivalry going on." Gill realized she was breaking her vow to take no interest in affairs at the house. The wine was making her head whirl, lowering inhibitions. Definitely a bad idea to drink on top of her pills.

"Oh, it's worse." Peta took a swig from her glass. "There was a thing."

"A thing?"

"When I first got here, Colin had a girlfriend with him, a girl called Tanya, another artist. They were meant to study with Juliana together. Apparently, though, Tanya was the jealous type and couldn't cope with Colin's attention being so taken up with teacher. So *she* starts flirting with Ned."

"What?"

"Actually, I think Ned's quite handsome in a way. He has a sort of . . . vampiric charm."

"All the same." Gill shuddered.

"Well, it was only to rile Colin, and it worked. He and Tanya had a big bust-up and she stormed out, never to be seen again. I'd only been here a couple of days when it happened. Then Juliana gave us all a lecture on how she would not tolerate this sort of behavior, and either we ran a smooth ship or we'd be walking the plank, to strangle a metaphor."

"Colin didn't go after the girlfriend, then?"

"I think he was relieved. Now he can concentrate all his energy on Dame J. All the students, too; the worship is unbelievable. I think some of them may be hanging on to the door by their fingernails when the course ends. She might have to call the police to prize them off."

Gill grinned at the image. "So you and Colin aren't . . ."

"God, no." Peta waved a hand in dismissal. "I might if I was bored, but I've already seen too much of him, if you know what I mean. I'm here to work, that's all."

Conflicting impulses roiled inside Gill, the brakes taken off by alcohol. Her grudging interest in Peta warred with her need to escape from people, to escape everything. "Are you a Dame-worshipper, too?" she asked sharply.

Peta's mouth became a tight bud; again, she seemed to bridle at personal questions. "Well. Who isn't? To work alongside a legend? It's fantastic opportunity, if only for a month or so. Here, let me clear up . . ."

Gill let her, since there was little to do. While Peta was in the kitchen, Gill switched on a lamp and lit some candles. Then her guest came back in, holding up the second bag she'd brought.

As Gill sat on the sofa, Peta knelt down on the rug at her feet, almost as if in apology. "Look, you may not like it," she said, putting her hand inside the bag and hesitating. "I won't be offended. It's supposed to be true, not pretty."

She drew out the mask, which was attached by the chin to a slim dowel. Gill took it and looked at her own face on a stick.

The mask was light, strong and smooth, like lacquered wood. In no way did it resemble the rough plaster mess that Peta had first shown her. It had the ivory-white blankness of Venetian masks, that porcelain-perfect yet bland and eyeless look . . . There was something horrible about it.

It had all the personality of a skull. The eye sockets were two black ovals against the creaminess, with holes bored through where the pupils would be. Lines of red gems radiated from the eyes, like tears of fire, or the legs of bloody spiders trailing out of the sockets. It was certainly powerful, and would not have shamed an art gallery. Gill stared at it in confusion and horror.

"Is this supposed to be me?"

"An interpretation. What do you see?" Peta leaned towards her, hands resting on her knees.

"Nothingness," said Gill. "With teeth."

"Interesting that you see teeth, when I didn't give it any."

The mask had smooth, white lips that seemed to express resignation. "Is this really how I come across to you? Someone blank, weeping tears of blood?"

"Far from it," said Peta. "The red lines are pain. The smooth face and black eyes say 'mystery.' I don't know you. Something's going on, and it's difficult—I don't know what it is, but that doesn't matter. Pain is what I see. Licking wounds."

Gill was so shocked she didn't know how to react. "That's true, you don't know me," she said softly. "Who asked you, anyway?"

"If I've upset you, I apologize." Peta sounded not at all remorseful. "You're right, I've no business forcing artwork on people who didn't ask for it. And it is a bit grim, isn't it? I should've made a panther, after all."

"It's beautifully made." She tilted it, so the light played over the satiny surface, glinted on the red tears. "I don't know how you got this amazing finish. But it's . . . disturbing."

"I know. Sorry if you don't like it. The point isn't to like it. Once in a blue moon, I'm compelled to model what I see, when I probably shouldn't; then I'm compelled to show it to the recipient, when I *definitely* shouldn't. And sometimes they get mad and throw me out."

"You make a habit of this?"

"Absolutely not." Peta smiled ruefully. "Only for special people."

Gill stood up and propped the mask—attached to its slender stick—in a vase on the mantelpiece, where it stood like a strange, threatening flower. "You needn't have done this." She sat down again and pushed back her hair with both hands, dropping her head between her forearms. Even without looking at the mask, she could feel its stare. The undercurrent of tension and fear within her, so tightly contained until now, began to seethe. "I don't know why you're curious about me, or feel you have to bring stage props to make me open up. It's not happening."

"You don't have to tell me anything. I told you, the mask's a gift, it's just a thing I do. Like sex."

"What?"

"It's fun, but it gets me into lots of trouble." Peta gave her small, mischievous smile again. "If you hate it, throw it in the stream."

"I don't hate it. It's just weird . . . someone doing that for me. You're weird." Gill realized she was slurring, the wine unleashing emotions. "I came here to be on my own. I do not need people trying to get inside my head!"

"I know." Peta kissed her very gently on the cheek. "You look interesting and I wanted to know you better, but okay, I'll back off. If you change your mind, I'll be up there at the house."

Gill sat back, shocked by the kiss, gentle as it was. It was too familiar, inappropriate. The room swayed, and the mask stared and stared, drawing her towards it. She rose to her feet and reached out, touching the satiny cheek before plucking it from its vase. She squared up to the mirror that hung over the mantelpiece.

"Er, Gill," said Peta, rising to her feet, "look, you're right, the mask is a bit grim and I had no right intruding on you with it. I'll take it away with me, okay?"

"It's too late," said Gill, her head swirling with a fearful energy. "You can't unmake it. I want to see myself as you see me."

Gill raised the mask to her face. Through the eye holes, she saw herself in the mirror. She was looking at her own soul. A cold white blank with black voids for eyes. Blood falling out like glittering tears. A torn, gaping nothingness full of pointless pain. She was falling into the chasm, scraped by its fangs as she fell. That was her true face staring back at her. All that was left of her: a wretched, hollow, broken nothingness.

Gill recoiled. She flung the mask down, where it lay flat on the rug, staring up at her.

All the anger she'd suppressed in hospital came raging out of her, along with a rolling stream of images. The dark bulk of someone in the corner of her room at night. Steve, her trainer and life partner—he who was supposed to love her—with his heavy-lidded, cold eyes and his chilling indifference as harsh truths came out. The grille of a 4×4, growling out of the darkness—that was the last thing she remembered before she woke up in a hospital bed, knowing at once that she would never race again. *Never again.* Pain and nightmare and breakdown . . .

"Gill?" said Peta, sounding scared now.

"Get out." Gill was struggling to control the drugged and drunken hysteria that threatened to spill out of her. "Go, go, just *go!*"

Peta, protesting and horrified, was backing away, hands out in appeasement—the scene was a blur. All Gill knew was that at last Peta stopped apologizing, and went, snapping the door shut behind her. Gill threw the bolts across and slumped down on the damp, bristly mat behind it.

"I don't want to see you again," she whispered to the closed door. "Don't come back here, don't speak to me. *Leave me the fuck alone.*"

Some time later, Gill came back to her senses, cold and shaking. She hauled herself to the bathroom and washed her face. Outside, thick grey clouds had brought an early dusk and the wind was rising.

"Was that supposed to be cathartic?" she said to her mauled reflection. "Well, it wasn't. Thanks, Peta. I didn't need you to demonstrate that I've had a nervous breakdown. I already knew."

Numb and drained, she limped back downstairs and stared at the tiny, empty parlor which was supposed to be a refuge, which now seemed a padded cell. Her behavior had been absolutely ridiculous. Something compelled her to pick up the mask again; to understand, now she was calm, why the hell it had freaked her out like that. Was it just the power of suggestion? Perhaps, beneath Peta's friendly veneer, there was active malevolence.

"You don't scare me," said Gill. In sheer defiance, she raised the mask to her face a second time and stared into the mirror again. This time there was no terror, no emotion. Instead, she felt something shifting, like some huge combination lock clunking into place somewhere in the universe. It was not a comforting feeling.

She placed the mask back into the vase, where it stood, silently watching her.

3

The Night-stone Angel

The toast she made for breakfast tasted of burnt cardboard. Gill stood at the sink to eat it, since it didn't deserve the honor of a plate. She still felt horrible about the encounter with Peta. However hard she tried to repair her fragile boundaries, she felt herself going under, all because of Peta and her wretched mask.

Not Peta. Me. She looked out of the kitchen window at the rock face behind the cottage and thought, *That's what my life's become. I've run into a wall and here I am, staring at a dead end.*

An hour later, Gill was standing on top of the rocks, looking down on the roof of Robin Cottage. It hadn't been easy; first a long walk downstream until the escarpment eased into a gentler slope, then an uphill trek as she doubled back through thick undergrowth, treacherous with brambles and rabbit holes. Now she was sweating, dizzy from a mixture of triumph and extra painkillers. Behind her, the tree-covered slope continued its gradual rise; in front, it dropped sheer into the tiny back yard of Robin Cottage. She'd done it. Defied the wall in order to see what lay beyond.

Ahead, through the treetops on the far side of the stream, she saw the roof of Cairndonan House, grey slates mottled with lichen. Farther away, smoke curled up from Juliana's enigmatic smithy. Presumably Peta was over there somewhere, prowling the studios for new mask victims, eager to expose their insecurities and phobias . . .

Gill turned away to seek an easier way off the escarpment, but soon found herself lost, enveloped by birch and ash and oak. Somewhat sheltered from sea winds by the lie of the land, they grew in profusion in their May greenery. She hadn't realized the woods extended so far behind the cottage.

In the past, when she'd trained cross country, her sense of direction had been terrific. Now it seemed to be broken. *Like the rest of me,* she thought. After a while she heard the music of water, slower and deeper than the stream she knew. A ruined building loomed through dappled light, overgrown and as green as the woodland around it. Fallen stones lay covered with moss and undergrowth beneath its towering walls. There was no roof, no doors. A water mill, once; now just a shell.

Her leg protested sharply as she picked her way through the gaping arch. Inside, the building was green, glowing like emeralds in a cloak of moss, fern and saplings. If there had been upper floors, they were long gone. The space smelled damp, and the high walls made it feel secretive, haunted. It was also hazardous, the floor heaped with overgrown masonry. There was a millstone, lying tilted under brambles. Pale green light shone through another open doorway in the opposite wall. Someone had placed a pole diagonally across the gap as if to warn off intruders.

Gill scrambled over some big fallen stones to reach the opening, realizing too late that it would be hell on her leg to climb back down. Outside, a small deep river flowed. That made the Robin Cottage stream a tributary, she guessed, joining forces farther down to rush towards the sea. There was a wooden platform that formed a bridge to the far bank. The planks were mostly intact, but the remains of a riverside path had vanished under vegetation.

The only way forward lay ahead, through masses of gorse, brambles and saplings, a neglected meadow with the hint of a footpath leading away through the long grass. Her hip ached vengefully and she felt a moment of panic. She'd walked too far again. What if she was stupidly stranded here? She'd always resisted using a walking stick, thinking it a wretched, geriatric accessory—but now she needed something, and the pole across the doorway would have to do.

She touched it and recoiled.

It wasn't wood but bone. Not human, obviously; it was five feet long, twisted along its length like a unicorn horn. The grooves were ingrained with black algae, the ridges crusted with green. It felt damp and disgusting. Still, as she grasped it, Gill couldn't deny the relief of leaning her weight on it. With its help, she crossed the slimy planks over the millrace and started along the meadow footpath. It seemed to aim directly at the church spire—a disused route to the village. A chance to buy the groceries she needed, if her leg lasted that long.

The footpath led gently uphill, with bushes on her left and the meadow lying to her right. Soon she lost sight of the church spire and there was nothing around her but greenery, insects and birdsong. Bliss. The gorse smelled like coconut.

A couple of hundred yards on, the track brought her onto a stretch of heathland with a stone circle. Gill's heart gave a leap of surprise. There'd been something about an ancient site on Juliana's web page, the Cairndo-nan Sisters . . . she'd forgotten about it until now. It would've been just her luck to run into Peta and her students, but, to her relief, there was no one here. Gill crossed the area, looking all around her as she went. Twelve chest-high stones stood around a central menhir. The air over the site shimmered, and she saw a chalice shape of ocean cupped in the distance. Strangely, the stones had a bluish tint, almost like lapis lazuli. Gill stopped to touch one. The rough surface under her fingertips felt as if it held cold electricity. Sounds of wind, wave or birdsong had faded. The silence was complete. She felt like a trespasser.

Beyond the circle, the footpath continued downhill along the edge of another meadow with a thick copse on her left. It was like walking along a deep green tunnel. Pushing through tall grass and cow parsley, she noticed a thigh-high stump of black rock standing to the right of the path. She parted the undergrowth around it and found a primitive, weathered figure with wings folded down its back. An angel? Her back tingled and she turned to see another, facing its companion across the path. Guardians at a gateway? Juliana's work?

Farther on, there was a horse in the meadow to her right: a tall, creamy-white beast with the feathered legs of a Clydesdale and a long mane rippling over a wide, arched neck. It stood as if waiting for something—perhaps for the return of its stolen horn? She grimaced to herself. Behind the horse rose a small hillock crowned by a tree that dripped yellow blossoms. Laburnum, mimosa? She wasn't good at plants. It was the sort of tree she would expect to see in the Mediterranean, not in the Scottish countryside. Gill went on, unsettled by the way the horse watched her as she passed.

At last the track curved down through whispering birch trees, and brought her into the village. There were scattered cottages, built from honey-yellow stone. These dwellings ran back into the hillside, almost as though they'd spilled out of the ground. The roofs had rounded contours, covered with colorful glazed tiles; red, blue, or turquoise. Vines clouded the walls, heavy with purple fruit.

Grapes? Gill thought vaguely. *Can they grow them in this climate, at this time of year?*

The weather, though . . . it had been a fresh spring day, but here in the valley the air felt balmy, and smelled of honeysuckle. The sky was very blue and the light golden, not a northern British light at all. The sun was like a swollen apricot. There was no proper road, only a broad green swath running between dwellings scattered in the trees, and not a soul in sight. The trees were heavy with nuts, plums, nectarines . . . the whole area an eerie, out-of-season orchard.

Presently the path brought her to a sort of village green, a great sweep of grass with a large house or pub along one boundary. No, not grass; a low springy herb, chamomile maybe. Dominating the green, where she might have expected a war memorial, a shining black statue towered over her. It was a stylized angel, all smooth simple curves, with wings arching high over its shoulders.

I have to get a camera, she thought.

Gill walked to the statue and touched the surface. It was carved of some shiny mineral, inky black glass or obsidian with mica sparkling inside; stars in the night sky. The angel watched protectively over the village. As she walked around it, tracing her hand over the cold curves and the wing tips folded down its back, she made out an inscription around the base. At first the characters were illegible cuneiform; then they jumped into plain resolution. The inscription read, TYRYNAIA, THE HEART OF US.

Past the statue, there was a broad tree-lined avenue and she saw, through a lacework of leaves, the sparkle of water. She began to walk towards the lake—*loch*, she reminded herself—the light and the mild air making her soporific, almost ecstatic, as if she were in a dream.

The dewy-violet water stretched to the horizon. She saw the faint shadow of land on the far side, where water and sky melted almost seamlessly into each other. Could there be such a loch, so close to the sea?

Turning, she looked back towards the village. In astonishment she saw, behind the green tiered hills that enclosed it, a mountain. A steep, slate-blue fang of a mountain with a cap of snow.

Gill stared. The mountains visible from Cairndonan were impressive but broad and rounded in shape; she'd noticed nothing as tall or close as this. How was it possible that she'd failed to notice such an obvious peak before? It would dominate the landscape for miles.

She followed the shore until the path curved around and brought her back into the village from another direction. Everywhere she looked, there were lush orchards. Sometimes she thought she saw figures in the distance, and her heart beat harder, but no one came. Soon she found herself at the green with the statue again. No sign of any shop or post office. Strangest of all, there were no cars. That was it—no roads, no cars! That was why it felt so surreal; that, and the golden light, the sense of desertion, the night-stone angel keeping watch.

Yet Gill accepted it all as if she were dreaming, or drugged.

One side of the green sloped up towards the great, rambling house of honey stone. It had the look of a country inn, with leaded windows, and greenery around the open double doors. She went towards it, every step releasing heady scents from the carpet of herbs beneath her feet.

At the porch, Gill propped her staff and went in.

A churchy scent of stone and the warmth of beeswax greeted her. Inside, she crossed a lobby and found a huge room with shadowy alcoves, lots of shiny dark furniture, high-backed tapestry chairs and a huge fireplace on the right-hand wall. With its gorgeous interior it must be a hotel rather than a pub, perhaps with an expensive restaurant. There appeared to be a bar on the far side; she saw gleams of rosewood in near-darkness. Along the left-hand wall there was a row of big, bright stained-glass windows.

In the center of the room, light streamed down from a glass cupola in the ceiling, pooling on a huge carpet of blue, green and gold. Entranced, she didn't notice the step down in front of her. Her foot went into thin air; she landed hard on her bad leg, and fell. Agony jarred her whole body. She lay on the cold flagstones, impaled on a spike of steel, her head filled with stars. Through the cloud she saw dream figures: a blue girl with wavy hair like an undine, a leaf-green tree creature, a lynx with its ears outlined by light . . . Peta's masks, come to life.

"Mind the step," said a man's voice.

He was leaning over her, a long-haired silhouette against the light. He was real, but the half-animal beings—she saw as blood returned to her head— were figures in the stained-glass windows along the far wall. She couldn't move or speak. The pain made her sob for breath. How long would it take a paramedic to reach her?

"What have you done?" he asked, sounding concerned now. "You didn't seem to land that hard."

"No," she managed to gasp. "Old war wound."

"Really, which war?" He sounded absolutely serious.

"Not literally." She indicated her left thigh. "Accident. Surgery."

Surely she'd ripped a muscle out of its bed, or a steel screw from the bone. This was bad. Hot sweat broke out all over her body.

"Where have you come from?" he asked in a steady, friendly voice.

"Don't know, I need a doctor . . . Oh, *shit* . . ."

"Keep still." A cushion was pressed under her head and then, to her shock, she felt a pair of strong hands on her thigh and hip. She nearly screamed. He ignored her protests. "This was the injury? Yes, I can feel it. You take too many painkillers. You don't need them here."

"What?" She uttered incoherent sounds, trying to say, "Call an ambu- lance—" Then she broke off in amazement. Warmth flooded from his hands; she actually saw a red glow around them, surrounding her leg. And the pain vanished.

Gone, absolutely gone. The man sat back on his heels, watching her as she sat up in shock. "Better?" he said.

She stifled a sob, rubbed water from her eyes. The departure of the pain was almost as shocking as its arrival. He helped her as she carefully climbed to her feet, although she didn't need help. Carefully she tested her weight. The limb held. Pelvis, hip and leg felt perfect.

"What did you do?"

He didn't answer, only smiled. He looked thirtyish and could have been a dancer or an athlete; he had that graceful, carved look, and an astonishing face, with strong bones and dark grey eyes under dark eyebrows. His hair was the longest she'd ever seen on a man. It hung well past his waist in dark brown ripples that shone red where the light slid over them. He looked like no landlord or hotel-keeper she'd ever seen. A rock star perhaps. Over black jeans and shirt he wore a garish waistcoat sewn with suns, moons and planets in rainbow colors.

"I'm Rufus Hart," he said.

"Gill. Hello, Rufus. Er . . . thank you."

He was studying her, motionless but for his eyes, which were flirtatious, lively and full of curiosity. He said, "I think you would appreciate a drink, Gill." He guided her across the room and sat her on a high-backed chair near the polished rosewood length of the bar. She was trembling, her mouth dry—but there was still no pain.

"Just fruit juice, please." Gill looked around awkwardly. "This is a public bar, isn't it? I haven't blundered into your house?"

The stranger grinned happily at her, his face aglow as if she was the most fascinating sight he'd ever seen. He was outrageously beautiful. She couldn't help noticing, despite feeling too bleak and damaged to be interested. "Absolutely, and we're always open. How did you find us?"

His rapt attention was disconcerting. Her barriers went up. "I'm staying near the village. Went for a walk and got lost. I was looking for a grocery store, actually."

"I see," he said. He turned and called out, "Leith!"

In the shadows behind the bar, someone stirred. Had the barman been there all the time, or slipped in through a doorway? It was too dark to see more than bottles glinting in alcoves between pillars of glossy dark wood. As the barman, Leith, slid a glass across the counter, she glimpsed a somber, carved-ivory face under a mass of black hair; then he was gone into the darkness again.

Rufus brought her the drink and sat in a chair beside her. The vessel appeared handmade; thick greenish glass with bubbles frozen inside, set into an intricate silver holder and stem. It crossed her mind that she shouldn't accept it; but she was too thirsty to resist. The liquid trickled down her throat, sharp and delicious, some exotic combination—mango and pomegranate, or the like.

"So, you walked here?" Rufus persisted. His voice was warm and his accent neutral, not a local brogue like Ned's. "Which way did you come? Across the stone circle?"

"Yes, that's it, and down the footpath. So, has your establishment got a name? I didn't see a sign."

A slight pause. "The sign is being repaired," he answered. "If you can guess the name, your drink is on the house."

"It would have to be the Angel." She shrugged. "Or is that too obvious?"

"The Angel." He smiled, showing white teeth. "No, that's a perfect guess."

"And this village is Cairndonan, right? There was something beginning with T on the statue."

"Well." He hesitated. "The natives use a different name. Boundry. And where are you from, originally?"

"London," she said.

"Ah, London. It's a long time since I was there."

"It gets dirtier and busier."

"I miss it," said Rufus.

"I don't," she said with a laugh. "Is it always this quiet here?"

"Lately, it has been far, far too quiet." He gave her another of those playful, thoughtful looks that were making her very uneasy. Like Peta, she thought. There was a shine about him, and a sort of knowingness, as if he took for granted that she'd be mesmerised by his unearthly beauty. How not?

"I should go."

"There's no hurry, surely? Rest until you've recovered from your fall. So, have you been in Cairndonan long?"

"A few days. Just visiting."

"And where are you staying?"

"Er . . . up near Cairndonan House."

"Ah, the great house. Who owns it now?"

The question startled her. Surely he knew. "Dame Juliana Flagg. The sculptor."

"Ah. It's such a long time since I was there."

"I think she's lived there for at least thirty years," said Gill, frowning.

"Well, time gets away from us here." Rufus's tone was enigmatically level. "Have you met her? What is she like?"

"I really couldn't say, I've barely spoken to her."

"Did it seem far, your walk from the house to here?"

"Hard to say. About an hour, but I kept stopping . . ." She stared, wondering why his questions were growing odder.

"And the weather, was it fine or raining?"

"It was . . . fine. It's warmer here, though. You know what the locals say, 'If you don't like the weather, wait a minute.'"

"Indeed," he said, laughing. "How interesting."

Perhaps he was only making conversation, but his questions were too probing, too weird. She continued to parry them as best she could, without actually being rude. After some minutes, she said firmly, "I really should go now."

"Must you?" Rufus's face became still, the eyes darkening as if he was on the verging of stopping her. "I suppose you must."

"Really." Gill hurriedly finished her drink. "What do I owe you?"

"As I said, it's on the house."

"Well . . . thank you. And as for my leg, I can't thank you enough." She stood up, light-headed, still incredulous.

"A little gentle manipulation, that's all." Rufus stood up with her, giving his alluring smile, his gaze hooked into hers. "Is there nothing else we can do for you?"

"Oh, yes, if you could just tell me how to find the shops?"

"If I give you a basket, you can pick all the fruit you want. There are fish in the lake, beautiful little goats to give us milk . . ."

She laughed. He had to be teasing. "Honestly, I'm from London. I can't do foraging."

"I know. Oh well. Go back the way you came," he said softly. "It was a pleasure to meet you, Gill. Have a safe journey. I hope we will see you again sometime."

Then both the impossibly godlike Rufus, and the unsmiling, black-haired young man behind the bar stood motionless, silently watching her as she left. The deities in the stained-glass windows watched, too, She felt she was swimming through shadows and syrupy light, as if she would never reach the door.

On her way out, she remembered to seize the unicorn staff. Suddenly it felt like a weapon. All the way back through the village and along the foot-path that snaked up through the birches, she sensed that something was following. It was a horrible feeling. Translucent figures with animal faces or waterweed for hair stalked her, and pantherlike shapes prowled in the periphery of her vision, yet whenever she looked around, there was nothing there.

The albino horse raised its head to gaze at her as she passed. The sense of menace was so strong that by the time she reached the stone circle, she was running.

Running! The miracle didn't strike her until she stopped for breath. As she stood there gasping, thinking, *I can run*, she noticed a track leading from the heath with a sign reading, PUBLIC FOOTPATH TO CAIRNDONAN, 1 MILE.

Ten minutes later she emerged onto a country lane which soon brought her between rows of stone houses and fishermen's cottages; a characterful, businesslike community bearing no resemblance to Boundry. Even the col-ors were different: grey and white beneath a sharp blue sky. She saw the elusive church, and farther downhill she found a post office, a pub called the Cairndonan Arms, an Indian take out, and her goal, the village store.

There was one other customer browsing the shelves: Ned Badger. Gill shot into a different aisle, pretending she hadn't seen him. Still disconcerted and shaking, she shoved the staff under one arm and began to grab milk, eggs, wine—everything she could think of. The till was manned by a blond local girl of around nineteen, who was pleasant enough but more interested in talking on the phone than in doing her job. She broke off long enough to take Gill's money and pass a plastic bag across the counter.

"Excuse me," Gill asked as she loaded the bag. "You know the other village, Boundry . . ."

The girl's frown barely dented her young forehead. "Where?"

"Boundry. It's about a mile away. There's a loch and a mountain and a hotel called the Angel. Is it . . . holiday cottages?"

The girl looked confused, and gaped at the twisted bone staff in Gill's hand. "Never heard of it. There's only the one village and this is it."

"But I was . . . never mind." Gill wasn't even sure what she was trying to ask. As she stepped out of the shop, she could hear the girl's voice from inside, "Still there? Aye, I've just had a right strange one in here . . . Oh, yeah, the weird ones are always English . . ." Laughter.

Everything looked ordinary outside. There were parked cars, locals strolling about, seagulls wheeling overhead. The far end of the street gave a glimpse of the harbor wall, bright fishing boats. She had only to walk back uphill until she found either a footpath to Robin Cottage, or the main entrance to Cairndonan House. At least she was confident that she could walk the distance. The lack of pain felt unnatural, too good to be true.

"Excuse me, Miss Sharma," said a low voice behind her. She turned and saw Ned Badger there, a bag of groceries in one hand. The sight of him set her heart thudding with anxiety. "Where have you been exploring?"

"I'm sorry?"

"I couldn't help overhearing. You were lost?"

She was tempted to ask what the hell business it was of his, but forced herself to be polite. To sound *normal*. "Oh, only a bit, but it doesn't matter. The estate is so beautiful."

"Indeed it is. I wouldn't like to think you'd walked anywhere hazardous. You could break an ankle and no one would find you."

Gill could see what Peta meant, that Ned had a sort of quirky handsomeness. With his aquiline nose, pointed chin, a shock of oily black hair streaked with white—standing there in his dusty-black, Victorian-looking clothes might have been a punk or a New Romantic twenty-five years ago. She guessed him to be around fifty. His face was etched by weather and by fine lines of worry and hard work, which made him seem older than he actually was. Some might see him as attractive, but in Gill's eyes, his youthful beauty had long since gone to seed.

"Well, I didn't. I'll try to stick to the footpaths in future. Bye."

As she made to walk away, to her horror he made a grab for the unicorn staff. "Let me take that."

"What for?" she exclaimed, pulling it out of his reach just in time.

"It looks dirty."

"It doesn't matter."

"Still, let me carry it for you." This time he grabbed the shaft hard, and she was suddenly in a ridiculous struggle for possession.

"There's no need!" She gave a determined yank and got it out of his grasp.

"I am trying to help you, Miss Sharma," he hissed.

She stepped back, holding up her grocery bag to put distance between them. "I don't need help."

To her disbelief, he then tried to seize her shopping. "Let me carry your bag and I'll walk back with you. You need to take it easy on that leg."

"It's fine," Gill said in suppressed fury. "I need no help, as long as I use this stick. Please. I'm fine on my own and I still need to, er . . ." she glanced at the post office a few doors along . . . "to buy stamps."

Her insistence shook him off at last. There was nothing more he could do without assaulting her in the street. With a shrewd, silent look he stepped away. His manner verged on obsequious; the light in his eyes was pure rage.

As she walked hurriedly away she heard him say softly after her, "Watch where you walk, and be careful what you pick up, and mind who you speak to. There is no other village, Miss Sharma. Don't speak of things you don't understand, lest you talk them into being."

In the Camellia House, as Juliana drifted from one easel to the next, she realized that she was completely absorbed in the moment. Worries about work, finances and other difficulties were distant, for a pleasant change. "Funny," she murmured, pausing by Colin where he lay, naked and re-laxed, on the couch. "Every year I half-dread the student influx, but once they're here, I'm surprised by how much I enjoy it."

"You should hold more courses, Dame J," he said.

She carefully looked only at his face, nowhere else. "Any excuse to dis-robe, Colin. I'm not sure my nerves could stand it."

He grinned as she shook her head and walked on. Perhaps he was right, but for so many reasons she hesitated to run the school more than once a year. Money, for one; it cost a fortune in food, laundry, bills; the fees barely covered it. And she needed to concentrate on *Midsummer Night*, if she were to stand any chance of bringing it under control . . .

"Dame J?" Ned's discreet voice issued from the palm trees framing the main doorway back into the house. He was hovering there with a familiar grave expression in his eyes.

"Yes?" she said, walking briskly to him. "Is there a problem?"

"Perhaps, Dame J." He paused. "A ward has been disturbed . . ."

She'd inherited Ned Badger with the house, Flora too; they'd been young then, hardly twenty, two villagers with flint in their eyes from living so close to the elemental powers of ocean and land. Ned in particular had always been full of superstitious beliefs. He still went around the estate placing tokens and charms to block the supposed pathways of the *Dubh Sidhe*. He'd even insisted on giving Robin Cottage a new door knocker, a horseshoe supposedly to protect the tenant.

Juliana's ex-husband, Charles, had dismissed such business as beneath his notice; he'd been one for material realities, country pursuits such as deer-stalking and fishing. She was immensely glad he was no longer around—the city gent acting squire of the manor—shooting at her wildlife. The room where he'd kept his guns and other sporting equipment remained firmly locked.

She was rather more sympathetic than Charles to Ned's beliefs, but she disapproved of his rituals, feeling them to be pointless. The dark ones cared nothing for herbs or iron or symbols, yet she couldn't convince him of it. Logic could not influence obsession.

Ned knew she disapproved, but he continued regardless, and so the matter was a thorny one between them.

"What do you mean?" She tried not to sound irritated.

He cleared his throat and spoke delicately. "Something I placed at the old mill. A staff. I saw the guest from Robin Cottage carrying it in the village."

"Well, I expect she picked it up while walking. Either that or you were mistaken."

His unreadable eyes narrowed. He persisted in the same soft tone, "I know what you think of this, Dame J, but it concerns me. She had no right; such actions disturb the boundaries . . ."

"Ned," she whispered, angry because she didn't understand why it was such an issue to him. "Whatever sinister power there is, or was, will not be stopped by flimsy props like sticks or horseshoes. You know that. Whatever there was, I've dealt with it."

"And you believe you can keep it subdued, packed away in the foundry?"

"I haven't time for this conversation." He flinched minimally, acquiescing, but his eyes remained stubborn. She added icily, "Leave Miss Sharma alone, Ned. She's come here for privacy. If she leaves because of you, how do you suppose I can afford to refund her rent? If she complains you've bothered her, I will dismiss you. Do you understand?"

"Yes, Dame J." He gave a slight bow, withdrawing. "As you command."

"Just what I need, a bonkers weirdo," Gill said to herself as she put packets of bread and cereal into cupboards, fresh fish, eggs and vegetables into the small fridge. Frozen peas went into the icebox, bananas and apples into the fruit bowl on the tiny kitchen table. She refused to let Ned Badger intimidate her. She was still marveling at how good her leg felt. The whole day had completely unsettled her. "Every time I set foot out of the door, some lunatic latches on to me," she muttered. "That's it. Tonight I'm going to lock the bloody door, watch TV and relax, and god help anyone who stops me."

She cooked a cheese omelette for supper, uncorked a bottle of red wine and poured a satisfyingly large glass. Television reception was hopeless. A storm was building. She tried to read instead, but couldn't get settled. She felt shivery, itchy, restless.

With a jolt she realized she was suffering withdrawal symptoms from oxycontin. Resigned, she went upstairs to fetch her pills. She took just one painkiller and her antidepressant, swilling them down with wine against all medical advice. It gave her heartburn. As darkness fell she found herself pacing the tiny cottage, checking over and over again that front and back doors were locked. Peta's mask stared at her, drawing her towards it repeatedly. She plucked it out of its vase, examined it and put it back. She wasn't going to try it on again, not even to prove she wasn't frightened of it.

She thought about Boundry. The place hadn't seemed real . . . but nothing had seemed quite real since her accident. Strange; when people were kind to her, as Rufus had been, it made her suspect that they wanted something, if only to have a laugh at her expense. Visiting Boundry had been like having soft, hazy golden cashmere pulled over her eyes . . . or was it all side effects of pain and medication? Perhaps she'd even imagined the encounter with Ned. The memory of his insinuating verbal assault left a vile taste in her throat.

Gill almost missed the fire in her thigh. Pain was real. Robin Cottage was real too, plain and down-to-earth, and that was good.

She went to bed early and lay curled up, thinking of nothing. As darkness fell, wind began to rattle the windows. The cottage was solid, but that only made the buffeting wind seem more violent, because there was no give in the structure. A banshee howl set up in the gap between the back wall and the escarpment. Sweeps of rain rattled the slates.

Gill lay listening to the storm for a while. Soon it grew so fierce that there was no possibility of sleeping through it. Instead, she got up to watch. Outside there was little to see; an impression of swaying trees, walls of rain blasting a pattern of silver mercury drops against the windowpanes. The wind sang discordantly.

It suited her mood. She'd poured all her emotions into the void and the void had received them. She had nothing left. Harsh weather was a welcome distraction that cleared her mind, washing her clean.

A sudden harsh banging noise made her start up in alarm. It sounded like someone pounding the door knocker, then the door itself, hard enough to break it off its hinges. The racket went on and on, while she stood in the center of the bedroom floor, frozen.

Looking out of the window, she saw a vague shadow on her doorstep. A voice was shouting incoherently above the wind.

Numb, she crept downstairs and picked up her ivory walking staff for self-defense. She daren't switch on a light. In shades of dark grey she could see the door shaking. The pounding went on and on.

"Who the hell is that?" she yelled.

A desperate male voice was panting, "Help me. Please. You've got to help me. Please, let me in. Before he comes. Please!"

Gill started back from the shuddering door. "Stop it!" she shouted.

She could hear his pained breathing—part-gasp, part-scream. Whoever was there sounded scared out of his wits, which scared her all the more. When the banging continued, she struck the door hard with the heel of the staff and yelled, "STOP IT!"

At that the knocking ceased. Instead, a face loomed at the window, making her start. She caught a brief impression of someone young and terrified. Then he was gone. She heard footsteps scuffling away.

Gill stared out into the darkness. His distress appeared genuine. Her instinct to protect herself warred against curiosity and guilt. She ought to help. Better to confront him face-on than to imagine him lurking in the night . . . She flicked on the porch light, unlocked the door and warily looked outside.

Rain buffeted her, throwing her hair around like a wild flag. The fan of light illuminated a wedge of stream bank; wet grass, rocks, fallen branches.

"Hello?" she called, her voice sharp with unease. She took a step or two onto the path. There were shadows, trees, raindrops shining in the light. The stream was high, rushing furiously between its deep banks. Then she saw him.

Saw the sole of his boot, at least. He'd fallen, as if he'd blundered towards the water, tripped and gone headlong down the bank. She approached warily, ready for the stranger to be faking; but he plainly wasn't. He was sprawled across some rocks, apparently semiconscious, his eyes fluttering. When she tried to ask who he was, where he'd come from, he only groaned.

Instinct took over, and she became the person she dimly remembered being, decisive and unafraid. When she tried to put him in the recovery position, so that he was lying on his side with his head tilted forward and one knee bent, he began to sit up, panicking, so instead she wrapped her arms around him for support and began to haul him towards the cottage.

Although slim, he was a dead weight, sliding on mud and grass, leaning heavily on her like a drunk. Rain ran down her neck. She got him to the doorway, where he collapsed spectacularly across the threshold, as if blown in by the wind that muscled past him.

Panting, Gill pulled him all the way in, fighting to get hold of the banging door and push it shut against the storm. Then she lifted and dumped him on the sofa, where he lay with his head back, hair dripping. She flicked on a lamp.

He looked youngish, early twenties; his face was colorless ice. He was around six foot tall, slim, with black jeans tucked into knee-high biker boots. His old-fashioned baggy white shirt, with its full sleeves and lacing, made him look like a drowned poet. He was soaked to the skin and looked in no state to be dangerous. She glared down at him, her unwelcome guest.

"Right," she said, "the door's locked, and no one's following you. What's happened? Do you want me to call a doctor? Police?"

His eyes half-opened, gleaming between dark, wet lashes. "No," he slurred. "Please help me. Don't make me go back there."

Then she realized where she'd seen him before. It was the barman from the Angel, the unspeaking young man with the pale, watchful face and dark hair, who had lingered in the shadows while Rufus beguiled her.

The man whom Rufus had addressed as Leith.

4

Leith

Rain swept out of the night to deluge the roof of Cairndonan House, overflowing gutters and streaming down windows. Inside her bedroom, Juliana watched silver trails dashing across the glass and listened to the wind wrestling with the trees. Although she could see nothing of the landscape, she sensed the ocean and the bleak humps of the Highlands beyond her estate, hidden behind veil upon veil of rain in the darkness. The feeling made her shiver.

Turning to her mirror, she swept back her hair and began to massage serum into her skin, concentrating on the fine network of lines around her eyes. It was a losing battle. She was sixty-six and couldn't expect to pass for forty. Everyone, especially her devoted students, repeatedly said how wonderful, how glamorous she looked, but even that was a sort of backhanded compliment, with the unspoken addendum, *for your age*. Really, her age didn't worry her that much; one's date of birth was just a fact of life, with nothing to be done about it. She would never contemplate plastic surgery; the very idea was grotesque. Still, it was a matter of pride to take care of herself. She was determined to remain the stately *grande dame* until the very end, and never turn into a frail old lady. *When the time comes*, she thought, *they'll have to fell me like a tree and lash me to the back of a truck.*

The course was going well. Perhaps Colin was right, she should do this more often. During the day, as she guided her students and watched them blossom, she felt fully alive. At night, though, alone in her room, old dark specters crowded in. Cairndonan Estate was an abyss, ravenous for money. The harder she struggled to complete her project, *Midsummer Night*, let alone sell it, the more it tangled her up and paralyzed her.

In the shadowy reflection of the room lying in near-darkness behind her, a figure stirred on the chaise longue at the end of her bed. Juliana did not turn round, only watched the woman's reflection in the mirror; a broad, striking face, dark lips, huge smoky eyes. A layer of some diaphanous, pleated material draped her body, with an outer garment of crimson velvet and fur lying casually open around her. The apparition looked like a silent film star, with an Art Deco–style feathered headdress rising from her forehead between the rippled waves of hair.

"There's only one way to fight the ravages of time, darling," said the woman in the reflection. "Die young."

Juliana briefly clenched her teeth. "Bugger off, Corah."

Corah laughed, her head tipping back theatrically. "You're so washed up, you poor old thing."

"Am I, indeed? With my alleged stature as one of the world's greatest living artists, an adoring flock of students and scores of successful exhibitions?" Her tone was self-mocking. "Being washed up looks pretty good from here."

"Your hideous marriage. Your lack of offspring. And the fact that you have done no salable work for the past ten years." Corah drew on a cigarette in a long holder and blew a jet of smoke into the air. "Is there such a thing as artist's block?"

Juliana's reflective mood turned bleak and hard. "You know nothing about me, or my work."

"*Au contraire*, I know everything. I see right through you."

"I could say the same," Juliana retorted. "At least I have done something worthwhile with my life, rather than spending it on my back. At least I haven't frittered my time away as a virtual prostitute."

Corah dismissed the insult with another gale of laughter. "And I could have made a damn good living, but the point was to have fun. Yes, I confess I spent time with one or two young men, several in fact . . . All right, many, many young men. So what? It was fun."

"It sounds desperate."

"You should try it. But you don't believe in fun, do you, Jules? Life for you is a very serious business. Heaven forbid you should ever let loose and enjoy yourself. God, how you take after Melody!"

Juliana opened another anti-aging potion, never taking her eyes off the ivory and charcoal figure of her aunt in the mirror. "What do you want of me?"

Corah's voice went flat. "You know what I want. What I've always wanted. To know what happened to our beautiful boy, my dear brother, Adam. Does he haunt you, as I do?"

"No, he doesn't. He died in the First World War. That's what I was told."

"Did he, though? So many puzzling stories about him being seen afterwards, both in London and here. It's this place, dear. Strange things happen. People vanish. Is it coincidence, a missing brother, a missing child? What was his name?"

"Don't," snapped Juliana, briskly applying a layer of moisturizer over the serum. "You must know what happened to your brother. If you expect me to find out the truth of something that happened over ninety years ago— You're the one who's passed beyond the veil, Corah. You should be the one with all the answers. But no. You never give me a straight reply to anything."

"How can I, darling?" Corah said huskily. "I'm a figment of your imagination. Since it's your mind conjuring me up, I can't tell you anything you don't already know."

"That's a shame, since you never stopped talking when you were alive. You owe me a few answers yourself."

"Such as?"

"Why you left me this money pit of a house."

"I explained all that."

"No, you didn't."

"Oh, come along. You love the house, Jules. If you didn't, you'd be long gone. You adore the house, more than your own husband, more than any lover!"

"Well, it's proving a very expensive love affair," Juliana said thinly.

"So, sell some work. Why don't you? Ah, but you can't. Imagine being afraid of what your own hands create. Imagine finding your own work so menacing that you daren't sell it! Ha!"

Juliana's shoulders tensed. "Leave me alone, Corah. I refuse to argue with hallucinations. Go."

In a chilling moment of lucidity, Juliana saw herself as deranged. Simply and starkly mad. Talking to a ghost! And even the ghost was telling her she was crazy.

"I can't go, and I can't rest, until I know what became of my brother," said Corah. She rose up suddenly, making Juliana start, her voice an accusing hiss. "Is Adam here? Have you got him? Are you hiding him from me?"

Juliana whipped round to confront her aunt. The chaise longue was empty. There was only the wind moaning outside, and the faintest hint of cigarette smoke on the air.

"You were there in the Angel this morning, weren't you?" said Gill. "What's happened to you? Your name's Leith, isn't it?"

No answer. The young man sat speechless, convulsed by shivering. Gill hurriedly fetched towels and a spare blanket. She helped him off with his shirt and boots and wrapped a bath towel around him, but drew the line at suggesting he remove his damp trousers.

Turning away, she quickly stoked the log burner, and then brought him a glass of water. He took a couple of sips, his hands shaking so much that he almost dropped it. Gill took it from him and placed it on the coffee table. A mixture of first-aid training and common sense suggested there was not much physically wrong; his pulse was strong and he didn't seem to be in pain. Was he on drugs? He had that glazed look of paranoia, as if he was not quite in the real world. She glared at him, hating him for invading her solitude.

"You should see a doctor," she repeated.

"No." The word shuddered out of him. "No doctor. Hide me. Please."

"What's happened to you?"

He only trembled, and stared past her with glassy eyes. His state of terror, whether drug-induced or genuine, alarmed her. Gill was frightened of him; it was that simple. "Make it stop looking at me," he whispered.

"I can't deal with you on my own," Gill said grimly. She grabbed her walking jacket from the back of the kitchen door and took a small flashlight from a cupboard. "Leith, I'm going out for a few minutes," she said. "I'm going to fetch help."

His eyes showed fear. "No! He'll come for me."

Gill took a couple of deep breaths. "Who will? Your boss, Rufus?"

No answer. He sat staring at nothing, hugging the towel around himself and rocking slightly. After a few moments he asked, "Where is this?"

The question puzzled her. "Cairndonan," she said.

"Cairndonan," he echoed. Then he began to repeat the word over and over again, still rocking. Gill put on her coat, pulling up the hood.

"Look, I can see you're upset, but try to understand that I'm not comfortable being alone with you in this state. You could be a serial killer, for all I know."

"Don't go," he said, so soft she could hardly hear him. "Make it stop."

"I have to fetch someone." She was growing annoyed now. "I don't know what to do with you." No response. "Don't worry, I'll lock the door. I can't make you any safer than that. It's a cottage, not a fortress."

Doubts flooded through her as she locked the door behind her. What if he ransacked the place? What if his pursuer was real? As she hurried through the storm, Gill struggled against a panic attack. She had little worth stealing, but that wasn't the point. Leith might be harmless, and there might well be no one chasing him, but strangers invading her home, her safe space—it had become a near-phobia for her. She thought angrily, *Can't I find* anywhere *truly safe and private?*

Ten minutes later she reached the house, her waterproof jacket streaming with water and her boots squelching. Still no pain in the leg; surely she would pay later. The bulk of the house blended into darkness, but light flooded the porch and lobby. She shook the water off her coat and went in.

The night porter was Colin. He greeted Gill with his infernally cheerful grin, a dozen questions in his eyes. "Greetings, Miss Sharma. Wild night, eh? How can I help?"

She wasn't sure where to start. Her whole body was vibrating with shock and she could hardly find her voice. "I need to speak to Peta Lyon."

"I'll call her room." Lazily he lifted the telephone receiver, saying as he dialed, "Everything okay?"

It struck her that she might need more backup than just Peta. But she could see Colin rudely hauling the young man out of her cottage and calling the police . . . which, although it was probably the correct response, seemed entirely the wrong thing to do. Her anger at the man's intrusion warred with her instinct to help. She empathized with his fragile state; she'd been there herself. Heavy handling was the last thing he needed.

She said, "Yes, I . . . no phone at the cottage . . . and I didn't realize how hard it was raining when I set out."

Colin shrugged and spoke a few words into the receiver. Gill waited impatiently. What if Peta refused to see her? No one could blame her, after the weird fit Gill had thrown last time they'd spoken.

"She says go on up," said Colin. "Top of the stairs, turn right, follow the corridor. Room 23."

"Thanks." Gill started to climb the stairs, with the stained-glass archer and his fallen friend looming over her. Rain rattled on the other side of the glass. In the dark, the window had little color and the design was delineated only by dull lead-lines. From the half-landing, the stairs climbed again to a corridor with a worn red carpet running down the center of molasses-brown floorboards. The house was silent and echoey around her. She wondered where Juliana was, and whether she was sound asleep or working feverishly through the night on some huge project, chiselling at some great block of marble or casting bronze . . .

Gill found Room 23 and knocked.

Peta answered, wearing a cream dressing gown, her hair sweetly tousled. She looked wary, which was unsurprising after their last encounter. "Hi, what's up? Wow, you look soaked, Gill. Is it about the other day?"

"No. I feel terrible about that, but it's not why I'm here. I know it's late, but I need your help. I've got a problem. This guy has turned up at the cottage . . ." Gill told the story in a handful of words, without mentioning that she'd seen Leith before. If it even mattered, it could wait.

"Come in," Peta pulled her arm, drawing her inside. "Tell me more while I get dressed. Please try not to drip on anything."

The bedroom was full of people. Gill stopped in her tracks. Seven figures with exotic animal faces were standing motionless in elaborate robes and cloaks. At first she thought she'd walked into a fancy-dress party or some magical ritual. It took her a moment to realize they were mannequins. There were masks everywhere, stacked on tables, hung from the corners of picture frames. The room glowed warmly golden and smelled of incense.

"Don't mind the guests," said Peta. She threw off her gown with no trace of embarrassment, pulling on a red satin camisole, black skirt and maroon sweater while Gill politely looked the other way. "It's what I do, masks and costumes. I'm a bit obsessive, as you can see. You say this guy isn't violent?"

"He doesn't seem it, but he's in such a state, anything might happen. Should we take Colin with us?"

"It's up to you," said Peta, "but Colin's bound to make a big macho fuss."

"That's what I was worried about." Gill exhaled through her teeth. "That's the last thing we need. This guy is a real mess, and I don't know what to do. He seems scared out of his wits. I don't want a big song and dance with the police, and anyway, if they take him away, we may never find out what's going on."

"You're a woman after my own heart," said Peta, hopping as she dragged on her hefty boots. She winked. "Just you and me, then. We'll sneak out the back way, okay?"

When they reached the cottage, wet and windblown, the lights had been turned out and the curtains drawn. Coldness trickled through Gill. She unlocked the door and stepped in, flicking the light back on. "Leith?"

For a few seconds she thought the room was empty. Then she saw the young man huddled in a gap between the side of the sofa and the wall, a white towel pulled around him. Almost like a child hiding.

"Oh my god," Peta said softly in surprise, as if she hadn't believed it until she saw him in the flesh.

"Hello?" said Gill. "I'm back. I'm Gill, by the way. This is Peta."

Leith stared up at them, his eyes glassy and bloodshot.

"Hey, mate," Peta said lightly. "What's happening?"

"Don't touch me," he murmured. Suddenly he thrust out his hands, making her jump backwards. "The *Dunkelman*! No, make it stop looking at me!"

He curled low over his knees, as if trying to disappear. Peta studied him for a few seconds, then said, "Wow, he does seem pretty well out of it, doesn't he?"

"Come on," Gill said cautiously. "Let's get you back on the sofa, at least. You're safe, I promise."

As she tried to help him up, he put one arm across his eyes and repeated wildly, "Make it stop looking at me!"

"Oh my god, he means the mask," Peta exclaimed. She took three quick steps to the mantelpiece, took the mask out of the vase and laid it face down. At that, the young man stopped protesting and let Gill help him up. He rose shakily and then toppled onto the sofa as if all his strength had gone. She thought he had passed out, until he stirred and moaned. His eyes were closed, his hair soot-black against the white of the towel.

"Oh, bloody hell, Gill," Peta said in a low, concerned tone. They stood looking down at the stranger. His shivering had subsided and he resembled a battle-weary soldier. "Hey, come on, speak to us." When he didn't answer, she sighed, "I wonder who he is?"

"No idea," said Gill. "All I know is his name, Leith. And I saw him in a . . . in a pub earlier today, serving behind the bar."

"So he's local?"

"His accent's English, not Scottish. I suppose he must live locally, if he works around here."

"How about we have a cup of tea?" Peta spoke pointedly, taking Gill's arm and ushering her into the small kitchen. As Gill filled the kettle and set it to boil, Peta added, "Doesn't seem very fair to stand over him, talking about him as if he's not there. When you saw him first, did you speak to him?"

They spoke in low voices so he wouldn't overhear. "No, but he seemed perfectly normal at the time," said Gill. "He doesn't seem dangerous, but . . . Do you think he's taken something, to make him freak out like this?"

"I'm no expert." Peta shrugged. "I didn't smell alcohol on him, did you? He doesn't look like a criminal or a drug addict. You might get demented strangers pounding on your door in a city, but it's got to be pretty rare around here. He looks exhausted. Might be having a mental breakdown of some kind." She stopped suddenly, her cheeks reddening.

"Like me, you mean?" Gill spoke tightly, dropping teabags into three mugs.

"I didn't say that."

"But you'd be right. I am cracking up." There was an awkward pause. Gill folded her arms around her waist. She looked at the floor, then made herself meet Peta's eyes. "I'm sorry about my behavior the other day. I was vile. You didn't deserve that outburst."

"Yes, I did," said Peta. "I crassly intruded on your privacy."

"True, I wasn't happy about it. All the same, I overreacted and I apologize."

"Me, too. I'm sorry." Peta gave a hesitant smile. "So we're okay? I've been worried about you. Do you want to talk about it?"

Gill turned away and continued tea-making. "No, I just want to forget it and decide what we're going to do with Leith. Not that I wish him any harm, but why did he have to pick on me? So much for my peaceful conva- lescence!"

"Try a monastery next time," Peta said wryly. "Look on the bright side: at least he's good-looking. Why don't I get cute young men in distress at my door?"

Gill rolled her eyes. "As soon as he comes round, take him, please."

As she stirred sugar into Leith's tea, Peta tipped her head, looking in- tently at her. "What do you want to do about him?"

"Do I have a choice? He can stay and sleep it off. Hopefully, he'll leave of his own accord in the morning. If not, we'll get him to hospital. What's bothering me, though, is if there really *is* someone after him."

Peta pulled a slim mobile phone out of her pocket and waved it. "If any- one else shows up, we'll call Colin *and* the police."

"If you can get a signal."

"If not, these boots have steel toe-caps."

"And they make you look like Olive Oyl. That's very scary."

"Fuck off," Peta said sweetly.

Gill managed a smile. "Whatever, thanks for being here." She went back into the front room, where the young man twisted restlessly on the sofa. "Tea," she said, "with plenty of sugar, for shock. Would you like something to eat?"

Leith gave a brief shake of his head, but he took the mug from her. He sipped it, then began to take thirsty gulps, gasping between each one. Gill withdrew to the kitchen again. Peta was near the back door, examining the twisted bone staff that Gill had left leaning there.

"Where did you get this?"

"Found it. I'm assuming it fell off a unicorn."

Peta's eyebrows twitched with amusement. She rested the staff back in position and looked at the palm of her hand. "It could do with a clean. I knew a witch who had one of these; hers was in rather better nick, though. They're supposed to have magical properties."

"Well, I do happen to know that these things actually come from nar- whal whales," Gill said dryly. "And explorers brought them back in me- dieval times to pass off as unicorn horns . . . damn, what's the special word I can't remember?"

"Alicorn," said Peta.

"That's it. They passed them off as alicorns."

"Still, it's a bloody funny thing to find just lying around. It could be quite valuable."

"It's just a walking stick to me. Help yourself if you take sugar." Gill briskly passed her a mug and they leaned against the countertop, watching the stranger through the doorway as they sipped their tea.

"I suppose we should call the Cairndonan Arms, or go up there in the morning," said Peta.

"What for?" Gill asked blankly.

"You said he was behind the bar. Ergo, they must know him there. Maybe he got into an argument with a drunken customer?"

"Ah. No. That's not where I saw him."

"Really?" Peta looked puzzled. "It's the only pub around here, to my knowledge."

Gill felt uncomfortable about elaborating, because the experience still didn't make sense. "It was the bar of a hotel called the Angel."

"The Angel?" Peta looked puzzled. "Don't know that one. Whereabouts is it?"

She was reluctant to tell the story because it sounded bizarre, but it flowed out of her regardless, coaxed by Peta's intense interest and relentless questions. She described the strange buildings, the sultry light, the great black angel statue and the steep mountain that was like nothing she'd seen in the Highland landscape.

"It must be a setup similar to Juliana's," said Gill, trying to rationalize. "A big house that's been turned into a hotel, surrounded by holiday cottages."

"And the strange mountain?" Peta asked.

Gill shrugged. "Optical illusion. Clouds, probably."

Peta's face was rapt with interest. "Any idea what the place was called?"

"Boundry, they said." Gill remembered something else. "I saw the word 'Tyrynaia' on the plinth of the statue. Maybe it was someone's name."

At that, Peta's eyes widened. "*Tyrynaia?*" she said, almost to herself.

"Yes. It said, 'Tyrynaia, the heart of us.'"

"Oh," said Peta. "Oh."

"Your face is saying you think I've cracked up."

"No. No, I don't," Peta said firmly. She seemed distinctly animated; her expression was thoughtful and alert, her hands fidgety. She put her empty mug aside. "Tell me again, whereabouts is it?"

"Hard to say." Gill waved vaguely. "About a mile or so inland from the village. The guy I met, Rufus—he looked like no landlord I've ever seen."

"How d'you mean?"

"He was like . . . a male model, or someone out of a painting. Hair down to his waist, and a hippie waistcoat covered in suns and moons." Gill paced to the fridge, put the milk away, turned and leaned on the door as she closed it. "This is the craziest part. I tripped down a step and I was in agony. Rufus put his hands on my leg and the pain stopped," she snapped her fingers, "like *that*. Afterwards, I almost had a panic attack and seriously felt I'd never escape . . ." She gave a deep sigh. "The more I think about Boundry, the more it feels like I was hallucinating."

"Why would you be hallucinating?"

"Because of all the jolly meds I have to take," Gill retorted. "They sometimes put me on cloud nine."

"Ah." Peta grinned. "As long as you don't drive or operate magical alicorns under the influence."

"When I had my loopy fit over the mask, it was because I was drinking with pills."

"If you say so, Gill, but you don't strike me as being the delusional type. If your medication's that good, can I have the name of your doctor?" She winked. Gill gave a short sigh. "Would you describe yourself as overimaginative?"

"No. Absolutely not."

"So let's assume that what happened was real."

"You don't seriously think I entered a supernatural village, do you?"

"Well . . . I hardly know you, so I take you at face value and assume you're telling the truth."

"Now you're humoring me."

"No," Peta said firmly. "I promise you I'm not."

Gill felt something uncoil inside her. "I didn't expect to be listened to as if I'm sane when I'm plainly crazy," she murmured. "So, I went somewhere real that seemed a bit peculiar because I'd had too many painkillers."

Peta touched her arm. The hand, with nails painted deep metallic burgundy, lingered. "You've stopped limping, and Leith is real."

"He was in the background. He didn't speak, just poured me a drink. Oh, now I wish I'd paid more attention to him."

Peta sucked her breath through her teeth; Gill often couldn't tell whether she was being serious or not. "You have heard the warnings about not eating or drinking in the faerie realm, haven't you?"

"For heaven's sake. There were no faeries. He's as human as you and me."

"Gill . . ." Peta hesitated.

"What?"

"Nothing." Peta let her hand drop. "Nothing. So he's running away from a rotten job as a barman, with a furious employer chasing him? Perhaps Rufus caught him with his fingers in the till."

Gill laughed, suddenly realizing how tired she was. "Maybe he'll tell us tomorrow." She looked at Leith, who was still cradling his mug, his head bowed. Crossing the room to him, she asked, "How are you feeling now?"

He looked up at her, his eyes large in their outline of black lashes. His panic had faded, but he looked as confused as a six-year-old waking from a nightmare. "Do you still want to stay?" she asked. "If you do, there's only the sofa. You might feel better if you get some sleep."

"I—I can't," he muttered. "*He* might come."

"Rufus?"

"The *Dunkelman*."

"I've got an idea," Peta said over her shoulder, making her start. "Why don't you take him upstairs and let him sleep in your bed?"

"What?" said Gill.

"I didn't mean *with* you." Peta gave a small, teasing smile. "But if he's upstairs and we're both down here keeping watch, he'll feel safer. Won't you, my friend?"

Leith didn't speak again, but let Gill guide him upstairs. She showed him the bathroom, then let him into the bedroom and grudgingly gave him use of the comfortable double bed. She helped him off with his boots, stripped her duvet off the mattress and folded a spare sheet and blanket over him as he lay down. He fell asleep almost instantly, his breathing deep and rhythmic, his face tranquil at last. Gill watched him, torn by a mixture of annoyance, unease and sympathy.

She bundled the duvet downstairs with a couple of pillows so they could take it in turns to sleep. She was startled to find that Peta had moved the coffee table and was unfolding a double bedframe with a thin mattress from the base of the sofa.

"You didn't know this was a sofabed, did you?" Peta smiled.

"No, I didn't."

"This place is full of surprises."

"You're telling me," Gill said stonily.

"So we can squeeze in together, honey," said Peta with a grin. "What's your preference, pajamas or unfettered nakedness?"

Gill gaped at her. "If you think I'm getting undressed, with a stranger upstairs and some theoretical maniac hunting for him, you're crazy."

"No, just an eternal optimist."

"I'm not even going to ask what that means. Bathroom's upstairs, on the right."

Gill lay down fully clothed on the thin mattress, pulled the duvet over herself and stared at the ceiling, all too conscious of the strange, terrified man in her bed upstairs. Presently, Peta reappeared, flicked off the light and slid in beside her, wearing just a camisole and panties. Gill stirred uneasily at the unfamiliar weight and warmth . . . How had she let this happen, this invasion? Suddenly she felt Peta's arm working its way beneath her shoulders. She stiffened. "What are you doing?"

"What's the matter, haven't you ever been to bed with a girl before?"

Gill coughed, not knowing how to respond. She said stiffly, "Not since my schooldays."

"Shall we take turns, then?"

"At what?"

"At staying awake to make sure our guest is okay. What did you think I meant?" Peta spoke with a smile in her voice. Her forefinger began to play gently in Gill's hair. Gill moved her head to stop her although, it fact, it felt soothing.

"Whatever, I won't sleep anyway."

She felt Peta's breath warm on her cheek. "You know, your body language says that you feel about as attractive as a garden fork, but it's not true. You're lovely, Gill, or will be when you learn to like yourself."

"I'm not gay!" Gill blurted, then felt foolish.

"That's a shame." A ripple of laughter shook Peta's slim body. "Relax, I'm only teasing you. Goodness, you're so touchy."

"I think I have a right, after the episode with your rotten mask."

"I noticed you still have it. You could have destroyed it or thrown it out, but you kept it." Peta was quiet, breathing gently in and out. She smelled deliciously of herbal shampoo, mixed with the comforting, earthy scents of paint and papier-mâché. Then she asked, "What are you afraid of, Gill? What did you see?"

Lying in the dark, feeling Peta's arm around her but not having to meet her eyes, it was all too easy to talk. The mask had swept away a barrier inside her and it was a disturbing feeling. "When I put it on and looked in the mirror, it was like looking into a void. Only the void was *me*. The next thing I knew, all the bad stuff I'd tried to forget came flooding into my head and I couldn't cope with it. That's why I went into hysterics."

"You didn't have hysterics. You just very emphatically told me to leave."

"Well, it felt like it, inside. Was that what the mask was intended to do?"

Peta's voice was steady and serious. "No, not as such. It's a sort of portrait that brings hidden attributes to the surface. But that carries a risk of stirring up stuff that needs to be released . . ."

"Maybe it did, but who the hell asked you to do that for me?"

Peta gave a small shrug. "No one. It was an impulse I should have controlled. Truly, I didn't mean to upset you. Sorry. I'm nosy and rude, with all the subtlety of a blundering bulldozer."

"You said it. In your gigantic hobnailed boots."

"Anyway, now the poison's out, won't you tell me about it?"

What was it about Peta that unraveled her? Her comforting touch, her refusal to be put off by Gill's prickliness? She'd intended to keep herself private, and yet every time she met Peta, she ended up giving too much away. It was like being seduced, manipulated. Self-control was an illusion.

Her intellect told her to clam up, but some part of her longed to confide in a sympathetic stranger. That was the weakness that Peta kept playing on. She hated the impulse, released by the mask, to spill her pain. She resolved to fight it. At the same time Gill was aware that her story was no big deal to an outsider. *I should stop being so precious about it*, she thought.

She lay in silence for a few moments, listening to the wind moaning outside. Okay, she would explain the basics, without emotion, as if it had happened to someone else. That would satisfy all needs, surely—Peta's curiosity, and her own urge to confess—without compromising her dignity.

"Running was all I cared about as a teenager," she began. "When I was sixteen—god, ten years ago—I found a terrific coach. Steve." The name felt unpleasantly solid in her mouth. She swallowed it away. "He was such a bully, but it worked; I started winning big races. It's very concentrated, that kind of relationship, coach and athlete . . ."

"I can imagine," said Peta. "Mentor and protégée."

Gill gave a sour smile. "We should have kept the relationship professional, but it was so intense. Every waking moment was about training, competing, winning. He even dictated what I ate and when. We got engaged; I thought we were in love, but what did I know? I'd never been with anyone else. Steve believed in me. We were a team. We were going to break world records, Olympic gold medals, total glory. That was the script."

"I take it your accident wasn't in the script," said Peta.

"Quite," Gill murmured. "Steve was very driven and that made him difficult. We argued a lot."

"What about?"

"Everything. My training schedule, mostly. I had a day job with a firm of accountants which I hated—my manager, a female, was always vile to me—but if I let off steam about it when I got home, Steve would lose his temper and accuse me of self-pity. If it wasn't about running, he wasn't interested."

"He sounds a complete arse," Peta remarked.

"Oh, he was, but when you're so bound up together, you don't see it. I trusted him; I assumed any problems we had were my fault. Now I can look back and see that I was actually terrified of him. He wasn't straight about training; for example, he started wanting to experiment with undetectable performance-enhancing substances and I wouldn't do it. He said it was state-of-the-art, I said it was cheating. He was just in a constant smoldering fury with the world, especially with me." She paused, cringing at the sour memories. "Every time we had a row, I'd assume it was my fault and

I just needed to get a grip and train harder. So one evening about six months ago, I was out for a routine run around the streets. As I turned into the parking lot of the apartment block, this huge 4×4 roared at me out of the darkness. The next thing I knew, I was waking up in hospital with a shattered hip."

"An accident?"

"Well, that's the thing." She shook her head to quell the disturbing images; a blare of headlights, the grinning metal grille surging at her; the faceless shape of the driver. "Later, I found out Steve was having a fling with the woman I worked for—the manager who'd been making my day job a misery. Finally I saw why she hated me so much! She'd gone to see Steve to give him the ultimatum—either *he* told me about her, or *she* would. But he threw her out, and she drove off in a rage just as I was coming the other way."

Despite her resolution to stay calm, Gill found herself shivering uncontrollably. "Hey," said Peta, holding her tight.

"It wasn't just the accident itself. It was what came after . . ." The memories were a painful cloud. She wiped her eyes with her knuckles, clawed her hair off her forehead. Peta's hands conveyed warmth as she waited for her to go on.

"I'm grateful I can still walk; it could have been so much worse—this pain-free episode is great, but it doesn't mean I'll ever compete again. There was a long blur of surgery, morphine and nightmares. When I came round, I knew my running days were over, but for some reason I thought, *I still have Steve and he'll put this right.* However." She drew a breath. "As soon as I came round and saw him beside my bed, I knew it was over. He looked at me and his eyes were dead. Then it came out, that he'd been seeing my boss behind my back, and that she'd been at the wheel of the vehicle that ran me down."

"So, she was driving off in a rage, and just didn't see you in time?" Peta put in cautiously.

"Exactly. I'm sure it wasn't deliberate. She wasn't *that* malicious—and from all I heard afterward, she was completely devastated and remorseful. It was a genuine accident, I'm certain." Gill took a breath. "And yet there's a dark, paranoid little corner of my mind that can't help wondering . . . I'm sure that, consciously, she would never have dreamed of trying to kill me. But did she have a split-second of blind fury that made her swerve towards me, or hit the accelerator instead of the brake? I'll never know."

"No, you won't," said Peta. "And you mustn't think like that, or you'll go mad."

"Even madder," Gill amended. "I know. Anyway, her affair with Steve ended that night. *He* was the problem, not her. After his first visit, he came to see me just twice, and he was so cold. Finally I caught on! I'd only ever been of interest to him for my athletic skills—the achievement, the reflected glory. And he'd already found someone new to coach. Someone younger, fresher and faster than me."

"Bastard. I guessed someone had broken your heart."

"Oh, I'm not heartbroken over *him*. No, it's the betrayal that tore this chasm inside me. My whole life with Steve was a lie. After he'd abandoned me, I started having a lot of nightmares about him, flashbacks. He'd be standing by my bed, this solid dark shape watching me . . ." Her heart rose into her throat with remembered fear and she struggled to get the words out. "A doppelganger in the shape of Steve, completely malevolent, horrible . . ."

"Perhaps not surprising, after what you'd been through."

"Yes. Post-traumatic stress, they said. After a long stay in hospital, I moved in with a friend from the athletics club for a while, but the nightmares wouldn't stop. I was convinced that Steve, or someone, was breaking in at night and standing over me, this horrible faceless shadow . . ."

"Hush, relax. You're as rigid as a board."

She tried, consciously flexing her limbs. "It sounds paranoid, I know, but I can't shake it off. I got good severance pay from my job and I fled. That's why I'm here."

"What about your family?"

Gill laughed. "What family?"

"Oh."

"So, I wasn't happy at all about Colin recognizing me. I understand how Leith must feel. Some horrific bogeyman is haunting me and I know it's not Steve, he's nothing and nobody to me now, he was just a catalyst to something worse. I know it's all in my mind but I can't stop thinking, what if this dark figure finds me?"

Peta took her hand, squeezed it. "You're safe, honey. We'll look after you."

Gill gave a long, near-silent groan. "I'm not really scared. I wake up with the dark man in the corner of my room and I think, oh, it's you again, just fuck off. If a stalker attacked me in reality, I'd fight. But it's the uncertainty, the bad dreams . . . I can't fight those."

"If I made it worse with the mask, I'm sorry," Peta said softly. "Have you really no family, no one you can trust?"

"There's only my mother, and we haven't spoken for years . . . that's another story. I trusted Steve. Now there's no one. That's why I've grown to like my solitude."

"Hey, go to sleep now." Peta hugged her gently. "You'll get through this."

Gill blinked, looking up at the darkened ceiling. For all her resistance to confessing, it had been a strange relief. And she hadn't broken down again. If anything, she felt calmer than she had in a long time. After a moment she said, "What about you, Peta? Why are you so concerned? You've been hell-bent on dragging my story out of me from the start. Why is it all me talking, and you listening?"

"I wanted to get to know you, that's all. I don't blame you for being suspicious after what you've been through, but that's all it is."

She said insistently, "Still, for the sake of fairness—let's talk about you."

"There's not much to know." Peta paused. "I'm from a village called Cloudcroft in the middle of England. Large family of loud redheads. I'm the quiet one."

"Oh, good grief," said Gill, smiling.

"I have four sisters. The eldest, Lydia, is a psychiatrist, and Jemima teaches physics at a college in London. Then there's me in the middle, then the twins, Molly and Maria, who intend to set up a veterinary practice together, assuming they don't kill each other first."

"Do you all have that lovely deep red hair?"

"All," said Peta. "Especially our mother, Cath. She's tremendously flamboyant; we call her Catherine the Great. My father, Peter, loves books and keeps his head down; he's so outnumbered."

The affection in her voice was plain. "It sounds as if you're very close."

"Yes, we are, although it can be a squabbling madhouse at times. We're all very proud of each other. I miss them a lot."

"So what brought you here?"

"Juliana advertised for an assistant tutor," Peta answered vaguely. "The chance to work with her was irresistible."

"But your style of work's totally different to hers. You don't seem desperate for guidance like Colin. Also, you sound decidedly evasive."

Peta laughed. "All right. I really did want to meet Juliana and I love teaching . . . but I had an ulterior motive, too."

"What?" An uneasy blend of cold fear and excitement washed through Gill. She clasped Peta's arm, hard enough to make her wince. "Come on. Tell me why you're so fascinated by my every move. What's going on?"

"Ow," said Peta. "Gill, you're being a bit scary now." She exhaled slowly. "Okay. I hadn't planned on talking about it yet. I'm perfectly sure you won't believe me."

"After what's happened to me in the last few days? Try me."

"If you promise not to repeat it."

"I promise."

"All right. Yes, I came to work for Juliana on a pretext. It's a long story, which I'll tell you tomorrow—but I have reason to believe that there's a strange and ancient gateway on Cairndonan Estate. A portal; a way to what some might call the Otherworld. I've been trying to find it."

Gill stared at her. "And?"

"And I think you have already found it for me, dear."

5

A Beautiful Prison

Gill slept, in spite of her conviction that she would not. She woke with a start. It was daylight, and she was alone on the sofabed. For a moment she was disoriented. Then she saw Peta—dressed and making tea in the kitchen—and she remembered.

She dragged herself upright, feeling stale in her clothes. There was a hint of pain in her hip, like a faint toothache. Her head ached from stress as she recalled the uninvited guest and her conversation with Peta last night. Anxiety stirred.

"Peta? Have you checked on . . . ?" She glanced up toward the ceiling.

"Not yet." The artist came over with a mug of tea, her hair resembling a crimson bird's nest. "Gill, it's past eight. I have to go and teach my students. And I need to shower and change first."

"You're not leaving me alone with him?" Gill hurriedly got up and began to fold the bed away, swearing as she caught a finger in the metal framework.

Peta helped her, swinging the frame back into the base of the sofa and pushing seat-cushions on top. "I don't want to, but I can't abandon my class. You could come up to the house with me . . ."

"I'm not leaving him here on his own! This is supposed to be my *home*, at least for a few weeks."

"We could take him with us . . . but then Juliana would want to know what you were both doing there . . ."

"Yes. I can appreciate that would be awkward."

Peta gave a rueful laugh. "However, if I leave and he murders you, that would be worse than awkward."

"You're reading my mind," Gill said sarcastically. Fumbling in her pocket, she found a couple of painkillers, popped them out of their blisters and gulped them with her tea, nearly scalding her throat. She recalled Peta's words last night. *I have reason to believe there's a strange and ancient gateway on Juliana's estate, a portal to the Otherworld . . . and I think you have found it.* No explanation. When Gill had pressed her, Peta had simply said, "I'll tell you tomorrow. I need to see for myself first." And then, soothed by Peta's fingers stroking her hair, she'd fallen asleep.

"Well, shall we go up and see how he is, for a start?" Peta suggested.

The young man was still unconscious, lying in a tangle of white sheets. With his chest and arms bare, his head tipped to one side and his hair a wild black halo, he reminded Gill of a painting she'd once seen . . . she couldn't recall the title . . . hair like soot against chalky, ivory skin . . . an image of death. Suicide. As her heart chilled inside her, Peta breathed, "Wow, isn't he beautiful? I'd love to sketch him. Have you got a camera handy?"

"You're sick!" Gill exclaimed.

"And you obviously haven't a trace of poetry in your soul," retorted Peta. "I hope he's okay. He doesn't look too good."

"Well, he's breathing," said Peta. "Leith?"

At her voice he woke with a start, raised his head and stared at them without recognition. "What is it?" he gasped. "Are they here? Tell him I'm sorry!"

"Who?" Gill asked. "It's just us two. Do you remember coming here last night?"

The young man gave the pained frown and sigh of someone regretting the night before. "I think so," he said, very softly. "Yes." He sat up slowly with his lean torso arched forward, weight resting on his braced arms, head drooping. "I'm sorry to have put you to such trouble . . . Am I in France?"

"No, Scotland," said Gill with a frown. "Why would you be in France?"

No answer. Peta said, "How about you come downstairs and have breakfast with us? You're safe. No one came looking for you last night."

The young man nodded, and put on the black robe that Gill handed to him. At least he was calm; that was promising. He followed Peta downstairs with Gill coming last. She noticed how cautiously he moved, looking around him as if everything was new and potentially dangerous.

They led him into the kitchen and seated him at the small pine breakfast table. Peta sat opposite, while Gill stood, since there were only two chairs. She quickly made more tea and some rounds of toast, which were hardly touched. All their attention was focused on the guest, who looked as nervous as a stray cat testing a new home. Was he on the run from the police? Gill wondered. Was he harmless, or would his disturbed state of mind lead to unpredictable violence?

"So, are you going to explain yourself?" Peta asked bluntly. "Your name is Leith, right?"

"That's what they called me."

"Is it your surname?"

"No. Just a name."

"All right, Leith, can you remember what happened last night?"

He looked down at his pale, interlaced fingers. "I remember."

"Can you tell us?"

A shadow fell over his face. "No. I can't."

"Is there anyone we can contact for you?"

"I—I don't think so. No. No one."

"So what would you like us to do for you?"

The pressure of questions seemed to distress him. "I don't know! Nothing. Please, let me stay awhile so that no one finds me. Then I'll go. Forgive me."

Peta put a reassuring hand on his wrist, looking up at Gill as she did so. "What do you think? Can he stay?"

Gill sighed. "I suppose so. Just for today. As long as he's not prone to violence."

For the first time there was a flash of life in Leith's eyes. "I would never do violence, never, it's not in me!" he said fervently.

Gill told herself sternly, *I must stop being scared. This is not another Steve. It's just a messed-up young man and I refuse to be frightened of him.* When Peta looked at her watch, Gill said, "You go. I'll be fine."

"Are you sure?"

"Completely. I've got my alicorn, and I've studied martial arts. I'll terrify him with my Tai Chi moves." She meant it lightly, but Peta still looked worried. "Really, it's all right," Gill said more firmly. "If he tries anything, I'll handle it."

"If you're sure." Peta headed for the front door, pulled on her boots and her coat, which still looked damp from last night's rain. As she stepped outside, she turned and added, "I'll be done with my class by three-thirty." She kept her voice down, Gill realized, so that Leith would not hear her. "I'll come back then, if that's okay? I'd like you to show me exactly how you found the way to Boundry."

"Why? What are you planning to do?"

"Nothing. I want to take a look, that's all. Take care, okay?" She gave Gill a reassuring touch on the shoulder, and went.

The morning was cool and still after the storm. Earth and rock and stream, great trees rustling gently in the bright air—all made Gill powerfully aware of nature's vibrant force. It overwhelmed her. She withdrew into the cottage and closed the door, uncomfortable with the burden of having this strange, vulnerable man foisted on her. Did he need medical help, or not? What to say to him?

Leith was standing at the sink, looking at the rock face outside. As she approached, he tensed visibly. He turned and asked, "Where has she gone? Would she betray me to Rufus?"

"Peta? No, of course not. She doesn't even know him."

"But she is one of their number." He walked past her and went to stare out of the front window instead. She followed him, caught between annoyance and curiosity.

"How d'you mean?"

"They shine," he muttered. "When they come to you, they . . ."

"You're not making much sense," Gill said abruptly. "She's an art teacher. I'm just here on holiday."

"I know this place," he said, as if in surprise.

"It's a cottage on Cairndonan Estate."

"Cairndonan," he repeated.

"Look, you still seem almightily confused. Why don't you have a bath? You'll feel better for it. Then we can talk, try to untangle what's happened to you. Yes?"

He was silent for a moment, and she wasn't sure he'd registered her words. Then his eyes cleared and he said, "Yes. A bath would be welcome. Thank you."

The way he spoke was formal and old-fashioned; it almost made her smile. She led the way upstairs and found spare towels for him, noticing the startled way he eyed her as if he thought she was going to stand there while he stripped off. His manner verged on prudish, which amused her. In fact, it was a welcome relief after Colin's brazenness.

"Don't worry, I'll leave you to it," she said. "Hopefully your clothes will have dried out by now; if not, I'll lend you something."

She closed the door and went downstairs, glad to be alone but not quite knowing what to do next. What if he did something crazy, slit his wrists or drowned himself? Shaking off her alarmist thoughts, she went into the kitchen, ate a piece of cold toast, then occupied time by washing up.

"This is absolutely bizarre," she said out loud. "I could walk away, of course, write off the money I've paid for this place. And go where? A hotel, a bed-and-breakfast in Glasgow? Maybe a big city's a better place to lose myself. Or I could head for Prestwick Airport and fly anywhere. I've got my passport. I don't *have* to be here."

Thoughts of escape soothed her. When Leith reappeared half an hour later—his hair wet, color in his cheeks from the heat of the water—Gill felt almost cheerful. Fully dressed in his dark trousers and white shirt, he had an athletic grace about him. She could appreciate why Peta had called him beautiful and wanted to sketch him.

She brought him coffee and biscuits—regardless of whether he actually wanted them—and excused herself for a quick, much-needed shower.

Afterwards, as she dressed in a fresh pair of jeans and black T-shirt, she fantasized about packing her few belongings. She could be out of there in minutes, if need be. The thought made her feel better as she pulled on a brown sweater, shaking free the damp inky ropes of her hair.

Downstairs, she found Leith again standing at the front window, gazing out. Without looking at her, he said, "I've done something terrible."

"Oh?" His words threw ice water on her mood. She asked cautiously, "How terrible? Murdered someone . . . You haven't, have you?"

"I might as well have done so." He didn't elaborate, only continued staring at the stream and the woodland beyond, where sunlight glittered on a million wet leaves.

Gill perched on the sofa arm nearest to the front door. "What do you mean?"

"Will you give me away?"

"To the police? Depends what you've done. If it's really horrible, I'd suggest you turn yourself in and leave me out of it."

"No, to him. To Rufus."

"Why on earth would I do that? I don't know Rufus, he's just some guy who touched my leg and bought me a drink . . . Oh, that sounded all wrong. Look, can we start at the beginning? It was you I saw in the Angel, wasn't it?"

"That place is not called the Angel," Leith said thinly. "Yes, I was there. I don't know how you found your way to us, but when I saw you, I thought . . . I thought that if you had found a way in, I could find a way out."

"*A way out?* Were you trapped there?"

"Yes. We all were. I wasn't sure there was anything still remaining outside Boundry. Perhaps the true world was destroyed in the war. I couldn't be sure."

"So . . . where is Boundry, Leith? *What* is it?"

He looked straight at her. His eyes were violet-grey and clear, like glass, and yet it struck her that they might as well be speaking different languages. Their minds were two separate universes. "It's a place . . . a terrible place . . . where nothing makes sense. And you can't leave."

"Sounds like my life," she remarked. "Boundry seemed very beautiful, though . . ."

"A beautiful prison."

"At least it had a bar." He didn't react to her lame jokes. Gill sighed. She hardly knew what to ask next. "Had you been trying to escape for long?"

Leith shook his head. "I never really tried before. I was too afraid. I always dreamed about it . . ." He looked around, as if distracted. "Is there a child here?"

"No," Gill said, puzzled. "What child?" He looked puzzled too, so she let it drop. "How did you find your way here?"

"I don't know. I followed you, Gill."

"Did you?" She was shocked. "But I . . . I can't explain how I found my way in. I was walking, and it just happened. There I was."

He reached out and held her wrist, making her start. "When you'd gone, I knew I must follow you. It was my only chance. I waited until Rufus left me alone and then I ran."

"How did you know which way I'd gone?"

"I don't know. There must have been clues, footprints in the grass, a thread of warmth, a trail of elementals disturbed in your wake—I can't say. I was afraid and it all happened so fast; the memories are blurred. I fled blind. I ran and ran into the storm. In my mind I sensed the way closing again behind me but I dared not stop to check, because I knew if I paused even for a second, they would catch me . . ." His chest rose and fell rapidly.

"They?"

Words began to tumble out of Leith in a stream. He paced the room, sat down, stood up again. Gill could barely make sense of it; she could only listen aghast, wondering if he would ever stop. There was no clear story, yet the words invaded her mind with vivid images.

Something about a forest swaying wildly all around him, like seaweed under the ocean. It was night; a procession of strange beings was moving within their own soft, firefly glow. Fear enveloped him as one of them turned its lovely, un-human face to stare at him. Someone was screaming. A tree root snared his feet and he was falling, pain tearing at him . . .

Glowing, translucent faces circled over him; hands clawed at his clothing. They looked like serpents and like angels at the same time. He tried to wriggle out of their grasp but his limbs were heavy and nerveless; paralyzed. Their leader loomed dark and dazzling out of the forest, reducing him to nothing . . . They were carrying him off like a prize, like a haunch of meat, and all the time their hard fingertips explored his skin, making him struggle helplessly for release.

The world turned inside out and went mad.

They surrounded him with their lovely faces and mocking smiles, hands caressing him as they would a pet cat. And always at their center, Rufus with his hair flowing like a river of dark blood, a king presiding over his court. They tipped delicious liquors onto Leith's tongue, bringing intoxication. Nothing made sense. Things would become clear for a single, poised moment, only to break up and swirl away into golden confusion.

Sometimes he was running in the darkness, and they were hard on his heels, hunting him as if he were a wounded hart. And he was sobbing with the tearing pain of his lungs, his heart threatening to burst with terror, but they only laughed as they pursued him without mercy and brought him back to his knees before Rufus again.

Boundry was a small corner of hell that cruelly masqueraded as paradise.

At the center of it was a tight whirlpool of agony that could not be expressed. He believed he was being punished . . .

Then, something about a glass wall, and a pale figure trying to break through from the other side, promising to help, but Leith was too afraid, looking over his shoulder for those dark and shining hunters who always came, the Dunkelmen . . .

These disturbing pictures took root in Gill's mind as Leith paced and muttered. After some twenty minutes, Leith's flood of words slowed to a trickle, and then to four that he repeated over and over again. He sat down with his head in his hands, shuddering, close to weeping. Awkwardly Gill sat beside him, resting one hand on his shoulder in a futile attempt at consolation.

He kept saying, "What have I done? What have I done?"

When Peta came back that afternoon, Leith was asleep once more, curled on his side on the sofa, apparently out cold with sheer exhaustion. Gill had passed the time by scrubbing dirt and algae off the unicorn staff; it polished up quite well, despite being badly discolored. Then she'd tried to read a novel, but, unable to concentrate, she'd given up and cleaned the kitchen instead.

"This," she said to herself as she scrubbed the sink, "was not in my vision of a retreat to the middle of nowhere."

She was caught between sympathy and frustration. True, she could simply have walked out . . . yet she hadn't. Not yet, anyway. Part of her wanted none of this to be happening, yet part of her was reluctantly intrigued . . . and, unexpectedly, Leith's presence wasn't as unwelcome as she'd feared. He gave her something to focus on, apart from her own difficulties.

When Peta's knock came, she hurried to let her in. The world outside was storm-cleansed and calm, with sunlight glowing through the woodlands and not a breath of wind.

"Ah, sleeping beauty," said Peta, smiling down at him. "How's he been?"

"Strange. Distressed, but not aggressive. At least he's eating and drinking. Not much, but it's better than nothing."

"Talkative?"

"Very, at one point, but not making a whole lot of sense. And . . ." She lowered her voice, taking Peta's arm to draw her away. "Sort of sweaty and restless, like I get if I forget to take my painkillers."

"Oh?"

"Let's not speculate about that. Maybe we can persuade him to see a doctor."

"D'you think it's okay to leave him for an hour or so?" Peta mused. "He's well away, isn't he? Come on, grab a jacket and your trusty alicorn."

Gill wasn't sure, but she obeyed, glad of an excuse to go out. She dithered over locking the door, but decided not to; it seemed wrong to lock him in. She would have to trust him in turn not to bolt her out. The air smelled so intensely fresh that it turned her dizzy. Rain-drenched leaf mold, wet earth, ozone, pine. She took one deep breath after another.

"I'd like you to show me exactly which way you went," said Peta, "when you found Boundry."

Gill shrugged. "I'll try."

The storm had left its signature on the woodlands in fallen branches and torn leaves. Along the stream bank, Gill guessed at the place where she'd begun to ascend the wooded rise to her right. Trees released showers of collected water on their heads as they pushed their way upwards.

"So, what's he been saying?" Peta asked as they went.

Gill, in front, was taking long strides with the aid of her staff, marveling that the pain had not returned. "Have you ever held a conversation with someone suffering a schizophrenic episode? They talk to you with absolute conviction about secret agents sending messages through the television? It was like that. Sort of. I wouldn't have believed a word, if I hadn't seen Boundry for myself." She fell quiet as they came to an impassable tangle of bushes and had to backtrack until they found another way through.

"So just because he might be drugged or psychotic," Peta said, slightly out of breath, "doesn't mean he's also delusional."

"I got the impression that he'd been abducted and held hostage in some way. Had a hideous time. It was hard to untangle what he was saying, but it sounded like he'd been used as a . . . a virtual slave."

"Slave?" Peta exclaimed. "That's a bit strong. Used, by whom?"

"You tell me." Threads of unease caught Gill's heart. She thought about the mask, about Leith's fear that Peta would betray him. "You're the one who seems to know all about portals to other worlds. He remarked that you were 'one of their number,' whatever that means. What did he mean?"

Peta went quiet as they pushed through bracken. She said, "I think I know what he meant, but I'll tell you later. It's too long a story."

Gill stopped and looked round at her. "Can I trust you? Can he? He seems to think you're going to tell Rufus where he is. How do I know your motives for being so fascinated with this Boundry place?"

"Of course you can trust me," Peta said firmly. Her face was solemn, her gaze steady. "Gill, I don't know anything about Boundry, or Rufus, or Leith. I'm as eager to find out as you are."

"Why?"

"I will tell you, I swear. But let's look first, and talk later."

Gill left it, at least for the time being. Without a track to guide her, she struggled to find the mill, wondering if she'd imagined even that. The woods were emerald-green and enveloping. Then the green-veiled ruins loomed through the mass of branches and her heart quickened. She heard the rush of water. "Here it is."

"Wow." Peta stared around her as they entered the eerie space within its overgrown walls. "Never knew this was here."

"It sits on a larger branch of the stream. There's a path that must have led to the village once, but it's completely overgrown."

"So you came through the center of the building . . ." Peta was agilely picking her way over fallen stones and brambles. Gill followed with more caution, catching up as she paused in the far entrance.

"And I found the alicorn wedged across the doorway here, then I crossed the old platform over the stream," she said. "Be careful, it's hellish slippery."

Before the words were out, Gill skidded on moss, and nearly went down. Peta grabbed her arm and steadied her. Amazingly, the jolt did not reawaken the throbbing in her leg. "Careful. Are you all right?"

"Yes, no damage done."

"Come on, then." Peta led the way past the creaking wreck of the wheel to the far bank. "I thought I'd searched everywhere, but the estate is so full of secret places . . ." She sounded excited. Gill, despite being damp and tired, realized that she, too, was beginning to enjoy the adventure. She indicated the wild meadow, with its tangles of bracken and gorse.

"Then we follow this footpath to the stone circle at the top."

The air was heady with the fresh, pungent scent of wet vegetation. As they walked, Peta asked, "Are you really hating Leith being at the cottage?"

The gentle way she asked the question made Gill feel churlish. "No," she said thoughtfully. "No, I don't mind as much as I thought I would. It's different, that's all. I was trying to work out why I can tolerate him, and I realized it's because he's so totally focused on himself."

"What?" Peta's eyebrows arched. "I've never heard utter self-absorption classed as a desirable quality before!"

"I know." Gill laughed. "What I mean is that he isn't hassling me, judging me, trying to control me. Because of the state he's in, he just accepts me being there. I like that. It's a pleasant change from the, er . . . negative attention I was getting."

"From the ghastly Steve?" said Peta.

"Exactly."

"I see why my nosy attempts at friendship were so very unwelcome."

"You weren't to know. I've been in a place where the most benign hint of attention seems threatening." Gill hesitated, aware Peta was working her usual spell, drawing too much out of her. "I'm a curled-up hedgehog. And you know, you don't seem quite benign, somehow."

"I'm pretty sure that's not a compliment," Peta said with a smile.

"Anyway, with Leith, it was all about *him*, and that was fine." To herself she added, *I wish I could've found some way to tell him, "I know how you feel. I've been there too." Maybe when we get back.*

By the time they reached the Sisters, Gill's heart was beating hard. The stone circle appeared as bleak and eerie as she remembered, with rugged cliffs meandering away to the north and the rounded purplish shapes of mountains inland. A bird of prey hung on the air currents far above. There was no sharp, snowy peak to be seen. She recalled the standing stones having a blue tinge, but now they were grey, lichen-mottled.

"Oh." Peta spoke in disappointed surprise. "Actually, I have been up here before and didn't notice anything. Mind you, I came from the other direction, from the village road. Great place for my students to sketch."

"Well, this is the way I came," said Gill. She looked around, puzzled. There was the signpost to Cairndonan village, apparently pointing along the path where she'd found Boundry. "Only one path," she said. "I could have sworn there were two."

She led on down the footpath on the far side of the circle, down the deep green tunnel with weeds dragging at her boots, until confusion made her hesitate. There were no stone angels guarding the track, no tree dripping with sun-yellow blossom, nor any strange white horse gazing at her. The church spire loomed, and she could see the backs of ordinary cottages. Fences, gardens, sheds.

There was no mountain, no misty violet loch. A car swished down the road towards the village main street, a hundred yards away.

"Oh, damn it!" Gill exclaimed. "Bugger! I *knew* I must have imagined it all."

She looked back. Her companion was not there.

"Peta?" She turned in all directions, looking around at the dense hedgerows and the meadow on her right, wondering how long she'd been alone. "Peta!"

Suddenly Peta was there again—only a few yards behind her, looking at something in the long grass. Gill's head spun; the world seemed to shift and crackle. She was certain the artist had not been there a moment ago. How on earth had she missed her? A momentary blind spot in her vision?

"I'm here. Look at this."

Sighing, Gill walked back to her. "I had a horrible feeling this would happen. Sorry if I've led you on a wild-goose chase but, let's face it, I'm completely cracked at the moment. I did warn you."

Peta looked thoughtful. Her lips were pursed, her eyes serious. "Again, if you hallucinated Boundry, where did Leith come from? Stop trying to rationalize it. Look."

She parted long stems of cow parsley to reveal a dark stump of stone; a crude angel figure. Gill gasped, then turned and made a swift, fruitless search for its twin.

"There were two!" she said. "I walked between them."

"And now there's only one." Peta fingered the worn head. "It means the portal is closed, that's all. At least I know where it is now. I wonder how you opened it?"

"I have no idea."

"Did the world turn strange—watery, or bluish?"

"Not sure. The air was sort of . . . ripply. Sultry. As if the climate had turned more Mediterranean than Scottish. Oh, and something else was different; when I was crossing the Sisters, the stones looked blue, not grey. Quite vivid, like lapis lazuli."

"Blue," Peta said under her breath. "That's a sign."

Gill raised the unicorn staff. "I know this sounds mad, but—was it something to do with me taking this out of the doorway at the mill?"

"I doubt it," Peta responded as if she'd asked a perfectly rational question. "There aren't usually magical artifacts involved. I think the alicorn was just a message of some kind, to say, 'The way is closed.'"

Gill recalled her encounter with Ned Badger. "In that case, I suspect I know who put it there." She described the ridiculous tug-of-war she'd had in the street; her description made Peta smile.

"I wonder what Ned knows?" said Peta. "Interesting."

Gill felt suddenly shaky with relief that there was no Boundry, no Rufus, no sinister spectral beings waiting to pursue her. Leaning down and pushing back the grass to reveal more of the angel figure, she felt the piercing pain of a thorn ripping her left palm. By reflex, she jerked her hand up. An arc of blood drops spattered from her hand. "Ow! *Shit.*"

"What have you done?" said Peta.

"A bramble attacked me. It's okay, it's nothing."

"Let me see," said Peta, taking the wounded hand. There was a half-inch tear in the palm, oozing and dripping blood. "You need to get this seen to. Have you had a tetanus shot?"

"Yes. I had every shot under the sun in hospital. Honestly, don't fuss. Let's get back to the cottage."

"Which is a good half-hour's walk, whereas the pub is only ten minutes away. Come on, Gill, let's at least get a bandage on it and sit you down with a drink."

"What about Leith?"

"He'll be okay for another half hour."

"All right." Gill gave in, unnerved by how much blood was coming out of such a small wound. "On one condition. Would you care to tell me what the hell is going on?"

"Sure," Peta said easily, taking her arm. "Come on, I'll explain over a drink."

When they entered the Cairndonan Arms, every head turned to stare as if the locals had never seen anyone from outside the village before. The place could not have been more different from the "Angel." Dark, nicotine-stained and full of character, it had old-fashioned red and green decor, low ceilings with oak beams, a brick fireplace with a coat-of-arms above it, and a heavily scarred dart board. The atmosphere was heavy with the pub scent of stale beer. Behind the bar stood a formidable woman of around sixty, a broad-bosomed matriarch with a helmet of grey-blond hair. The shelf behind her was stacked with at least fifty different types of Scotch whisky.

The proprietor, although stern-faced, turned out to be surprisingly help-ful and friendly. Gill was taken into the pub kitchen, where her wound was bathed, disinfected and dressed. With the bleeding staunched and a bandage protecting the cut, her hand felt comfortable again. Then Peta ensconced her in a nook by the fire, and brought two large glasses of red wine. "It's a bit early," said Gill.

"It's nearly six. Shut up and drink."

"Thanks. I need it." She paused to take a couple of large gulps. "Sorry I couldn't find the place. Typical. You must think I'm an idiot."

"I don't think that at all." Peta lowered her voice. The murmur of the pub had risen again, now that they were no longer the center of attention. Tucked away in their snug corner, they could talk without being overheard. "Portals can be capricious. If that particular one has been closed for some years, it might be . . . rusty, so to speak."

"Leith said he sensed the way closing as he fled," said Gill. "I imagined it sealing itself like a giant zip behind him."

Peta's mouth curled at one corner. "That might not be so far from re-ality."

"But who opened or closed it? Rufus?"

Peta shook her head. "I don't think any *person* did so. These gateways have a life of their own; I hesitate to say a *mind*, but definitely a life . . . like a flower, perhaps." She lifted a hand, palm cupped like a lotus, closing and opening her elegant fingers. "A personality, definitely. Someone might *in-fluence* a portal to open or close—but control it, never. Actually, that's not true; there are exceptions, but generally speaking, it's down to the unseen powers of the cosmos, my dear."

There was a gleam of amusement in her eyes, but Gill felt left out of the private joke. She asked bluntly, "So how come you know all this stuff?"

"I love the way you're so direct," said Peta. Her innate good humor made it hard to dislike her.

"Being mangled under a motor vehicle left me shorn of all the social niceties, I'm afraid. What's your excuse?"

"No excuse at all, beyond my natural charm," Peta replied. "What I'm telling you isn't secret, exactly, but people don't generally know the truth. There's a different race, older than humankind . . ."

"What race? Like Neanderthals?"

"Yes, like that, only better-looking." Peta laughed. "All the myths of elves, angels or demons, the Shining Ones who were here before mankind arrived? They're still here. They call themselves Aetherials, or older names such as Aelyr and Vaethyr. And they can move between this world and realities humans can't usually see."

"The Otherworld," Gill said flatly, as Peta took a drink.

"That's the generic term for it, but more often we call it the Spiral. In Cloudcroft, where I'm from, there stands the greatest of all gates into the Spiral, but there are many lesser ways all over the country, small portals hidden in hollow trees, springs, woodland glades, ancient paths . . . I came to Cairndonan to search for one portal in particular. The one you found."

Gill was staring, caught between the desire to believe Peta, and the fear that, despite her worldly-wise air, she was just a flake. She resisted the idea of her experience in Boundry being used to support someone else's web of delusion. Yet there was an aura about Peta; a feeling of light and shadow gathering around her, a door being opened in the darkness.

"I'm simplifying," said Peta. "The Otherworld isn't a single solid world like this one. It has layers. We call the first layer the Dusklands, and even humans glimpse it sometimes; you know those magical times at dawn or dusk when the Earth seems alien, eerie?"

"Yes. But that's just . . . atmosphere, isn't it?"

Peta gave a quick shrug of her shoulders. "Or a deepening of perception. Then there's Dumannios, the deeper layer of the Dusklands, where things can become quite dark and out of control . . . and its sister dimension, the Crystal Ring, which is said to be the realm of the subconscious made physical, where vampires and other archetypes originate."

"I hope there isn't going to be a written test," said Gill.

Grinning, Peta took a swallow of her drink. "I don't expect you to accept all this in one go. I'm just telling you. Reality's deeper than it seems, but you've already experienced that."

"I can accept Boundry as a unique weirdness. But you're saying that this weirdness is normal to you? Look, I've just left London. Dog-eat-dog lifestyle, zillions of commuters, traffic, dirty pavements, no mercy. This is culture shock."

"Really? So when you've been pounding the streets at dead of night, or felt the cold steel glare of your boss on your spine, or woken up convinced there's a Steve-shaped intruder in your bedroom, you've never felt an *otherness*?"

Gill shivered, violently enough to spill a drop of her wine. She put the glass down. "I'm not sure it's the same as what you're telling me."

"What you dismiss as 'atmosphere' may, to an Aetherial, be an actual dimension that he or she can enter physically. Do those dimensions seep into our subconscious to become dreams? Or do our dreams create them? A bit of both, I believe. Only in the Dusklands can you find a Gate, and only through a Gate can you enter the Otherworld proper, the Spiral itself."

"Like going through the back of a wardrobe?"

"Exactly, yeah." Peta nodded enthusiastically. "I always loved the idea of a portal inside a wardrobe. Haven't found one yet, but you never know."

Gill gazed skeptically at her. "The rational bit of me insists you must be making this up. But why would you bother? So either it's real, or you're crazy."

"Gill, I am crazy, but that's a totally separate issue. Indulge me. Ask questions as if it were all true."

"I'll try. So . . . have you entered the Dusklands?"

"All the time."

"And the Spiral itself?"

"Oh, yes. Many times."

The way Peta looked as she said it—unfocused, as if remembering something intensely personal and bittersweet—sent a great wave of coldness over Gill. She remembered how Peta had vanished and reappeared as if nothing had happened.

"So, what's it like in the Spiral?"

"Raw. Rural. Beautiful. Elemental. The stars sing. The standing stones there are as blue as lapis lazuli and they are said to be sentient. My dear, you've been there yourself."

She looked straight into Gill's eyes as she said this. Gill was left wordless for a few seconds. She saw that to Peta, it was absolutely real. She took several swallows of wine to quell the strange feeling rushing though her. With her left hand, she gripped the narwhal tusk to ground herself, feeling its ridges smooth under her fingertips. "Humans can go into it, then?"

"Not usually, but sometimes. You haven't asked me the most obvious question of all, yet."

"What?" Gill hesitated, knowing exactly what she meant but hardly able to form the words. "You're not trying to tell me that you are one of this ancient race yourself . . . an Aetherial . . . are you?"

Peta answered softly, "Well, yes. I am. I'm Vaethyr, which simply means I'm an Aetherial who dwells on Earth, which the Aelyr call Vaeth. It sounds very much to me as if Rufus is one, too."

"So you're not human?"

"Hey, don't look so horrified. Honestly, when we live on Earth we become so very, very close to human that you'd hardly know the difference."

Gill recoiled. She didn't mean to but it was a visceral reflex. The idea that Peta was *not human* chilled her in some part of her brain so primitive she couldn't rationalize the fear at all. She experienced a head-rush that made Peta, in her pool of light and shade, look completely eldritch.

"Does Juliana know?" It was the first question to jump into her head.

"Of course not. There's no need for her to know, as long as I don't frighten the locals."

Out of some impulsive desire to control the situation, Gill seized Peta's wrist, her nails making imprints. "What are you made of?"

"Ow." Peta snatched her arm back, startled. "Flesh and blood."

"So how—how do you know you're Aetherial?"

"Same way you know you're who you are," Peta said lightly. "I was brought up with it; my family, our heritage and experiences . . ." Again the faraway gaze. "Vaethyr live among humans because we love the Earth, not because we intend any harm. Maybe some did in the past, but not now."

Gill knocked back the last of her wine, went to the bar and came back with two tumblers of expensive single-malt Scotch. "Cheers," said Peta. "Say something. It's all a bit weird, I know."

"Understatement."

"Do you believe me?"

"Do you care?"

"Yes, because I don't want you to think this is an elaborate joke. Gill, one thing you mentioned that told me absolutely you'd been in the Spiral; you saw the word *Tyrynaia* on the statue. Tyrynaia is the name of a legendary Aelyr city. The statue was obviously a tribute to that, to our origins. It's not something you could have made up. I'm telling the truth, too. I can prove it, if you want."

"You don't have to prove anything to me." The first sip of Scotch gave Gill the fiery shock she needed. "I've seen Rufus and Boundry. I've listened to all the stuff Leith came out with, which made my hair stand on end. Apparently Ned Badger is aware of something. And now you tell me about it as matter-of-factly as if I'm sitting in a classroom! So okay, it's hard for me to digest. The jury is out."

"That's fine. At least you're still here listening to me."

"But where did they come from, these Aetherials?"

"From the Earth," said Peta. "From the raw matter of creation. Only a lot earlier than humans. There's a lovely creation myth involving the Big Bang, goddesses and primal beings. At one time we dominated the world . . ."

"Naturally."

"But as the human race rose, we faded. Many withdrew to the Spiral, but some of us remained here."

"And what do Aetherials *do*?"

"What d'you mean, what do we do? Wow, you're a tough audience!"

"I'm not sure my poor brain can take this," Gill said waspishly. "Think of me as the drunken heckler, and continue."

"We're not completely alien. Our life cycles can be strange; we tend to vanish, rather than growing old. But in many ways, we're just like you. We eat and sleep, we have families and conflicts, our own ceremonies and traditions. We work for a living, we fall in love, get jealous and behave appallingly . . . all that stuff. We live among humans in a way that doesn't attract attention. The differences remain below the surface . . . Gill, you're hugging yourself and edging away as if I'm giving you the creeps. Please don't. I have feelings, you know."

"Glad to hear it." Gill made an effort to relax, to accept what Peta was saying. "Sorry. And what about Leith? Is he one of you?"

"I'm pretty sure he's not," Peta answered, "Usually, Aetherials recognize each other, but sometimes—if the other person is holding in their aura really tight—you can't tell. Perfect camouflage. I think Leith's too ill to exercise that level of discipline, though."

"He and I are human, yet we both entered the Otherworld . . . is that possible?"

"The official line says not. Aetherials can be pretty snobbish and elitist. Around Cloudcroft, they're very cliquey and I'm as bad as anyone, I admit. The official stance is that only Aetherials can experience the Dusklands, only Aetherials can pass into the Spiral. Humans simply can't, by virtue of their utter lack of magic. But as you've seen, it patently isn't true. It's unusual, but it happens, especially in places where the Dusklands manifest strongly, and they are *really* powerful around Cairndonan, incredibly intense." Excitement glowed in Peta's face. Gill wanted to trust her, but the damaged part of her still warned, *Be careful.*

Peta looked at her watch. "Speaking of Leith, I suppose we should go back."

Gill's head was whirling from finishing her drink too fast. The evening was cool but the late sunlight glowed golden. Gill felt too mellow to hurry, and didn't object when Peta linked arms with her. As they made their way up the twisting road out of the village, she said, "So you came here looking for this portal and yet you know nothing about Rufus or Boundry?"

They were a few paces on before Peta answered. "There was a . . . a conflict in Cloudcroft that led to the Great Gates being sealed shut for fourteen years, and all the minor gateways with them. A difficult time for Vaethyr . . . Eventually the ways were opened again, and a group of us decided to search out all the lesser portals in the British Isles, to examine and map them. It's never been done before. Since portals are so elusive, it's a never-ending task." She gave a slight smile. "I've found quite a few so far. Cairndonan is especially rich in rumors and tales and, because Dame Juliana lives here, I couldn't resist the opportunity to take the job—of course I didn't tell Dame J my secret interest, or she'd never have employed me. I'm doing this for my mother, actually. It's her project. So, to answer your question, yes, I suspected there was a portal here but no, I had no idea what lay within it."

Still there was an edge in Peta's voice that suggested she'd told only part of the story. Gill felt a pang of envy at her sunny nature, her confidence and her close, more-than-human family. "You must be quite the team, you and your fabulous flamboyant mother."

"Bitter, Gill. Come on, tell me why."

Half-drunk in the soft evening, Gill realized her resistance to giving personal information was low. Again she felt the tug between her desire for privacy and her need for friendship. She remembered how she'd lain in the dark with Peta and told her almost everything, and the world hadn't ended. So, the bare facts.

"My mother's English, my father from India; he was a newspaper reporter in Delhi. I don't remember him. It was one of those senseless deaths; a dog bit him and he died of blood poisoning. I was only two. I like to believe my mother loved him, even though she was married to someone else at the time."

"Were you born in India?"

"Yes, romantic, eh? My mother, Christina, traveled a lot so my dear grandfather brought me up for a while; he was a sweet, gentle man, a widower. The family were Hindus; that's what I remember of India, the temples, the festivals . . . Then my mother returned when I was five and whisked me back to England. Christina . . ." Gill hesitated. "She was a journalist. She went all over the world, worked in war zones, drank too much. It was a wild life."

"She sounds very brave and intrepid."

"Oh, she was. Fantastic woman. Unfortunately, we loathed each other. She divorced her first husband—the one I got the name Shaw from—after the love affair with my father, and then she worked her way through a string of losers before settling on my obnoxious stepfather. He was the last straw. I left when I was sixteen, never saw her again."

"Are they still alive?"

"The stepfather died a while ago. The last I heard of Christina, she was working in a bar in Spain, spending her days drinking and roasting in the sun. Good luck to her; I don't think of her as family now. All I had was Steve and my running . . ." Gill shrugged. "So much for that. When I decided to leave London I took my father's surname, Sharma. Left the wreckage of my old self behind, as it were."

Peta squeezed Gill's arm tighter with her own, conveying understanding. Affection, even. Something inside Gill could not deal with affection. She tensed and didn't respond. Then Peta asked quietly, "Where will you go, when your lease on the cottage is up?"

"I have no idea."

As they reached the edge of the estate, Peta detoured into a forest, where a track brought them onto a footpath that ran along the ravine towards Robin Cottage.

"My secret shortcut," Peta explained. "So, you've vanished from your old life. Hidden yourself away like a pupa, waiting to reemerge."

"I don't know about reemerging. Can't see past the next hour, sometimes."

Peta was quiet for a time; the only sound was of water surging over rocks beside them. Presently she said, "I knew someone who disappeared. This boy, a friend of mine, Mark Tulliver. When he was sixteen, he went into the Spiral and never came out again."

"Oh." Gill hardly knew what to say. "How long ago?"

"About eighteen years. We were the same age."

"Boyfriend?"

"Sort of." Peta colored. "He was lovely. But, you know, we were young so I don't know if it would have lasted. He went through the Gates in Cloudcroft . . . It was his first time in the Otherworld, his initiation. The Spiral can be dangerous. He may not even have survived, at least not in a form we'd recognize. His poor mother, Maeve—she's my mum's closest friend—she was at our house in tears so often, we couldn't bear it. I've searched for him on and off ever since, but the Spiral is a vast, confusing place and the geography rarely obeys any rules we'd comprehend . . . It's pointless, really, but I can't let go of that tiny filament of hope."

"That must have been hard, not knowing what became of him."

"It happens. Loved ones go into the world beyond and sometimes they don't come back; but we still have to let them go."

"I feel as if the world's gone porous," said Gill. "As if it's not enough that I've already cracked up, I've got all this to contend with!"

"That's probably the best time."

"You wouldn't normally tell humans these things, would you?"

"Never before," Peta said somberly, "but you're part of it now, my dear."

"I don't want to be."

"Well, that's tough, because it's too late. Let's hope Leith's managed to calm down and sort himself out by now."

As they reached Robin Cottage, they found the front door standing wide open. Gill and Peta looked at each other, abruptly sober with alarm.

"Leith?" Gill called softly. She cautiously stepped in but the small front room was empty. She checked the kitchen, while Peta ran upstairs only to reappear seconds later, looking pale.

"He's gone," she said.

6

They Gather for the Feast

"Juliana?" The velvety, insinuating male voice on the other end of the phone was familiar. She exhaled. She could only deal with her ex-husband by pretending they'd never been married at all, that he was merely some acquaintance who must be tolerated, like an accountant or a solicitor.

"Hello, Charles."

"How are you, dear girl? Have you a summer school on this year?"

"Always. We're all in fine fettle, thank you."

"Delighted to hear it."

"And how are things at the seat of government?" she said. "Still there, presiding over the halls of power like a cockerel over a particularly noisy chicken coop? Or should I say, some ghastly Shelob-sized spider at the center of its web?"

He chuckled. "You sound almost proud of me."

"I suppose I am, in a weird way, you arrogant old devil. So, what do you want?"

"Jules, dear, you always assume I want something. No, nothing except to see your dear old face. I'm going to be in your neck of the woods. I have some meetings at the Scottish Parliament so, while I'm in Edinburgh, I thought I'd drop by."

"Charles, Edinburgh's hardly my neck of the woods, and I wouldn't refer to a several-hundred-mile detour to the northwest as dropping by."

His smooth tone was unperturbed. "It's still a darn sight closer than London. Really, the extra drive is nothing and it would be so nice to catch up."

Juliana sighed through her teeth. "When?"

"In a couple of weeks. My secretary will let you know the precise date nearer the time."

"I may not have a window in my diary."

Again the soft, annoying laugh. "Oh, Juliana, don't be like that. It will be so pleasant to catch up, like the civilized beings we are; like a pair of old pals reminiscing. We're lucky that our separation was mostly so amicable. Anything that *wasn't* amicable is very far in the past, isn't it?"

"I suppose so." The receiver of the old-fashioned telephone seemed to weigh a ton in her hand. There was no reason to refuse. "Yes, come for dinner, Charles, by all means. Have your secretary call Flora to make arrangements."

"Lord, is she still with you? No trouble. I'll see you soon."

After she'd put down the phone Juliana stood at the window of her private sitting room, looking out into the dusk. She half-expected to hear Corah's voice making some sarcastic comment. *"Of course he wants something; why do you always take him at his word, give in so easily?"* Corah, though, did not appear; the words were only in her own mind.

She knew the answer. She gave in because Charles was her weak spot. Her anger with him had run dry long ago, but there was still something about his charm that amused as much as it exasperated her. Also, she prided herself on the fact that they had managed to remain on reasonably civilized terms. Snubbing him might have implied that she still cared.

Although she referred to Charles as her ex-husband, they had never actually divorced. Neither of them had wanted to remarry so they'd just let matters drift without resolution. Juliana didn't want a divorce at this late stage. The last thing she needed was a large legal bill.

It was time for the evening meal, but Charles's call had taken away her appetite. Instead, she made her way down through the house towards the studios. All was quiet; distantly she heard the faint murmur of voices and footsteps as her students converged on the dining room, chatting about their day, brimming with the pleasure of creativity. Juliana smiled. She didn't want to think ahead to their departure, to being alone with Ned and Flora once more. Nor to the tension that would ensue from Charles's threatened visit.

Dusk filled the Camellia House and rudimentary sculptures stood like ghosts in the silent forest of palm trees. Juliana moved between workstations, studying sketches, running her hands over wood and soapstone. Quiet contemplation of her students' work would help her to guide them the next morning—she thought of it as guiding, more than teaching. Their enthusiasm gave her energy. It even warmed the chasm within her, at least for a time.

Juliana was a swan gliding serenely on the surface; that was all she allowed outsiders to see. No one—except Ned and Flora, to some degree—suspected the frantic paddling that went on beneath. It was a near-impossible task to run the house and estate with just two staff—plus Colin, who was temporary—but they were all she could afford. While the school was on, two women came up from the village to help with catering, but otherwise, it was mostly Ned and Flora. *A skeleton staff,* she thought, *almost literally.*

She heard Ned's voice behind her. "Dame J, will you be coming in to supper?"

"Ah, no, I'll have something later. Go, help Flora serve! Don't hold up the meal on my account."

He gave his habitual sardonic bow, and left.

Ned was edgy, which got on her nerves. He hated having visitors at the house, she knew. It upset his routine of patrolling the boundaries, his rituals of reinforcing the net of charms and talismans with which he fancied he was protecting Cairndonan Estate. He believed that strangers tore holes in the protective web. He couldn't keep up with the mending and so he was restless, sullen and suspicious.

Juliana had long given up arguing with him, and simply left him to it. He tried her patience, but at least he was loyal, as was Flora. Both more loyal than ever she deserved.

Looking out across the gardens, she saw twilight gathering above the sea, silhouetting the foundry. A shadow of unease passed over her. Secretly she understood Ned's dread of invisible intruders. She realized that her own urge to patrol the silent house came from precisely the same disquiet.

Unlike Ned, she had been able to exercise her own peculiar control over the mysterious invaders, but the fear was always in the back of her mind.

"What if more turn up, *Winter?*" she murmured. She visualized the statue's pale face in the foundry, serene and luminous as snow. "What if they came seeking revenge? Are we strong enough to fight them off?"

Gill's first reaction was relief. If Leith had left, he was not her problem anymore.

That feeling was chased by one of resignation. She couldn't shrug off responsibility so easily. She and Peta stood looking at each other.

"Where would he have gone?" asked Gill.

"Anyone's guess," said Peta. "I didn't realize we'd been out for so long—my fault for talking too much." Gill went into the kitchen and drank a glass of water to wash away the whisky taste. As she did so, Peta added, "I hope Rufus, or whoever was chasing him, didn't drop by."

Gill turned. "I can't see any sign of a struggle, can you?"

"No . . ." Peta's gaze drifted. "Hey, look at this."

She reached down to the floor and straightened up again with the mask-on-a-stick in her hand. The twin black voids stared, crystal blood leaking onto the cheeks. "This was on the carpet. Did it fall, or was it thrown?"

"Do you think he tried it on, and freaked out like I did?"

"I didn't make it for him, so it wouldn't have any . . . resonance." Peta placed it back into the vase as she spoke. "Still, he didn't like it."

"He was muttering about a *Dunkelman*. What did he mean?"

"I've no idea," said Peta.

Gill groaned. "I suppose we'll have to go and look for him."

"Come on, then," Peta said, laughing. "I suspect that behind that misanthropic exterior, dear, you're starting to like him."

"I don't like him," Gill said acidly. "He's a lunatic. But he's *our* lunatic, at least until we find someone else to look after him."

This time, Gill locked the cottage door behind them. They walked along the stream bank—Gill carrying the alicorn—over the footbridge and along the path that wound through the trees towards the house. All the way, they watched carefully for any hint of movement between the curtains of foliage. Now and then, Peta called out softly, "Leith?"

As the woods blended into the gardens, there was a place from which the foundry could be seen poised between the folds of the estate and the rugged edge of the cliffs. Gill saw the briefest glimpse of a dark figure in motion.

"Peta, down there."

By the time they reached the foundry, he'd gone. Gill saw a rough grey wall ahead, heard the pounding of the tide not far away. The building looked like an old smithy, with smoke drifting from an industrial-scale chimney. They made their way around, over broken ground and thistles, until they reached the big double doors at the front. Here was a broad slabbed area, and a concrete track leading off it, presumably so that large-scale sculptures could be removed from the foundry by forklift. No sign of Leith. They paused, looking around.

A door creaked open and Colin stepped out, wiping his hands on a dirty rag. He looked disheveled, with a welder's mask pushed back on his head. "Evening, ladies," he called. "How's it going?"

By reflex, Gill began, "You haven't seen . . ." Then she thought better of it and trailed off, "No, it's okay. Nothing."

"Just having a stroll," Peta added, unconvincingly.

"You're missing dinner, aren't you? It's gone seven."

"You too."

"Oh, that's okay," said Colin. "I have to use my off-duty minutes to do my own stuff. I'll grab leftovers from the kitchen later. You want to come inside and see what I'm working on?"

Gill and Peta glanced at each other, and at the slice of darkly glowing foundry they could see through the doorway. Fires sparked, and there was a smell of hot metal. "I'd love to," said Peta, "but like you say, we'd better get up to the house. Another time?"

"Sure, whenever," he said, sounding only mildly disappointed. "Take care, girls." He withdrew with a cheery wave. They went on their way, following a narrow path that led towards the gardens, twisting between rocky outcrops as it went.

"Perhaps I was mistaken," said Gill. "I saw a flash of something dark—his hair, I thought. Maybe it was just a crow."

"He could be anywhere by now." Peta sighed. "Let's try the house."

"You think he's gone up there?"

"Who knows? It's worth a try. Half an hour, then I quit. Let him fend for himself. I'm starving."

"Oh, Aetherials get hungry, do they?" Gill said crossly, aware of heartburn and a sharp headache from drinking on an empty stomach. "You're not superhuman, then."

"Never said I was, honey," Peta retorted.

The path brought them into the grounds behind the house, curving around lawns and bushes that shielded them from view of the windows. Gill glanced up at the lofty white framework of the Camellia House. Above it, the sky was still bright but losing color, blue fading to lavender.

Peta said, "Everyone will be in the dining room at the front, so hopefully no one will see us. Not that it matters, but I'd prefer not to be faced with a load of questions about what we're up to. Especially if Ned Badger catches us. I see what you mean about the creepy factor."

"Oh? Has he said anything to you?"

"No, but he *lurks*. I was picturing him trying to wrestle the alicorn off you. The house has some grim old Victorian artifacts around, stuffed dead animals under glass domes, that kind of thing. I think the tusk must have been part of the collection, and Badger borrowed it."

"To ward off the scary faerie folk?" said Gill. "Was that its purpose?"

Peta gave a scoffing laugh. "Its purpose was to make Ned feel better; if he *believed* it worked, it did, in his own mind. What blocked or unblocked the portal was not an old whale tusk. But it makes me wonder what he knows, or thinks he knows, about this place."

"Do you think he realizes you're . . ." Gill was saying when all at once she saw Leith, his slender form slipping along one wing of the house, some twenty yards to their left. "There he is."

"Leith!" Peta called out.

He glanced over his shoulder, but didn't stop. Instead he walked to a side door, opened it and vanished inside. "Great," said Peta, hurrying in pursuit. "Let's see if we can fish him out before Ned or someone finds him wandering around."

Inside, they followed Leith along a corridor, past an opulent drawing room that appeared to be set up as a television lounge for guests. There was no one around. To Gill, the house seemed a tangle of passageways running off everywhere. She was lost, until she recognized the way to the studio where Peta had held her mask-making workshop. The young man paused at the door, staring in through a glass panel.

Before they could reach him, he pushed open the door and went in. They followed. Inside, the studio was deserted, made eerie by a dozen half-finished masks hanging along the walls. The students had obviously tidied up as best they could, but there was an air of creative chaos about the area; stacked plastic bowls and bags of plaster, paint-stained benches scattered with fabric scraps and wire.

Leith halted in the center of the room, staring at the dentist's chair. He appeared paralyzed—rather as someone might look in the grip of a dental phobia, Gill thought. "Why is this here?" he asked softly as they approached him. No preamble, no attempt to explain what he was doing.

"Er, it's for people to sit in while they have molds made of their faces," Peta answered. "So we can make masks. You really shouldn't be in here, you know."

"You make death masks?" He traced the headrest with a pale fingertip. He looked lividly pale in the gloom, his eyes feverish. "Why?"

"No. Living masks." said Peta. "It's art, Leith. For theater or dressing up or just for fun. Like the mask in Gill's cottage? I made that for her."

"That was fun?" Gill gasped.

"Sometimes a mask can show what's inside you," Peta added.

"Or hide it," Leith murmured. He raised his chin and looked around the studio. "I thought I knew this house, but I don't. I can see what used to be, but it's all changed."

Gill went closer to him, moving cautiously in case he fled again. "So you knew this place before you were in Boundry? Are you remembering what happened?"

"No," he said, and struck his forehead with the heel of his hand. "It happened to someone else." He stared down at the chair for a moment. Then he looked up at Peta, his eyes burning. "Make a mask for me!"

"Oh." She looked from him to Gill, her eyebrows arched. "What for?"

"To hide me. To help me see through the shadows. So that when the *Dunkelmen* come, they won't recognize me. I'll see them, but they'll go straight past, looking for someone else. That's what a death mask is meant for, isn't it? Transformation."

Peta visibly floundered for a few seconds, while Leith's stare remained fierce and steady on her. "Well, um, who told you that?"

"I don't know. It came to me."

"Masks can represent all kinds of things . . . Don't call it a death mask, though; that's so misleading. It's about transformation, yes. Passing from one state to another. But no mask is literally going to hide you, Leith."

He raised his fingertips to his cheek; Gill noticed that the nails were clean and trimmed. A small detail, suggesting he hadn't been held in a dungeon in Boundry. Not recently, at least. "But if it changed me, and frightened them . . ."

"Are you serious?"

"Yes. A different face. You will know what face to give me because you're of the same kind."

"Same kind as what?"

He hesitated, eyes glinting with suppressed dread. "You're like Rufus, a shining one, but not cruel like him. At least I hope my sight doesn't deceive because if it does, I'm lost."

"I promise you, I'm a friend," Peta said firmly.

"Then help me. Please!"

Gill expected a flat refusal, but Peta stood with a thoughtful glimmer in her eyes. "Ahhh . . . well, all right, we can try."

"Peta!" Gill broke in. "What are you thinking?"

"I'm not thinking. I'm *seeing* a mask for Leith, which means I need to create it. Sit down." He obeyed, sinking warily into the dentist's chair.

"You can't!" Gill persisted. "The whole process sent me over the edge. What might it do to him?"

The artist looked at her with an expression of mischievous determination. "It should be interesting."

"Oh my god, you're loving this, aren't you? Who cares about the chaos it causes, as long as it's *interesting*?"

"Ever considered a career in health and safety, Miss Ooh-too-risky?" Peta moved to fetch a plastic bowl, a small bag of plaster of Paris, strips of muslin. "Don't let's get overexcited. It's not an instant process, Leith; this is just a rough. I have to take it away to finish it. It will be a day or two. As long as you realize that?" He gave an uncertain nod. "Gill, could you fetch me a jug of water? Sink's just there."

"This is ridiculous," she hissed, but she propped her ivory staff by the sink and did as she was asked anyway. However surreal and wrong this was, it was weirdly exciting at the same time.

As Peta put an old towel over him, another under his head, she said, "Leith, do you know the word *Aetherial*?"

He gave a slight shudder. "Yes. I know it."

"You're right, I am of the same race as Rufus—assuming that's what he is—but you need to realize, we're not all wicked. I want to help you."

"I believe it. Gill told me. I wouldn't ask otherwise. I don't possess the power to fight Rufus, but you do."

"Steady on," said Peta. "I can't claim that. Don't expect too much. It's just a mask, not a magical suit of armor."

The summer evening glowed outside, but light was gradually bleeding from the studio. Soon it would be pooled in twilight.

"Peta, he's going to freak," Gill whispered. "I nearly did, and I knew what was happening."

"So talk to him," said Peta. A soft cloud went up as she tipped plaster of Paris into the bowl. "Keep him calm."

Sighing, Gill kneeled beside him and took his hand. It felt tense and bony in hers. She saw the nervous, liquid gleam of his eyes as he glanced sidelong at her. "Leith, it will feel a bit strange; you'll feel the plaster stiffen and warm up, but it's nothing to worry about. . . . Just hold still for a while. It won't take long."

He lay rigid, letting Peta comb back his long fringe with her fingers as she put a plastic cap on him to keep his hair clear. As the first strip of wet plaster touched his forehead, he flinched, but otherwise lay quiet. Peta sang in a low, soft voice as she worked, which filled the silence and seemed to soothe him almost to sleep.

"Okay, that's it," said Peta after a time. "It's starting to set, so I'm going to remove it."

As the plaster cracked away from his flesh, he gave a stifled cry. The mask moved, but failed to come free.

"Oh, damn," said Peta, "I forgot to grease him up first. I *never* forget that stage."

"Always a first time," said Gill.

Leith reached up to grab Peta's wrists, trying to stop her pulling the mask off. It was stuck. All he was doing was to hamper Peta's efforts to free the mold without hurting. Gill encircled his wrists in turn, trying to make him loose hold of Peta. For a few moments they struggled in an awkward three-way wrestling match.

"Okay, okay," said Peta, letting go of the mask in order to stop the struggle. Leith, however, held on to her wrists and, as she stepped back, he rose with her, his blank white face like that of a ghoul in a horror film. Although his voice was muffled, Gill made out the words "No, it's too soon, the bones are not healed. What kind of nurses are you?"

"Leith, stop it," said Gill, gently pushing him back into the chair. "We're not nurses. We're not plastering broken bones. It's a mask, remember?"

"Yeah, keep still, for heaven's sake," Peta snapped. "If I rip it off, it will damage the cast and maybe your pretty face, too. If I do it gently, the natural oils of your skin will help me, but I can't if you keep thrashing around."

Her stern tone had the desired effect. He let his hands drop and lay still, his breath puffing against the inside of the mask until Peta, with careful probing fingers, eased it free. Beneath it, his face was flushed, with flecks of plaster and lint stuck to his cheeks.

"It's fine," said Peta, inspecting the inside. "Just a couple of ragged areas. I can soon fix those. Sorry about forgetting the Vaseline, but I don't usually try to work under these circumstances."

She looked more amused than sorry. Gill, resting a hand on Leith's shoulder, felt the rapid rise and fall of his rib cage. He felt hot. She could physically feel a furnace of emotion inside him, ready to explode. "Peta, I did warn you. All we've done is scare the hell out of him."

"All in the service of trying to find out *what's* scaring him," said Peta, briskly tidying away the debris of her task.

In a faint voice he said, "How can it hide me, if you take it off?"

"Sweetheart, I can't leave it stuck to your face," said Peta, giving Gill a glance. "I told you, I'm going to smooth it and paint it for you. You're really in a bad way, aren't you?"

Gill stroked his shoulder, trying to soothe him while imagining how the situation appeared from his point of view; the studio lying in half-darkness, and two strange women pressing him into a dentist's chair while apparently trying to suffocate him . . . she guessed, from Leith's wild expression, that this was not among his favorite fantasies. "Come on, Peta. Let's get him out of here now."

There was a soft click. Gill saw the shine of glass as the door swung open. She froze; Peta froze. The figure coming towards them with slow, firm footsteps was Juliana. For a moment she was a shadow, grey on grey; then a light flicked on, flooding the room with blinding whiteness.

"Ladies?" she said coolly. "I don't mind you working late, but at least put some lights on. What on earth are you doing?"

Peta exhaled. She and Gill stood like a pair of naughty schoolgirls, caught by a ferocious headmistress.

"Nothing, Dame J," Peta said with an apologetic smile. "Sort of an extracurricular project. Gill and um, er . . . both agreed to model for me."

Juliana glided towards them. In a grey velvet kaftan that glittered with swirls of beads, she was a tower of silver. Her eyes resembled thousand-year-old glacial ice. "I thought we had intruders! And where did you find 'um, er,' whose name seems to have slipped your mind?"

She moved closer, peering at the young man. "I can smell alcohol on someone. Miss Lyon, I do trust that you didn't think it was acceptable to pick up a strange man in the pub and bring him into my house?" Her tone was at once sardonic and serious. "I'm sure no assistant of mine would dream of conducting herself in such a manner."

Peta looked indignant. She opened her mouth.

"It was me," Gill said hurriedly, wanting to defuse the situation before Peta said something she'd regret. "We met him . . . in the pub and . . . We got chatting and he wanted Peta to make him a mask, that's all. It was just . . . a laugh."

Leith, meanwhile, did nothing normal such as looking embarrassed, mumbling an apology or scuttling towards the door. He only stared; first at Juliana, then at Gill. He looked ethereal, and definitely not of this world. Juliana studied him, curiosity lighting her eyes under severe iron-grey eyebrows.

"I don't see anyone laughing," she said. "And I don't believe a word of it. The truth, please."

Her authority was compelling. Peta's expression turned sober and she looked Dame Juliana in the eye. "I don't think you'd believe us."

"Oh, really? I'm willing to bet I've eaten stranger things for breakfast. I'm telling you, no one is leaving this house until I get an explanation." Juliana's frown deepened. "You look a little familiar, young man, though I can't think why. What's your name?"

He didn't answer. His eyes gleamed with a fearful light. Gill had a sudden jolt of fear that the mold-making had worked some irreparable harm.

"He's not very talkative," said Peta. "His name's Leith, apparently."

"He sort of found us," Gill added. "I met him yesterday in . . . in the village. Then he turned up at Robin Cottage later, in the middle of the rainstorm, as if he was terrified for his life. We've been trying to find out where he's from, but he seems to have lost his memory."

"Or he's too traumatized to explain," said Peta. "That's why I'm making the mask, you see. It can, er . . ." She glanced at Gill. ". . . reveal things that aren't otherwise obvious. Release emotions."

"And has he consented to this dubious therapy?" Juliana spoke crisply, turning to focus on Leith again.

"I asked them to do so," he said in a low voice. "To camouflage, not to reveal . . . but it's hopeless. Nothing can conceal me from him."

"Who are you?" Juliana asked, her eyes softening with concern. He didn't answer; she went on studying him for a few moments, unspoken thoughts clouding her face. Then she looked at Peta and demanded in a brisk tone, "Have you eaten?"

"No, I missed the dinner gong, I'm afraid," said Peta, exchanging a puzzled sideways look with Gill.

"Me, too. Well, you can all come up to my private quarters and I'll have Ned rustle up some scraps from the kitchen. Yes, you too, young man. Come on. We shall have a friendly chat over supper."

Gill, startled, began to demur, but Juliana held her with a steel gaze. "I insist. Please understand that I can't possibly let any of you leave until I've received a full and satisfactory explanation."

Dame Juliana's apartment lay on the upstairs floor behind a door marked PRIVATE. Beyond lay a series of large rooms that struck Gill as well-preserved Victorian: all shabby grandeur, with a lot of dark polished wood, red velvet, antique furniture, dim table lamps. Juliana showed them into a dining room that had a large walnut table set with silver and white china with an elaborate candelabra as a centerpiece. At her invitation, they seated themselves; Leith beside Gill, Peta facing them and Juliana at the head of the table.

Ned Badger entered, as if materializing from the shadows.

"Unexpected guests," said Juliana by way of brusque explanation. "Whatever's left from dinner, bring enough for four, would you?"

He nodded, self-contained and unreadable. "There's still some fresh salmon and a few of the langoustines I purchased straight off the boat this morning, bread and cheese of course, a lemon soufflé . . ."

"Perfect. As I said, anything." Juliana waved him away. In the difficult pause that followed, she got up to fetch a bottle of Merlot from a sideboard. She poured four glasses, then took her time lighting candles on the many-branched candelabra. Each new flame added sparkle to the pearl-grey flow of her hair. Light pooled on the table, making the umber darkness of the room seem cavernous.

Gill sat tense and quiet, overwhelmed by embarrassment, longing to flee. Peta gave her a small, rueful grin behind Juliana's back, but Leith was looking around with wary eyes as if he'd forgotten the others were there.

Juliana began some neutral banter with Peta—was she enjoying herself, how was her class progressing?—which filled the silence until Ned returned. This time Flora came with him, each of them bearing a laden tray. Gill avoided eye contact as they set out the dishes, but she was acutely aware of their spiky presence, Flora's tired, stern face and the stiff upsweep of her hair, Ned's watchfulness. The air bristled with unvoiced questions.

"Thank you," Juliana said mildly. "I won't need you again tonight. Get Colin to help clear up in the kitchen; the sooner you all finish, the sooner you can go off duty. Have an early night." Gill noted the kind subtlety with which she told them to mind their own business. As they left, she went on, "Well, do dig in. I'm trying to make this an informal chat, not an interrogation."

In spite of Juliana's menacing presence, and Leith's introversion, Gill ate. She was so hungry she could almost have consumed the place mats. The only item she didn't touch was the langoustines, which stared from their dish like tiny lobsters; Peta and Juliana shared them. Beside her, Leith picked at his food, occasionally glancing up from beneath half-lowered lashes. He looked tired and beautiful and out of place, the candle-light brushing him with a soft unearthly glow. . . A sensation stirred inside Gill that she dared not identify.

Peta appeared relaxed. Trouble entertained her, and nothing seemed to daunt her for long; Gill envied that quality. To her, the atmosphere felt artificial to the point of pain. She'd expected Juliana to react more predictably, to summon Colin and Ned and expel both Leith and herself from her property. Instead, this strange gathering. At first they made only the smallest of small talk; how did Gill like the cottage, wasn't the scenery magnificent? A line from a half-remembered song kept repeating in Gill's head, *They stab it with their steely knives, but they just can't kill the beast.*

"Now, let's try again, from the top," Juliana said after a while. "Feel free to chime in at any time, Leith, if you think you can shed light on things. Miss Sharma?"

Peta said, "This is a delicious supper, Dame J, and we're very honored, but to be frank, Gill's not under any obligation to explain herself to you."

"That's true," Juliana responded evenly. "However, this is my house, and my estate, so I feel it is very much my business if strange men with amnesia come stumbling onto my property. No, I can't force you to explain, it's true. But I would truly appreciate it if you would."

"I'll try," said Gill. Mellow from food and wine, her resistance to giving answers dissolved—no doubt that was what Juliana had intended. She began a hesitant explanation, but her own words sounded false as she constantly edited what she was saying, referring only to an unnamed hotel bar; not to Boundry, and certainly not to the Otherworld.

Juliana sat back in her chair, placing her knife and fork neatly on her empty plate. "Can we have the uncensored version, please?"

"Not really." Gill sighed. "It would sound ridiculous. Leith, you tell her."

He made no response. He looked uncomfortable, out of his depth. It struck her it had been a dreadful mistake to bring him here. Although, in fact, he'd brought himself.

"Miss Sharma," said Juliana, "if you'd spent as long as I have in these parts, you'd know the rumors of a vanished settlement, strange apparitions, processions of what the locals call the *Dubh Sidhe*—from which, they say, you must turn away and make the sign of the cross lest they take you with them. Is that where you came from, young man? Have you been away with the faeries?"

He stirred, his face turning pale.

Juliana straightened up, looking at Gill and Peta with grim fascination. "That got a reaction. Look, you should know I'm pretty much unshockable. I know the stories. Strange encounters in the woods. Children disappearing. I didn't grow up here; I came here thirty years ago from London when my aunt left me the place in her will, and I resisted these superstitious tales as rigorously as the greatest cynic imaginable. But the atmosphere of Cairndonan has a way of seeping into you. Intellectually, I'm still a skeptic. Emotionally, though . . . I know that things happen. Things do happen."

Gill cleared her throat, not knowing what to say. Suddenly feeling bone-tired, she took a drink of wine, and began again, this time describing Boundry and all that had happened since. Peta made interjections, carefully leaving out any mention of her own motives. From Juliana's reactions, it appeared she had no idea of Peta's true nature. On the contrary, Peta seemed stunned to discover that Juliana knew so much.

Leith himself said nothing, until the very end. Then he whispered, with exquisite politeness, "Please don't let Rufus find me. He will know what I've done. I can't go back there."

"What have you done?" asked Juliana. When he didn't reply, she reached across the table and touched his long white hand. "We won't, I promise. If he comes, we'll send him away." And she went on gazing deeply at him, pressing his hand even when he made a slight attempt to pull free.

Gill thought, *What the hell . . . ?* She added hesitantly, "When I left Boundry and found myself back in Cairndonan, I tried to ask a young shop assistant about it. Your, um, Mr. Badger overheard and challenged me. He seemed a bit . . . upset."

"Oh, Ned," Juliana sighed. "I really can't comment on my staff, but he is steeped in local belief and that makes him a little overzealous. I'll speak to him."

"No, don't," Gill said, horrified. "I don't want him thinking I've complained to you. I dealt with it."

"Well, I certainly don't want him hearing any more about your experiences. The less he hears, the calmer things are. Don't speak to anyone about this."

"So what do *you* know, Dame J?" Peta asked, looking the great woman squarely in the eyes.

Juliana's gaze slid away. "No more than you. Rumors of eerie sightings.

Disappearances. Leith's appearance is unprecedented, though." Juliana shifted, as if some electric wave of excitement were passing through her. "I don't know what to make of it. It's astonishing. Well, well."

Gill hadn't expected this reaction from her. She felt on safer ground, oddly reassured to find Juliana receptive rather than dismissive. But still there were endless unanswered questions about Leith, and he was giving nothing away.

"I'll make coffee," said Juliana, rising. "I have a little kitchenette area, just a kettle and mini-fridge, but it saves me bothering Flora every time I need refreshment. Help yourselves to dessert, cheese, whatever you fancy."

"Could I use your bathroom, please?" asked Gill. A growing discomfort made her realize that despite several glasses of wine and water, she hadn't visited the loo for hours.

"This way." Juliana took her across the sitting room next door and directed her into a wood-paneled passage with more rooms leading off. Here she found a huge bathroom with old-fashioned white fittings. There were framed photographs on the bathroom walls, and in the passageway itself, Gill noticed as she emerged. Photographs everywhere, mostly monochrome views of the house and surrounding scenery. As she retraced her steps across the sitting room, she was drawn to some framed images grouped on the striped wallpaper.

A table lamp cast a dim light, enough for Gill to make out stiffly formal portraits typical of the 1900s, soft greys edging into sepia. A patriarch with bushy sideboards, his wife equally stern and proper beside him, three charming wide-eyed children: a boy and two girls. There was an image of a man with earnest eyes behind spectacles, a moustache and neat beard. There were further portraits of the same three children, older, grown up. Each looked out from a separate oval frame; a fair young woman, attractive except for a mouth pursed as if she'd sucked a lime; a dark-haired girl whose eyes shone with mischief, so vivid that the photo could have been take a minute ago. The last was a young man with the kind of effortless, unself-conscious good looks that must have had females swooning over him. Dark languid eyes, sable hair.

Gill's breath caught in a suddenly dry throat. The man in the photograph looked strikingly similar to Leith.

"Ah, you've found the ancestors," said Juliana, right behind her shoulder, making her start violently.

"Sorry, I didn't mean to be nosy. They . . . caught my eye."

"Really?" Juliana said mildly. "Anyone in particular?"

"Er . . . all of them. I like old photographs."

In lamplight, Dame Juliana's face had a silver-gold glow. She didn't seem annoyed, as such, but there was something sharp and probing in her expression. "Well, the very Victorian couple are James and Agatha Montague. My grandparents. The other gentleman is James's brother, John, who used to own this house. And the children of James and Agatha are Melody—she's the fair-haired one with the broom handle stuck up her backside—and the Byronic beauty, Adam. The dark girl, the one who looks as if she's just sold her grandmother to the gypsies, is Corah. My aunt Corah, may she rest in peace, inherited the house from her uncle John and in turn bequeathed it to me. This pair . . ." She indicated an older Melody with precisely waved hair, standing beside a smiling man in British army uniform. The greys of the image were smooth and crisp. "Melody again, with her husband, Captain Robert Flagg. My parents."

Gill felt hot and cold, her heart pounding in her ears. "There are no pictures of . . . No pictures of you."

Juliana gave a dismissive grunt. "One doesn't want pictures of oneself about the place."

Gill forgot to be afraid of Juliana. Her fingers hovered near the photo of Adam, wanting to touch it but conscious of leaving fingerprints. "Don't you think that Adam looks a bit like Leith?"

Juliana's eyes hardened. "There is a passing resemblance."

"I think he looks exactly like him. They could be twins."

"Indeed, if twins can be born about ninety years apart." Juliana fell quiet. Gill couldn't read the thoughts moving behind those lively, glistening eyes. She began to feel increasingly uneasy. Dishonest. Somehow they caught each other's gaze and held it just a little too long.

There was a sudden, paralyzing moment of awkwardness, as if a silent bomb had gone off between them. Gill turned hot, cold, panicky. She realized then that Juliana knew, she *knew* and had known all along and had chosen not to say anything and now one of them had to say *something* before the atmosphere between them was poisoned forever. If it was possible to die of embarrassment, Gill knew she'd be the one to expire where she stood. Not Juliana, who stood there in cool, disapproving speculation.

Gill thought feverishly, *If I didn't want this to happen, why did I come here?*

Juliana was the first to speak. She cleared her throat and said mildly, "Miss Sharma, I don't wish to pry and I may be mistaken, but is your mother's name Christina Shaw?"

Gill drew and released a breath. "Um, yes."

"Née Flagg?"

"Yes. I'm sorry, Dame Juliana. I should have said something, but . . . Yes, my mother is your sister."

Juliana's expression made her heart stumble. "You are sorry?"

"For not telling you, I mean."

"Why didn't you?"

Gill's face felt red-hot. "Because—because I didn't want you to think I wanted something from you. That's not why I came, not at all." The stony face tilted slightly, inviting her to elaborate. "Things have happened to me that I need to forget. It was a bad time. I had nowhere to go, so I ran here. I thought I'd feel safe, camouflaged. I wasn't going to tell you . . . I didn't want attention or sympathy from you, honestly. I just wanted to hide."

"Gill, I realized who you are," Juliana said crisply. "I suspected, when you made your booking. I knew for certain, as soon as I saw you. Even if I hadn't, Colin recognized you anyway. He doesn't know we're related, but he knew your sporting identity."

"Oh." Her heart rate began to settle. So her anonymity had been an illusion from the start. "Why didn't you say something?"

Her aunt paced to the window, turned and folded her arms, framed against crimson velvet curtains. "Because *you* didn't. I was a little annoyed, I suppose, first that you'd come here at all, and then that you seemed to find subterfuge necessary. My attitude was, 'Right, if that's the way she feels, let's leave her to it.'"

Gill set her chin, feeling that she didn't like Juliana very much. "I'm sorry. Bad decision. I honestly didn't think you'd recognize me."

"I can see why you'd make that assumption. Christina and I went our separate ways long ago. We lost touch entirely. I couldn't keep track of her husbands, her lovers, her family situation; I heard on the grapevine that there was a daughter—you—but I never got the chance to meet you."

"I know. It's sad."

"Is it?" Juliana looked at Gill with a cool, probing expression. "Family is overrated. Fraught with jealousy, competition and hostility. It was my choice, since you were wondering, to have no pictures of my sister or myself on the wall. Our 'family' was a bad joke. Why waste time with people you can't bear for the sake of some gratuitous blood bond, when you could be with friends of your own choosing?"

Gill gave a thin smile. "So the fact that I'm your niece is absolutely irrelevant to you? I'm just . . . some random person who showed up?"

"Exactly," said Juliana with a laugh.

"Suits me."

"However, it's not irrelevant at all, is it? One tends to hear things, even when one tries not to. I became aware that the athlete Gillian Shaw and my unknown niece were one and the same. You were picked for the Olympic team, weren't you? Then your name dropped out of sight . . . a car accident . . ."

There was no hint of sympathy in Juliana's voice. Gill found that a relief. "Yes, well, my running days are over. Also I lost my job. And my fiancé. And everything."

"That's unfortunate. And you're calling yourself Sharma now?"

"It's my father's name, not that he and my mother were ever married. When I came out of hospital I didn't know where to go, so I came here. But as I said, I don't want anything from you. Just peace and quiet."

Juliana was quiet, her face unreadable. Then she said, "And how is Christina these days?"

"I don't know," said Gill. "We don't speak. She married this vile man— I hesitate to call him my stepfather—but because I hated him, she turned against me. Things got worse and worse until we stopped speaking. The stepfather died a while ago. She retired to Spain to soak up the sun and get drunk and harass Spanish waiters."

Juliana gave a bark of laughter. "That sounds like Christina." Then, "I can't charge you rent for the cottage, it doesn't seem right. I'll refund the money for your booking."

"No!" Gill said fiercely. "Don't you dare! I didn't come here looking for charity. I can pay my own way."

"All right. Thank you for that; the money doesn't go amiss. But Gill, please do stay in Robin Cottage for as long as you wish. I'm glad to have you there. As long as we can let this family stuff lie?"

"That's fine by me."

Juliana's measured reaction and lack of sentiment was a huge relief to Gill. Afterwards, she wondered where else the conversation might have led; nowhere, possibly, since neither was the type to initiate a gushing re-union. But then Leith came in, followed by Peta, who shot Gill a strange look. He moved as if sleepwalking, his gaze roving around the room, glancing off Juliana and the others as if they were no more than furniture.

"Leith," said Peta. She looked at Juliana and Gill, opening her hands in a helpless gesture. "I was trying to talk to him and he just walked off, like he's in a trance."

"He needs to rest," said Juliana as he came to a halt before the family portraits. With no trace of unease, she followed Leith and placed a hand on his shoulder. He did not even look at her.

Gill said, "I'm sorry we intruded on you, Dame Juliana. We're all tired. We should go. I'll take Leith back to Robin Cottage. He can sleep there while we decide what to do next."

"I won't hear of it." Juliana spoke in the same commanding tone she'd used to summon them upstairs. Light glinted on the silvery beaded velvet, sparked in her hair and glowing eyes. "There isn't room for him at the cottage, whereas I've got acres of it. I have a massive spare room, Leith." Her hand on his shoulder tightened in a proprietary way. "You must stay with me until we untangle the mystery of who you are."

As she spoke, Leith was staring at the grouped portraits of the family.

Gill saw something change; the others didn't seem to notice, but she did. As he gazed at the photograph of Adam, she saw his restless eyes turn to glass, as if his mind, overloaded, had switched off. She didn't know what had happened, but a chill began in her spine and swept through her.

"I'll get Colin to see you back to the cottage," Juliana said to Gill. Her manner would allow no argument. "Come along, Leith. Let's get you settled in."

"What is she playing at?" Peta asked in a low voice as she and Gill went downstairs to the reception area. Arms linked, they descended in step.

"You're asking me?" Gill gasped. "I've no idea."

"That was quite a talk you had with her. One thing you should know about Aetherials, we have terrific hearing. So, you're her niece?"

"Yes," Gill said wearily. "Why do you sound annoyed about it?"

Beyond the hall windows, the night was blue-black and desolate. They reached the outer doors and stopped there, just inside. "I'm not annoyed," Peta said, shaking her head. "Really, not. We had a couple of heart-to-heart conversations, yet you never mentioned it—but why should you? It's your business, not mine."

"Quite," Gill answered. "I didn't want anyone to know, least of all Juliana. I wasn't going to mention it, and if it wasn't for Leith and your mask-making antics I probably never would have. I could be equally mad with you for eavesdropping, you know."

"Unavoidable." Peta gave an apologetic dip of her head. "Sorry. Well, it's out now. So tell me, what did you learn about Auntie Juliana from your mum?"

"Nothing."

"Nothing? Oh, come on!"

"I think I left my alicorn in the studio."

"We'll go and fetch it, then." Peta turned her around and they walked across the hall, down the darkened passageway. "Seriously, nothing?"

Gill gave a tight sigh. "She was spectacularly bitter and twisted, my mother. Never mentioned Juliana, or their childhood. Truth is, I only found out that Juliana was my aunt when I was twelve; it was the stepfather who told me, not my mother. I didn't even know she *had* a sister until then."

"Wow," said Peta. "*Wow.*"

"If ever she mentioned my grandparents at all, her lips would go thin and she'd start chain-smoking for England. She was angry with my grandmother—that was Melody—for reasons I never fathomed. She was even angry with my grandfather for getting himself killed in the Second World War! How inconsiderate! Even when her relationship to Juliana came out, she wouldn't talk to me. No, we were like beings from different planets, Mother and me."

"Sounds rough."

"So you understand, I wasn't sure what sort of reception I'd get from Juliana," Gill added. "I shouldn't have told her. But she already knew, so . . ."

"But you must have been curious, or you wouldn't have come here."

"Was I? I think I was unconsciously searching for security that doesn't exist. Stupid."

"No, not stupid at all. Natural. Don't you want to find out about your family?"

Peta pushed open the door to the empty studio, letting Gill through. "Juliana and I have one thing in common, at least. The concept of 'family' was a bad joke to both of us. Now I've got Robin Cottage to myself again, maybe I can get on with my plan for complete solitude."

As Gill scouted around the workbenches and dentist's chair for her alicorn, Peta said, "Aren't you curious to know why she was so very eager to take Leith in?"

"Yes, but mostly I'm relieved."

"Well, I'm seething." Peta's eyes shone through untidy strands of hair. "He was our concern, but she's exercised her authority and just whisked him away from us. She had no business doing that. Don't you feel she's effectively . . . hijacked him?"

"I suppose she has."

"Well, I'm not letting it rest until I find out why. How about you?"

"I don't know," said Gill. "I'm tired. I didn't want to get embroiled in dark conspiracies. Right now, all I want is my bed."

"Well, grab your staff and clear off then," Peta said, rolling her eyes. "You're right, it's been a long day."

Gill turned by the sink, one hand resting on the wooden draining board. "I left it leaning against here, I'm sure I did," she said. "It's gone."

"It's quite a nice room," said Juliana, opening the door to the spare bedroom that was just off the entrance hall in her own apartment. It was a big room; it had been a study in John Montague's time, but some years ago she'd pushed the old furniture to the walls and put a double bed in. She flicked on a light. "It even has its own little bathroom. You'll be all right here, won't you . . . Leith?"

He gazed at her, or past her, as if he had no idea who she was or why he was here. He was pliable, passive. Juliana studied him. There was a name for the state he was in . . . catatonic, was that it? Or dissociative? Where the mind was so stressed it simply shut down, unable to endure any more thoughts or feelings. Probably she should call the village doctor, but she had no intention of doing so. As long as he was not agitated or violent, she wanted no outside interference. He needed time to heal; that much was plain.

With one hand held out, as if to calm a nervous cat, she said softly, "Your real name isn't Leith, is it?"

His lips parted.

"Can you tell me what it is?" No answer. She turned her hand palm down, to show it didn't matter. "That's all right. People have gone missing, you see, and we have to unravel . . . Do you remember the house? Do you remember me?"

Tears swelled like liquid glass in his eyes, turning them silver. For all she was trying to be rational and detached, a dreadful turmoil of hope swirled inside her. She saw herself stepping forward with outstretched arms to clasp him to her bosom . . . it took all her strength to suppress the urge. No, no displays of emotional incontinence, she told herself in disgust. *Get a grip, Juliana.*

She managed to stop herself asking more questions, braking on the very precipice of saying too much.

"It doesn't matter now. Go to bed, Leith, sleep and don't worry about anything. You're safe."

7

The Serpent Stones

Colin, dispatched by Juliana, took Gill back to the cottage on the electric golf cart. She hadn't wanted an escort, but once out in the dark, she was grudgingly glad of his presence. As the vehicle rocked and shuddered its way along the track, she found herself thinking about Peta's words. Had Juliana hijacked Leith? Yes, that was exactly how it seemed.

Why had she been so very swift and eager to take him?

"So, who's the guy that turned up?" Colin said through his teeth.

"We're not sure."

"Bloody funny, Dame J taking in some random guy that wanders up from nowhere. Maybe she knows him."

"I expect she'll tell you all about it. You're part of the sacred inner circle, aren't you?"

He gave a hollow laugh. "Whatever that means. I'm sure she's got her reasons, but who the hell is he? Some stray nephew?"

Gill didn't reply at first, only watched the deep shadows of hedgerow and woodland rolling past. Then she said, "You almost sound jealous."

Colin gave a gruff laugh. Once, she might have found him attractive, in an earthy kind of way. Since her time in hospital, though, she felt like a stone block; dead inside, but *gladly* dead to all romantic possibilities. It saved a lot of pointless yearning and pain.

"Well, that's the thing about Juliana," he said. "She's the center of the universe. She's the queen bee and we're the drones circling around her. She's the goddess and we're her acolytes. You can't help but fall a bit in love with her. Magnificent, isn't she?"

"Completely," said Gill.

"She was married, you know. Some geezer called Charles Sandford-Barnes; he's something big and important in the government, apparently. They separated years ago. Hell, you'd think she'd be grateful for a younger man's attention, wouldn't you? One of these days she'll notice me. I swear

that Ned Badger thinks he's in with a chance; he's overdue for a sharp reac-
quaintance with reality. Smarmy creep."

"You've got designs on Juliana?" Gill said with a shocked laugh. "She
must be thirty years older than you, at the very least."

"So?" Colin grinned, not the slightest bit abashed. "Don't knock older
women. Look at her. She's gorgeous. Look how she glows."

He was right. Gill had seen that from the start. There was nothing elderly about Juliana; nothing fake, either, nothing stretched or lifted. She
wasn't especially beautiful, but what shone from her was energy, passion,
character. "Hope I'm like her when I'm sixty, seventy-odd," said Gill.

"The point is that she isn't her *age*. She's a goddess. Goddesses don't get
old. Look at Greta Garbo, Marlene Dietrich, Sophia Loren, Helen Mir-
ren, Judi Dench; they're glorious. They're immortal."

"Colin, are you sure you're not gay? What are your feelings about Judy
Garland?"

"Ha bloody ha." He swung the cart over the bridge and onto the
stream-side path with reckless speed. "Ned Badger and Flora, his missus,
they're like a pair of guard dogs around Dame J. Like, 'Keep off, she's ours!'
Who do they think they are? They're housekeepers. I'm an artist. And then
all these students who are here for all of three weeks and think they own
the bloody place! They all want a piece of her."

"So everyone in the inner circle feels threatened by everyone else," said
Gill, hanging on as the vehicle bounced. "You're all competing for her attention, her favor. Feelings must run high."

"Yeah, all that's true." Colin's tone suggested an unkind desire to shock
her. "But I really would like to get my hands on that magnificent flesh. Picture this; you see her on an arts documentary and she looks like a bloody
duchess carved out of ice, dispensing grace and favor all over the place. But
you'd think to yourself, I've had her. I know what she likes, I know how
she smells, I know what makes her howl. An aristocrat like her needs a bit
of rough, don't you think?"

"Plus it would raise your profile," said Gill, resolutely trying not to take
the bait. "In twenty years' time, when *you're* a famous sculptor and they
write your biography, your infamous liaison with Juliana Flagg can only
boost your notoriety."

"Too right," he said with a grin.

Gill wondered how Colin would react if she revealed that Juliana was
her aunt. He'd find out eventually, no doubt, but for now she still felt the
need to keep it to herself. Lightly she said, "Can I draw a halt, before you
go into any more detail about what you'd like to do with her? You don't
want to leave me with images I can't get rid of."

"Absolutely not," Colin laughed. "A gentleman never tells."

Gill closed the door behind her, instantly feeling the stillness of empty rooms around her. In a dark corner of her mind, she entertained a fleeting thought of what it might have been like—if she'd been a different person, someone altogether more reckless—to invite Colin in. It was many months since she'd had sex, and as for *loving* sex, she couldn't even remember. Steve had been controlling, not affectionate. In theory, a sweaty, anonymous encounter in the dark might have made her feel alive again. The reality of it, though—she shivered, knowing she couldn't have handled it. First there was potential rejection; she imagined an expression of horror on Colin's face as he spluttered refusal, "You must be joking. You're not my type, love; I'm into glamorous older women, not limping stick insects."

But then, if he'd accepted—there would have been boundless opportunity for embarrassment, disappointment, bodies and minds disastrously out of sync. And even supposing the sex went well, how to get rid of him after? Would he come creeping around the cottage every night, expecting the same? Or would he ignore her afterwards, as if she was some tissue he'd used and discarded?

No. Gill let out a whoosh of breath, glad that she had no urge to take such risks. Being alone was comfortable, simple and orderly.

And yet. Last night, she couldn't wait for Leith and Peta to leave her space. Now that they were gone, the cottage felt desolate, lifeless. Her conversation with Leith yesterday, although she hadn't welcomed it at the time, now seemed pleasantly intriguing. There was something tender about the memory. Remembering, she began to share Peta's resentment that Juliana had swept him away. She'd laid claim to him, just as she insisted on owning everything and everyone here. Leith was a mystery, *Gill's* mystery, and now he was gone she felt . . . sad. Frustrated by unfinished business.

She went to bed, trying to ignore the unfamiliar scent of Leith on her sheets. It was pleasant, warm and musky, yet there was something of fear in it. She would have to wash the sheets. Three times she woke with her heart thudding, convinced that there was someone in the room with her; the dark bulk of an unknown but unspeakably menacing intruder. And once she dreamed she was walking around the cottage in a panic, searching for a child whose distressing cries were always in another room.

For almost a week, Gill had the stretch of peace she'd hoped for. A couple of days after the evening with Juliana, she returned from a walk to find a note pushed under the cottage's front door: "Dropped round to see you—come up to house if you want to chat, okay? P."

Gill stalled, caught between an impulse to seek Peta's company, and the stronger desire to stay free of entanglements. If she went up to the house, that would make her the one pursuing the friendship, and she wasn't ready for that. So she procrastinated. She didn't chase Peta, nor did she seek news of Leith. Least of all did she try to find Boundry again. At last she had the solitude she wanted.

She spent her time walking along the cliffs, the seashore and the harbor, reading, watching television when reception was not too snowy, subsisting on meager meals of soup or canned beans. Occasionally she went to the Cairndonan Arms for a glass of wine and a ploughman's lunch. Steve would have been horrified at her diet.

The landlady, Fiona, always greeted her with a cheerful word. The villagers were friendlier than she'd first thought, and Fiona proved quite gossipy. Even the rude teenage girl in the grocery store thawed towards her. Gill liked to stand on the quay and watch the fishing boats, despite the small chance that she might bump into Ned. A couple of times she'd seen him there, buying fresh-caught fish, and had to make a swift diversion to avoid him.

Gill was certain it was he who'd swiped her narwhal tusk from the studio. She dared not challenge him about it, since it hadn't belonged to her in the first place. Still, the idea irritated her. She'd found it, she'd been making good use of it, so how *dare* he snatch it away?

One afternoon as she was walking along the quay, she bumped into Fiona, who'd just bought fish from one of the boats. They exchanged a few words; it was a bright, calm day. The bay shimmered bright turquoise. It was a day to wash away Gill's night terrors. "It's beautiful here, just so beautiful," she said.

"I'm glad you think so," said Fiona, preening a little. "How's your hand, did it heal okay?"

"It's much better, thanks." Gill flexed the scarred hand. On impulse she asked, "I suppose you know lots about local folklore, do you?"

Fiona gave a dismissive chuckle, her broad bosom shaking. "Ah no, not me. Silly stories. That fellow up at the big house, he's the one to ask. Ned Badger."

"I'm not sure I could," Gill said, startled. "He's a bit . . ."

"Eccentric?"

"Intimidating."

The landlady laughed. "Oh, he is. A little bit touched. They do say it runs in the family."

"Oh?"

Her voice fell. "It's a sad story. When he was a young boy, his mother vanished for a couple of years. No one ever knew where she'd been. One day she returned in a dreadful state and she's spent the rest of her days ever since in a psychiatric hospital. Still there now."

Gill took this in. "That's terrible."

"Aye, tragic. Some people are a wee bit scared of him, and turn their backs, but I try to look on him more kindly. When you think what he went through, it must have warped his mind."

"Did they never find out what had happened to his mother?"

"Well." Fiona shifted her packet of fish from one hand to the other. "It could have been anything. No one spoke of depression in those days. People sometimes just run off, don't they?"

"Oh, yes," said Gill.

"But some folk will persist with stories. The *Dubh Sidhe*, the dark elves; they're said to walk through the woods up by the house and snatch anyone foolish enough to cross their path—and, believe me, some still speak of them in hushed tones, convinced they're real."

"You're a skeptic?"

"I keep an open mind, dear; don't want to offend anyone. Ned's mother was not the only one, far from it. We've had more than our fair share of disappearances, going back decades. Some reappeared, some didn't. The truth is, it was probably all coincidence, just a set of random events—but they get lumped together to prove there's something uncanny going on."

Gill smiled. "The estate at night can be so spooky that it's impossible not to believe it."

"A quiet warning, though; if you start asking questions, don't be surprised if folk clam up on you. They don't like being seen as superstitious, even though they are. They don't like outsiders passing judgment, and most of all they believe that *talking* about you-know-who is . . . dangerous."

"I'll bear that in mind. Thanks. That's fascinating."

The following day, Gill was still pondering the conversation as she ate a good breakfast of eggs and toast, then pulled on her walking boots. Determination seized her. For the first time in a week, she took the route through the woodland behind Robin Cottage and through the ruined mill. She had to return, if only to break the spell.

Her leg was stronger, her pain hadn't returned, and she'd all but stopped taking her medication, breaking pills into tiny fragments as she weaned herself off.

Up at the stone circle, there was no hint of the Otherworld today. The wind blew strongly into her face as she took in the view of purplish mountains and a glittering sea. The Sisters remained grey—ancient, mysterious, but completely of the landscape. There were two footpaths only: one that

led to the ruined mill and one that led to Cairndonan village. No mysterious third way.

Voices broke her reverie. The multi-hued form of Peta appeared, followed by half a dozen students, from the village footpath. "Marvelous
weather, isn't it?" said an older women, brushing past Gill and setting up a
stool and easel almost on her feet. It was the woman who'd nearly stormed
out when Juliana questioned her skills; she plainly recognized Gill, in turn.
"I've learned so much from Peta," she confided. "More than I ever could
from Dame Juliana herself, she's too rarefied for me. Peta's so down-to-
earth, in tune with real-world artists if you know what I mean . . ."

She was still chatting away as Gill politely withdrew. Again she had
an uneasy feeling of watching people at a wonderful party to which she
hadn't been invited. While the students wandered among the stones,
seeking good viewpoints, Peta slipped up beside her and said, "Hi. How
are things?"

She seemed a little reserved—presumably because Gill had not responded
to her invitation. "Fine. How about you?"

"Great," said Peta, "apart from you ignoring my note. Surely you're curious to know what's happening with Leith?"

"I wasn't ignoring it," said Gill. "Yes, I'm curious, of course, but . . . when
you let yourself get interested in people, that's when you get into horrible
tangles with them, which is exactly what I vowed to avoid. I needed . . . space."

Peta gave a wry grin. "Enjoying it?"

"Yes, I am, actually."

"I didn't mean to pressure you, Gill. I'm in an awkward position,
though. If I don't try to see you, it might seem I've lost interest, but if I *do*
try, it seems I'm being too pushy. I can't win."

Gill occupied herself by trying to scrape mud off her boots on a protrud-
ing ridge of stone. "And that's exactly the reason I wanted to keep myself
to myself. Too much can go wrong, and I haven't got the energy for it."

"Nor me," Peta said with her usual good humor. "So let's be honest,
okay? I like you and I still think there's a good friendship waiting to happen. So you'll have to endure me, until one of us leaves."

"You like me?" Gill began to smile, despite herself. "Even though I'm so
miserable, prickly and moany?"

"It's part of the fascination." Peta moved away as she spoke, making her
way over rough grass to the nearest menhir. She pressed her hands to its
rough, licheny surface.

"I'm sure I'm nowhere near as fascinating as Juliana."

"You'd be surprised." Peta smiled. "Still, she's in a class of her own." She
drifted away to glance over her students' shoulders, checking that they'd

chosen good viewpoints, making suggestions. Her circuit complete, Peta came back and said, "Have you seen Dame J's sculptures?"

"Only in photographs," Gill answered before she remembered the chain-saw carving Juliana had made and destroyed.

"When you see them in the life, there's something really odd about them," Peta said thoughtfully. "Something . . . I can't put my finger on it. Shivery. Disorientating. Just . . . weird. What's it about?"

Peta perched on one of the lower stones, her ankles crossed, the wind tangling her messily tied-back hair and bright Indian scarf. Gill leaned on the stone beside her. "God, I wish I'd brought a camera with me. Everywhere I look, there's a wonderful landscape or image and I've no way of keeping it."

Deadpan, Peta reached into a pocket, drew out a camera and placed it in Gill's hand. "Don't say I never give you anything."

"What?"

"Borrow it, my dear. It's digital, dead easy to use, just point and shoot."

Gill felt a spurt of happiness, like a child given an unexpected toy. She stepped back and, after a moment's fiddling with the buttons, took a shot of Peta atop the stone. Turning, she took more; the cup of shimmering ocean, the mountains, students amid the stone circle.

"So, what is happening with Leith?" Gill asked at last. She wasn't sure why she'd put off asking. "Have you seen him?"

"No. He's still in Juliana's rooms. She's told everyone that he's her godson, and that he's recovering from an illness. Apparently he's resting, eating a little, still not speaking. But he's calm. So she says."

"You sound annoyed."

"Argh! I could slap her for grabbing him like that! I tried to sneak in a couple of times, but the door to her quarters is always locked."

"Surely the fact that he's being looked after is more important than our nosy need for information," Gill said primly.

"Oh, come off it." Peta laughed. "You're dying to know every detail, just like me."

"Well . . . What about the mask?"

"I finished it, but she won't let me see him, so . . ." Peta jumped down and began another circuit of her class, pausing behind each in turn to inspect their work. It was plain how much they all liked her, responded to her. Gill began an idle walk to the north edge of the stone circle, taking more photographs as she went; intending simply to wander away rather than distract Peta from her teaching duties. She felt tranquil today, felt she could walk and walk without needing a rest, simply keep going to the desolate cliffs of the coast, walk off the edge of the world.

"So what happened between Juliana and your mother to make them fall out?" Peta was at her shoulder, as if she'd appeared out of the wind.

Gill mentally shook herself. "I don't really know. I never met my grandparents; Robert Flagg died in 1943. As far as I can make out, Melody wasn't around much, so Juliana and Christina grew up like war orphans. I suppose they grew apart. The only time my mother was forced to acknowledge Juliana, because the vile stepfather mentioned it, she went into a sort of burst of spitting resentment. 'That overrated, overprivileged poser is no sister of mine' sort of thing."

"Neglect, competition and jealousy?" said Peta. "Sounds like a nice toxic combination."

"Before I entered Juliana's apartment, I'd never even seen a photo of my grandparents before."

"Oh. That's quite something," Peta said softly, looking intently at her. Gill wondered if she was planning another mask, one to express this new layer of knowledge. "It must be quite momentous for you, coming here. I hadn't realized."

"I never wanted it to be a huge deal," Gill said, briskly bundling up any sense of *momentousness* and pushing it away. "You saw the family portraits, didn't you?"

"Yes, I did."

They looked at each other. Gill said, "Do you agree with me, that the one of the young man called Adam was the absolute image of Leith?"

"You thought that?" Peta turned thoughtfully to look at her students scattered among the standing stones. "So did I."

In the days that followed, Gill obeyed her urge to walk and walk. She climbed rough hills alongside burns that rushed through deep, stony fissures towards the sea, got lost in glades of dense, emerald woodland, climbed dramatic rock bluffs to gaze in exhilaration at the greater mountains beyond. She watched birds of prey hovering over the mountains, seals playing in the waves. She still couldn't believe that Rufus's healing of her leg had held. How could the man who'd done that be the same one who'd so terrified Leith?

She pondered it as she walked, and thought of the confessions she'd made to Peta, and shivered. Her past seemed a cold void, the chasm into which the mask had plunged her. Anyway. It was all behind her now: painful childhood, frantic ambition, failed relationship. Once, Steve had been the furnace that powered both her life and her running career. Now, though, she saw that period as a dark time, a smothering black tunnel. For it all to end in a car accident seemed poetically inevitable.

There was one speck of light: faint memories of India. Even now, if she glimpsed Hindu imagery—a blue-skinned god, a red spot on a forehead, many-armed Kali, bright garlands around a man's neck—it filled her with a shuddering excitement as if, after all, there was a spark of warmth and love in the void, something long lost. Her dear grandfather.

Anyway, there was nothing in Cairndonan to remind her of India. Even her confessional moment with Juliana had been an anticlimax. *If only she hadn't guessed and I hadn't told her . . . the secret was far more fun,* she thought, sighing.

It struck her that the summer school was already half over if not more. Peta would be leaving. They met casually for a pub lunch and a chat—there was still no news of Leith—but Gill continued to resist letting her too close. Yet to think that Peta would soon be gone brought a wave of dismay. Gill's efforts to fend her off suddenly seemed like time wasted. They didn't, after all, have leisurely months to forge a friendship.

By the fourth evening, Gill had taken endless photographs. The day was otherworldly, as though she waded in the first layer of—what had Peta called it? The Dusklands. It was nearly seven when she returned to Robin Cottage through the glowing evening. Peta and her students would probably be sitting down to supper now. Would Leith join them? What on earth did Juliana plan to do with him?

As Gill entered her front room, she had the camera in both hands, so eager to review the day's images that she didn't pause to close the door or remove her boots. The photographs were astonishing. Scrolling back to the afternoon at the stone circle, Gill saw that she'd captured a special event, a magical time that would never come again. Peta's red hair tangling on the wind, the way the light slanted across the menhirs, the concentration and enjoyment of the students. Gill bit her lip, wondering, *Why didn't I appreciate how special the day was while it was still happening? I never . . . immerse myself. Never have. Why?*

Still, she had photographs now to help her reconstruct the past. It would be like creating a mosaic, making memories into art, a new and separate entity. . . A quick flame of excitement went through her. *Juliana must have a computer,* Gill thought. *I wonder if she'd let me use it?*

Some of the shots had strange light effects, a faint shimmer around the stones that made Peta's hair seem tipped with fire. One image in particular caught Gill's attention. There was Peta, leaning on a standing stone, hair streaming out like a sunlit cloud. On the stone itself was a faint worn carving in its surface that she hadn't noticed at the time: a crude relief of a serpent, winding vertically up the stone. The head and most of its length appeared blue, like lapis lazuli. And behind the stone and Peta, she could see that the Cairndonan footpath looked strange, blurred by a double image in that one place. *Two* tracks, one overlaid on the other.

She focused until her eyes hurt. Yes, there was the path to Cairndonan village, but there too was the subtly different, elusive path to Boundry. Gill released the breath she'd been holding. She needed to see this on a full-size screen . . . was it possible the portal had reopened without them noticing? Perhaps you never would see it, unless you approached by the correct route, through the mill . . .

As she studied the image, she became aware of a dull rhythmic sound, a slight shaking of the earth. It barely registered at first. Then she realized she was hearing the four-time beat of hooves at walking pace.

Gill stepped into the doorway to look. A large white horse was approaching along the stream bank from her right. Its neck was arched, the mane rippling right down over its shoulder, the tucked-in muzzle curtained by a long forelock. It lifted its feathered, dinner-plate hooves high like a Lipizzaner. The horse had only a rope halter, no saddle or bridle. The rider on its back was in jeans and a bright patchwork jacket. No riding hat, either, just a thick, shiny flow of dark hair to which the sun lent a red halo.

Rufus. Oh god, it was Rufus. The sight of him sent her heart into spasms. Her feet shifted in panic, but it was too late to withdraw and close the cottage door. Even if she'd been able to move, he'd already seen her. As the horse drew level, Rufus shortened the halter rope and the beast stopped placidly, standing square and magnificent as if in a show ring. She caught its horsy aroma.

"Hello, Gill," said Rufus, leaning down with one arm across the muscular ridge of its neck. "We meet again." When she only stared, he indicated himself. "I'm Rufus Hart. You can't have forgotten me? You came into my . . . er, my hostelry some days ago."

"Yes," she stammered. "I know. I was just . . . surprised to see you."

"I don't suppose . . ." He paused, casually swinging one leg forward over the withers. Despite the unconventional dismount, he landed neatly, both feet together, and stood facing her, smiling. "I don't suppose you've seen a young man, mid-twenties, same height as me, thick dark hair? We call him Leith. You probably noticed him during your visit?"

Gill had the presence of mind to appear puzzled and innocent. Not fast enough, though, for Rufus's razor-keen wits.

"Your barman. Yes, but . . ." She folded her arms and gave what she hoped was a concerned frown. "I haven't seen him since. Is there a problem?"

His eyes narrowed at little, glistening. "Well, possibly. He seems to have gone missing. I have looked everywhere and, to be honest, I'm growing more than a little worried about him."

There was nothing about him to suggest he was any kind of monster or slave-keeper. He seemed normal; a concerned friend. "Why are you worried?"

Rufus paused. His smile fell away. "He's my brother. He's been ill."

"Your *brother*? I didn't realize."

"No reason why you would. Are you sure you haven't seen him? Strange. I had such a strong feeling that he had come this way."

"Well, if he did, I didn't see him." She looked him straight in the eye, daring him to accuse her of lying.

"Thank you anyway, Gill. I'll continue my search."

With a light movement he was on the horse again and riding away, leaving her standing there stupidly, wondering what she should have said or done. She watched as he reached the main bridge over the small gorge. As he rode across, turning side-on to her, she held up her camera and captured him. He was some distance away by then and there was no time to use the zoom. She watched him making his way at a walk up the track that led to the estate's main drive.

The moment he was out of sight behind trees, she turned the opposite way, crossed the footbridge and took her shortcut to the house, with her camera in one hand.

She was out of breath and aching when she let herself in through the first side door she came to, the weariness of her long day catching up with her. It would take Rufus probably only five minutes to arrive, assuming he was making for the house. In the dining room, a few faces turned to look as she entered. Ignoring them, she crossed to the table where Juliana sat chatting with Peta and a handful of her adoring male and female disciples. Leith was not among them.

Juliana looked up sternly, an unholy fusion of headmistress and empress. "Gill," she said, "to what do we owe this pleasure? Do join us, won't you?"

"Rufus is coming," Gill blurted.

"What?" Peta was on her feet immediately. Juliana rose more slowly, pressing a hand on Peta's arm as if to quiet her.

"Come into the hall." Juliana spoke in a brisk, soft voice, dropping her napkin on the table and asking her dining companions to excuse her. She led the way across the lobby and into an empty office. Gill made her hurried explanation, suddenly aware that her head was pounding from tiredness and hunger. "He's looking for Leith. He said Leith's his brother." For emphasis, she fumbled with the camera until she called up the image she'd just taken; a horse on a bridge. It was like a blurred Pre-Raphaelite painting, horse and rider a drifting shape of light; a medieval knight on some enigmatic quest. The upright figure of Rufus with his flower-meadow jacket and flow of dark hair was unmistakable.

"You just took this?" asked Peta.

"About ten minutes ago. He might not be heading this way, I don't know, but what if he is? I had to warn you. Or rather, warn Leith."

Juliana, who had been studying the image, gave the camera back. "Warn him of what, exactly? No, I appreciate what you're saying, Gill. But really, what can Rufus do if Leith refuses to go with him?"

"I don't know," said Gill, looking to Peta for an answer that wasn't forthcoming. "But Leith was scared of him for a reason."

"Wait here," said Juliana. "If Rufus arrives, stall him. I'll go and talk to Leith."

With that, she swept out. Gill felt a pang of annoyance that it was Juliana again who took it on herself to warn Leith. Peta said, "At least if Rufus turns up, we might get some answers."

They moved into the lobby to keep watch on the drive. There was no one manning the desk. For once, Gill wished that Colin or Ned or Flora was around; presumably they were busy in the kitchens. "If you're Aetherial, how come you don't have any answers? Do you really not know who Rufus Hart is?"

"Why should I?" Peta gave a small, apologetic shrug. "That's like me expecting you to know some random man from New York, just because you're both human."

"But might he have . . . supernatural powers that make him dangerous?"

Peta looked serious, her eyes and lips very dark against her chalk-pale complexion. "Our creed is to do no harm. After some nasty Otherworld conflicts in the past, we said enough is enough."

"Ohh-kay . . . and are you telling me that no one ever breaks it?"

"Sadly not. Just that we have no strange powers aimed *specifically* at hurting or scaring people. I'm fairly sure Rufus can't hurl bolts of lightning or throw a magical barrier around the house."

"Oh, good. As long as you're *fairly* sure," Gill groaned.

"He may well be no more dangerous than a human. But all it takes for a human is a knife, a gun, a can of petrol or an attitude to cause havoc . . ."

"This isn't the slightest bit reassuring!"

"Shame you lost your unicorn spear."

"Yes, because I think the unicorn is on his way to claim it back."

Outside the front doors, nothing moved. The estate lay green and still, mountains timeless in the distance. After a few minutes, Juliana came softly down the stairs, a flow of silver-grey. Her face was pale, her expression withdrawn, preoccupied. "I've seen the white horse from an upstairs window. They're heading this way."

"What about Leith?" asked Peta.

Juliana shook her head emphatically. "Oh, he most definitely does not want to see Rufus. Poor boy turned as white as ash when I told him. He's terrified."

"Oh, god," said Gill. "Can I go up and see him?"

"No, leave him be. It's no reason for the rest of us to lose our heads, is it?" said Juliana. "Ah, reinforcements."

Ned Badger appeared from the dining room, a noiseless ebony shadow; Colin came from one of the passageways, all swaggering energy in pale blue jeans and a khaki shirt. "Problem, Dame J?"

"You might say that. There's a visitor on his way who wants to see my, er, my godson, but he's not welcome."

"Right, I'll see him off," said Colin, hands on hips.

"No, Colin, hold fire. I want you to hover discreetly in the background."

"You're kidding."

"No, I am not kidding," she stated, silencing him. "This Rufus may leave willingly, in which case I don't want him to think he's caused the remotest stir. But if he's difficult, I will need you to escort him, very gently but firmly, off the premises. Got that? Flora and her helpers will finish serving dinner as normal. No fuss. And I've reassured Leith that there's absolutely no reason for him to see this person if he doesn't want to."

The sound of unshod hooves clomping on the drive drew near. A pale shape passed one of the windows framing the front doors. Then the extraordinary form of Rufus came striding in, shadowy against the liquid gold of the sky behind him, light streaming through his hair.

He completed his entrance with a slight, ironic bow. "Gill, we meet again," he said, "unless you have an identical twin? I'm so pleased to see you. Ladies, forgive me; my name's Rufus Hart. I'm looking for someone who has gone missing."

"Gill told us," Juliana said. "Please, come into the office."

She signaled Ned and Colin to remain in the lobby; Peta and Gill pushed into the office after her, before she could prevent them.

"This is so very kind of you," Rufus said as Juliana closed the door. He didn't look threatening, Gill thought. He looked like an ordinary, personable young man. Well, not *ordinary*; he was too striking. But bright, friendly and self-possessed. "Leith's my brother. Did Gill describe him to you? He would be hard to miss, since he is very nearly as good-looking as me."

Somehow he managed to pull off this line with an incredibly charming grin.

"Shorter hair," he continued, leveling one hand at his collarbone. "He was wearing, let me think, dark trousers and a white shirt and black leather boots . . ."

"Mr. Hart, when did you lose him?" Juliana cut him off, her tone businesslike.

He hesitated. "A few days ago."

"And you've only just started looking?"

He replied in a quiet, grave tone, "Madam, I began as soon as I realized he was missing. I've tried all the places where he would usually be found. If you haven't seen him, tell me and I'll be on my way."

He glanced at Peta as he spoke. Gill saw that she was looking straight ahead, carefully not meeting his eyes and remaining deadpan.

"I'm very sorry, Mr. Hart." Juliana spoke in a warm, firm tone. "We haven't seen anyone answering that description. Being so remote, we never get anyone on the estate who isn't an official guest; a stranger would be spotted immediately. Can you leave a number where we might contact you, if anything happens?"

"Alas, we live without modern technology," Rufus replied without blinking.

"Do you live in Cairndonan? I'm amazed I've never met you before."

"No. Further afield."

"Where, in some remote croft up in the hills, you and your brother? Here to escape the rat race?"

"You could say that." Every subtle question Juliana threw at him, he simply evaded, as if he were made of air. "Are you sure he hasn't been here?"

"Quite sure. I'm sorry." With that, Juliana raised an ushering hand as if to see him out. As she did so, Rufus collapsed. His head dropped, his hands went to his face. His long hair fell forward and he staggered slightly, groping backward until he found a small hard couch that stood just inside the office door. He sat down, head in hands, apparently distressed. Gill's preconceptions about him wavered.

"Damn," he said, voice muffled. "God, I can't lose him. I can't."

Peta sat down beside him, as if the quick impulse to help had overridden her caution. Juliana and Gill stood looking at him; Gill nearly laughed to see how very similar their demeanor was: arms folded, all measured wariness where Peta would jump straight in.

Rufus let his hands drop onto his thighs and looked up. He was quiet for a moment, his face turning pale, his gaze unfocused. Lines of pain webbed his brow. He looked human, broken and scared.

"Um," said Peta, "can we ask what this is all about?"

"There's only the two of us," Rufus said softly. "I'm his . . . carer. God, I hate that word. Leith has suffered since childhood with mental illness. He was diagnosed with psychosis at fifteen; how accurate the diagnosis was I couldn't say, since the medical profession have done nothing to help him. It's just a label. What's true is that he suffers prolonged bouts of intense mental distress, confusion and paranoid delusions that can make him a great danger to himself. I hoped that a new start in a remote area might help. He seemed better for a while, but now I'm afraid that the unfamiliar surroundings have only unsettled him . . ."

Tears ran from his eyes. Gill stared, her heart giving a jolt of uncertainty. Peta frowned up at her. Juliana said, "Have you called the police?"

"Of course." Rufus sprang to his feet and said hoarsely, "Oh my god, what if he's gone over a cliff?"

"Please try not to think the worst," Juliana said stiffly. "If he had, surely he would have been found by now."

"You're right." Rufus pushed his hair off his face, drew a breath and composed himself. "Excuse that moment of panic. I'm grateful for your time, but I'll trouble you no longer."

He moved toward the door, to their collective relief. As they followed him out of the office towards the doors, Juliana said, "Really, is there no way for us to contact you?"

"Unfortunately, there isn't," Rufus answered. "But I'll come again in a day or two, just to check if you've heard anything. If that's all right?"

"Of course," Juliana said through her teeth.

"Thank you," he said as she held the main door open for him. Gill was aware of Colin and Ned hovering like sentries. "If you do see my brother . . . he may spin all manner of dreadful tales about his circumstances, but they aren't true. It's his illness speaking. Sometimes he stops communicating altogether. He needs kindness, that's all. If he does turn up, please would you look after him until I come back?"

"Naturally," said Juliana.

Then Rufus left at last. He'd been there only a few minutes but it felt to Gill as if he'd filled the whole mansion with crackling light and tension. They watched as he sprang onto the horse's back and rode away.

Juliana flicked a hand at Ned and Colin, telling them to stand down. She had to do so twice before they obeyed; Ned slipping reluctantly into the dining room and Colin stepping outside, presumably to make sure that Rufus left. The three women looked at each other.

"Well, now I don't know what to think," said Peta.

"Nor me," said Gill. "He was pretty convincing."

"What?" Juliana snapped. "Surely you weren't taken in by that performance? Disingenuous garbage, from start to finish!"

"But where's the evidence that Rufus has done anything wrong?" Peta asked reasonably. "When Gill met him, he was perfectly nice, wasn't he?"

"Well . . . yes." Gill frowned, confused. "He was . . . unusual, but to be fair, all he did was offer me a drink and work a miracle on my leg pain. He didn't try to stop me from leaving."

"I'm only suggesting that we can't discount what Rufus said," Peta added. "What if he's telling the truth and Leith's ill?"

Juliana glared at Peta; an imperious look that might have made birds drop from the sky. "Leith is clearly ill, but I'm convinced they're not brothers."

"That does seem unlikely, it's true," said Peta.

"He sat there and told a series of blatant lies! Letting us think they live in a croft when we know they don't."

"Actually, Dame J, it was you who suggested that."

"He didn't deny it. That's as close to dishonesty as makes no difference."

"While we sat there and told the biggest lie of all," said Peta, "that Leith's not here. And I'm sure he knew."

Juliana's stare turned glacial. "Fine. Run after Mr. Hart and bring him back. See how Leith likes it."

Peta opened her hands in mild exasperation. "I wasn't suggesting that. I'm only saying, maybe we should be handling this differently . . . I don't know."

Gill broke in, "Can we see him?"

Juliana hesitated. Gill saw the tensing of her shoulders, the way her face closed. Again she wondered what game her aunt was playing. "Why?"

"Just to make sure he's all right."

A long pause, then Juliana sighed. "Very well. Just you, Gill." She added with achingly polite firmness, "Peta, do go back and finish your supper."

Peta's face showed stoic disappointment. "I'm concerned about Leith, too, Dame J."

"I know, my dear, but I would like a quiet word with Miss Sharma alone. Come upstairs, Gill. There are a couple of things I need to explain."

Leith was in Juliana's sitting room, standing in near-darkness. The curtains were drawn, the lights off. When Juliana flicked on a lamp, he jumped. Gill saw how pale he was, the expression of numb terror blanching his face. Her heart went out to him.

"It's all right, he's gone," said Juliana. "My dear, there's no need to be anxious. We won't let him near you, I promise."

"You won't be able to stop him," Leith whispered. "He'll come back."

"Still, I think there's something I can try."

Gill said, "Rufus claimed that you're his brother. Is that true?"

Leith didn't answer. His forehead creased. He moved to the window, opening the curtains a sliver and peering out. He was dressed in clothes that looked baggy and incongruous on him, dark jeans and a scruffy pale blue shirt; Gill guessed they'd been borrowed from Colin.

"I'll fetch some brandy from the other room," said Juliana. "Won't be a moment."

Cosy in our fire-lit cocoon against the winter, it seemed possible to stay as we were forever. The three of us, growing up, chasing each other through the great cavernous rooms of the house, startling deer in the heather, running through the woods, along the cliff-tops to the sea.

But then came the Great War.

Adam went in 1916, at the age of sixteen. He came back to us in 1918, changed.

Juliana gasped to see a picture of Adam, a wide-eyed youth in army uniform. It was one she'd never seen before. He looked so young. The uniform looked too big, making him appear unearthly, like a sprite dressed up.

A bullet had gone right through him, missing the vitals; he recovered and lived, physically at least. I don't know what he suffered, what he saw. He would never speak of it. One can use one's imagination. But it was so hard to see him afterwards; his bright face washed-out and gaunt, the light gone from those sparkling eyes. The way his gaze would lose focus when no one was speaking to him, the slight tremor of his hand when he lit a cigarette. Sometimes he would flinch at nothing. Oh, how my soul chilled to see him flinch at shadows!

It was the first time Father had cause to be proud of him. But he was embarrassed, too, because he did not know how to deal with this son, this stranger who had visited Hell and survived. That was the defining feature of the family, it must be said; stiff, embarrassed, strangers even to each other.

So we brought Adam to Cairndonan, Melody and I—she was seventeen then, I sixteen—thinking that if any place on Earth could reawaken the old Adam, it was here. We would have fun. We would be children again. He would be healed.

"Healed," murmured Juliana. "So it's true, he did come back from the war."

At Cairndonan House, in 1919, it was as if time had stopped in 1860.

As a child, I used to wonder what on earth occupied our uncle in his study. He was always there among old books and papers, reading, poring over photograph albums or staring through a microscope.

Well, Uncle John was a collector. He kept stuffed dead animals under glass domes, drawers filled with shells and fossils that gave off a scent of old churches when they were opened, yellow old whale tusks, shelves full of photograph albums and boxes of slides. We were a little afraid of his

oddness. But while Adam was away, I started paying more attention to
our uncle and he began to trust me.

His great thing was photography. Many of the fine black and white
portraits you will see about the house are his. What is less known is that
he was using a color process called 'autochrome', a really early form of color
photography that gave most vivid results. That was how he occupied his
time.

Degenerate that I am, I confess it gives me pleasure to see that you
share such a passion—he with his photography, you with your art.
Treasure it, my dear. It's worth more than all the cheap thrills in the
world, believe me.

Anyway, that summer, aged sixteen, I discovered his secret. I was
growing too old now for childish pursuits and bored, bored, bored with
the labyrinthine house and dreary wilderness outside. I would slip into
Uncle John's study and, instead of running from him, ask questions. And
at last he revealed his secret.

He was trying to photograph a species of faerie folk, the 'dubh sidhe'
as they are known in these parts. You will have heard of other 'fairy
photographs' from those times, hoaxes lapped up by eminent persons, who,
you'd think, should have had the wit to know better. Look, here are the
'Cottingley Fairies' cut from a magazine—you'd have to be half-blind
not to see these are cardboard cut-outs with drawings on them! I'm sure
John knew nothing of such goings-on; no, this was an idea he'd cooked up
for himself. It was more than local rumour or folklore to him. He claimed
to have seen things. And he was determined to capture them on film.

He showed me his early efforts; blurry shots of woodland, standing
stones, shadows. He took them from a locked cabinet and spread them out
on his desk for me. I could see nothing in them, but he insisted that this
blur or that was the trace of some supernatural entity passing before the
lens. He rambled about new techniques he was developing, a more sensitive
emulsion, a better type of flash device, on and on, while I tried to look
serious and suppress my laughter.

'There is something on the estate,' he said. 'It must be possible to
photograph it!'

I remember how he stammered with the excitement of describing what
he'd seen. Usually he was a quiet, dry man, wrapped up in his own
thoughts, but now his hands trembled and his eyes gleamed behind his
spectacles.

When I asked if he had faerie specimens pinned in cases like butterflies,
he did not even know that I was teasing him.

'I don't know that these beings are what we'd term faeries at all,' he
said. 'We should not think of them that way, but as something unknown.

They are not tiny—they're the same size as us. I have seen them—half-seen, I should say. Some appear human, others . . . not. It's as if they're on their way somewhere. You won't see them clearly; they are dark like midnight, somewhat hunched over—almost reptilian—and some are winged, look—' He flicked through the pages of sketches he'd made and drew a shaky breath. 'I call them Dunkelmen.'

That word. It made me shiver. My foolish sixteen-year-old self stood there stifling tears of laughter, but in the midst of mockery I felt a chill of pure fear.

'Like bogeymen?' I said.

John replied, 'I don't know where I got the word from. I thought it was from folklore but now I can find no reference to it. Perhaps it came from my own mind. Still, the name's as good as any. Dunkelmen. The dark men.'

I didn't quite think him mad, not that, but definitely eccentric, deluded, so passionately focussed upon this need to photograph figments of his imagination that he'd lost his grip on reality. I offer no excuse for my cruel, secret mockery of a harmless old man. We weren't close to him; he was self-absorbed, awkward, more like some dry schoolmaster than a proper uncle. In other words, he was ripe meat for our immature pranks.

I was on the edge of growing fond of him. However, I ignored those higher feelings in favor of childish high jinks. I told myself that it was only to see Adam smile again; and that was great part of it, but it's also true that much of it was pure mischief.

So I confided in my brother and sister and soon I had caught them up in a giggling conspiracy. Uncle John believes in faeries, what a lark. I cringe now to think of it—but at the time, it seemed the most hilarious practical joke ever staged.

On Midsummer Night, Uncle John went deep into the woodlands beyond the garden and positioned his cameras and flashes, concealing the setup with branches like a birdwatcher in a blind. He was determined to remain all night, and we were determined that he should have something to photograph.

It beggars belief that he did not suspect us—but he trusted us, dear old fool, and was so set upon his ideas that he never suspected a hoax. Or perhaps he did realize—actually, he must have in those last moments—but of course, there was no chance to ask him afterwards.

Adam, Melody and I dressed up in curtains and armed ourselves with a lantern and some small bells. The summer nights stay light, so far north, but let me tell you the darkness was thick enough as we tiptoed through the trees towards his hiding place. We hid in the shadows, just far enough away that he'd perceive only a glimmer of movement or the unearthly tinkle of bells. Such a struggle we had to stifle our laughter! But it was the first time I'd seen Adam smile since he'd come back from war. I saw his eyes brimming with light again and I felt joy welling up inside me because I saw the old, innocent Adam again and I thought yes, he'll be all right from now on.

Our presence sent Uncle John into a fever of activity. We heard more than saw it, because there was little to see; just an agitated shadow setting the leaves aquiver. Shaking with stifled laughter and delicious fear, we began to perform a 'faerie procession' for him. A flash lit up the night like a flare, which quite blinded us. After that, all was confusion.

An unnatural procession came, for sure. Suddenly the forest was full of moving things, dark shapes rushing all around us. I was knocked down. I heard screams. I remember nothing clearly—a whirl of strangeness—then I fell insensible, knocked out by a tree branch perhaps—and I woke at dawn to three things.

Melody, sitting on the ground and staring, dumb with shock, her face deadly white and wet with dew. Uncle John, lying dead on the forest floor—his heart had failed. And Adam—gone.

Juliana paused, got up to pour herself some water. She turned over the page and there was a strange double-page spread, bordered by wavy lines and disturbing little sketches of figures with wings and cloaks, people falling with terrified faces. There, Corah had written a second account of that night. *It was all I could do to stifle my laughter. The forest at night was frightening . . .* It was longer and more vivid, as if the first attempt had not satisfied her. Then the narrative continued as before.

Everyone was astonished to discover that Uncle John had willed Cairndonan to me. It was the wonder of the family. But think; who was it who paid him attention, looked at his photographs, and asked him questions day after day? He never realized I was humouring him. He thought my interest sincere. I shudder to think of it now—all I can say in my defense is that I was a child and a fool. And that, beneath my schoolgirl idiocy, my jeering was meant more in affection than cruelty.

Still, I can't deny the bald truth. I conceived the prank. Thus, it was I who killed him.

It must be said that Melody and I both went clean out of our minds after that.

We could never forget that night. Uncle John lying dead, his face grey and purple and contorted, eyes staring like a fish. The darkness full of rushing creatures like a hurricane of wings and claws and mad laughter. Night after night, I dreamed of them and woke thrashing, full of excitement and terror. Melody, by contrast, fled daily to church to scourge herself with prayer and penance. I believe that I disgusted her. I moaned in the night and would not set foot in her damned church.

Still, we were bound together by this awful Thing, the fact that our dear brother Adam was gone.

He simply vanished. We never found him. The only answer I have is that when the Dunkelmen came, they snatched him up and carried him away with them. Whatever the truth—we never saw him again.

Even now my throat closes up and tears fall. I still can't bear it.

We searched and searched. For years we searched. For the rest of our lives. What did outsiders see? Two mad old women who went to mediums and stage hypnotists. Two eccentric, mad old biddies in hats, yes. Even now I go out in the forests calling his name, and the locals shake their heads and say, there is poor mad old Corah Montague, still searching for her brother. They turn away from me in sympathy and fear, because they know.

The whole damned business destroyed us.

Our parents entered a state of denial. I think they believed Adam had committed suicide, and that was certainly the rumour that grew in London. So they countered it sternly with their own version: that Adam had died in the trenches. That became the official story; their son Adam died bravely, defending king and country. He'd never come home at all. They came to believe it as truth.

Not Melody and me, oh no. We dared not speak of our search, but it went on, always there feverishly beneath our everyday activities. Oh, we worked; I as a nurse, Melody as a military secretary. She met and married your father, Captain Robert Flagg, in 1936, and soon two girls came along; you and your sister. By 1944, Robert was dead.

An image in crisp shades of grey showed a smiling man in uniform beside a thin, blond, upright woman. They were posing with two girls of around three and four: Juliana, the elder, and her sister Christina. Beneath, Corah continued,

He was a dear, long-suffering man, Robert. Taken from us too soon. Bloody war.

Robert was good for Melody; he was a protective barrier between her and the loss of Adam. He was sensible and balanced her neuroses. Once he was gone, there was nothing to keep her from the abyss of obsession. When the second war ended, we resumed our quest, but now it had the taint of desperation.

As you know, during World War II, Cairndonan was used as a military hospital. I went a little wild with the soldiers and doctors, it must be said. Melody was horrified. The more she disapproved, the crazier I became. I smoked and drank and fornicated and I loved every moment! But, you know, I used fun as she used religion—to mask the eternal nightmare of That Night.

The night of the Dunkelmen.

Well, and then you arrived, and you know the rest.

Your father dead, your mother always dumping you and your sister on friends, relatives, schools—it's a wonder you didn't grow up as crazed as us. How did you emerge so level-headed? Christina—well, I'll say no more.

We owe you an apology, of course. I'm not good with such sentiments, though, and I don't think there's an apology big enough—will a house do?? It would me, but then I'm shallow. As in, 'Never mind sorry, just give me some bloody diamonds!'

Instead, an explanation.

That's why your mother and I were always vanishing together, why her mind was forever elsewhere. We could never give up the hope that our beautiful, beloved brother would one day reappear. Or that we might glimpse again the Dunkelmen in a different guise and persuade them to release Adam to us! To take pity on us.

But there is no pity in the faerie heart.

Juliana, one last thing. As I write this I realise that the years are no buffer after all, and at forty or sixty you may find it all as raw as you would have at twenty. Sorry, sorry, my dear girl. There's a truth I'm trying to tell you which I realise I can't, because it will change the way you view everything. I can't, and yet I must. It's not good, not nice, not 'proper' as Melody would see it. So after long thought, I've decided to make a little game of it. I am going to write it and seal it in an envelope within this book. Then it will be up to you whether to open the envelope, or to decide it's safer not to know. Burn it, if you like. But knowing you, you'll read it. Well, you're a grown-up, and you can't say you haven't been warned.

So what I would like you to do is this. Write down on a piece of paper what you think it says in the envelope. Have a bet on it among Charles and your friends! Then, however horrified you are, at least you'll have had the pleasure of a little flutter along with it.

The narrative ended there. If Corah had meant to write more, she had forgotten, or not known what else to say. Juliana turned to the last page, but there was nothing else in the scrapbook.

There was a thin, rough patch on the inside cover where clearly something had once been pasted and torn away; but no envelope.

"Of course not," hissed Juliana, pressing her fingers flat to the place where it should have been. "So where is the envelope, Ned?"

Gill sat on the end of Peta's double bed, exhausted from the soreness of her leg. It felt like an electric wire touching a tooth, while the muscles around it shrieked with cramp. She was still seething at Rufus, at what she'd allowed to happen. She was verging on self-pity, she knew, but she felt justified in indulging it for once.

Peta's mannequins stared at her with the faces of half-human exotic birds, wild cats, demons. The room was all color: shimmering greens, raspberry red, cobalt blue and rose gold. Jewels sparked, feathers danced. It was like having a migraine.

She heard voices in the corridor: Juliana and Peta, coming closer.

"I was just trying to be fair, to give Rufus the benefit of the doubt," Peta was saying, "but he has stepped way over the line now."

"I'm not surprised in the slightest," Juliana said waspishly. "I assumed he'd do something like this. I could see it in his eyes. He's what they call a loose cannon."

The door opened and they came in.

"Gill," said Juliana. She looked weary, stressed and distracted. "Sorry I couldn't speak to you sooner. I've had a hellish day. Flora's in hospital. Ned's still with her."

"I heard. I'm sorry."

"So, I'm two men down, as it were, and she isn't there to field the endless bloody phone calls from my accountant. Meanwhile, we try to keep the classes flowing so the students don't suspect there's a problem. And now I understand you had a visit?"

"What's Peta told you?" Gill said warily.

"The crucial bit," said Peta, giving her a firm, wide-eyed stare that conveyed, *Don't worry, nothing embarrassing.* "How Rufus showed up and left you in screaming agony."

"I wasn't actually screaming," Gill said dryly.

"You know what I mean."

"Well, this is all we need," Juliana sighed. "I'm sorry, Gill. How are you now?"

"Surviving. I can hobble about a bit, which is good; I couldn't even stand up when it first happened."

Juliana smiled, her face briefly radiant. "That's the family spirit; stiff upper lip, look on the bright side. You're happy to share with Peta, for the time being?"

"Yes, it's fine," Gill said through her teeth. "This is ridiculous. I feel like a refugee."

"Let's hope it's not for long. To the best of my knowledge, Rufus has not been here again. No one's seen him."

"That's strange," said Peta. "I thought he'd come straight here after he left Gill. Where is he? It's ominous."

"Perhaps he's given up and gone home," Gill suggested without conviction.

"That would be great, and also incredibly unlikely," said Peta.

"So what's he waiting for?"

Juliana moved to the window and looked out. "I don't want word of this reaching Leith. I don't want him upset, especially if it's for no good reason."

"Isn't that treating Leith like a child?" Peta remarked.

"He *is* a virtual child, in this state of mind. Please, Peta, don't break ranks. You two and Colin are the only ones who know, until Ned and Flora return. You're my little army. We need to keep Leith calm. Agreed?"

They nodded. Gill said, "I have a dreadful feeling that Rufus will get in, whatever we do to prevent it. We know he's not afraid to hurt people. He's unstoppable."

"We'll see about that," Juliana replied. "All doors and downstairs windows will be locked before dark. The fire exits can't be opened from outside, in any case. Colin will be on patrol."

"It won't be enough."

Juliana's expression was stern, her tone emphatic. "I swear to you, if Leith doesn't want to leave, no power on earth is going to take him away."

Gill shivered. She felt tired and defenseless. "Don't make promises you can't keep. Don't put yourself in danger, either, please."

"We'll see."

Later, she and Peta ate supper in private with Juliana. Gill had little appetite and felt woozy with pills, but no one noticed that she was only picking at her food. To her surprise, Leith joined them as they sat down. He was dressed in dark trousers and a white shirt, his face colorless but for the dappling of scabs and bruises on his forehead. Seeing him, Gill felt desperately ashamed that she'd slept with Rufus—his tormentor. She pulled her high-necked sweater a little higher around her throat.

His bandages had gone. Seeing this, Peta exclaimed and caught his hands between hers, turning them over to inspect the palms. "Wow, these are healing really well." Looking curiously into his face, she asked, "How long were you in Boundry, Leith?"

He gave a shadowy, self-conscious smile, but didn't answer. The conversation was stilted, since they were carefully not mentioning Rufus in front of him; but later, when the meal was over, he said suddenly, "Rufus is coming for me."

"No, dear." Juliana put her hand on his. "He won't find you."

"He always does. He'll make me go with him."

"No." Gill winced to hear her aunt make the promise. "I swear on my life and on my dear father's soul, Rufus will not find you."

Juliana knew she would not sleep that night. Peta and Gill had retired to their room and Leith also had gone to bed, but she sat on the couch in her sitting room, alert to the slightest noise. The more she thought about it, the more ridiculous it seemed that Rufus would try to break in at night. It would be easier by far for him to sneak in during the day. Perhaps he would come tomorrow. She hoped he would, so that they might have a final showdown and impress upon him that Leith wanted nothing more to do with him.

Juliana had brought Corah's scrapbook to her own rooms, but she'd drawn the line at searching Ned's domain for the missing envelope. She'd have it out with him when he returned. All evening she'd thought of showing the book to Gill—it was her heritage, too—but the time had not been right. It could wait.

And Leith—dare she let him read it?

Every few minutes, Juliana rose to look out of the window. Colin had left the outside lights on, as she'd asked, so no one could approach Cairndonan House without walking into a curtain of white light. All the time, she stacked her problems in her mind as if making a sculpture from them, a shape she could understand. (A twisted column with a figure trying to push out of it, haloed by black rings, flat and tilted like the rings of Saturn . . .)

Add up the income from the summer school. A nice sum, until you realized that the money had already been swallowed up by bills. She literally could not afford to let the course slide and have students demanding their money back . . . She pushed the nightmare of money aside, but all her problems circled around the arrival of her Otherworld guest.

"Does it really matter who you are, Leith?" she murmured, staring into the dark. "Leon, Adam, someone else entirely. You're a beautiful boy and I want you to stay. It's a matter of principle, now, that the Aetherials don't get you back. They have always thought that they can play with us, deceive us, torment us; they've been at their game for centuries. But they have not reckoned with me."

Juliana thought she was wide awake, until the darkness lurched and swayed around her like a ship. Corah's voice was a snake hiss in her ear, *"Wake up, you idiot, they're here! Don't let them take Adam again!"*

She caught her breath and sat upright. All around her, the air rustled and whispered. All through the house, she could feel invisible movement, like a wind through dark woodlands, like a host of unseen night creatures, searching.

Invasion.

11

Inside the Foundry

Gill could not sleep. She lay gazing at the ceiling, feeling less safe than she had at Robin Cottage. For a while, Peta had lain awake beside her with one hand folded around hers, like two schoolgirls in the dark. Now Peta was asleep, but Gill still lay in an uncomfortable haze as a small demon repeatedly poked hot forks into her hip. The costumed mannequins were watching her, whispering to each other . . . the very darkness seemed to be in motion, full of shadows, jostling and prowling.

In her usual nightmare, a single intruder stood silently watching her in the darkness. This was different . . . as if the fragments of the night itself had come to life. She couldn't see them, but she could *feel* their energy and sinister intent. A soft weight held her down and she couldn't move, let alone break the spell.

"Gill, wake up!" someone hissed.

She sat up by reflex, drawing a huge gulp of air as if she'd been suffocating. Peta was shaking her. Gill felt her heart thudding heavily, her whole body aching. She grunted, trying to push Peta off and slip back into sleep. Such a struggle to wake, like drowning in tar . . .

"Gill!" Peta pulled her arm, dragging her right off the bed. She couldn't arrange her legs in time and collapsed like a rag doll towards the carpet. Pain woke her up like a slap as Peta caught her. "Wake up!"

"What the hell . . ."

She heard the click of a light switch, but no light came on. In the faint starlight that penetrated the window, it seemed to Gill that the whole room rippled, as if seen through a thick veil. "Great, the power's gone off. Something's happening." Peta's murmuring made little sense. "Bloody hell, Aelyr, *dysir* . . . I heard they could do this enchanted sleep thing, but I've never seen it . . . Gill, listen. There's something in the house. Gill!"

Water hit her face. Gill flinched, feeling coldness trickle down her face, into her mouth. Blinking water out of her eyes, she found Peta staring at her, holding an empty glass in her hand.

"Sorry, but you have to wake up! Can't you see them?"

"See what?" Gill felt thick-headed, disoriented in the most surreal and unpleasant way. "It's my medication," she slurred. "Let me sleep."

"It's not your medication. It's Dumannios."

Peta's eyes were as round as an owl's in the near-darkness. She was pulling a cardigan over her pajamas, then wrapping a dressing gown around Gill's shoulders. Gill wrestled into the garment, still unsure if she was hallucinating. The more alert she became, the stronger the impression grew of specters roaming loose in the room. Even the walls seemed unstable.

"What are they? Why can't I see them?"

"They're Otherworld creatures, half on another plane," said Peta. "I'm only catching glimpses. This must be Rufus's doing."

"Are they dangerous?"

"I don't think they'll hurt us physically but they have power over the psyche . . . so let's assume they are. Come on. The good news is that my night vision is excellent. Bad news, even in the dark I can see that this purple cardigan clashes with red pajamas."

"Never stopped you before . . . Where are you going?"

Peta was heading for the door. "To find out what's happening. Get your shoes on, quick—if you can walk?"

"I'll manage," Gill said tightly. She grasped the alicorn for support, wishing she'd swallowed her pride and left the hospital with a proper set of crutches. "Wait. I'm not staying here on my own."

"Colin!" said Juliana. Slumped over the reception desk, head resting on his arms, he was sound asleep. She'd tried every light switch on her way, nothing. Starlight through the lobby doors cast a wan aura around him. She squeezed his shoulder and gave him a rough shake, raising her voice. "Colin. Wake up!"

Still he slept, insensible. She looked around the cavernous hall; the stairwell and the great stained-glass window looked strange, as if a greyish pall hung in the air, full of shifting shapes. There was an odd, green scent like rosemary. She felt drowsiness stealing over her, an urge to fall where she stood and surrender to deep, delicious sleep . . . With all her will, she resisted, holding steady against a tide of panic. All around her, the hall was filled with elusive, moving specters. If only she could see them clearly. That was the most unnerving thing, *feeling* the ghostly invasion but being unable to see it.

This must be Rufus's doing, that the Otherworld was forcing its way into her domain. He couldn't know she was fairly resistant to such manifestations. She thought, *Where the hell is Ned?* As soon as the thought occurred, her heart sank. He was still at the hospital with Flora, of course. *Damn.*

A last try. "*Colin!*"

He slept on, snoring lightly.

Juliana groped her way into the office and located a large, heavy flashlight on a shelf. She flicked it on, aware that she was breathing hard. Not frightened, exactly, but possessed by urgency. The dark house felt huge around her. The invaders must be searching for Leith and she would protect him at any cost.

By the fragile beam, she mounted the stairs and tried the first guest bedroom she came to. She'd wake her students first and explain later, but now she needed help. The door was unlocked and in the bed lay her most talented protégé, tall skinny grey-haired Reg; dead to the world. Like Colin, there was no waking him. She backed out of the room and closed the door.

So, unnatural sleep had claimed her students, too. She was on her own. *It's for the best if they don't see anything*, she thought. *So be it.*

The only thing that mattered was protecting Leith.

She hurried along the landing towards her quarters. Was Rufus here, or had he sent in this demon pack to do his dirty work for him? "D'you really think I'm going to fall for your wiles, Rufus?" she muttered as she went. "Think again."

Entering her apartment, she called out, "Leith?" She expected to find him unconscious as she'd left him, and was startled to find him awake and dressed. He came swaying towards her out of the gloom of the bedroom, his eyes huge and dark with terror.

Perhaps his long exposure to the Otherworld had given him immunity to its narcotic effects.

"Is it Rufus?" he said. "He's here, isn't he? His *dysir* are hunting me. I can smell them. They'll hunt me out and lead him to me."

"It's all right," said Juliana. "Let them come. They'll be sorry." Taking his arm, she bundled him through her rooms to the passage by the bathroom. There she opened a small door concealed in the paneling. "I'm going to take you somewhere safe. No arguing, just do as I say."

Behind the panel, she angled the flashlight to illuminate a staircase, an old, hidden way for household servants. Chivvying Leith in front of her, Juliana descended the musty wooden stairwell to the ground floor near the kitchens, down again into the cellars where the walls became stone and the narrow space smelled of earth, mildew and cobwebs. Reaching a small oak door, she drew a bunch of keys from her pocket, unlocked and pushed opened the door onto a tunnel.

"In there?" Leith whispered. "Please don't lock me up here!"

There was panic in his voice. She said steadily, "No one is going to lock you up, Leith. It's just a service tunnel. It leads to the foundry. My workshop." She took his arm and urged him forward as she spoke. "It used to be a gas plant to light and heat the house, you see, and this was a way for them to reach it when the weather was bad."

"Yes," he said faintly. His breathing was fast and shallow. The flashlight beam played eerily over the stone walls, over his frozen face.

"So I'm going to hide you in the foundry until Rufus gives up and goes away." That was the best explanation she could provide.

"He won't give up," said Leith, but he went with her anyway.

The tunnel ran underground, angling downwards as it followed a natural rock fissure that traversed the gardens towards the cliffs. The air was thick with dampness, the air turning ever colder as they made their way towards the far end: the secret door to her workshop.

Time and space elongated. Behind, pursuing Leith's trail, the spectral predators flowed like floodwater; Juliana could hear them, smell their narcotic scent. She moved as if through molasses, too slow to outpace them, while the end of the tunnel seemed miles distant, too far ever to reach.

"Dysir," said Peta, holding Gill's arm. They worked their way towards Juliana's rooms as fast as her sore leg would allow. "They're elemental beasts, somewhere between guard dogs and hunting hounds. Only they're not canine, not even corporeal. They . . . they scare the crap out of me, quite frankly."

"You don't fancy one as a pet, then?" Gill remarked. The house felt hostile; too quiet, its dimensions all wrong, boundless.

"No thanks, but people do keep them like that. They're a phenomenon of Asru—that's part of the Spiral—but an elitist one, a status symbol. You might be *granted* them, if you're important enough. In Rufus's case, maybe stolen."

"Since he apparently sees himself as the most important being ever to grace the Earth, he obviously thinks he's entitled."

They found Juliana's door unlocked; Peta gave a perfunctory knock and walked in. Inside, the rooms had an air of sudden desertion. The door to Leith's bedroom stood open and there was no one inside. Gill tried a light switch; nothing.

"Dame J?" called Peta. "I thought Colin would be around, at least."

They groped their way to the far end of the apartment, to the passage where lay her bathroom and bedroom. Those rooms were deserted, too, but Gill felt a waft of cold air and heard Peta's fingernails scratching at wood. "There's a door here," she said.

As she spoke, the floorboards began to shake with the thunder of heavy paws. The space around them was suddenly full of movement, invisible yet muscular. Something struck Gill, like the shoulder of a small horse or a large dog, shoving her back against a wall. She cried out. At the same moment, the door sprang open, hitting the paneling. Peta staggered back, colliding with Gill; a herd of dark shapes came flowing past them. Gill got the impression of a wolf pack, bustling and unstoppable—only these were bigger than wolves, just inky silhouettes, confusing to the senses. She couldn't pick out individuals. Occasionally she caught the bulk of a head or a fiery eye; then only busy darkness again.

They poured through the secret door like floodwater into a well.

"They're not solid," Peta said grimly. "Come on."

Tugging her arm, Peta waded into the flow. Gill followed, thinking how unutterably foolhardy this was. It was lightless and there were steep stairs leading down; she would have turned back but now there were more *dysir* behind her and she was trapped, had to go with the flow, cursing as her hip twanged with every step.

Walking amid the *dysir* was like walking in a blustery wind or a strong river current. She could pass through them and yet she was buffeted at every step. Gill gripped her narwhal staff in her right hand and clung to the stair rail with her left. Adrenaline carried her through the pain.

"Where the hell does this lead?" she gasped.

"Kitchen," said Peta, then, "Oh . . . and cellars, apparently."

They found their way into a narrow tunnel, led by a dancing flashlight beam some way ahead. The mildewed stench of stone swallowed them. In the close press of the walls, the *dysir* seemed huge, chest-height almost, and the tunnel was full of their scrabbling paws and their breathing.

For a time they pursued the retreating light. Then the passage straightened out and Gill glimpsed Juliana at the far end, and Leith with her. The end of the tunnel was filled by a flight of open wooden steps leading to a trapdoor in the tunnel roof. Juliana was near the top, struggling to undo bolts and arguing with Leith at the same time.

"Leith!" Juliana snapped. "Help me open this bloody trapdoor, will you! Quickly."

He hung back, plainly terrified. Gill saw him staring from Juliana to the onrushing *dysir* and back again. Light wavered around the walls as Juliana battled with the weight of the trapdoor, her flashlight held awkwardly in one hand.

Gill sprinted forward. She squeezed past Peta and Leith, stumbled up the steps to help her aunt. It wasn't clear what Juliana intended but there was no time to ask. She had to help her aunt haul the trap open before the ravenous shadows reached them.

Peta cried out a warning—and the whole tunnel seemed to erupt.

"Keep them back!" Juliana cried hoarsely. "Leith, up here, now!"

The trapdoor fell open with a bang.

The tunnel was full of raging shadows. Gill descended a couple of steps, caught Leith's arm and dragged him upwards until she could pass him into Juliana's hands. Then she was being pushed about by a tide of furious beasts.

Suddenly they were visible.

They had vague, brawny forms reminiscent of gryphons or wild boar, eyes of yellow fire. Gill gripped her alicorn, beating at them, but they parted and swirled like water. Walls, floor, everything seemed to move and writhe and lunge at her. She looked back for Peta, couldn't see her—but in Peta's place—

There was a figure resembling one of her mannequins. A tall fire creature, all scarlet flame and feathers in a whirl of orange light, a bird of paradise. This creature fought the *dysir*, intimidating them, appearing to hurl flame at them. They cowered. When they tried to muscle past her she appeared to seize them, one after another as if lifting a dog by the scruff of its neck, and *threw* them back into each other.

It bought Juliana the time she needed.

Gill saw her now pulling Leith through the open gap and into the space above. Gill glimpsed the inside of the foundry; a sort of nothingness, filled with sooty mist and gleams of fire.

Then Juliana called out, "Stand back, let them through!"

Gill hardly had a choice. She was flattened against the wall as the tide of *dysir* came surging past her. She saw the fire-bird that was Peta falling, vanishing under the stampede. Up the steps they poured, through the open trap and into the darkness in pursuit of Leith.

It was like being caught in a small tornado. Gill shut her eyes, held her breath. It was over quickly. The last of them slipped out of sight. Silence fell. There was no sign of Juliana, or of Leith.

She paused a moment, dazed. By instinct she began to make her way up towards the trapdoor until her head just breached the gap. Above was a dark, roiling space. It must be the inside of the foundry and yet it wasn't; it seemed too big. It had no walls, no edges. It was smoky and shadowy, with red fires glimmering through the pall. There stood a handful of Juliana's statues, half-seen in the swirling fog; briefly shining pale and motionless, before being veiled again.

"Juliana?" she called.

She took in the scene for a second or two; then Juliana and Leith reappeared as if from nowhere. Gill had to descend and stand aside to let them through.

"It's all right, Leith," Juliana was saying. "They're gone. You did well."

He looked chalk-white, numb with shock. Above him, Juliana let the trapdoor down and it slammed shut, severing Gill's view. Dumannios vanished. The stone walls around them were solid again.

Where the fire-bird had been, Peta was on her hands and knees, panting as she stared up at Juliana. Gawky in boots and pajamas, she rose to her feet, pushing back her hair. 'Dame J? Where are the . . . the creatures?"

"Gone," Juliana said brusquely. "Thank you for your aid. Let's go back into the house and speak no more of this."

"But what happened?"

"Nothing." Juliana's face was grim, her eyes narrow and icy. She towered like a steel empress. "Go back. It's over."

In daylight, Gill and Peta stood outside the big double doors of the foundry. The morning was crisp and clear, the sky bright over the sea, waves glittering and rolling into white froth on the rocks below. The stony cliff paths around them were patterned with lichens, jeweled with alpine flowers of yellow and white. Seagulls cried. Gill saw a bird of prey hovering above the headland to the north. It was a glorious morning. Difficult to believe what had happened a few hours earlier.

Over breakfast—served by a pale Peta and a rumpled-looking Colin—the students had muttered about nightmares, restlessness and strange apparitions. There was a veritable buzz of excitement over this shared psychic weirdness. Some, who had at first claimed heavy, oblivious sleep, miraculously began to remember strange events after all.

Juliana was saying nothing.

She'd become a stranger again, coldly magnificent and as close-lipped as a statue. Raising the subject of the incident was so completely out of the question that even Peta dared not try it. Dame Juliana would discuss only art, or even the weather, as if nothing had happened.

"Why wouldn't she talk about it?" asked Peta. "We were the only ones awake and we helped her, yet she's treating it like a military secret."

"Too many people around."

"No. She's had every chance to speak to us alone and she's avoiding us. It felt almost . . ."

The world was so fresh, wild and beautiful, it was difficult to accept that the night's terrors had been real. Gill was limping badly, but the pain had settled to a blunt ache. She could bear it, as long as she took her pills and didn't dwell on it.

"Almost—what?" she prompted.

Peta answered slowly, "As if, rather than the *dysir* entering the surface world, the house itself had shifted through the Dusklands into Dumannios. They didn't enter our reality; rather, we went into theirs."

"Could Rufus do that?"

She shook her head. "Only if the house already straddled both realms, as I suspect it does."

"And what's Dumannios again?"

"A state of chaos, of fear." Peta seemed to be struggling for the right description. "The Dusklands is what lies beneath the everyday surface. Dumannios is more of the same only . . . spicier. Absolutely not benign."

"Dream versus nightmare," said Gill.

"Good analogy, but those layers are . . . real to Aetherials. Not always in a good way."

"It all seemed pretty real to me. I saw you change, Peta. That was the weirdest thing of all."

Peta smiled. "I had to, in order to have an impact on the *dysir*, to fight them on their own turf, as it were. That was my Otherworld form you saw. You approve? I think it's rather fine, myself."

"God, you're so vain." Gill couldn't help laughing. "Should I have been able to see you like that, though?"

"Not as a rule, but this place is so steeped in the Dusklands, anything is possible."

"So Juliana saw you, too."

"Probably. She knows so much more than she's letting on. It looked as if she was using Leith as bait, with the *dysir* all pouring after him like greyhounds after a hare . . . and then they were gone. But where? How did she banish them? She seemed to know exactly what she was doing. I need to understand, Gill."

"As long as Leith's all right. That's the main thing."

"Mm." In her easy, affectionate way, Peta stroked Gill's arm. "How's the leg today?"

"A pain in the ass, literally. It's made me realize that there's no magic shortcut to recovery. I have to go the hard way, and start doing my physio exercises religiously instead of hoping for some angelic-looking, sadistic, manipulative Aetherial to put me right instead."

"I assume you're talking about Rufus," said Peta, eyes narrowing. "You haven't been doing your exercises? You're a bad, bad girl."

"I know. I was too angry, or impatient. But speaking of *him*, where was he last night? Was he there spectating, and we just didn't see him?"

Peta gave a *who knows* gesture with her hands. She turned to the foundry doors, moving closer and sliding her fingers into the narrow gap between them. "Hey, it's unlocked," she said. "Must be someone inside."

The *someone* was Colin.

He was sitting on a toolbox near the mouth of the unlit furnace, smoking a cigarette. His jaw was rough with stubble, his eyes red-rimmed. Around him loomed a large, dusty space housing a huge metal press, workbenches, all manner of equipment. In one corner, a structure of curved metal spars stood beside a wide, open doorway with another vast workroom beyond.

"Hi, girls," he said. His voice sounded gritty and tired.

"Juliana's not here, is she?" asked Peta.

"Nah, unless she can manage to be in two places at once. She's getting ready for her class."

"I thought it was your turn to wash the breakfast pots," Peta said lightly.

"Screw it," he replied. "It'll get done eventually. Looking for something?"

Colin was not in a good mood, but she seemed to think better of starting an argument with him. "We thought we'd take you up on your invitation to see your work in progress, Colin."

"Well, there it is." He gestured with his cigarette, at the metal structure dropping ash. "It's one of those things, I'm never quite sure if it's finished."

"What's it meant to be?" said Gill, feeling a philistine as soon as she asked.

"I dunno. It's about the futility of war, or something."

"It looks like two giant rib cages that have crashed into each other. Sorry, I could write what I know about art on a postage stamp."

" 'Sall right. Rib cages, that's fine. I was seeing something like two gods locked in battle, slaughtering each other, crashing to the ground and just rotting there where they fell. Good. Maybe I got it after all."

"Impressive," said Peta. "Mind if we look around? Could be my only chance to see the inner sanctum."

"Be my guest. What the hell do I care?"

Gill followed Peta into the second workspace. It was a shell, about forty feet by thirty, with stone walls and a high, raftered ceiling, light falling through windows in dusty beams. The room was filled with sculptures; some covered in burlap, others on show with sheets pooled around them as if Juliana had recently been working on them. There were shapes of gleaming marble and bronze, big gnarled excrescences of glass. It was like a strange, petrified forest.

Gill realized what this was. The unfinished, unseen work, *Midsummer Night*.

The sculptures stood between seven and ten feet high; smooth, sensuous shapes hinting at humans trapped inside. Some figures leaned towards each other, as is to form a series of arches. There were two shapes entwined. A set of three figures, caught as if in a stately dance. Another, like a struggling mass of beings trying to escape each other. All spellbinding to look at yet subtly disturbing . . .

She could visualize Juliana, halfway up a stepladder beside a limestone monolith, dressed in grey overalls, headscarf and plastic goggles, working away with hammer and chisel. She shivered, disturbed without knowing why. Moved, too, to think that her aunt had created all this with such strength and passion.

Peta began stalking very slowly between the carved forms like an uneasy cat with its fur on end. She seemed transfixed. Gill watched her inspect the long trapdoor in one corner, its old planks the same grey as the concrete floor. That must be the way they'd come last night, through the service tunnel from the house . . . and this was where Juliana had brought Leith to lure the *dysir* . . . so what had become of them?

There was no sense of them in the room.

While Peta was occupied, Gill went back to Colin and found him working his way through another cigarette, filling the foundry with the reek of smoke. He offered her the pack, but she shook her head.

She leaned on the alicorn and said, "I don't mean to be personal, Colin, but are you all right?"

"Yeah, fine," he grated.

"Where were you last night?"

"Don't you start." He hissed a jet of smoke between his teeth. "Look, I probably shouldn't tell you this, but I'm leaving."

"What?"

"Think I'll go to London. Maybe back to New Zealand."

"Oh no." Gill felt dismayed, for her aunt's sake. "You can't. Why?"

"I didn't tell you any of this, okay? I've had enough of being Juliana's dogsbody. She doesn't even pay us, you know? Not that it matters. All I wanted was to learn from her, but you have no idea how frustrating it is trying to help her with her work when all she does is nitpick and destroy perfectly good stuff we've made. She says it's not perfect, but what the hell is perfect? No, there's something really wrong when an artist refuses to finish their work, not because there's anything wrong but because they're scared to let it go." He paused for breath, raking a hand through his hair. He looked sideways at her, eyes bloodshot. "Sorry, I'm ranting."

"No, go on."

"And this sounds crazy, but the house has been creeping the hell out of me. It's one thing doing a night shift to make sure the place is secure. A burglar, I could deal with. It's another thing when you *know* you've locked every door and window, you *know* you're on top of everything, but the house is invaded by . . . things you can't even see."

"I know. I was there last night."

"You stayed awake? Not me. I let her down."

"Surely not."

"I did. Fell asleep right there in the lobby, had a bunch of hideous dreams, slept right through whatever it was. And then she gave me a right dressing-down this morning. Why wasn't I there when she needed me? Perfect Ned wouldn't have slept through it if he'd been there. Fuck!"

"Hey." Gingerly she put a hand on his shoulder. "Ned wasn't around, so who knows? Everyone slept. I only woke up because Peta made me."

"The stuff I saw last night . . . because I thought I *was* awake, not dreaming . . ." His voice fell to a gruff near-whisper. "Nothing fazes good old Colin, right? Wrong. Nothing's ever freaked me out like that before. I can't get it out of my head. That Rufus guy, it's not as if you can get hold of him and give him a good beating. It's like he's made of soap. I don't know, I need to get out of here. Maybe you should go too."

The suggestion sent a surge of anxiety through her. In theory she could walk out any time; yet she felt tied here, locked into a dance that wouldn't cease until she understood.

"Colin, you can't leave," she said firmly. "You did not let her down. You're not the sort who walks away when things get a bit difficult, are you?"

"I thought I wasn't, but this . . ."

"Juliana needs you. You need her. She's your goddess!"

His hunched shoulders began to straighten by degrees. "Always will be."

"Then stay. You're just feeling a bit down. If you go, you'll regret it forever."

He looked up with the start of a grin. "Wow, you've got strong feelings about it. Such passion."

Gill pulled back, a touch embarrassed. "If you go, you'll be letting Ned Badger win."

At that, his eyes became gleaming slots. "All right. All right. That does it. I'll give it some more thought. Now clear off, will you? I'm really not supposed to let anyone in here and I'm in enough trouble as it is."

"Well," said Peta as they stepped outside. "That was interesting."

As she turned to close the heavy door, Gill gazed out towards the cliffs, not looking at anything in particular, just taking in the view.

She found herself looking at Rufus.

Terror plumed inside her. Time slowed and her gaze locked upon him like rifle sights. He looked back, straight into her eyes. He was no more than twenty paces away, standing easily on some rocks like a sightseer out for a stroll. Narrow dark jeans, a raspberry-red T-shirt, a white stone on a black cord around his neck. The breeze lifted his prodigiously long, glossy hair, which glowed red around the edges. He looked completely otherworldly; lean, angelic, heartless.

Her fear twisted into a cascade of memories: ghosts of lust and pleasure, shame, disbelief as he casually speared her hip with fire because she wouldn't bend to his will. His golden-tinged face was pallid, his eyes full of speculation, anger and sadness mixed. All the menace in the world was distilled in his face as he stood there, holding her with his eyes.

She heard a whisper that seemed to be in her head. *What has Juliana done? I will have my brother!*

"Peta," Gill croaked.

In the eyeblink it took Peta to turn round, he'd gone. "What?"

"Rufus was there. Really, I saw him!"

"I believe you," Peta said quietly. "Come back up to the house. You can help me with the washing-up while we talk."

Back in the kitchen of Cairndonan House, the students had already cleared up after breakfast; all was tidy, spotless. Normally, Flora would have been here already preparing lunch, but now the room was empty. Peta made a pot of coffee and sat down with Gill at the kitchen table.

"The workshop we entered this morning, and the workshop where Juliana took Leith and lured the *dysir* last night, were not the same place," Peta stated.

"Eh?"

"That is, they occupied the same space, but they were different."

"Is this a riddle?" asked Gill. "Stop it, before my head explodes."

"You went partway up the steps. What did you see?"

Gill closed her eyes, trying to remember. "A cold dark space, like a cave. Some pale, statue-like shapes, standing in a fog. There was light coming from somewhere . . ." She opened her eyes. "A red glow. Fire. That must have been from the furnace, though."

Peta's gaze was intense. "The furnace is in the front section, and anyway it wasn't lit. And what did we see this morning?"

"A big old workroom, with a trapdoor in the far corner. It must have been the same space, mustn't it? The foundry isn't big enough to have a third room of that size. It looked different because of the angle, or the light . . ."

"That's what I'm saying. It's one space, which changes according to the route from which you approach it. Enter from the regular door and it is just Juliana's studio. Enter from the tunnel and it's different, deeper. Two planes, overlapping."

"No. I can't get my head round that."

"Yes, you can. It's the same as Boundry. It occupies the same space as Earth, but you can only find it if you approach it in a particular way. It's a *portal*."

She jumped up and left the room. Gill sipped the powerful coffee, trying to push Rufus out of her thoughts. Two minutes later, Peta came back with an ordnance survey map, a ruler and a pencil. Pushing cups out of the way, she unfolded the map on the table, flattening it with her hands, her forefingers and thumbs forming a diamond over the area in question. Gill saw the jigsaw outline of the coast, the curve where Cairndonan village lay north and slightly east of the house, the snaking lines of small rivers, tiny beige oblongs denoting the house, its outbuildings, Robin Cottage, even the ruined mill. Peta placed her ruler on the map and drew a light pencil line along it.

"Wow," she said. "Look at that. The foundry, Cairndonan House, the mill, the stone circle and the footpath to Boundry . . . they all lie in a dead straight line."

Gill looked. The pencil line ran clean through every feature, like a connect-the-dots diagram. The old mill lay at the center. "You wouldn't realize it from the ground," Peta went on, "because of all the twisty paths, streams, woods, general ups and downs of the landscape . . . but there it is."

"Like a ley line," said Gill.

"Yes, exactly," Peta looked gleeful. "An ancient path . . . between two portals."

They looked at each other. "What does it mean?"

Peta's eyes lost focus. Judging by her expression, she was as puzzled as Gill. "I don't know yet. But I know Juliana's more than she seems to be. And that she's doing something . . . Honestly, I don't know what she's doing. I can't put it into words. But it feels . . . wrong. I need to speak to her."

Gill sat back, folding her arms. "Are you sure that's a good idea? You know how she is. If you ask anything she wants to keep secret, she'll cut you dead."

"The alternative is to snoop around behind her back," said Peta, "which isn't easy with Ned and Colin forever lurking. Damn!"

"What?"

"The course finishes on Friday. There'll be an end-of-school exhibition and a last-night party—you are invited, by the way—and then . . . it's the end of my contract. I've no excuse to be here any longer. How can I snoop around her property when I'm not supposed to be here?"

"Well," said Gill, "you could stay in the village and wear a disguise."

"It's a thought. Hey, nice work talking Colin down off the ledge." Peta smiled, then glanced at her watch with a groan. "Damn, I'm horribly late for my class. Have to go. They're in a frenzy to finish everything for the exhibition, so I won't have much time between now and Friday—but I will see you, won't I?"

"I'm sure you will," said Gill.

———————

When Peta had gone, Gill sat for a while, turning the alicorn slowly between her hands. Then she stood up, deciding to go to Juliana's quarters. If Juliana herself wasn't there, at least she would have a chance to speak to Leith.

The door marked PRIVATE was open and she saw Ned and Colin there, apparently wrestling a statue of a male figure into position just inside the entrance. She heard grunts, soft curses. She was nearly at the door when Ned Badger stepped out to meet her.

"Hi, I thought you were still at the hospital," she said, hiding her dismay at seeing him. "How is Mrs. Badger?"

"I've not long returned from Flora's bedside. There's little I can do and I'm needed here. Can I help?"

"No, it's fine. I'm hoping to see Leith." She looked past him at the statue. "Can I help you to move that?"

"No, it's done. Thank you." Still he stood blocking her way. She was unbearably tempted to shove past him regardless. "Miss Sharma." Ned's face looked as pale as old bone and more deeply graven with lines than before, skin sheened with sweat and his dark, white-streaked hair slicked back with oil. "Everything I do is in the service of protecting the house and its guests. I can't let you in at this time."

"Why not?"

"Because I won't let anyone enter Dame Juliana's apartments without her permission, or while she's elsewhere."

Gill wanted to ask so many questions: *Did you tell my aunt that Rufus was at the cottage with me? Were you trying to protect me when you attempted to get rid of him? (And I wish you'd succeeded, by the way.) What must you be thinking of me? Why did you hide the scrapbook? What do you know?*

Ned, however, seemed too menacing to be approachable. Expressing curiosity, she felt, would make her vulnerable to him. She didn't trust him.

Instead she said, "Well, I hope Mrs. Badger is feeling better. Will she be coming home soon?"

"Not soon," he answered in a tone like ash. "She has developed pneumonia."

"I'm sorry. I didn't know. I hope she'll soon be on the mend."

"So do we all," said Ned. Still he glared at her with grey pain in his face as if to say, *This is all your fault. It all began with you.*

There was nothing she could do but retreat, leaning heavily on the alicorn that she'd effectively stolen from him, feeling his stare like cobwebs on her back.

Defeated, she returned to Robin Cottage and let herself in. It felt quiet, ordinary.

She'd had such a painful walk to get there that she sat down and cried with sheer frustration. She fancied that the mask's expression, too, was one of tearful anguish. It seemed a dream, that she'd ever been walking around freely, even running, without pain. The experience had given her an entirely false sense of hope.

Bloody Rufus. But where was he? Would he come back?

Let him come, thought Gill. *I've run out of energy to be scared of him.*

A few days passed and all was quiet. Gill stayed at Robin Cottage, defying Rufus, Ned Badger or anyone else to frighten her away. She rested for a couple of days; then she set about forcing herself through the punishing set of physical therapy exercises that she should have been doing all along. Then she began to take short walks, always with her borrowed camera.

She was learning patience.

She saw Peta every day, albeit briefly. The students were in a frenzy to finish their projects before Friday, so she had little spare time.

"You must come to the last-night party," said Peta. "All the work will be exhibited and there'll be nibbles and drinks and, no doubt, floods of tears."

"I have nothing to wear." Part of her still recoiled from the prospect of socializing. "I didn't bring any party clothes with me."

"You don't have to dress up," said Peta. "Anyway, I can lend you something. You must come, Gill. Everyone goes home on Saturday."

"Including you?"

"I'm staying until Sunday, to help Juliana tidy up and that. Then I'm going, yes."

"It'll seem strange without you."

"I know." Peta gave a sad smile. "I'm just a casual employee, I've got no excuse to hang around. So, on Saturday morning, what d'you say we take a proper look at Boundry together?"

A thrill of fear went through Gill. She hesitated. "All right."

"Great! We'll go early, about eight, okay?" Her eyes lit up with conspiracy. "It's a date, honey."

The exhibition had been set up in the Camellia House. There were huge, striking abstract paintings on easels, life studies arranged along the back wall—a dozen different views of a naked Colin, each so individual it could have been twelve different men. Gill thought how sensual and confident he looked; not like the man she'd met after the night of the *dysir*. There were sculptures of wood, clay and carved sandstone; some attractive, some ugly, but all striking. Between two palm trees stood a totem covered in

colorful, staring faces; the fruits of Peta's mask workshop. The local landscape had been rendered in scores of watercolor landscapes and pencil
drawings.

All this creativity was interspersed between tropical plants and trailing
vines, transforming the Camellia House into a shining rain forest that had
exploded with color and light.

"It's tremendously *busy*," she overheard a female student remarking to
Juliana. "Like a wonderful, vibrant outrush of energy."

"Indeed," Juliana said with a dry smile. "Well, minimalism is so over."

Gill was wearing a long, clingy maroon dress borrowed from Peta. Even
though her friend had assured her it fitted like a sheath and looked amazing, she felt gawky and self-conscious. Her hair hung in indigo waves over
her shoulders, one side pinned back with a large crimson silk flower—
Peta's touch again. She had also glued the jeweled dot of a bindi between
Gill's eyebrows.

The event buzzed with the students' radiant fulfillment. All around Gill
there were reminiscences and hugs and tearful promises to stay in touch.
She floated around, feeling like the outsider she was. Again she felt a brush
of envy, but she didn't really mind. It was like being caught up in some
wondrous dream. For a time she occupied herself by taking round trays of
drinks and food, since Flora was not there to do so. When her leg grew too
sore to continue, she began drinking instead.

Peta was busy talking and laughing with her students, but now and then
she'd catch Gill's eye and give a wink or a grin. Gill drank far too much
wine and talked nonsense to complete strangers. Occasionally, when her
orbit intersected with Juliana's, her aunt would take her elbow and introduce her, "This is my niece, Gill."

"Where is your godson?" asked a sixtyish lady with kind eyes and retro
pince-nez-style glasses perched halfway down her long nose. She peered
over the top of the frames. "I heard he wasn't well."

"He's much better," Juliana answered smoothly. "He's resting."

The evening began to blur. Gill swam in a strange sea of green light filtering down through foliage, an underwater grotto with splashes of color,
strange images, dizziness and laughter. At one stage, Peta was beside her,
and they were sharing an intense, private conversation.

"So, we're on for Boundry tomorrow?" Peta was saying.

"I'm up for it if you are, but what about Rufus?"

"What about him?"

"Just the fact that he's a psychopath! What if we meet him? What if he
tries to imprison us, like he did Leith? I wouldn't put anything past him."

"We can't run scared of what *might* happen, Gill."

"I'm not scared," Gill slurred, full of drunken courage. "I'm just being practical. If he comes I'll fight him off with my unicorn staff. I think I was a warrior in a past life. A warrior!"

"I bet you were." Peta was amused. "But we must find out everything we can, before it's too late. We've only got tomorrow left. I have to know what Juliana *is*. If it's the last thing I do, I'll find out. I'll ask her right now."

"No, don't." Gill was pulling at her arm.

Peta was not deterred. "I will, I'll make her tell me!"

She couldn't remember how the conversation ended. Some of Peta's acolytes joined them; she heard the woman whom Juliana had turned away saying, "I'm so glad I stayed. I've learned so much from Peta, she's taken me right back to basics and made me realize I couldn't draw to save my life!" A gale of laughter, but Gill was slipping away, excluded by their banter . . . At one point, she had an impression of Leith moving softly through the crowd, a mask held up by its slender stick to cover his features. Instead he presented a face concealed by black rubber and goggles, staring through tendrils of ivy . . . Gill tried to speak to him, even tugged at his arm, but he moved on without answering, lost in a world of his own.

Afterwards, she was not sure he'd even been real. The whole evening was a fluid sea-green blur, as dreamlike as Boundry itself. Eventually she became aware that most lights had been turned off, that people were drifting away, the party winding down. Beyond the jewel box of the Camellia House, the night felt endless above the cliffs and the ocean.

Someone had opened the outer doors to the garden, and a fresh salty breeze off the sea blew in. Gill saw Peta and Juliana framed in the doorway; she wasn't far from them but might have been part of the greenery for all the notice they took of her. Ned Badger was in the background, clearing away plates and glasses in the manner of a surly waiter willing his last customers to vanish. Peta was saying what a triumph the summer school had been, and how much she'd enjoyed working there . . . Juliana nodded and smiled, her cordiality as impenetrable as the steel door of a vault.

"You've been . . . refreshing, Peta."

"So, what are you going to do with Leith?" Peta asked bluntly. She'd taken far longer than Gill to show the effects of drink but now it seemed she had caught up.

Juliana's smile turned to stone. "Keep him safe, of course. Please lower your voice."

"We saw you 'keep him safe' the other night. How did you do that? We deserve an explanation."

"Perhaps, but I'm not obliged to give one."

Peta dropped her head back with a huff of exasperation. "If it wasn't for my help in that fucking tunnel, you might not have succeeded in the first place! They were *that* close to catching him!"

"Peta, please," Juliana hissed. "You've had too much to drink."

"Who hasn't? Don't change the subject. What's in your foundry, Dame J? Because I sensed something very weird, very wrong. Dangerous. How did you know Rufus's *dysir* would vanish if you lured them in there?"

"Rufus's what?"

"*Dysir*. It's what they're called. Well, a sort of folklore nickname, actually, but it's what the Aelyr generally call that type of shadowy guardian."

Juliana went still. The whole tableau seemed to freeze in Gill's eyes, caught in sudden icy focus. The two women confronted each other like enemy queens. Then Juliana said, "I know what you are, Miss Lyon."

"Oh, really?"

"You're one of Rufus's kind. Unfortunately, it took me too long to see it." She added vehemently, "You know, if I'd realized you were one of them I would not have employed you in the first place!"

One of the stragglers, the woman with pince-nez glasses, was approaching as Juliana made this remark. She paused in a double take, then diverted hurriedly in another direction. Gill winced.

"Why not?" asked Peta.

"Because the *Dubh Sidhe* are always trouble," Juliana said grimly.

"We don't call ourselves that."

"They steal children and kidnap people and bring madness and chaos."

"And we are not all like that!" Peta retorted. "Why would we kidnap humans? Most Aelyr who live in the Spiral aren't even interested in humans. We're not child-stealing demons! All right, it's true that young Vaethyr who wander into the Spiral for the first time can get into trouble, but that's really mischief on the part of the Aelyr, not outright wickedness . . . you know, there are rules, rites of passage . . . but that's a separate issue."

"What are you rambling on about?"

"I'm saying that abducting humans is not common Aetherial behavior. It's something specific to this location."

"And what is it to you?" Juliana said frigidly. "Who are you, Peta Lyon, an Aetherial placing herself covertly in my house with the intention of spying upon me and asking questions? What do you want?"

Gill was abruptly sober, if only for those few moments.

"Who are *you*?" Peta retaliated in a voice like snow. "That's the real puzzle. That's what I want to know, Dame J. What gave you such power over *dysir*, and what are you hiding in your workshop? Your sculptures . . . your sculptures are . . . You're the one with questions to answer!"

Her words washed over Juliana like sea foam. "No. I'm not. How do I know you're not in league with Rufus?"

"I promise you, I'm not." Peta was indignant.

"Then all I can tell you is that I am trying to protect my house, my community and Leith from the likes of Rufus, and those who went before him."

"But if you're a danger to Aetherials, I can't let this rest."

"Then it's just as well you're about to go home," said Juliana. Never before had Gill heard such menace in her voice. "Not all Aetherials are powerful, Miss Lyon, and not all humans are weak. I don't know what makes you think you have the right to interfere, but you must get it into your dizzy head that what I do is *no concern of yours.*"

That was Gill's last clear memory. The dregs of the night frayed and she had no awareness of going to bed . . . only a whirlpool taking her down into a void.

She woke in a haze of discomfort. Head thick and pounding, pain all the way from the heel to the top of her skull, horrible taste in her mouth. She groaned and rolled over. The light in the room looked murky; where was she? With difficulty she raised her head and tried to focus. Eventually she realized that she was in Peta's room.

Alone.

Groaning, she sat up, breathing hard for a few seconds to quell her stomach, which felt like puppies fighting in a sack of acid. There was also someone swinging a lead weight around in her head and she had to wait for that to settle, too. She wondered miserably what had possessed her to drink so much.

She was fully dressed, apparently having discarded only her shoes on the way to the bed. Her watch showed ten o'clock. *Ten!* Where . . . where was Peta?

Gingerly, she limped to the bathroom, feeling fractionally better for using the loo and then pressing cold water onto her face. Pain settled over her left eye. She drank from the tap and took two painkillers. Once she was confident they were going to stay down, she groped her way to the window and pulled back the curtain.

Below, on the front drive, she could see Colin hefting suitcases into cars, students clutching their carefully wrapped artwork, a general bustle of departure. A mini-bus-sized taxi waited, Ned Badger helping the driver to load luggage. Juliana was there too, conducting her farewells. Gill looked for the bright blood-splash of Peta's hair but couldn't see it.

Perhaps it was the hangover haze—fragments of memory from last night throbbing like heavy, fiery mosaic across her mind—that worsened her anxiety, but this felt wrong. A glance at the bed told her that Peta had not even been in the room last night. Perhaps she'd decided to have a last wild fling with Colin after all, but Gill knew in her bones that, even if she had, she would have reappeared by now.

We'll explore Boundry tomorrow, Peta had said. *We'll go early, about eight* . . . Yet it was past ten.

She would have woken me, thought Gill. *She wouldn't have gone without me.*

The mannequins and masks stared at her, keeping their secrets; but Peta, their creator, was gone.

12

Pathway

Gill found Juliana in the office. The door was closed and so she knocked first, not even sure her aunt was there until she heard the clipped command. "Yes, come in!"

Juliana was all steel and thunder behind the big desk, her demeanor un-approachable. "Yes, Gill, what is it?" she snapped as if her niece were some irritating minion.

"I can't find Peta. She's vanished."

In the pause before Juliana replied, Gill registered the drift of bills and letters spread before her on the desk. Some had urgent red lettering on them. Juliana's face was like granite; perhaps to disguise embarrassment, but she made no attempt to hide the pile.

The steely eyes focused on her. "What do you expect me to do about it?"

Gill took a breath and tried to sound sane. "I'm sorry to intrude but I thought you might know where she is. I've looked everywhere."

"Gill, I expect she's gone home. Everyone went this morning. Miss Lyon and I had a regrettable argument last night, no doubt fueled by too much booze and emotion. I wouldn't be surprised if she went early, without a word. It's a bloody nuisance because she was meant to be helping me tidy up today, but if she's gone I will not be shedding any tears over it."

"She wouldn't leave without saying anything to me."

"Perhaps you're wrong about that."

"No." Gill's head began to throb painfully again. "She can't have gone. Her car's still parked outside. We'd arranged to meet."

"At what time?"

"About eight, but I didn't wake up until after ten. I had way too much to drink last night."

"And so did she," Juliana said tersely. "There is your answer. She must have looked in and decided not to wake you."

"No," said Gill. "I slept in her room. She wasn't there. Was she at breakfast?"

"No." Her aunt gave a sharp sigh. "I really don't have time for this co-nundrum. If her belongings and her car are still here, then so is Peta. Have you looked in the studios?"

"I've looked everywhere. She asked me to . . . to go somewhere with her, and she wouldn't forget."

"Well, she is rather scatter-brained. Lovely artist, inspiring teacher, but hardly the most organized person."

"You don't understand, she wasn't in her own bedroom last night. I'm really worried."

Juliana was silent and only glared at her. Gill felt unaccountably afraid of her. Since the night of the *dysir* she'd sealed herself away like some inaccessible stone tower; sealed Leith away, too, as effectively as Rufus had once done. Eventually her aunt said, "Gill, as you see I am up to my eyes in paperwork, Flora has developed pneumonia, and I simply don't have time for this. I haven't seen her. I don't know where she is, but I'm sure there's a simple explanation. Get Colin to help you search, if you're so worried, but please, take your problems away!"

Cut dead, Gill made a stiff retreat to the door. She kept thinking of Juliana and Peta arguing in the doorway, Juliana letting the *dysir* into the foundry as if sweeping them into a chasm . . . Gill said tightly, "I'm sorry to have disturbed you."

As she left, she heard Juliana speak in a weary, placating tone, "Gill," but it was too late. She closed the door behind her and dizzy with pain and frustration, kept walking. She thought, *Why is Juliana behaving like this, just when I was so close to trusting her, even liking her?*

The hangover was now a full-on migraine, and walking one more step seemed too exhausting to contemplate. She struggled down the woodland path to Robin Cottage, where she forced down some muesli to soothe her ravaged stomach, swallowed more pills, stripped off the borrowed dress and sank into a hot bath.

There were two possibilities. One, that Peta's flippant attitude to life was so ingrained that she thought it perfectly acceptable to swan off to Boundry without a word to Gill. The second, that something bad had happened to her . . . that she'd met Rufus . . . or even that Juliana herself was responsible for her disappearance . . . no, no, no, that was madness.

Although Gill didn't remember a great deal of the party, she remembered her aunt's accusation, *You're one of Rufus's kind.* She'd been furious to discover that Peta was Aetherial, as if it had been a deliberate deception. Which, in a way, it had.

Gill shampooed her long hair, sinking right under the surface to wash the suds out. When she resurfaced, the answer seemed clear.

"She *must* have gone into Boundry. She wanted to go early to make the best of the time she has left . . . but I was unconscious, and in no fit state. Maybe she did come in and try to wake me, and was pissed off with me for being insensible. So she decided to go on her own . . . anything could have happened to her. Idiot!"

Gill rose out of the bath in clouds of steam, water cascading down her body. The painkillers were working at last, making her feel numb and pleasantly detached. She wrapped herself in a towel, squeezed the inky wet ropes of hair. If Peta had gone to Boundry, there was no choice but follow her.

After her niece had left, Juliana looked over the array of red bills, tax demands and solicitors' letters spread on the desk in front of her. Sighing, she swept them all into a messy heap and tucked them away in a box file. Too daunting to contemplate. She had to prepare accounts for the summer school—a job Flora would normally have done—but the task was dispiriting. Any profit would go straight to pacify whichever creditor was the most litigious.

The last of the students had left and the place was too quiet. Always, when a course ended, she had this sense of anticlimax, a sort of postpartum depression. In a few weeks, summer would be finished, autumn on its way and then the storms of winter to face. No money to heat the place, of course. With a pang, she remembered that Charles had threatened a visit in the near future. *Thank you, Charles, that's the last bloody thing I need.*

As for Rufus Hart and the business of Boundry, she couldn't spare them a thought. She was certain that he'd been present that night, that he'd seen his hound pack vanish and made a tactical withdrawal. He must have realized that she was a foe to be reckoned with. At the same time, she knew Rufus would be back.

Juliana wasn't emotional by nature, yet the few passions she had were wholehearted. Three things mattered: Cairndonan, her work and now Leith. He wasn't Leon, and he apparently didn't want to be Adam—fine, let him be whoever he wanted to be. Her only desire was to help him adjust to his new life on the surface world. Thinking of him, she smiled. Against all her intentions, she regarded him more and more as a son.

Yet this monster of debt threatened everything.

Sell Cairndonan House? That was an option, but it was absolutely unthinkable. No doubt if she ran more art courses, students would flock to her—but she couldn't afford even the outlay on food, let alone to pay the extra staff she would need. It was a miracle they'd got through the last week at all.

Something had to give. Her whole world was stretched to its breaking point. Juliana knew she must act, but she seemed paralyzed. She felt like a diver poised on a high cliff, trying to raise courage to dive into the sea far below. She simply could not bring herself to make the leap. She knew she never would, until she received the right signal, the little prod in the back that took choice away and sent her plunging down. She would recognize the moment when it came, but it wasn't yet.

Juliana would die before she sold her beloved Cairndonan.

She tried to concentrate on her accounts, but it was hopeless. The business of Peta was bothering her. She felt bad now for being so short and dismissive of Gill's concern; her niece hadn't deserved her sour attitude. She uttered a long sigh of resignation and pushed back her chair. It was no good. She had an idea where Peta might be and conscience compelled her to act.

A few minutes later, she was opening the trapdoor from the service tunnel into the foundry. (She did so one-handed; strange that it had seemed to weigh a ton that night. Panic would do that.) Around her lay the strange, boundless space that her workroom became when she approached it from this special direction.

She entered a pale forest; not true woodland, but a group of tall shapes carved from stone, yearning upwards. Twisted columns, arches, abstract yet semihuman statues contorted in pain. Beyond lay blackness, but within the group itself a faint light glowed, emanating from the sculptures and from the white mist that drifted among them.

Step by step Juliana went deeper in. It was cold and absolutely silent. All she could hear was her own breathing. She had created this, and still was not sure what she'd done. It had grown from her subconscious, from the sinister Aetherial gift she'd been given.

Each subgroup had a name: *Pathway, So Little Time, Harvest, Let Them Steal Away* and *Return*—and each told its own story. *Pathway* was about venturing into the forest, *So Little Time* showed lovers clasping . . . and each group, each tale formed part of the larger whole. She still kept adding to it, refining it. This was her master creation, the set of sculptures she called *Midsummer Night*.

Since the invasion, she'd had one piece moved to her private apartments: her favorite, *Winter Came to the Wood.* Now it stood sentry outside Leith's door. It was the only one small enough to be moved up there, and the only one that—to her knowledge—had no stray entities trapped within it. Its purpose was to protect Leith from Rufus. Not that it could come to life and attack Rufus—but he would be wary of it, she believed, as if it were a scorpion. It wasn't the rational part of her that believed this, but the wordless subconscious depths from which *Midsummer Night* had issued. She'd learned to trust it.

"Peta?" she called. No reply. She went farther and called again: "Peta, are you in here? Please show yourself. I'm not angry. We need to talk."

Still nothing. She wove between the formations for a time, going as far as she dared. In her "real world" workshop, *Midsummer Night* had a finite area and a precise number of components. Here, it wandered on indefinitely, although she had found—from an occasional bold foray—that it repeated itself, and eventually brought you back to the same place.

Knowing that made her no less uneasy.

"Peta!" she called, one last try. Obviously she was not here after all, unless . . .

Something moved in the gloom, and touched her shoulder.

She jumped violently. Her usually sturdy nerves were shattered.

It was Leith. His face was luminous ice; his eyes were lustrous with awe and anxiety. "Dear god, you frightened the life out of me!" she said.

"I apologize, Dame Juliana."

She put a hand to her chest, to steady her heart. "What are you doing here?"

"It's . . . it's the one place I am sure Rufus won't find me. He won't dare come in here, will he? Because of the others."

"What do you mean?" Surely he didn't know.

"The others," he whispered. "Can't you hear them?"

She could.

She could block them out for a time but, if she spent too long in here, their presence became increasingly obvious, like tinnitus growing louder and louder in her ears. They were *inside* the carved shapes, trying to force their way out. They sighed and clawed. Now she could hear their muttering voices, ebbing and rising . . . she fancied she could see eyes glowing just beneath the surface of the stone, aware but unthinking like those of animals, staring at her from their prison . . .

Now they had been joined by the *dysir*. Juliana saw trapped shadows flowing around the base of each sculpture. They wandered restlessly round and round like spiders trapped under glass, not understanding why they couldn't escape.

Shuddering, she turned away, trying to block out their spectral writhing.

"They keep calling to me," said Leith.

"You can hear them?"

"*I know them*," he said.

He backed away, hands rising as if he wanted to cover his ears. She put a hand on his shoulder to steady him. "Dear, I think you should come back to the house with me."

"They're calling my name. They remember me."

His fear was contagious. Juliana kept an iron grip upon herself, but the floor beneath her feet felt insubstantial, as if it were full of holes; a mere web, holding her up. Inside the moon-pale formations she glimpsed faces appearing and fading like fish under water. Ghostly, accusing faces.

She got her breathing under control, reminding herself that she was their jailer. Their master.

"You know, don't you, that while they're in this place they can't escape? They are under my control. You're not in danger. That's why Rufus would never dare come in here. If he did, he would be trapped, too."

"I know." His head drooped, nodding. "I know they can't touch me. But they can still taunt me."

"So come back to the house. I've put a statue at your door. There are no spirits inside it, but Rufus will be afraid of it."

"They can't escape, but they want to."

Juliana shivered. He might sound as if he was hallucinating but he wasn't. She knew something of the Otherworld, but he was more steeped in it than she could imagine. Who knew what he perceived, that she couldn't? The cold mist penetrated her clothes, wreathing around her until she feared it would hide the way out. "Have you seen Peta?"

"No."

"You know who I mean, the red-haired girl? Did she come down here?"

"I know who she is and no, I haven't seen her."

"All right." Juliana took his arm firmly then and began to guide him towards the way out before she lost her bearings entirely in the eerie fog.

It was still possible that Peta had come here before Leith, or that he simply hadn't seen her . . . Last night she would have been glad to see the deceptive Peta Lyon trapped within *Midsummer Night*'s coils, but today she was appalled at the idea.

"You can't stay here. It's cold and uncomfortable, not to mention horrendously creepy. Come along. The statue, *Winter*, will watch over you." *And I cannot spend any more time worrying about Peta Lyon's whereabouts,* she decided as she guided Leith away. *She's a grown woman, for heaven's sake. Probably Gill has found her by now.*

Dressed in jeans, walking boots, sweater and waterproof jacket, her pockets full of medication and chocolate bars, her trusty alicorn staff in her hand— Gill was as ready as she could be.

The walk felt familiar now: a couple of hundred yards along the stream bank, leave the path and climb upwards through the trees. The woodland canopy glowed above her as she clambered over fallen masonry through the mill, gasping with effort . . . She ignored the persistent throb of her leg, but it was always there in the background, a steady battle that drained her energy.

Across the slippery planks to the other side of the millrace she went. Then along the overgrown path to the Cairndonan Sisters, watching for a cobalt glow and snake symbols around the stones . . . catching her breath in terrified wonder when she saw these signs.

On the far side, the footpath did not this time bring her to the disappointing rear of Cairndonan village. Instead she passed between two black angels and saw the tree dripping yellow blossoms—only Rufus's white horse, Chamberlain, was missing.

Next she found the serpentine track leading down through the silver birches, between the honey-colored stone dwellings and along the wide grassy path towards the heart of Boundry. The light was as rich as egg yolk, the colors seductively luscious. She felt triumphant and terrified. Soon she reached the broad green swath where both the night-stone angel stood . . . and Rufus's house. It was real, it was still here! He'd let her believe it was some kind of country pub, all the while mocking her attempts to rationalize what was happening.

"Yeah, hilarious, you bastard," she said under her breath.

If Peta had come to Boundry, she must be here.

Approaching, Gill noticed it had only a single, high story, but there was structure of sorts on the roof, a sort of lookout like the top floor of a lighthouse. The double door was closed but unlocked. Taking a firm grip on her staff, she went in, determined not to fall over any unexpected steps.

In the center of the big hall, she stood in the pool of light falling through the cupola and called out, "Rufus!"

Her voice echoed, making her wince, but no one answered.

"Anyone there? Peta?"

Nothing. She went all the way across the space with its tall stained-glass windows of strange deities and its graceful furniture, past the "bar" where Leith had poured fruit juice and passed it to her from the shadows. There was a door of dark oak in an ivory-white wall. She sucked in a breath; her throat was so dry it hurt. She opened the door.

On the other side was a hallway that reminded her of Cairndonan House. It was dark in here, so dark she hesitated to go any farther. She paused a moment to let her eyes adjust.

"Rufus?" she called. Then, more loudly, "Peta?"

Her eye was caught by some pieces of paper pinned to a panel, as if to a notice board. The first read, *The next one of you to desert us, DO NOT expect anyone to come searching for you! Don't bother coming back, don't send a postcard, see you in the Abyss.*

There were others, with cryptic announcements—*Eight-folders, join me to push out the cell walls!*—and quirky sketches of several male and female Aetherials, no one she recognized. There must have been others here . . . Now the house had a feeling of sadness. She imagined it full of beautiful Aethe-rials, a household presided over by Rufus . . . an echo of Juliana's house, the queen bee with her court of admirers. Where were they now?

Leading from the hallway she found a series of beautiful rooms, with high carved ceilings, curtains like soft shimmery waterfalls of soft teal and laven-der and ruby red. In some there were couches with jewel-colored cushions, while others had low beds covered in gorgeously embroidered covers that made her think of gardens in full flower. The place reminded her of stately homes she'd visited . . . yet everything was imperceptibly wrong, the layout odd, the styles and proportions unfamiliar. It was like architecture in a for-eign country. Another *world*. Yet all felt deserted. The words *Mary Celeste* entered her mind.

Presently the necklace of rooms brought her in a circle and back to the inner hall again. The hall was shaped like a Celtic cross: one axis leading between the main room and the bedchambers, the other having a window at one end and at the other, a staircase. There was one door she hadn't tried. She half-opened it and froze; all that lay within was darkness. A cel-lar? The prison where Rufus had kept Leith for a time? Quickly she closed the door, backed away and hurried to the stairs instead.

She climbed cautiously. There was only one room at the top, a large octagonal chamber, perhaps twenty feet across, with windows on every side. This was the tower room she'd seen from outside. Rufus's bedroom? Floor, ceiling vault and window frames were all made of warm golden wood, and there was a broad sleeping platform covered with russet silk and furs. There were chests of drawers, a couple of chairs; it had a warm simplicity that she would expect of someone more normal and human than Rufus. Beneath the window opposite, stood a desk, a baroque-looking thing with decoration picked out in gold leaf.

Gill went to the desk and looked at the view. To her left she saw the sharp white tooth of the mountain and, to her right, the violet lake melting into a misty horizon. Between the two, a path wound towards low, blue-green hills. The scene was one of peace, its colors of melting beauty.

The chamber gave a panorama of Boundry as she made a complete cir-cuit, but there was no glimpse of Peta's bright hair.

She returned to the desk, feeling like a spy, or worse. There was a stack of handmade paper, thick and mottled with fiber. There were quills, small pots of powder pigment in blue, black and red, a mortar-and-pestle and an inkwell. There were also some pencils and plastic ballpoint pens standing in a stoneware pot, which looked out of place amid the archaic items. A tall, slim decanter of blue glass held a clear liquid that smelled mildly alco-holic, like vodka. People who insisted vodka had no smell had never actu-ally sniffed it, she thought, replacing the stopper.

It struck her suddenly that she had no idea where Rufus was. He might walk in at any second, for all she knew. Her heart began to hammer. All she'd thought about was finding Peta. What on earth had given her this idiotic sense of security?

More urgently now she opened a drawer and saw drifts of loose paper covered in writing. Letters, notes, journal entries . . . She picked up the top one, which looked as if it had been written yesterday, the black ink fresh on rough creamy paper. The slanting, extravagant handwriting was hard to read but, like the notices downstairs, it was in English.

Everyone to foregather in the Lady of Stars Chamber at dusk for the purpose of anointing our guest! Bring your unguent of choice, be it wine or honey or oil— that which is as pleasurable to lick from the skin as it is to apply! Mmm.

"That must have been some party," she whispered.

There were a couple of sketches, drawn in loose, quick ink lines, but plainly recognizable as Leith. Head tipped back, eyes closed, the hint of bare shoulders. Shivers went through her. Seeing sketches of him seemed profoundly shocking.

Result of vote to send the little fisher girl home: in favor, seventeen; against, two. Someone had written underneath, *At last! Throw her back! A dying fish would have provided more entertainment!* Another wit had added, *And tasted better.*

Gill unconsciously put her fingers to her mouth. She was thinking of Ned Badger's mother, who'd vanished and returned, out of her mind. So Rufus and his cronies thought it was a joke, did they, to kidnap people, toy with them and drive them mad?

Copernica, darling, I must insist that you stop screwing our guest! The poor boy can hardly stand. Let someone else have a turn! A different hand had added underneath, in red ink, *Jealous, Rufus! Join us!* And below that was a tiny drawing of three naked figures; one reclining, the other two leaning over him like vampires.

She looked at the next sheet, which held only five stark words.

Leith = channel of the dead.

She dropped it hastily, as if it held a curse. The room felt cold. Trickles of panic ran over her skin, as if to warn her that if she did not hurry, Rufus would catch her. In his house. Spying on him.

The next few sheets were different. At first she thought they were a letter, but the tone was more like that of the writer musing to himself. *We were there together at the start of all things, sharing the womb, sharing the Source. Always, always together. Sinking claws into each other's flesh. Hating and loving. Surely you must remember. I am not asking for love. All I ask is that you remember!*

Another page was entirely covered in the same word, written in different sizes and styles, like a calligraphy exercise. *Mist. Mist. Mist. Mist. Mist.*

And on the next, jagged and blotched as if written in temper, with holes in the paper where the nib had torn right through, a single word.

Mistangamesh.

There were pages of melancholy scrawl, written in ballpoint pen on lined paper torn from a manufactured notebook. No time to read it all, so she skimmed a few pages, feeling horrible for intruding on someone's privacy— even if that someone was Rufus, it was still wrong—but unable to stop. *All gone to leaves and animals, to gossamer and dust. Only I carry on. It will be just you and me, then. Now you MUST come back!*

I thought that if we drowned you in pleasure, you would remember. If love didn't work, perhaps hate would? How I taunted you! Remember, so long ago, how I used to plough into our sweet sister, both of us crying out our pleasure loudly so that it would make you furious—How you raged with jealousy! But no, even the memory of hatred wasn't strong enough to stir you.

I thought that if I left you deprived of light and sound and food, with no distractions, some recollection must wake in the darkness. Nothing! Pain, then— nothing concentrates the mind like a little torture, does it? Strip away the human mask, layer by layer, with pleasure and pain and fear, eventually there is nothing left but the essence. Then you would have to remember, and come back!

Why are you making this so difficult?

I've stripped away the layers, it's true. There is almost nothing left. Yet still your real self hides, down there in the darkness.

Gill stopped, slipped the papers back into the drawer and shut it. She couldn't read any more. The act had made her feel contaminated; partly from the violation she'd committed, partly from the words themselves.

Time to go, she thought. Panic rose; she had no idea how long she'd been here. She must find Peta.

Gill left the russet glow of the chamber, limped stiffly downstairs and across the main room—not a hotel bar, after all, so was it their Lady of Stars Chamber? Outside, she made her slow but determined way past the angel statue and down the long green avenue to the lake. The water barely seemed to move; a fine mist floated across the surface, obscuring the violet hills on the far shore. The thin strip of sand along the shore was bluish, with larger polished pebbles like blue-lace agate.

Gill stooped to pick one up and slip it in her pocket, turned left and followed the shoreline. As she went she studied the relative positions of the dwellings behind her, the curve of the lake and the steep, ethereal white mountain that reared on her left-hand side. The sky was rich blue, full of stars even though it was day . . . the mist flowing off the lake was fresh and bright in her nostrils. It was hard to stay focused. She paused to watch a pair of long-legged herons gliding over the water. The air was making her feel light-headed, drowsy.

Now there was a fork in the path that she hadn't seen last time. The track beneath her feet curved back into Boundry, but there was another way, faint and silvery, that branched off to her right.

She followed it until the nearby hills rose around her, their slopes softly green with a bluish cast, rocks along their crests catching the same peach-gold light as the mountain. As long as she kept walking, the pain was manageable; it was when she rested that she'd be in trouble.

The path snaked into a narrow pass between the high ridges, a sort of gorge. It had taken her perhaps ten or fifteen minutes to reach it. By then the light was going. There was a definite red-gold cast to the landscape, a cobalt flush to the sky. Even as she watched, the mountain peak turned to deep apricot, and all around her lay indigo shadows. How had evening fallen without her noticing? And so early? It couldn't be much past noon, on Earth.

On Earth. What a crazy thought.

"Peta?" she called. "Peta!"

An echo bounced back, *Peta!*

No answer. She shivered, horribly aware of the silence, of how exposed and alone she was in these strange hills. *Just a few more steps along the path, just to see what's around the curve. Then I'm going back.*

Something swallowed her.

It happened in an instant, as if she'd hit a soft, translucent barrier; as if thin air had thickened like gelatine. All at once she was caught up in a swirl of fog; a greyness that felt as dense as goose down, thickly cloying like treacle. Panic grabbed her. It was like falling into deep water and starting to drown, her throat in spasm . . . She was asphyxiating.

Gill thrashed helplessly. She was struggling through molasses, through quicksand. Her feet came off the ground and she was actually floating in the gel, sinking, utterly disoriented. She got both hands around her ivory staff, raised it and started to push and stab at the barrier. She was fighting for her life.

The next few moments were a blur of frantic movement. She was slashing at the solid fog, trying to shred it and swim through it at the same time. Her sight turned black with pressure; her ears roared. Then there was a soft *snick,* as if something had shifted, two parts of a lock slipping into alignment.

The barrier gave, and spat her out. She felt her head burst out into cold air; then the rest of her body pitched forward and landed heavily on the gritty path.

She knew how to fall, and rolled on her shoulder with the impact, which saved her from breaking an arm or collarbone. She lay on her back, panting, staring up at an indigo sky full of stars and swirling nebulae.

Gill pulled herself into a sitting position and cursed as she waited for the spearing pain in her hip to subside. As she sat there, winded, she looked up at the U shape of the steep gully sides and the track passing between them. What the hell had stopped her? As she stared, the air rippled and she saw that the track petered out at a dead end, a translucent rock wall veiling the path.

Only she was on the wrong side of it. Somehow she'd forced herself all the way through. Beyond the barrier, the path back to Boundry was unreachable.

"Oh, shit," she whispered, dragging herself painfully to her feet. "How the hell do I get back?"

Limping, she approached the barrier again with the alicorn held two-handed, like a weapon. She used it to prod at the opalescent rock. Air could feel as solid as a brick wall, in a strong wind . . . so perhaps in the Otherworld there were forces that could create an illusory barrier? It had let her through like quicksand yet now she could not penetrate it even with the tip of her staff. The quicksand had set to rock.

Gill recoiled. She was drenched in sweat and shivering. *Fuck*, she thought. *Where the hell am I? What do I do now? What in god's name made me think that this was a good idea?*

There was nothing around her but rock walls, blue darkness and silence.

Then she heard something . . . *breathing*. She held her own breath, stood motionless. It wasn't her imagination. The sound was soft, slow and intent. It came from the shadow-shape of a boulder lying four paces from her in the darkness.

The boulder moved.

Gill cried out, or tried to; the cry was a rasp. The thing that crouched in front of her was not rock but alive, an indistinct blue-black bulk. She saw the hint of scales glistening on a long skull, spines that might be wings or armor curving from its shoulders, molten reptilian eyes burning into her . . .

The beast rose and unfolded to an alarming height. Now it was a solid, breathing shadow, looming towards her. She froze. Her mind and body went to stone, abandoning her. And then it uttered a word.

"*Leith.*"

"It's been a long time, Juliana." Charles Sandford-Barnes, her estranged husband, sat facing her across the dining table. Tonight of all bloody nights he'd turned up unannounced. Still she'd swept all her difficulties out of sight, put on a front of cool poise and welcomed him. Colin and Ned had produced a quick and surprisingly edible meal. Leith was in his room; he seemed more than content to stay out of sight with only books for company. That he'd started reading was a good sign.

Charles knew nothing of him. Juliana intended it to stay that way.

The long face with its strong nose and watchful expression had changed very little; the half-moon pouches beneath the eyes were more pronounced, but the grey eyes themselves hadn't lost their keen, shrewd sparkle. His hair, like hers, was silver-white, but unlike hers was satisfyingly thin on top.

"Indeed it has," she said. The dining table was in near-darkness, candle-light glinting on silverware and glasses of red wine. The light made his head seem to float disembodied on the darkness, like the face of a narrator in a ghost story. "You were supposed to let me know when you were coming. It's too bad of you to turn up without phoning."

"I did try. No one answered. My secretary left a message on your answering machine for Flora to call my office, but no one did."

Juliana paused, releasing a breath. "Flora's in hospital."

"Oh." That surprised him a touch. "Oh, I'm sorry to hear it. Is it serious?"

"She collapsed with a severe asthma attack. They took her to Inverness. Now she's developed pneumonia . . . she doesn't seem to be recovering very well. I don't think she wants to." Juliana was surprised to feel tears prick her throat. "Her health hasn't been good since . . ."

"Of course." Charles cleared his throat, having the grace to look uncomfortable and sad, or at least to fake it. Then he smiled. "You look wonderful," he said. "You never look any older; how do you do that?"

"Made a bargain with the faerie folk," Juliana said dryly. "What do you want, Charles?"

"Just because I'm a politician doesn't mean I always have an ulterior motive."

"No. You have an ulterior motive, just because you're *you*."

He gave a soft laugh. "I miss your bluntness, Jules. Can't a fellow pay a social call on his ex-wife?"

"Not when she lives out in the wilds, no. Just passing, were you?"

"In a sense, yes. Business at the Scottish Parliament. Edinburgh's hardly a million miles from here, almost local compared to London. One forgets what a remote spot this is; can't say I miss the never-ending drive to and from civilization."

"No, you never really took to this place, did you? Any excuse to bolt back to London, pausing only to impregnate the housekeeper on your way." She spoke sardonically but a flicker of pain stirred; memories of their hideous breakup, although more than twenty years ago, never quite faded.

He smirked. "Oh, come on. We don't need to live in the past. We're older and wiser; can't we be friends again, Jules?"

"Please stop calling me Jules. You know I hate it." She sipped her wine, taking her time to avoid answering. *Friends? Not in a million years*, she thought. Conversing with him was like fencing with tiny, icy scalpels.

"Forgive me. Habit. But how are you, Juliana? Busy, as ever? How is the magnum opus? What was it called again?"

"*Midsummer Night*," she said through her teeth. He knew perfectly well what it was called.

"Good heavens, it's a long project, isn't it?"

"It will be finished when it's finished."

"I'd like to see it."

"What?" She almost choked on her wine. "Why would you want to see it?"

"Oh, you know. To see how it's developed after so many years. I'm interested, my dear."

Coolly she held his smug, insinuating gaze. "Sorry, Charles. No one is allowed to see it until it is ready for exhibition. I'm keeping it under wraps until then."

"That's a shame. All that aside, I wouldn't mind purchasing a small sculpture from you. Anything lying around that you can spare."

She snorted. "What for? You don't even like my work!"

"That's not true. Have you something in marble, say about six or seven feet high, just big enough to make a statement without being too ostentatious? Your work still holds immense interest and kudos, Jules."

"I don't think I have anything suitable."

"Indeed, you do. That piece standing by the doorway to your spare room would be perfect." He nodded at *Winter*, the graceful marble guardian that stood outside the door to Adam's room. When he'd first arrived, he'd paused to stroke the sculpture as if it were a cat. She gritted her teeth.

"That's staying where it is. It's part of *Midsummer Night*."

"I'm not asking you to give it to me! I'll pay you. Name a price, and I'll double it. It would make a fine talking point in my office."

"Ah. A status symbol," she said contemptuously. "Something else to show off with, like that red middle-aged crisis of a Ferrari Testosterone that you pulled up in."

He laughed. "If that's what you want to think. For your information, it's a Lamborghini."

"Name a price and you'll double it? Clearly you are swimming in more money than you know what to do with."

"I couldn't possibly comment," he said archly.

"It's not for sale."

"Well, if you change your mind . . . Call it an advance. A little something to tide you over this difficult time."

She went still. "What?" she said. "An advance? What is it you actually want, Charles?"

She stared at him, until he shook his head and put down his wineglass, becoming intent on centring it precisely on its coaster. "To help you." He reached across the table to take her hand, but she stiffened.

"Have I asked for your help?"

"No, and you never would; you're too damned proud."

"It's not a matter of pride," she hissed. "I do not need help, from you or from anyone."

"Really?" The sardonic eyebrows twitched. "That's not what I've heard. Financial troubles are nothing to be ashamed of, Jules. These are difficult times."

Fury poured through her, congealing. "I don't know who you've been speaking to but I am not in any kind of trouble. How dare you? Don't try to turn me into some kind of victim to be patted on the head and helped. Now I'm remembering why we separated."

Infuriatingly, he chuckled. "So, you are sound. My sources, suggesting you are on the brink of bankruptcy, are entirely wrong. I'm glad to hear it."

"What sources?" She could imagine, only too well, the web of contacts he must have across the legal system, the Inland Revenue, every layer of the system. Of course he could find out whatever he wanted, just a small exchange of favors . . . he'd always been the same. Yet, naively, she'd never expected him to turn it against her. "You've been spying on me?"

He spoke across her, his voice velvety with compassion. "You have sold almost no work for the past fifteen years. Creative block is the favored theory among the cognoscenti, but I hold no truck with that; I know that you've been slaving over your masterwork. However, selling only a bit here and there is not enough to feed this famished money pit of yours." When she said nothing, he added, "I am right, aren't I?"

"My situation is absolutely no concern of yours, Charles."

"Well, it is, in a sense. I have a proposition. Let me buy Cairndonan House from you. All your problems will be solved at a stroke."

Everything inside her went rigid and cold. She took an inward gasp. After a moment she managed to answer. "It's not for sale."

"I intend to make you a very generous offer, old girl."

"I don't care. It's not for sale, especially not to you, not under any circumstances."

He persisted in the same mellow, menacing tone, "Surely you understand the gravity of your situation, Jules. The day is coming when you will be *forced* to sell. On that day, I will be there, checkbook in hand. I expect I'll snap it up at auction at a bargain price, probably a third of what I'm about to offer. With the property market as it is, you'd be a fool to take chances. This is the best offer you'll get. Truly, I couldn't bear to see you forced to the precipice, left in reduced circumstances. The humiliation . . ."

"Do stop talking like a Charles Dickens novel," she snapped. She looked into her wineglass, but couldn't subdue the storm that was churning inside her. "It's not for sale."

"I would really prefer to do this by fair means."

"What? Are you implying that you might employ foul ones? God, why am I even asking that question?"

"I have claims on this place." He let the words fall softly. "The fact that we're still married—that's why you wanted to avoid divorce, isn't it? So that the estate wouldn't be torn apart. And I went along with that. I let you stay."

"*Let* me?" she cried. "It's my ruddy house!"

"Which you can't afford to keep. Accept my offer, Jules. Otherwise . . . well, there are all sort of legal tangles we could get into. A divorce could be messy. There could even be a challenge to the legality of Corah's will . . ."

"You wouldn't! You'd lose, Charles. You don't have a lawful leg to stand on."

"And you are probably right, but do you have the resources for a protracted court battle? Solicitors' fees can run into hundreds of thousands of pounds. No, I thought not."

Again the sinking feeling in her heart, the horrible sense of her whole life unraveling. She mastered her emotions before she lost control altogether. "Why now, Charles? Why do you want it now?"

"An opportunity has arisen. A business opportunity. Imagine what Cairndonan House could become, Jules: a luxury hotel. A golf course. Hunting, shooting, fishing. This area of the Scottish coast is an undeveloped tourist gold mine!"

"A *golf course*?" She spat the words in contempt. "You want to turn my home into a bloody leisure complex? And how have you got the millions required for this project?"

Again the devilish smile. "I have . . . investors."

"Oh, of course." She sat back. "I should have guessed. Is it the old cash-for-honors racket, or backhanders for amending the odd law here and there, something in your back pocket for nodding through some dodgy planning application? Favors in return for you scattering knighthoods and peerages all over your sponsors. You must be sitting on quite the cash mountain by now. How long before you become *Lord* Sandford-Barnes?"

His grey poached-egg stare did not waver. "Don't knock it. D'you think you'd have been made a Dame of the British Empire without a nudge from me?"

"Don't you dare," she hissed. "I earned that honor in my own right. Don't you dare try to devalue it." She glared ice and fire at him, but knew that nothing she said would stem the flow of his little smiles and insinuating head tilts. The more she defended herself, the weaker her argument would sound. "That's how it is, is it?" she said flatly. "It's not what you've achieved, but who you know."

"It was ever thus." He raised his glass to her and took a gulp. The wine turned his lips wet and red.

"You always were jealous of my career. I see that hasn't changed. The only reason you want Cairndonan is because it's *mine*."

"Not for very much longer, at this rate."

"You'd never get planning permission . . . Oh. What am I saying?"

"Precisely." He leaned back, the candlelight reflecting small flames in his eyes. "I have friends everywhere, at every level, on both sides of the border."

"One great shining web of corruption."

"So you will have to consider my offer, old girl. I'd let you stay, of course."

The last remark, lightly thrown down, shook her. Despite her indignation, she wavered. Her financial problems would be solved at a stroke, and she could stay!

Even as she thought it, every cell of her body recoiled. The idea of renting her home and studios back from Charles, of being forever more beholden to him, while her beautiful wild estate vanished under a *golf course* around her . . .

"It's not going to happen, Charles. Not in a million years. Now I would like you to leave."

He sat there as if she hadn't said a word, which made her want to leap up and stab him with a steak knife. He reached into an inner pocket, brought out a wallet and opened it. "Here, I'm going to give you my legal team's business card. To pass onto your own solicitor. You're going to need it."

As he passed the white oblong across the table, she saw the photograph contained behind a small plastic window in the wallet. It was a picture of Leon. Two years old, chubby-cheeked and smiling. Her blood turned to ice. He still carried a picture of Leon! Of course he would. It was his son. Juliana sat absolutely still while a carnival of pain and confusion rioted through her.

Charles flipped the leather leaves shut, not realizing she'd seen.

She thought of Leith, her secret, and caught her breath in sudden wild joy. That was one thing Charles could never share. Leith's presence might yet mean that Leon, too, would come back, a fine, handsome young man—but if he did, she decided, she was damned if she'd ever tell Charles. Let him suffer all the way to his grave!

A smile reached her mouth, and he appeared, mistakenly, to take it as assent to his plan. He raised his glass to her. His mistake amused her more; she felt fierce and reckless. How horrible this was, this bullying intrusion, and yet—this was it. The catalyst. The prod to send her flying off the precipice.

"To the future," he said, smiling back. "Cheers."

"Cheers," she answered. "And now it's time for you to leave." She threw her napkin on the table and rose to her feet.

He looked shocked. "At this time of night?"

"It's nine o clock. You can be back in Edinburgh by midnight—earlier, the speed you drive at. Take your Ferrari 'Testostero-tosser'—"

"Lamborghini."

"Whatever, take it and leave, go, get out. Cairndonan House is not for sale. My work is not for sale. I am not for sale. Good night."

"As you will." He stood up, looking sardonically amused and furious at the same time. "Don't leave it until you are completely destitute with bailiffs at your door. Keep in touch, old girl. Make it soon."

13

Lashtor

"Leith?" The low male voice spilled from the silhouette above her.

"I'm not him." Gill felt a rock wall against her shoulder blades. She'd crept back as far as she could, but there was nowhere to go. She was trapped.

"No, I see that," said the voice. "Where is he?"

She heard the leathery rustle of wings. "Not here."

"But you know him?"

All she could see of the creature were hints of indigo; the proud wings upswept like a pair of harps, a bluish sheen on a high cheekbone. His eyes appeared to be lit from inside, changing from blue to gold with the slight movement of his head. She felt her clothes sticking to her clammy skin. Even through her terror, it struck her how absurd this was. Here she was, trapped in an unknown realm with some species of winged demon . . . What was the correct answer to its question? "I . . . I've met someone called Leith, yes, but . . ."

The creature reached out to her with a large, long-fingered hand. Poised on the edge of horror, she looked down at it as if it were a deadly scorpion alighting on her shoulder. The hand was human-shaped but thick-fingered and scaly, with long black claws for fingernails. Blue and green lights shifted on the scales, reflecting the star bright sky above.

The hand fell away. "Human, like Leith," he said.

"Yes."

"Were you imprisoned by Ephenaestus?"

"Sorry, I don't know what you mean. I wasn't imprisoned, no."

"How did you come to be here?"

The night was black crystal with stars spilled across it like blossoms, scents of damp rock and greenery rising around her. A tornado of amazement was working its silent way through her, terror mixed with delicious wonder.

"Really long story." She was shaking so hard she could barely speak. "The short version is that I don't know. I'm lost."

The eyes expressed puzzlement, even contempt. She thought, *Surely he wouldn't have a conversation with me if he was going to kill me . . . would he?*

"Who are you?" he asked calmly.

"Gill. You?"

"Theodorus." He drew back a pace, as if to give her breathing room. "There's no need to be afraid, unless you try to run from me. I can't let you go until I know how you came here, you understand? You must come with me"

"Oh." Gill folded her left hand to grip her opposite elbow, a reflexive gesture of shielding. Her right fist tightened on her unicorn staff, ready to use it as a weapon if necessary. "So you're . . . arresting me? Look, if I'm trespassing on your domain, I'm sorry. I promise you, I can't run anywhere."

The dark face tilted. "You're hurt?"

"It's from an old accident, but it still aches. Right now I can barely hobble."

"How did you come through the *geatus* from Boundry?" He indicated the dead end of the gorge. It appeared a seamless wall.

"Is that what you call it? Do you mean a portal?"

"Of a kind."

She sensed she would get no clear answers. "I'm not sure. I didn't even see it; I found myself tangled in a kind of fog, felt like I was drowning. I struggled and then something seemed to shift and I fell through onto this side. That's all I know."

"The barriers are breaking down," said Theodorus. He raised his head to stare at the blank wall through which she'd come. It seemed to waver as she looked at it; rock, ice, mist, rock again. "And before that, how did you reach Boundry?"

"Again, not sure. The first time, it was accidental. I followed a certain path and there I was." As she tried to embellish this raw statement, she became aware of how incredibly tired she was, stumbling over the words.

"And you met Leith?"

"Yes." She added warily, "And someone called Rufus."

She had no idea whether Theodorus was ally or foe of Rufus. The smoky, feathery shape looming over her brought her close to panic, the same fear that she'd felt of Steve—not *caused* by Steve, but by a terror dredged up from deep in childhood. Theodorus raised his head, as if scenting the air. He crossed to the place where she'd encountered the *geatus* and pressed his hands to the unyielding surface. He was ten feet from her, presenting his winged back to her . . .

On impulse, she ran. It was an animal response, beyond thought. Some reserve of adrenaline kicked in and she was stumbling along the path as if surging desperately towards a finish line.

She made twelve paces before her leg gave way. More than pain, it was sudden loss of muscle tone. The leg simply wasn't there. She fell and rolled with an explosive grunt. No sooner was she down than Theodorus was there above her, like an owl gliding effortlessly after its prey.

Gill lay trembling with shock, sobbing, cursing herself, Rufus, Steve, Peta, Juliana, fate, everything that had brought her to this. She thought she was facing her last moments and didn't want to die so suddenly, without answers. She cringed in a ball . . . yet no attack came. Instead, Theodorus knelt beside her and helped her to sit up.

His gentleness came as a shock. "Where did you intend to go?" he asked.

"I don't know!" Gill said savagely. "I want to go home, but I'm fucked, apparently!"

"You promised you would not run away."

"No, I told you that I *couldn't* run. And as you see, I can't. There is a difference."

He exhaled and sat back on his haunches, the spoked canopy of wings swaying and whispering with every movement. "Gill, I can't leave you here. The *geatus* to Boundry has re-sealed so we can't go that way. You have to come with me."

"Oh my god." She imagined him taking her to a dank cave. She imagined never finding her way back to her own world.

"Hold tight to my back. Arms and legs around me. Here, let me help you."

He turned his back, crouching to make it easy for her. In a haze of shock, she obeyed. She felt awkward, mounting him like a horse then leaning along his spine, fitting her body between what seemed two folded calfskin sails. He was wearing some kind of simple garment as dark as his skin; she couldn't make out detail, but felt a fluid, textured fabric under her fingers. The hard ridges of his vertebrae, pressing into her through her jacket, felt like the spine of a small dinosaur. It was bizarre and unnerving to be physically close to such a creature, to find he was real and solid. The scent of him was dry and clean; a hint of grass and earth, no more scent than a cat or a bird might have. She wrapped her legs around his hips, slid her arms around his neck as he rose and began to walk with a long-legged rolling stride.

She hung on, trembling, like a tired child being carried home. Despite everything, Gill felt like laughing. *So much for dignity*, she thought. *Anyway, what home have I to go back to? A rented cottage and a demented aunt. Being taken prisoner by a demon can't be much worse, can it?*

Suddenly she realized her unicorn staff was no longer in her hands. She had dropped it in her panic. Too late; he was striding at speed through the darkness.

"Tell me what you were doing in Boundry," he said.

"What are you, the Aetherial police?"

"Please. It matters."

"I was looking for someone," she said to the side of his head. There were bone ridges covered in glistening scales, folded-back shapes that she assumed were ears. "A friend. A young woman with red hair—true red, like blood—and I'm not sure what she was wearing but it's usually bohemian-looking, big boots, long purple dresses, that sort of thing. You haven't seen her, have you? Did she come this way before me?"

"I haven't seen her, no. I have seen no one since I last saw Leith."

"Oh, god." Gill went light-headed with renewed anxiety. "I was so sure she'd come into Boundry—where is she? How stupid of me to jump to that conclusion. Where, where did she go this morning?"

One other place, Gill thought. She drew a breath that burned her lungs. *The foundry. What if she sneaked off to take a look after the party, and didn't come back?*

"This is a nightmare," she murmured.

"It's not so terrible," he said, clearly not realizing she meant the loss of Peta rather than her immediate situation. So, he couldn't read minds—that was something. "Hold firmly to me. I will not let you fall."

He began to run. Folded wings unfurled on either side of her with a powerful *whump*. There was a muscular movement near her thighs, like a pair of oars sculling . . . a second pair of wings? Further pinions sprang from his arms . . . Six wings?

Gill hung on with a silent scream. They were airborne. Flying!

Her stomach leapt and swooped as if on a roller coaster. She'd been on a hang glider once and it was the same feeling, breath-taking loss of control, the air hard in her face and nothing, nothing beneath her. Her breath came in high gasps beside the Aetherial's ear. Hyperventilation made her hands and feet tingle. She thought she would pass out.

"Nothing to fear," Theodorus said firmly, his voice muffled by wind currents. "You won't fall. I'm taking you to—" He said a word that sounded like *Lashtor*. His firm, strong wingbeats lifted them and she had no choice but to cling onto this strange, weightless ebony creature who was all wings, holding her breath because it was the only thing she could control.

Gradually her terror receded as she grew used to the sensation and realized it wasn't going to kill her after all.

Gill sobbed then. It was partly from exhaustion and the cruel ache of her leg. Mostly, though, it was from astonishment. Above her were more stars than she'd ever seen; drifts and shoals and spirals of diamonds across an infinite vault. She saw what appeared to be Saturn, as big as the moon, and Mars too, a cloudy purplish red. Beneath her, an array of folded peaks lay indistinct in darkness like an ocean realm under deep blue water. Not the bulky, bleak summits of the mountains near Cairndonan, these, but attenuated peaks, tall and impossibly ethereal.

She looked down at this hostile expanse with dismay. Wherever Theodorus was taking her, not in a thousand years would she find her way back. A fearful sense of resignation slipped over her. Behind the rhythm of wingbeats she became aware of an infinite, cosmic silence . . . no, not quite silence. There was a background song, a faint crackling hiss blended with pure high notes . . . the song of the universe itself? she wondered.

Gill drifted in a kind of rapture, her mind and body almost ceasing to function.

For a while she was warm from exertion. Later, with little heat penetrating her clothes from the Aetherial's body, she turned bone-cold. Unbelievably, she almost fell asleep.

When she opened her eyes again, the mountains were suffused by pale blue light. Theodorus was gliding in a wide arc above a valley, swinging towards a sheer steep slope that fell and fell towards the gleam of a river far below. The flank was silvery granite, all columns and crags and precariously rooted trees. Perched on a kind of terrace below the summit was an edifice fused into the higher slope behind it; fortress or temple, she couldn't tell. Everything was white and pearl and silver. It was happening too fast, the scene swinging and rushing towards her as Theodorus swept in to land.

He planted his feet squarely on tessellated marble tiles, six wings folding, his body sinking into a crouch. Gill realized this was her cue to dismount, but for a few seconds she couldn't move; she was set in position. He uncrossed her wrists, began to push her gently off his shoulders. Then with a groan she fell, landing stiffly curled up. She was so cold she'd stopped shivering. She felt like a dead thing, rigid. She only knew she was alive because everything hurt.

There was movement above her. A blur of black, sapphire and gold, wings stirring a muscular breeze. Voices. Then someone was leaning down beside her, wrapping a silky blanket around her as they helped her to sit up.

The man helping her was human in form but obviously Aetherial; she saw it in the sheen of the skin, the glow and glitter of the bright blue eyes. He was around thirty—if Aetherials had an age as such; she suspected they reached the perfect prime of life and stopped there—and he was six feet in height, strongly built, his skin the color of tawny-gold silk. Clean-shaven, he had none of Rufus's exaggerated beauty but his features were handsome, regular and youthful; he might even be attractive if he smiled. His head was entirely shaved, a golden-brown dome. His large but shapely ears lay close to the skull and his eyes were two electric blue lamps.

"Gill," he said. "We'll warm you up. Don't worry about anything."

Don't worry, she thought. As she unfroze, the insanity of her predica-
ment brought her close to panic again. Lost, stranded on a mountain in another world, a thousand miles from discovering what had become of Peta.
She swallowed the fear. She wondered if she looked as numb and demented
as Leith had when he'd stumbled out of the storm.

As the man drew the quilted blanket around her, she noticed his clothes.
A soft, loose tunic over trousers, the black fabric textured with deep blue
embroidery. The patterns made her think of runes. They disturbed her on
some neurological level, like the start of a migraine.

Looking past him, she saw two figures dressed in white, standing near
an arch in a salt-white wall. She captured the image, as if taking a mental
snapshot.

"I'm going mad," said Gill. "Is she here?"

"No, I'm sorry, we haven't seen your friend," said the man. "Let me help
you to stand. Just a few steps inside and you can rest."

"Where's Theodorus?" she asked, hobbling with him. Everything looked
ice-white and cold; the terrace beneath her feet, the building with its cloisters and pointed arches in front of her. This was most definitely not Scotland,
nor anywhere she recognized as part of the British Isles. "The being with the
wings? If he was real. If he wasn't, don't ask me how the hell I got up this
mountain."

The man replied, "That was me. I'm Theodorus. Theo."

"No." Cool shadow folded over her as they crossed a cloister and entered a sort of cell. Warmth licked her, making her shiver. "You can't be.
He was scaly and huge and covered in wings . . ."

"And I frightened you, for which I apologize."

His voice sounded clearer, but otherwise . . . it was the same voice. She
remembered Peta in the tunnel, the night of the *dysir*.

"Your Otherworld form."

"Yes."

"But you're not wearing it now."

"We have many forms," he said.

He set her down on a hard couch. She pulled the blanket around herself
and stared at him. The cell, she realized, was a cavern. Firelight bathed the
walls, so it seemed they were inside an amber sphere. Other openings led
off; she became aware of echoing spaces, a honeycomb of caves lying above
and beyond.

"I wasn't frightened," she said tightly. "Just . . . startled. It's hard to believe."

"Of course." He sounded, she thought, a touch condescending. "Most
Aetherials can change form, although it's usually harder for the Vaethyr—
those who live on Earth. It's safer at night to take a predatory shape."

"And the wings come in handy for a fast getaway," she said.

"Well, yes. But this is my . . . everyday form."

"Like the default setting."

She thought he wouldn't know what she meant, but he gave a hint of a smile. "The one I was born in, yes. Rest; I'll return in a few moments."

He left her alone, and she heard voices speaking a language she couldn't understand. Arguing, or explaining to someone else how he'd found her? She huddled under the warm blue fabric of her quilt, feeling drowsy and content to stay here indefinitely. When Theo came back, another man came with him and gave her a tall glass in a holder. He wore white clothing with a dark tunic over it, and had a similarly shaved head and grave, gracious manner. She thanked him. Steam issued from the glass and its warmth nearly burnt her fingers.

Some kind of fruit tea with honey and a kick of ginger. She wasn't a fan of such teas, but at this moment it was the best thing she'd ever tasted. "I'll let you rest for a while," said Theo, "but I must talk to you. If you wish to relieve yourself and to wash, go through the inner doorway and to the right. You'll find a bathing cave."

"We can talk now," said Gill, between sips. "I just need to thaw out. I'll be fine when I've had my pills. Where have you brought me?"

"Lashtor. In Sibeyla."

"Where the hell is Sibeyla?"

"The realm of air." Theo seemed a touch impatient with her questions. "In the Spiral. The Aetherial realm."

Was Sibeyla one of the places Peta had told her about? "And what's Lashtor? It reminds me of a monastery . . . A Buddhist monastery, or a hermitage . . . if you understand what I'm talking about."

"I understand." She suspected that she'd offended him, but he went on, "Call it a hermitage, then. You're seeking Vaeth equivalents that you recognize. That's understandable."

She frowned over the rim of the glass. "Are Aetherials so different to us that your way of life is absolutely unrecognizable?"

"No," he said softly. "Not at all."

"I'm not the brightest person in the world, but I can understand most things if they're explained properly."

He nodded silently, almost apologetically. "And I will answer, but first you need to sleep."

She used the last few sips of tea to swallow the painkillers she'd once hoped not to need again. Theo looked reprovingly at her and said, "You don't need those here."

"Thanks. I'll be the judge of what I need."

He rose from the cross-legged position, fluid as a gymnast. "Rest. Then we'll eat. That will do more good than chemicals."

The truth was, she was almost too tired to take herself to the bathing cavern. She made the effort and found the strangest bathroom she'd ever seen; a sort of grotto bathed in a dim, rippling light. Everything glistened like wet limestone. Folds of rock screened a tiny side cave with slate seats poised over a dark, narrow chasm. It was almost but not quite private, since there were no doors. She used it hurriedly, aware of the fathomless drop beneath, more nervous that someone might walk in. In the main area, fresh water gushed down channels in the walls into natural basins. Deeper in, she glimpsed pools of hot water bubbling and steaming.

She had no energy to explore further. A quick wash, then back to the amber cell to take off her boots and jacket and lie down on the couch.

That was the last she knew for a long time.

She woke, aware that many hours had passed; half a day, perhaps. She was curled up on her side, the quilt wrapped around her, warm and soporific with sleep. Her leg didn't hurt, exactly; it felt like something leaden that didn't quite belong to her.

After ten minutes of yawning, she managed to peel off the quilt and sit upright. Gingerly, she tested her legs, wobbling like a fawn. Stiff, aching, good for nothing; situation normal, then. With a pang of dismay she remembered dropping the alicorn in the wilderness; it had become like a friend to her, and she felt vulnerable without it. Leaning on walls, she hobbled her way to the inner corridor, which was lit by filtered daylight and the occasional yellow splash of a candle, and thence to the bathing grotto again. There she washed her face and hands in an ice-cold glassy stream. There were bowls of fragrant salts and soap granules, piles of soft, cottony towels. Those small touches made her mind reel with disbelief, the sense that she was actually in some expensive spa artfully built to mimic a natural cave.

Returning, she wrapped the quilt around herself and limped outside onto the terrace, continuing all the way to the edge. Only a low wall separated her from the drop beneath. A sharp dry wind filled her eyes with tears.

All the rapture and terror of the flight returned.

She found herself in a bright, floating landscape, with high peaks soaring above the lower summit on which she stood. The scene dazzled her with its melting whites and silvers and violet-blues. Clouds rolled in slow majesty through the valleys. It was as she'd imagined the Himalayas, vastly magnified. Nothing looked quite solid. All this massive folded bulk of rock might easily have been made of frothed clouds, floating in a void.

Three birds swooped past—storks, or winged Aetherials? She followed their path with her eyes, down into the valley, losing them in a lace of mist.

The world seemed to swoop and tilt. Gill stepped back, so light-headed she feared she'd fall, or even drift away like an untethered balloon.

Turning, she looked up at the pale walls of the hermitage, which followed the contours of the rock mass against which it was built. There was greenery up there, tough vegetation carpeting the rocks with violet flowers. Even its narrow, arched entrances echoed mountain peaks. She saw figures moving within the cloisters, and others on roof terraces above her. It was so quiet; she barely heard a voice. Ineffable serenity lay over everything.

She whispered to herself, "Perhaps I've died. This is the afterlife that I didn't believe in."

"Gill?" Theo's voice made her start. "We'll breakfast outside, if you're ready."

He beckoned her to a small trestle table set farther along the curve of the terrace wall. Two other male Aetherials were helping him to set out a meal. All three wore similar clothes, long blue-embroidered black tunics over loose white trousers and shirts. "Monks" didn't seem the right term for them, she thought. Brothers, then. That would do for now.

"Gill, this is Berenis and Fleorn."

Berenis was the one she'd seen before; he had a narrow face and velvet-black eyes. They inclined their tanned, serene faces to her and withdrew. Warily she sat down on a bench facing the valley, keeping the quilt tucked around her. As Theo sat down opposite, she noticed that he had a pen—some kind of fountain pen with a carved crystal barrel—and some sheets of paper. He tucked these under his elbow to keep them from blowing away.

"Please, help yourself," he said.

There was a round brown loaf full of grains and nuts, creamy curd cheese, fruit resembling apricots and dates, more gingery tea. Theo tore the loaf of bread in two, offering half to her. She took it, broke off a piece and hesitated, even though the rich, nutty smell made her stomach growl. "There's something about not eating or drinking in the faerie realm," she said. "If you do, you lose your memory, get stuck here for seven years, or something like that."

Theo gave a quiet huff, looking unamused. "That might begin to happen if you *stayed* here for seven years. When the stuff of Aether becomes part of you, then you might lose your ties to Vaeth . . . but a few meals won't hurt. Especially since you're human, not Vaethyr."

She scooped some curd cheese onto her bread, took a tiny bite. It tasted fine. Not strange, not laced with poisons or drugs, as far as she could tell. And she was famished, light-headed as much from hunger as from the dizzying views. She sat gazing out at the unbelievable realm of Sibeyla, sipping hot tea in between small mouthfuls of food.

Theo said, "I hope you enjoyed your long sleep."

"Yes. Amazing, thank you. I feel much better."

"Good." He ate sparingly, watching her. "Again, I apologize for seizing you, but I need to know all you can tell me about that place, Boundry."

Gill frowned. "Why should I tell you? I don't know who you are."

"I can't help that. If I explained, it would mean nothing to you."

"Try," she said.

The blue eyes flamed into her. "I'm a defender of the Spiral."

"What does that mean?"

"Purity," he said. "But it's irrelevant. I serve the Spiral Court."

"Okay. You're right, I don't understand. Can you put it in plainer language? You're a policeman, a monk, a warrior—what?"

"All and none of those, in a sense."

"Are you the good guy or the bad guy?"

Again, she sensed his tightly controlled impatience. He leaned forward, the sleeve falling away from the bare forearm he rested on the table. She saw the flex of powerful muscles and, too late, tried to stop a mental image of him lifting her one-handed and hurling her like a spear into the void. "That's not for me to judge. Let me just say that Rufus Dionys Ephenaestus is the focus of my attention. He is a wanted man. I have been trying to find him for years. Others tried and failed before me. They have tried and failed for centuries, for millennia, but I will not give up."

"Millennia?" A chill slithered down her back. "What's he done?"

"What hasn't he done?" He folded his hands. "That's more the question."

Gill took her time eating an apricot. It was fleshier and more flavorful than any earthly apricot—of course. She was shaking with waves of awe and fear that kept coming, however rational she tried to be. At last she said, "Look, this is awkward for me. If I tell you anything, I could be getting an innocent person into big trouble."

"You imagine Rufus is innocent?"

"No, but I don't know the facts. There *might* be a different explanation for his behavior. You could be the Aetherial Gestapo for all I know."

The sky-blue eyes pinned her. He sat very still, apart from the interlaced fingers tapping against the backs of his hands. "If you must use terms like that, think of it as hunting down a war criminal," he said crisply. "Talk to me, Gill. You won't be leaving Lashtor or returning to Vaeth until you do."

"Perhaps I like it here," she said defiantly. "What are you going to do, dangle me over the drop? Torture me?"

"No. One of our Aelyr codes of conduct is that we do not harm humans."

"Good." She shivered slightly. The intensity of his gaze suggested he might be happy to abandon the code.

steam, revealing for the first time without shame the purplish red ladder of staple marks that ascended her left leg from knee to hip.

Peta reached out and traced up the length of it with a finger, sliding on a glaze of soapy water. "Wow," she said. "That *is* good."

They slept, but Gill was awake long before Peta stirred. It was four in the afternoon; she felt woozy from sleeping during the day. She dressed in jeans and a sapphire-blue sweater, combed out her hair, which had dried in a tangle. Once she'd teased the blue-black ripples into order, she went along the corridor to Juliana's private rooms.

The house was so quiet around her, it felt uninhabited. She felt a need to see her aunt, even though she had no real idea what to say, even half-hoped she'd still be asleep. Colin let her in. To her surprise, Juliana was already up and dressed, looking surprisingly fresh; she was sitting at her dining-room table with Leith on her left, a familiar book lying closed in front of them. Her hands rested on the cover, as if she were unsure whether or not to reveal its contents.

The mask Peta had made for Leith stood propped in a vase on a side table. The sight of it made Gill start. The face was so skilfully rendered that it appeared three-dimensional: a face in heavy black goggles with a canister covering the entire nose and mouth . . . an unknown soldier in a gas mask, peering through a dense curtain of ivy . . . It was like another presence in the room.

"Ah, Gill. Come in, sit down," said Juliana.

Leith looked up with haunted eyes. There was something in his expression, as if he wanted to speak to her and couldn't. She said, "Sorry, if I'm interrupting . . ."

"No, your timing is perfect." Juliana stroked the marbled cover of the book. "I've been hesitating, but you both need to see this. I meant to show you separately—no favoritism involved, Leith just happened to be here—but come, sit with us."

Colin excused himself, saying he was going to prepare sandwiches for the meeting. Seating herself next to Leith, Gill said, "Wow. Corah's scrapbook. Ned gave it up, then?"

Juliana sighed through her teeth. "I found it and took it, I'm afraid. I have no idea if he's noticed, because he's been preoccupied visiting Flora. To be frank, I'm more than a little annoyed with him. You were right, Gill. This book was left for me and he had no business hiding it from me . . ."

Juliana slid the book in front of Leith, who was in the center, and she opened the heavy cover and began to read aloud in a gentle, steady tone. Gill and Leith followed the words, studied the photographs. A story of two sisters and a brother, innocent and lively, sent to stay with their uncle John . . . A picture of Adam in army uniform. *A bullet had gone right through him . . . Oh, how my soul chilled to see him flinch at shadows!*

Leith listened to the words in silence, as still and bloodless as wax. The night of the *Dunkelmen.* A practical joke that went horribly wrong . . . And then the story that followed, Corah and Melody's endless search for their lost brother Adam.

As it unfolded, Leith seemed to be unraveling before Gill's eyes. Juliana paused, looking at him in concern. "You recognize this, don't you?" she said gravely. Wordless, he nodded. "Do you want me to stop?"

Shaking his head, he made a helpless gesture for her to go on to the end. She did so.

Leith broke down then. He put his face in his hands and shuddered with soundless sobs. Gill put one hand through his arm, stroked his hair; she didn't know what else to do.

"Told people I'd died in the trenches!" he exclaimed. His voice was raw. "How I wish to God I had! I didn't know. I didn't know. Why did they go on and on searching for me, when there was nothing I could do?"

"Because they loved you, Leith," said Gill. "I would have done the same."

"Don't call me that anymore. My name is not Leith."

"Adam, then. Adam."

Juliana watched and waited, her expression grim. Adam rested his head against Gill's, as if to hide the anguish in his face; he didn't try to fend her off, but let her hold him as if she was all that anchored him. Discreetly, Juliana rose and brought him a glass of water. Gradually he quieted.

"Adam, I'm sorry. If you had been Leon—as I hoped—this would have meant nothing to you. I knew there was a risk it would upset you. Perhaps I was wrong to show you this, but I had to be sure. And you had to know."

He nodded. "Please forgive my outburst. I've been away . . . somewhere very strange . . . for such a long time. I've returned to a world I don't recognize and I don't belong here."

"Yes, you do," said Juliana, her fingers spread on the last page. "This is the connection. This shows that you do belong, that we are your family."

He took a series of gulping breaths. "I was so afraid to remember."

"Do you want to talk about it?"

"No," he said. "No. I never forgot anything, truly, but I couldn't think about it—I wasn't in my right mind. The mask helped me look clearly at things, but . . . this, about my sisters—to me they're young women who stepped out of the room a minute ago—to think that they grew old and died, looking for me . . ."

"I know," said Gill. "But it's all right, you're strong, we'll help you." Platitudes, but she didn't know what else to say. Her voice and her hands seemed to soothe him; that was enough for now. Looking at Juliana over his bowed head, she said, "What about the envelope?"

"Ah, that." Juliana rubbed at a furry patch in the back cover. "It is missing, naturally."

"Did Ned take it?"

"I presume he must have. What could it have said, that Corah couldn't write in her main narrative? Something not good, not nice, not proper. Up to me if I read it or not. Or burn it, safer not to know. What am I to make of that? Ned may have destroyed it, for all I know."

"Have you done what Corah suggested?"

"What's that?"

"Written what you think it says and had a bet."

Juliana guffawed. "No, I have not. And I absolutely forbid speculation of that kind. Anything that's worth suggesting is almost certain to cause me grave offense."

"I don't know what Corah could have done that's worse than all the stuff she's already admitted to," said Gill.

Adam was shaking his head vehemently. "That's not the Corah I knew. She wouldn't drink and smoke and fornicate with dozens of men! She wouldn't."

"She was sixteen when you last saw her. People change, dear." Juliana shut the scrapbook, squaring it on the table. "If you'll excuse me, I need to make a phone call. I'll see you both downstairs at six? If it's any consolation, Adam—if you weren't prepared to read Corah's memoir, I am most definitely not ready to know what was in her envelope. However, I am just about ready to kill Ned Badger when I see him."

She rose and gave Gill a meaningful look, as if to say, *Look after Adam.*

When she'd gone, Gill went to the small kitchen area and boiled the kettle. She hardly knew what to say to Adam, but it didn't seem to matter. The barrier of awkwardness between them was gone. She returned to the table with cups of tea and sat beside him again.

"That was probably the hardest thing," she said. "Hearing what happened after you'd," she nearly said *died*, but caught herself, "after you'd been abducted."

"No. The hardest thing was the trenches. And living when all my comrades died in the mud around me—Corah was right, my father would much have preferred me to die with them. Much tidier. And not knowing how to tell Corah and Melody I couldn't live anything like a normal life after that. And not having the chance because I was carried away into some insane netherworld that never made one ounce of sense, all the time I was there. It was our punishment, wasn't it, for tormenting a harmless old man to his death."

She put her hand on his upper arm. "What you did was a bit mischievous, but you couldn't have known the *Dunkelmen* would come, nor that your uncle John most probably had a heart condition."

"Gill, one of my fruitless ambitions was to be a priest, so I know that it doesn't work like that. There was no excuse, no mitigation. We did wrong and we were punished."

She watched the light glittering in his restless eyes, and waited for him to go on. Although he'd said to Juliana that he didn't want to talk, the words now came tumbling out in a soft stream. How he and Corah and Melody, old enough to know better, had tricked their uncle John in the woods, pretending they were the *Dubh Sidhe* he believed in . . . until true Aetherials had come, dragging Adam away into darkness, leaving devastation behind them.

"I thought that Rufus was the devil, or at least one of his lords, sent to drag me into the absolute pits of degradation and sin. I prayed, but heaven had abandoned me. Not that I thought myself any more precious and holy than the next man, but I had made up my mind to be a *priest*." His voice turned hoarse. "But these creatures, Rufus and his cohorts, they took me and . . . I'll spare you the details." He shuddered. "It was unspeakable."

She was quiet for a moment. Shaken, she didn't know how to react. "Look, Adam, I know things were different in your day, that certain matters were never to be mentioned, but times have changed. Nothing is taboo anymore. I won't be shocked by anything you say. Horrified on your behalf, maybe, but not offended."

Adam closed his eyes as if in pain or shame. Gill cleared her throat and went on, "I went into Boundry again, and I looked around the house where I first met Rufus. No one was there. I found some papers, notes and stuff that Rufus had written. It sounded as if he'd tortured you. Imprisoned you in the dark, dosed you with drugs, I don't know what else . . ."

Adam opened his eyes again, uttered a sigh. He couldn't meet her gaze. "Yes. He did all those things. You have to realize that I was already mad from the battlefield . . . I couldn't sleep. Each time I closed my eyes I was there again, in hell; bodies everywhere, and barbed wire and mud, men screaming and the sky exploding . . ."

She put her hand on his. "They had a name for it, shell shock. Now they call it post-traumatic stress disorder . . . but you weren't mad."

Adam gave a short, humorless laugh. "By any name, I was insane. At the beginning, while I still had some fight in me, I would argue and plead to be taken home. But they laughed at me, gave me sweet-tasting liquors that took me out of myself and made the pain go away . . . time blurred, I didn't know who or where I was. When the potion wore off, I'd wake screaming. Craving oblivion again."

"So Rufus kept you drugged, all the time you were there?"

"Much of it, yes. It's hard to remember."

"There were others there too, weren't there? Who was Copernica?"

Adam flinched. Gill felt an odd pang, recalling the explicit sketch she'd found of two figures leaning over a third. *Jealous, Rufus? Join us!*

"She was one of them. Vivienne, Idro and Idrina, Nicolas, Ekaterina . . . oh, Sylvynus; he was one of the few kind ones. There were so many in the early days, I never learned all their names. I tried to fight, truly, but they kept me drugged, and I was so afraid of them, with their shining hair and laughing mouths . . . They would come to me in their animal forms, one after another. It was worse than carnal sin; it was like a kind of bestiality."

He squeezed his eyes shut. A couple of tears splashed onto the table.

"No, don't think that." Gill frowned. She was struggling to comprehend what he was telling her. When Adam had first fled to her out of the storm, she'd thought he had a kind of innocence and untouched beauty . . . It caused her inexpressible pain, to think he'd not only been imprisoned but violated. "They can change form, but they're not *animals*, Adam. Don't think that. It wasn't your fault. Rufus kept you drugged, imprisoned, beaten and abused for however many years passed in Boundry; it's no wonder you're . . ."

"A lunatic?" He smiled sourly.

"I didn't say that. I'm trying to understand why Rufus would torment you. Maybe he gets a kick out of cruelty for its own sake, but I got the impression he had a bigger goal in mind."

Adam shook his head. "It wasn't just from cruelty, I'm sure. He wanted something more from me. He kept insisting I was his brother, someone called—"

"Mistangamesh." She spoke the name in unison with him, causing him to look at her in surprise. "I saw it written in his notes. He seemed to be saying that whatever techniques he tried on you, kind or cruel, you wouldn't admit to it."

"Because I'm not! How could I be? I'm just Adam Montague. But he continues to insist that I am his brother, and that I'm willfully refusing to remember."

"So he tried to break you down to nothing, in the hope that you'd confess, or remember?"

"Yes," said Adam. He gave a faint smile, as if unutterably relieved that she understood. "But what could I do? I couldn't pretend, because I don't know what it is I'm supposed to be remembering. There's nothing there to recall. He scraped the blackest corners of my soul and found nothing. Yet still he won't give up!" His head dropped. "When he gets me back, it will continue and I can't endure it."

"He won't get you back," she said firmly. "We'll protect you. Theodorus will catch him and you'll be safe."

"I should have been a man, and protected myself and my sisters."

"It's all right, Adam. You're still as shell-shocked as any soldier who survived the trenches. There's no shame in it."

He sat upright, rubbed his face and groaned quietly. "That's why he named me Leith. He said that the name means 'river'—like the river Lethe, associated with death and the underworld. He said that that is what Adam was to him; a channel for a dead man to come back to life. That's why my suffering didn't matter."

"God," she breathed. A cold, violent tremor went through her. "You know, Adam, I'm thinking it's Rufus who's out of his mind, not you."

He sipped the tea she'd made him. The cup rattled on the saucer as he put it down. "The worst, the most horrible thing . . . no, I can't say it."

"It's okay. Whatever you want to say, or not, it's fine."

"But if this is a confession, I can't leave it unfinished. I don't want the others to know, but I need to tell someone and I can only tell you, Gill. I can't live with what I know. Your revulsion will be my punishment. Your loathing will be the scourge I deserve."

"Oh—steady on. I doubt it. I'm listening as a friend, not a judge. It can't be that bad, can it?"

"It is to me." He met her eyes as if forcing himself; color flushed his cheekbones. "When they took me, when they used me worse than any whore, however bitterly I hated them and hated myself . . . some part of me . . ." He struggled and tried again. "Some base, animal part of me . . ."

"Enjoyed it?"

He flinched as if mortified that she'd said it. He looked away, hair falling forward to obscure his face. "So you see how complete my illusions were, that I could ever be good, ever become a man of God. It was all to show me the truth of how utterly weak and rotten with sin I was, rotten to the core. I was pulled into a nest of demons, and I *enjoyed it*."

"Ah." Gill was feeling completely out of her depth. "Is that what you really can't live with? The fact that you found pleasure, not just misery?"

"It's unpardonable. My soul can't be redeemed. I have no soul."

"That's not true." She folded her arms, leaning on the table. She took a raw breath, thinking, *This is all wrong. I'm attracted to him. He's an ancient relative of mine who should not even still be alive. He looks so perfect and untouched with his ivory skin and beautiful eyes, and now he's telling me he's spent years having wild demon sex and I'm jealous! He's a mess, I'm a mess. This is so, so wrong.* "Look, Adam, I'm rubbish at this. Giving wise counsel, I mean. You should probably talk to Juliana or a doctor or even a priest at the local church. Anything I say will sound completely lame and it probably won't help you anyway; it's just words, isn't it? I can't persuade you to think differently. If I say that you're not wicked, simply human, that's not enough to stop you loathing yourself, is it? But it's all I've got. *You're human.* You're a young man. If a group of beautiful creatures ply you with sex and drugs, yes, you're probably going to enjoy it. Wow!" She faced him, simmering with emotion. "I don't know why you're even surprised!"

"I should have been better! Stronger."

"Oh, well, shouldn't we all. I don't know what to say." Her growing anger seemed to startle him. She pushed her hands through her hair, a gesture of frustration. "Look, Adam, I know how you feel. Can I tell you something without you going all Angel Clare on me?"

"Going . . . what?"

"Did you never read *Tess of the d'Ubervilles*? On their wedding night, Angel confesses that he had an affair with another woman. Tess is relieved and says of course she forgives him because her sin is just the same. Only, when she tells him that she was seduced by another man, he's all righteously shocked, and rejects her."

Adam gave a laugh, very soft. "Oh yes, I read it. I'd forgotten. So long ago."

"Well, Rufus seduced me too. It was only for one night. Afterwards, I so wished it hadn't happened. But at the time, yes, I enjoyed it."

That threw him. He stared, as if seeing her for the first time.

"Don't give me that old-fashioned look!" she said. "That's exactly what I'm talking about! I didn't want to tell you, but I couldn't sit here with you thinking I'm someone I'm not. I had to be honest."

He lowered his eyes; looked up again with a gentler gaze. "I'm in no position to judge you. I'm only sad. Rufus taints everyone. He can leave no one alone."

"I thought I'd sworn off sex too; not for religious reasons, but still, I felt I was above and beyond all that, and no one was going to break into the ice fortress to reach me. But Rufus did. He melted straight through my defenses. And afterwards, I hated him and hated myself for surrendering, and despised myself worst of all for loving every moment of it. So yes, I understand what you're saying, Adam. But you've made me realize that feeling *bad* about it is the biggest waste of time on the planet. He can only taint us if we let him! Sorry, I'm ranting."

"So he's hurt you too."

She hauled the heavy, unruly length of her hair over one shoulder and said, "No. I thought so, at the time, but actually he didn't. I made a mistake, but that doesn't make me his victim. And you couldn't help what he did to you, but you can walk away and know it wasn't your fault! I'm sorry,

Adam, I'm talking rubbish. I'm just frustrated because you've been through hell and I don't know how even to begin to help you."

"No one can." He glanced at the eyeless, ivy-wreathed mask that stared from a side table. "I've been poisoned, Gill. Who knows if I'll ever be clean again?"

Juliana went downstairs to the office, steadfastly ignoring all the aches and bruises that made her feel every one of her sixty-something years. Still not quite able to believe what had happened—her brief and perilous visit to the Otherworld—she'd bundled the whole experience to the back of her mind. She couldn't afford to falter now. She had the distinct feeling of being mid-battle, under siege. Or halfway across a fast-flowing river—the worst possible time to stop swimming.

She had the receiver in her hand, about to phone the hospital, when the door opened and Ned Badger stepped in. He looked like a black and white ghost; the dark, unwashed hair flopping forward over the strained pallor of his forehead. Juliana quietly replaced the receiver and stood up.

"Ned," she said gravely. "I was on the point of calling you. I know I said I'd come to the hospital with you and I can only apologize. Something cropped up that was out of my control . . ." She gave a brisk shake of her head. "I won't go into detail. I will come tomorrow instead, armed with flowers and chocolates."

He said nothing, only lowered his head in glowering acquiescence.

Under normal circumstances, she would have been more apologetic, but the matter of the scrapbook stood between them. She couldn't bring herself to say the word *sorry*. Coolly formal, she went on, "I realize you must be tired, so I'll be brief. It's come to my attention that you were keeping a book that was intended for me. Corah's memoir."

Ned's face fell. He stared at her from narrowed, pink-edged eyes. She continued, "Flora's situation being as it is, I'll leave it at that for now—except to ask you this one thing. I will need you to surrender the letter." He was silent, frozen like a waxwork. "Do you understand? A letter was taken out of the book. I must have it back."

His thin lips parted. "Yes, I understand," he hissed.

"Good. Come to the downstairs drawing room at six." She snapped at him like a sergeant major, firmly suppressing the anger that boiled inside her. To think he'd stolen her aunt's papers and kept them secret, all these years that she'd trusted him! "Go on, then. Go and rest, and think up a bloody good explanation while you're at it."

Ned did not move. His eyes became stormy with rage she'd never seen there before. "So, now you find time to visit the hospital, Dame Juliana? You are too late. Flora is dead."

All the breath left her as if she'd been kicked. She sat down heavily. The shock was visceral. Not once had she allowed herself to think that Flora might die.

"She can't be. She was getting better!"

"How would you know? You have not been near her. She deteriorated overnight. I tried to phone, but there was no answer."

"Oh, my god. Ned, I am so, so sorry. I had no idea it was so serious. People recover from pneumonia . . ."

"And they also die of it. They die of broken hearts, too. Hers was broken for a long, long time."

Juliana exhaled, her anger melting into shame. Strange grief; it felt all wrong, riddled with guilt. She was certain Ned had never truly loved Flora, that he'd only married her out of a kind of pity after Leon had vanished, but still, his grief was real. Anyone could see it. Perhaps he'd felt more than he'd ever shown.

"She was so much part of this place . . . I can't believe it. If only I'd realized how ill she was."

Ned went on glaring at her, his eyes dry but as red as fire. There was so much roiling beneath his taciturn surface, it alarmed her and frightened her. How had she been so oblivious as not to notice?

"If only you had, Dame J. Instead you greet me ranting of scrapbooks and letters! What do I care about that, when I've sat and held Flora's hand as she died? When will you understand that everything I've done, I did to protect you?"

With that he stormed out, leaving her in shock. The draft of the door slamming sent papers and bills swirling off the desk like fallen leaves.

17

Harvest

Gill checked her watch. She was early for the meeting, but as she approached the room in which Juliana had asked them to gather, she realized she wasn't the first there. She could hear voices; Peta talking to Theodorus, evidently having caught him on his own at last.

Glancing in, Gill saw Theo standing motionless, composed, while Peta paced about, looking animated, rosy-cheeked and fresh in a maroon velvet top and patchwork skirt, garnets and amethysts glinting around her neck. Her hair, loose, was a bright red flood. The room was a sort of luxury common room provided for her students—full of squashy floral sofas, with a television in one corner and art books lying on a large coffee table. Lamps in the corners gave the room a faded golden-ivory glow.

Gill hovered, but they didn't see her. Theodorus was a larger-than-life presence, blue eyes shining in the golden-hued face, light burnishing the sculptural shape of his shaven head. No wings were in evidence and his loose garments looked unremarkable; you could imagine he'd just finished teaching a martial-arts class. Still, he had a more-than-human sheen about him. He had all the grace and unconscious disdain of a lion.

Gill saw him as a calm, white and golden figure; Peta, by contrast, was red with fire, almost visibly bristling with it.

Uncertain whether to walk straight in or hang back, Gill did the latter, drawing back against the wall just outside. She felt uncomfortable, listening in, but it was hard to avoid hearing them unless she walked away. The temptation to stay got the better of her.

"So, Mark Tulliver," Peta was saying. "Marcus Theodorus Talovaros. You were a boy when I last saw you and you had hair in those days—lovely thick dark brown hair—but I could never forget you. I'd know those eyes anywhere. And you must remember me." She raised her chin and said wryly, "No one ever forgets me!"

Theo very nearly smiled. "Of course I remember you, Peta. I didn't expect to meet you on a mountain in Naamon—but I knew who you were the moment I saw you."

"So why didn't you say something?"

"Because I'm not Mark anymore. It was a long time ago. I'm someone different now."

"What happened to you?"

"Nothing *happened*. It's what I chose. I'm not sure I can explain."

There was a pause, as if Peta were reconsidering her approach. "So, where have you been all day? Resting, I hope?"

"No. Searching for Rufus," Theo answered, his voice heavy with failure. "He was ever elusive. Notorious for it. But we're closing on him. It's only a matter of time."

"Well, I'm sorry you've had a wasted day," Peta said with an edge. "Rufus is bound to turn up again, yet you still thought chasing him was more important than talking to a long-lost friend for five minutes?"

"I'm sorry, Peta, but it is important. I'm here now."

"That's something." Her voice was mild, for all its complex, painful undertones. "So, Mark Tulliver, what happened to you? We stepped through the Great Gates to Elysion for our initiation—and no one ever saw you again. People thought you'd perished, swallowed up by the Spiral—such things have been known to happen, after all—or . . . really, we didn't know what to think."

Theo gave a low-key laugh. "I was swallowed. You could say that. The fire of the initiation brand brings strange visions, not so much madness as revelation . . ."

"I managed to get through mine without running wild and vanishing," Peta retorted.

"You were always more closely bound to Vaeth than me."

"Clay-footed, you mean?"

"I didn't say that."

"So, this revelation—what was it?"

"Nothing sudden or blinding. Only that when I saw the Spiral for the first time, I saw reality in a different way. I had to go deeper and deeper in." His tone was warm and amused; not apologetic in the least. "I kept going; that's all; when others turned back, I simply kept going."

"And you forgot all about me?"

"No, I never forgot you. Of course not. But I fell in love."

"With some beguiling Aelyr maiden?"

"With the Spiral," he said mildly.

Peta's voice changed, as if she were moving around the room. "I thought we had something, you and me. Of course, we were only sixteen; I don't suppose it would have lasted. But I never got the chance to find out."

Theo lowered his head. "I'm sorry."

There was a pause, long enough for Gill to risk glancing in. She saw Peta in front of Theo, stretching up in a quick graceful motion, Peta stretched up to kiss him. Embarrassed, Gill tried not to look, but her gaze was caught. Peta's mouth rested gently on Mark's. Then his hands came to her upper arms, and he gently put her away from him. "It was a long time ago. I'm a different person."

"No kidding." Peta gazed at him with bright eyes.

"I'm sure you are, too."

"Not really. I'm older, wiser and better off, but underneath I'm still the same dotty idiot who used to hang around with you pretending to like your dreadful poetry."

He laughed. "Now, that I had forgotten."

"And your family?" Her voice hardened. She folded her arms, widening the gap between them. Still they took not the slightest notice of Gill. "How easy was it to forget them? Your lovely mum, Maeve, who never knew what the hell had become of you? Because it was *my* mother, and me, who had to sit holding her when she broke down. Did you even know the Gates were barred for fourteen years or more? Did you ever think of her, or guess that she would hold a vigil for you at the locked Gates on every festival?" Peta grabbed an old-fashioned black telephone from a side table; its jangle made both Gill and Theo jump. "You should call her, perhaps?"

He drew back a pace, looking stunned. "I can't. It would be pointless. The son she lost no longer exists."

"I'll do it myself, then!" Peta noisily set down the telephone, and made a gruff noise of exasperation. "Later, when I understand, I'll call her and I *will* make you speak to her. You owe her that, at least."

"I never meant anyone to be hurt by what happened." His low tone was contrite, but there was stubbornness in it, Gill noticed. He sounded, she thought, as if he privately thought their grief had been an overreaction, irrelevant.

Peta clearly heard the same. She said sardonically, "But you had something more important to do?"

He opened his hands, uttered a groan. "Peta, you've entered the Spiral yourself! Didn't you see it, feel it? It sounds pedestrian to speak of wonder and mystery, but what other words are there? It's ineffable. *It's where we belong.* And I had to stay there."

"Yet you didn't care to share the wonder with me," she said dryly. "You didn't come back and say, "Peta, you have to see this!" That's okay; you weren't obliged to. We were just mates, weren't we? Occasionally we got carried away and had impulsive sex, which we both seemed to find rather enjoyable at the time, but most of the while we were just mates. But I lost you that day. We stepped through the Gates together. The Aelyr hunted us down in the fields of Elysion and branded us and when I came round, you were gone. I didn't feel very much wonder that day, Mark, I can tell you."

"I can't change what happened. And I wouldn't change it."

"Must have been good, to break Maeve's heart."

"I trust she will understand."

"Why should she?"

"Because she's Aetherial. She knows we take flight and vanish like birds; it's in our nature, even with Vaethyr. For her to feel otherwise is sheer sentimentality."

"I see." Peta ran her finger along the edge of the mantelpiece, as if skimming a line of dust. "What happened to gentle, Melusiel Mark? I didn't realize it was so easy for us to change our elements of affiliation. You were a kindly, watery Tulliver but now you've gone all cold and Sibeylan, like you've frozen to ice vapor. I liked the wings, by the way. I'm not quite so sure I like the new you."

"When we were on Mount Khafet, you couldn't change shape." A harder note entered his voice.

"So?" She tossed her head defensively. "I happened to be in shock, because of Juliana's sculpture, and because I'd just nearly gone hurtling off a mountain. I never could fly, in any case. It's a nice trick for those who can do it, but it's not who we are. We can alter our shape, but we're not shapechangers, Mark. We're Aetherials. Some of us transform, others not. It doesn't define us."

"And if you would let me finish—I didn't mean it as a criticism. It's what happens when Aelyr try to live on Earth. We become divorced from our true natures. We lose touch with our *fylgias* in the inner realm, lose our natural abilities. Vaethyr become too human, like blind mud creatures. It's not your fault, Peta. I'm just saying that it is a shame."

Peta gave a short laugh. "Oh, this is familiar. I'd forgotten, thanks to my rose-tinted memory, that you could be quite obnoxious at times. You've gotten worse, Mark. Thanks for giving me the rather patronizing benefit of your opinion, but let me tell you, however blind and muddy I may be, I'm quite happy in my Aetherial skin, thank you."

"Are you?" he said.

"Do you know that you sound as if you're trying to convert me to something?"

He smiled. "No. Well, perhaps."

"How did you end up at Lashtor?"

"I went deep into the Spiral, deep into the heart of Asru, the innermost realm. Certain Aetherials I met there . . . those who weren't interested in physical indulgence, or feasting upon the human world, or creating their own dynasties . . . who were only dedicated to the Spiral itself, seeking to model themselves on Estel the Eternal who only contemplates infinity . . ." A flush of passion tinted Theo's face. Peta was watching him intently, listening with a slight frown of concentration. "I realized I'd met folk who felt as I did. I discovered Lashtor and I stayed there. That's all. I became who I was meant to be."

"Well, I'm glad for you," Peta said, with forced sincerity. "You found your vocation, and it wasn't me. That's fine. All I ever wanted to know was what happened to you."

"So, are we at peace?" Theo said hopefully.

"We'll see about that."

At that point, Gill heard voices in the corridor; Juliana and Adam were approaching, with Ned and Colin. It was when Gill saw Ned that she remembered: she had left the alicorn in Juliana's apartment, and given it no thought since then. She thought, *Perhaps that means I no longer need it. Ned can have it back. But I don't want to make a song and dance about giving it to him so I'll just leave it for him to find . . .*

She cleared her throat, but Peta was still too preoccupied to notice her there, or simply didn't care. She was saying, "So, how does contemplating the infinite square with chasing Rufus around?"

Theodorus took a few steps to the fireplace, suddenly restless. "It's not enough just to meditate on the Spiral—we have to earn that right by actively protecting it. It came to my notice, through Albin and others, that the search for Rufus Ephenaestus had been all but abandoned. I took it up again. Not everyone agrees I was right to do so, but most do. The renewed policy of the Spiral Court is to bring him to justice, once and for all. I'm carrying out their will."

"Well," said Peta, apparently running out of words. Gill had only known the crusading side of Theo; she couldn't imagine what a shock it must be to Peta, who'd known him as someone quite different, her first love . . .

Drawing level with Gill, Adam met her eyes and gave a subdued smile, acknowledgment of their earlier talk. Juliana simply swept straight into the room, attended by Ned Badger and Colin. Gill and Adam followed.

Juliana appeared brisk, businesslike and ghost-white. She began, "Sorry to have kept you waiting. We've had some bad news. Ned returned from the hospital earlier and told me that his wife Flora, my dear housekeeper, has died . . . As you know, she was in hospital and the chest infection that landed her there proved fatal." Pushing back silver skeins of hair, Juliana absorbed the murmurs of sympathy, raising one hand to acknowledge them and cut them short. She spoke for a few seconds more about Flora, while Ned stood as stiff and grey as old wax beside her. Gill was stunned; she'd hardly known Flora, had no feelings for her, yet she saw what a shock it was to the household.

"I still can't quite believe she isn't coming home," Juliana went on, "but there will be due time to mourn her later. For now we have more urgent matters to consider . . . erm, Colin and Ned will serve supper, just sandwiches I'm afraid, after we've talked." She put her hands together. "I'm afraid I have quite a lot to tell you and, to be frank, I'm beyond caring who knows my grim secrets. I need your help. All of you."

Gill and Peta sat down on the couch next to Adam, and Colin perched on the arm of a chair while Ned, Juliana and Theo stayed on their feet.

Juliana cleared her throat. "I need to talk to you about *Midsummer Night*, the sculpture group in the foundry that I never seem quite able to finish. Ned has always known this, and I've recently told Peta, but to give the abbreviated version: A small boy, Flora's son, went missing and it triggered . . . painful inspiration in me. For the first few years, my work was just disturbing enough to be tremendously successful." Juliana's tone was dry. "I had no qualms about selling those early works, but things began to change. My work took on a warped darkness, a sort of invasive, vampiric quality . . . really, I can't describe it. I loaned the first piece to the sculpture garden at Loch Tornan . . ."

"*Go Not into the Forest*," said Peta. "Oh, there was something weird about it, all right; I couldn't work out what it was."

"Another, called *Harvest*, was bought by a private collector, who returned it to me a couple of years later . . ." She gave an ironic smile. "Saying that it terrified his children. However, I continued to work on the series because it became a compulsion I couldn't or wouldn't resist. All the time, my doubts grew. Offers came in but I deferred selling or exhibiting. I couldn't keep myself from working on *Midsummer Night*, even thought I came to consider the work too dangerous ever to see the light of day . . . Colin, would you pour us all some brandy?"

They declined; it was Juliana who needed it. She took a gulp and cradled the glass between her hands. "There are Aetherials trapped inside the sculptures. I didn't set out deliberately to capture them . . . but it became a kind of revenge, a way to protect the folk of Cairndonan, even a bargaining counter in a way. However, over the years I became alarmed at what I'd done. Still I keep *Midsummer Night* in the foundry, always adding to it, perfecting it . . . wondering what the hell to do next. You might lure a dozen tigers into a cage, but then what do you do with them? It's wrong to keep them, but if you set them free, they may tear you to pieces."

Adam said suddenly, "They are Rufus's lost followers."

"We can't know who they are," said Peta, but she sounded uncertain.

"They must be. I was telling Gill earlier—when I was first there, there were others. Gradually they left. They quarreled with him."

"What about?" Theo asked.

Adam hesitated, lowering his gaze. "I think, in part, it was about me."

"And as they deserted him, they were drawn in and caught by Dame Juliana's statues," said Theo.

"Peta has pointed out, and I agree, that the right thing to do is to let them go," said Juliana. "Ah, but that's the dilemma, isn't it? Dare I?"

"They're members of my own ancient race," said Peta. "How would you feel if I told you I'd created a work of art by imprisoning various human beings? Wouldn't you think I was maybe a bit . . . crazy? Dangerous? In need of locking up myself?"

"I'm not defending what I did," Juliana said steadily. "It all happened in a fever of creativity, in a rather hellish period that I can now only describe as madness, a sort of breakdown. I know what I've done is wrong. I've painted myself into a corner, so to speak. As long as I keep them in the foundry, caught between worlds, they are ensnared. But if I move the work into the public arena, all bets are off. They may stay bound inside the work, or they may escape and wreak havoc."

Ned Badger murmured, "Don't do this, Dame J."

She raised a subtle hand to quiet him. "My concern is not really for myself but for those around me. However, a situation has arisen."

Colin hurriedly refilled her near-empty glass and she paused to take a drink. Squaring her shoulders, she took a breath and announced, "The time has come for *Midsummer Night* to be exhibited."

There was a murmur; Gill, Peta and Adam glanced at each other, not knowing whether to be pleased or worried. Colin actually clapped his hands together. "Wow, that is great news, Dame J! Finally! How long have I been trying to persuade you to put on an exhibition, get back in the saddle?"

Ned made a kind of hissing noise between his teeth, turning away.

"The fact is," Juliana continued bluntly, "I've been having certain . . . cash-flow problems. Either I sell *Midsummer Night*, or I lose Cairndonan altogether."

There was a whisper of dismay; Gill suspected that it was no surprise to anyone—except Theo, to whom it was of no concern—even if Juliana had never quite spelled it out.

"No, Dame J." Ned's voice fell like an ax. He looked fierce and red-eyed. "Don't do this. We won't let you lose the house!"

"Don't argue with Dame Juliana!" Colin exclaimed. His shirtsleeves were pushed back, his arms folded. "She's got a waiting list of buyers going back years and you're telling her not to exhibit? What's wrong with you,

Badger?" He reddened and bit his lip. "Look, I'm sorry about your wife and all, but the show must go on."

"This is nothing to do with Flora," Ned hissed. "There can be no exhibition. The *Dubh Sidhe* are too dangerous."

"This is too weird. You're crazy."

"Stop it!" snapped Juliana. "No arguments. It's decided. I've no choice. If I don't raise some money, I will be made bankrupt in a matter of weeks. My charming estranged husband has offered to buy me out and let me stay as a tenant—"

"He's *what*?" they said in near-unison.

"Let me say that I'd rather marinate my own head in hydrofluoric acid than accept his offer. I've lain awake at nights for years, worrying about this moment—but *Midsummer Night* is the work I have created and so it's the work I have to put on show, and take the consequences. Seeing as I have no money and no time to orchestrate a proper event in London or another major city, the opening will take place here, on the twenty-fourth of June—that gives us precisely eight days to prepare. Will you all help me?"

"Midsummer Day." Peta looked speculatively from her to Theo. "This is very sudden, Dame J. I know I said you should release the Aetherial hostages, but are you sure this is the right way to go about it?"

"Perhaps not, but it's the only way I know. I believe I know how to release them—which I will not attempt to do until after the exhibition—and I don't think they'll be able to escape until I do, but what will happen then, I can't speculate. I'll choose a suitable site on the estate and we'll forklift the sculptures to it. I'll have my agent—the poor woman must think I've expired—put out invitations to all the right people, the art critics, collectors, general cognoscenti."

"It's a long way to travel, and very short notice," said Peta. "Will they come?"

"Oh, they'll come, all right," Colin said gleefully. "It'll be a sensation."

"A disaster," murmured Ned.

"But you will help me, Ned?"

She looked hard at him. He looked at the carpet and said through his teeth, "Of course. As ever."

"Peta?"

She shrugged helplessly. "I honestly don't know what to say or do for the best. This is crazy. But yes, Dame J, of course I'll help. Curiosity will kill me one of these days. But I wouldn't miss it for anything."

"Thank you," said Juliana. "Gill?"

"Er, yes," She stirred, straightening. "What do you want me to do, though?"

"Oh, goodness—hand out leaflets and canapés, ply people with champagne, make yourself generally useful. Just *be there*."

Ned said stubbornly, "And if the *Dubh Sidhe* break loose?"

Theo answered. Gill realized that he must already have discussed this with Juliana in private. "Bringing *Midsummer Night* into the open may well mean its prisoners are let loose. We can but trust Dame Juliana to control them, at least for a time. I also believe that it will attract Rufus Ephenaestus."

"Oh, he's certainly not one to miss a party," said Peta.

"When he comes," said Theo, "and when his followers emerge to meet him, I and my comrades from Lashtor will be standing ready to arrest them. Yes, there may be danger and it will take courage for all of you to brave Rufus's creatures and Rufus himself; but we will be on hand. He and his cohorts will be taken before the Spiral Court to answer for their crimes. So there is no need for any of you to be afraid." His eyes were steady, lit up like twin pale fires. "I thank all of you for bringing this to pass. We have been awaiting this chance for centuries."

That night, Juliana stood outside Adam's room before the snow-pale form of *Winter Came to the Wood*, the most nearly human of her sculptures; an exquisitely detailed head, neck and torso emerging from the rougher shape of a tree trunk. Juliana looked up into the beautiful stone mask of the face. She shivered. This was the only piece that had no living Aetherial trapped within it and yet it still seemed to have its own watchful spirit. Only now did she notice that it, too, looked like Adam. The cold scent of churches arose from the statue and seemed to penetrate her to the bone.

"What would you have me do?" she said. She raised a hand to stroke the smooth marble cheekbone. "An Aetherial came to me in a dream and offered me this bargain. Yes, I turned it against them, but what did they expect?"

Winter gazed down, implacable.

"I'm going to remove you from here and place you at the center of *Midsummer Night,* where you belong. Will you watch over it for me, as you've watched over Leith?"

Next, she trod the length of the garden tunnel with only a flashlight beam to guide her. She unlocked the trapdoor and ascended into the eerie stone forest that was *Midsummer Night.* In the darkness and strange fire-tinged mist, she walked between the forms of stone, glass and bronze that she had created.

Pathway. So Little Time. Harvest. Let Them Steal Away. Each statue or group had its own name, its own story. She paused to touch each one, sensing the latent Aetherial trapped within. Their presence manifested as a faint glow, a sheen that had a holographic property of hovering just above the surface; something moving within the solid form, like fish swimming beneath a thick layer of ice. Something silver or greenish or dark would swell to the surface then fall away again, amorphous, unutterably disturbing.

The *dysir* were there too, a multitude of shadows flowing around the base of each piece, mindlessly seeking escape.

Each shape hinted at someone trying to fight their way out of the matter that constrained them—and there was something real and sentient within, trying to do exactly that. She felt presences watching her, as sharks might watch her from an aquarium. Were they aware of what she'd done? Did they hate her, and plan revenge? She couldn't tell. They simply watched, silent.

"It was only to protect mortals from being abducted by you," she said under her breath. "No, more than that. I meant to offer you in exchange for Leon being given back to us. Can you understand that? Well, we have Adam back, at least, so perhaps it is the beginning of the end of this stalemate. And it was because you add such mysterious beauty to my work. I have not dared to show the world until now."

She spoke out loud. "I'm going to bring you out of here and into the light of day on Earth. Vaeth, you call it. I will release you, and after that your fate is out of my hands. Others may have business with you, I'm afraid. I ask that you vent your anger only upon me, no one else. On me alone."

There was no answer. The eerie silence drifted around her like mist. She had no idea if they could understand her or not.

"Well, I have told you," she murmured. "If you choose to remain in this form out of sheer respect for my art, I bless you for it."

She broke off, startled by movement. Peta's white face loomed out of the darkness, circling the statue as she came to Juliana's side.

"I hope you weren't planning to incorporate me into your work of art," she remarked wryly.

"Of course not. You're altogether too down-to-earth and human."

"That's what Mark said." She gave a sour laugh. "How many individual sculptures are there? I make it a different number every time I try to count."

"So do I, to be honest," Juliana said grimly. "I might have known you'd sneak in again. You're very brave. Aren't you afraid, knowing that you might be drawn in?"

"Well, because I'm aware of the danger, I can resist it." Peta hugged herself, shivering. "It's still freaking me out to hell and back. Feels like . . . being trapped in some Victorian lunatic asylum, walking down a dark corridor between the cells with no idea how to escape."

"And yet you came."

"To see if I could understand what you've done."

"And can you?"

"These Aetherials have gone into elemental form, as they would to attach themselves to a tree or a rock. It's a kind of . . . hibernation, in a sense. But how you've compelled them do it, I don't know. That's what scares me, Dame J. Your power."

"You're very honest," said Juliana.

"If I learned to bite my lip, I'd get into less trouble," said Peta.

"And now I think we should leave, don't you? I've told them they will soon be set loose. Whether they can hear or understand is another matter. It's all I can do. Now I don't want anyone setting foot in here until the pieces are moved out ready for the exhibition. Agreed?"

"Yes, Dame J," Peta sighed. She looked solemn, overwhelmed. "It's no good, I still can't work out quite what this is or who you are. But if I put all that aside, these works . . . it's hard to believe they were made by human hands. They're beautiful, incredible."

"Thank you," said Juliana, unexpectedly warmed.

Peta gave a wry grin. "It's why worshippers gather around you, and around Rufus too. Doesn't matter how good, evil, high-minded or amoral you actually are; they're drawn to the fire of your life force, and nothing else matters. Genius. We can't help but follow genius."

Later, as Juliana sat before her dressing-table mirror, rubbing serum into her skin, she felt very far from being any kind of genius. In the half-light, a familiar face rose over her shoulder. Peta had been pacified, but Corah was not, and never would be.

"You lied to them," she drawled.

Juliana started. "No, I didn't."

"You omitted the truth. Same thing." Corah drew on her cigarette, blowing a stream of phantom smoke into the air. "You neglected to mention the bargain you made, that you gave a child in exchange for your artistic powers."

"There was no need for them to make that connection."

"Your guilty secret."

"For god's sake, Corah. Say something useful or go."

"You're going to die," Corah said crisply. She put out her red tongue to remove a strand of tobacco from it with a fingernail. "That's what dear old Ned's so afraid of, isn't it? Your own work might come to life and kill you. You could lock up the sculptures, lock up the house and flee. Then you'd be safe. But you won't, because you have a death wish."

"Oh, that is absolutely not true." Juliana glared at Corah's reflection. Did this seem like the same woman who'd written her cynical, frank story in the scrapbook? Oh yes, it did, but unrestrained, elemental. She felt fear rolling through her like a physical weight.

"You have to play out the story to the end, Juliana, no matter *how* it ends. I'll tell you something. If you let anything bad happen to my beloved Adam now you've found him, you will be spending eternity here in limbo with me."

"Go," Juliana said firmly. She closed and opened her eyes, but Corah was still there, leaning close over her shoulder now; putting a smiling second head beside Juliana's own. She could even smell Corah's perfume, and the alcohol sharp on her breath.

"You admit the beautiful boy is Adam, at last."

"Yes. Yes." Juliana thrust her hands into her hair, tugging until it hurt. "That doesn't mean Leon isn't still out there somewhere!"

"You would know more, if you had read my letter."

"It is not my fault it went missing. I think Ned's destroyed it. Tell me what was in it, if it was so important."

"Can't, darling. Could only do that if I were real, and not a figment of your guilty imagination." Corah smiled, her cupid-bow lips near-black like those of a siren from a silent film. "I could have told you, though, that my lovely brother was not your Leon."

"How do you know?"

"Because he's here with me."

Juliana's heart jerked as if electrified. Corah was suddenly farther back in the shadows of the room, and beside her stood a small, pale child, holding her hand. Juliana felt caught in a spiderweb nightmare, her heart on the edge of failing. All she had to do to escape was turn away from the mirror, but she was frozen in place.

At the sight of the child—an innocent little specter—she was close to fragmenting. Only by a huge effort of will did she hold herself.

"You lied to them, darling," Corah repeated. "Failed to admit that you bartered for your power, then turned it against the *Dubh Sidhe* who sold it to you. And, oh dear, what is going to happen when they break free? You should know better than to toy with angels and gods . . ."

A knock at her door broke the spell; Corah was gone. Juliana shook herself as if emerging from a trance and called, "Yes, come in."

Ned entered, his face pallid in the dim light. He looked like another of the undead, worse than Corah; scrawny, soft-moving, his hair part of the darkness except for its lightning streaks of white, his eyes bloodshot. He held a large, stiff envelope balanced on his fingers, like a waiter presenting a tray.

Juliana stared. He didn't know that Corah had been urging her to read it . . . *but Corah's only my inner voice*, she reminded herself. *She's not real.*

"Take it, then," he said.

Juliana studied him for a moment, wondering if she'd ever known him at all. From the moment she'd met him—inherited him with the house—he had devoted himself entirely to her. And to protecting Cairndonan, however ineffective the talismans and prayers he'd used to do so. What more was there to know?

"I thought you'd destroyed it."

"I wanted to, but I couldn't."

Juliana took the envelope. The stiff paper was turning yellow. It bore her name in Corah's writing, embellished with swirly flourishes, *Juliana*. The flap was open. Anger stirred as she saw the evidence that Ned had not merely taken it, but opened and read it. She placed it on her dressing table.

"You had no right to conceal it from me."

"I know," Ned answered.

"Still less right to read it! How dare you!"

"I did wrong," he said quietly. "I am guilty. But I had to know what poison she had written to you. I could not risk the damage her words might do."

"You had no right, Ned. It was none of your business. The letter was for me!" Her protests were lame; she simply couldn't find words adequate to express her outrage.

"I had to choose between two wrongs," Ned said, unperturbed. "Which was the worse? I did it for your sake, Dame J. All I have ever done is try to protect you! To keep the underworld at bay, so that it didn't take you as it took . . . others. I even wed Flora to protect you!"

Juliana tried to control the huge cauldron of rage simmering inside her. She'd always known that Ned married Flora—after Leon had gone—partly out of pity, partly to negate the damage Flora had done to Charles and Juliana's marriage. Ned was astute; he saw that an unmarried Flora, abandoned by Charles, lonely and grief-stricken, would be a constant reminder and torment to Juliana. A married Flora was neatly tidied away. It had worked for Ned, too; he no longer appeared a loner, a servant unhealthily obsessed with the lady of the house. Married, Ned and Flora became a safe, neutered entity. Truly a marriage of convenience all round.

Still, it was something they'd never acknowledged out loud before. So sordid, unspeakable. "Don't," she snapped.

"If only I'd done so *before* the boy went missing. I tried, you know. Even before he was born, I asked her repeatedly, but she always turned away. Said I was only asking to protect *your* feelings."

Mastering herself, she said steadily, "Isn't that exactly what you were doing?"

"Yes, of course, but only to do the best for everyone! And I believe it was Mr. Sandford-Barnes"—Ned always referred to Charles excoriatingly by his surname—"who persuaded her to refuse, so that he might more easily retain control of the child. If we'd been already married, and I'd been living with her at Robin Cottage, the boy would never have disappeared."

"You can't know that."

"I would not have been so careless with him. I would have kept him safe! We were all to blame, every one of us. I have devoted my entire existence to protecting you from the darkness."

Cold acid spilled through her. His tone of voice woke a horrible premonition. She kept seeing the pale little figure at Corah's side. "Ned, do you know something about Leon?"

"If only I'd been there, that night. For all the grieving you did over him, you can't deny that a little part of you wanted him gone."

"That's not true! Tell me."

Ned shook his head, his eyes red-rimmed. "Don't ask. Don't read the letter. Don't hold this exhibition. I'm imploring you, Dame J. There's only one way to deal with this Rufus, and that is to trap him inside *Midsummer Night*, bolt the foundry doors and throw away the keys. If you put on this exhibition, you are playing into the hands of the *Dubh Sidhe*. This is what they want, to be unleashed again! And you'll let them do it, out of entirely misplaced guilt! If you put your work on display, if you let them have their way—your doom will be on your own head. Don't do it. I know you won't listen, but I'm begging you. Don't read your aunt's letter. Burn it!"

She could barely find her voice. "Ned, do you know what happened to Leon?"

"Now Flora's gone, I can tell you." He paused, then said softly, "He was dead when I found him."

The whole universe seemed to be crammed inside her chest, and she felt it tilt and fall. "*You found him? I* don't believe you!"

"It's true—but I hid the fact, so that you and Flora could go on hoping that one day he might return. Flora knew that Leith, Adam, wasn't him and that's why she gave up and turned her face to the wall. Nothing you or I said to her could make any difference, because her hopes had died." He spoke softly, his voice fervent but controlled. She could do nothing but listen, stunned, as he spilled more words than she'd ever heard from him in thirty years.

"Hate me if you like, curse me to hell. But don't you forget this— everything I have ever done has been for your sake. *Everything.* I'm your faithful dog, Dame J, to the death."

———

After he'd gone, Juliana began to read the letter.

My Dearest Juliana,

Well, did you have your bet? I hope this won't come as too much of a shock. Perhaps you guessed it already, or learned it from someone else, in which case, let me not make it too much of a song and dance.

There's something you need to know about your sister, Christina. She knows—though I doubt she's ever told you, or anyone—that she's adopted. Her real parents, as I understand it, were a hard-working couple who ran a pub near Melody's church. They died when a German bomb destroyed the pub, but a baby was pulled out of the rubble. Melody saw it as her Christian duty to adopt the child. It seemed to me that she didn't like children very much, just the idea of them.

At the next line, Juliana stopped. She tried to skim the rest but couldn't. Her mind closed down. She couldn't read it, couldn't take it in, couldn't accept what Corah might be telling her. Instead, she folded the letter back into its envelope. After the exhibition, maybe then she'd try again, but not now. She wasn't ready.

Tomorrow, she would have to tell Gill what they had already suspected. As for the rest—Juliana half-wished that Ned had burned the letter after all.

18

Midsummer Night

Juliana chose the space for *Midsummer Night* with care. The exhibit was to stand on a broad flat sweep of ground just to the north of the house; an area that lay between the forest edge and the cliff tops of Cairndonan Point, a perfect amphitheater encircled to the west by sea and misted islands, to north and south by mountainous coastline stepping away into the distance. A backdrop of pine and cedar completed the area, veiling the house itself from view.

Gill observed the proceedings, doing whatever she could to help. Colin and Ned between them couldn't handle such a weight of materials, so Juliana had brought in a team of contractors from Inverness, at considerable expense—*"Just another bill to worry about later,"* she'd muttered. Temporary paths were laid to support a miniature crane that would lower each piece into position. Gill watched as the sculptures were forklifted one at a time from storage, then lifted by crane and painstakingly eased into position, swaying precariously in a cage of chains. *Winter* was brought from the house, and *Go Not into the Forest* transported from Loch Tornan. The process took an entire day. Juliana Flagg was a perfectionist. Gill did her best to mitigate her demands on the long-suffering contractors by providing an endless supply of coffee, sandwiches and cake.

When it was done, *Midsummer Night* stood as if it always had been there.

Even the great landscape failed to dwarf it. It was a like a small Stonehenge, an echo of the Cairndonan Sisters, eerie and ageless. Swaddled in thick protective burlap, the sculptures resembled shapeless Egyptian mummies against the vast, liquid sky. Or papery brown chrysalises.

Gill wondered what, if anything, would emerge.

She stalked the area, taking photographs, but the lens failed to capture anything she couldn't see with her own eyes. Juliana's work made stark, dramatic shapes against the landscape, but no fugitive elements appeared on the digital screen, no strange lights or ghost figures.

As evening fell, Juliana stood with folded arms and surveyed her petrified forest. Peta and Gill, Adam, Ned and Colin stood in a loose group
around her. Theodorus was there too, standing apart. He stood as motionless and composed as a court usher, hands clasped in front of him. He and
Peta were barely speaking at present, thanks to his reluctance to discuss the
past, and her annoyance—but sometimes, when Peta wasn't looking, Gill
caught him giving her long, sidelong looks.

Over the past few days he'd been disappearing for long stretches; travel-
ing to and from Lashtor, Gill assumed. He'd told them almost nothing of
his plans. He insisted that the less they knew, the less they could tell Rufus
if he reappeared. But there had been no sign of Rufus since the fight in the
foundry.

"Well, it's done," said Juliana. The breeze lifted strands of her silver
hair, which she'd fastened in a loose chignon. "Perhaps nothing will happen. Maybe they're trapped inside forever, *dysir* and all. Outside in the surface world they might lose their magic, or whatever it was that animated
them. Perhaps it was only inside the foundry that they seemed . . . alive."

"At the interface between Earth, Dusklands, and Naamon?" said Peta.
"Possibly. We'll have to wait and see."

"Letting them loose is madness," grumbled Ned, still relentlessly un-
happy with her decision.

"Letting *what* loose, though?" said Juliana. She gave a grunt of laughter.
"My prisoners might already have slipped out and blown away on the wind
for all I know—in which case, good luck to them."

"No," said Theo. "They are still inside."

Gill shuddered involuntarily.

"And what are they waiting for?" Juliana raised her hands. "I believe
they will stay bound until I call them out—but I can't be sure. If they
choose their moment to escape, I don't suppose an apology is going to cut
much ice."

"You owe these creatures no apology!" Ned said through his teeth. "You
were protecting Cairndonan from them!"

Peta raised her eyebrows, but said nothing. Gill wondered if Ned even
knew that she was one of *these creatures*. Colin was looking at Ned, shaking
his head in exasperation. "Y'know—no disrespect Dame J—but all this
stuff's going right over my head. The important thing's the exhibition,
isn't it? Getting you out there in the public eye again, where you belong!
None of this other stuff really matters, does it?"

Theo spoke coldly, ignoring his remarks. "Whatever befalls, keep in
mind that I and my fellow Lashtorians will be watching. You won't see us,
but we'll be there. Just go about your business as usual. All I ask is that,
when the moment comes, you give us your full cooperation."

"We'll see about that," said Colin, but Juliana put a quieting hand on his arm.

"Colin, don't be awkward. Theo is here to help us and we're in his hands. Just trust me, will you?"

Gill looked at the sculptures and said, "It feels as if they're sleeping, or waiting . . ."

"Waiting," echoed Juliana. "For what, I wonder? Well, let them stay so. The covers will stay on overnight. Tomorrow, we'll unveil them, for good or ill."

When morning came, a cheerful bustle overtook the estate. A canopy was erected over the main path that wound through the gardens towards the cliffs, so that guests could pass from house to exhibition regardless of rain. This walkway brought them into a hospitality tent where food and drink would be served. One side was open to the sculpture arena so that if the weather turned, at least they could still view the exhibit from shelter. The canvas was dark green, to blend with the trees. There was nothing to jar the eye, nothing to detract from the appearance of *Midsummer Night* in its wild setting. Paths of bark mulch had been laid down, weaving between the sculptures so that people could walk without churning up the grass or getting their shoes muddy. It gave the feeling of a forest floor.

Two television crews arrived in huge white vans; one a news crew, the other filming for an arts documentary. Juliana had allowed them in only under the strictest conditions: handheld cameras only, no trailing cables, no getting in the way of her guests, only a brief time to set up. Apparently she knew from experience that they'd take over the whole day if they were let loose.

Gill sensed her aunt's tension. She didn't show obvious signs of nerves—it wasn't her style—but rather seemed to be containing an enormous, coiled mass of energy. It made her more brusque and bossy than usual.

A few days ago, Juliana had taken Gill aside and told her what the beginning of the re-discovered letter contained; Corah's assertion that Gill's mother, Christina, had been adopted. Gill had been startled, even saddened, but not greatly shocked. "I can well believe it," she'd responded, eager to reassure Juliana that she wasn't devastated. "Christina was so different from you. So, we're not even related, you to my mother or me to you. I feel doubly out of place now."

"Why?" Juliana said crisply. "I'm sorry you had to find out like this, but please don't think I feel any less that you're my niece. I hope you're not too upset."

"No," Gill said firmly. "I'm really not. Like I said, my mother and I weren't close. No, actually, it makes sense of things."

"For me, too," said Juliana. "This strange, stretched-out family . . . it's as if we're hardly connected at all, just motes of dust in an abyss. Weirdly, it makes me feel you and I have more in common, not less."

"Really? What else did the letter say?"

Juliana had been evasive. "Do you know, I . . . I haven't quite been able to read it all yet. There was yet another description of the infamous Night of the *Dunkelmen* and I quite lost the will to go on. Later, I'll read it. Once the viewing is over."

"It certainly doesn't stop me wanting to be like you," Gill said, smiling. "Fearless."

"You think I'm fearless?" Juliana had replied with a hollow laugh. "Let me whisper my greatest fear. That, without Aetherial inmates to add magic and beauty, my sculptures would be nothing at all. Just dumb, dreary stone."

This conversation ran through the back of Gill's mind as a backdrop to everything else; but it was painless. It had only confirmed what she'd suspected. Juliana had not rejected her because of it, and that was all that counted. Today, the only thing that mattered was the exhibition, and Gill was more than happy to forget everything else.

Juliana's timetable was military. The event—a preview, by invitation only—was to begin at two in the afternoon and end at six—the last guests to have left the premises by seven at the latest. Those who needed to stay overnight had been directed to accommodation in Inverness or other towns; no one was invited to stay at the house itself. Juliana wanted to keep things on a formal basis, keep her guests at a distance rather than have anyone still hanging around the next morning. Mainly, though, it was because of *Midsummer Night* itself. She insisted she would not put outsiders at risk of . . . anything.

Something would happen, Gill was sure. Peta and Theo—everyone except Colin, in fact—were convinced of it. It was like anticipating a hurricane, a simple matter of waiting.

As preparations intensified, Gill and Peta did all they could to help, rushing back and forth to set up trestle tables with white cloths, glasses, crates of wine and champagne, platters of canapés—incredible, the amount of work involved. The two village women who helped Juliana with catering were there. All this activity was good, Gill decided. It made the Otherworld recede, taking all its nebulous threats with it. The world became ordinary, busy and purposeful—just as Colin apparently preferred to view it. She wished she could still share his matter-of-fact outlook.

Juliana introduced her to a tall, sleek woman with glasses, bright red lipstick and a dry but friendly manner; this was her agent, Megan Folds. "I never knew Dame Juliana had a niece," Megan said with a broad smile. "She always was one for surprises."

"This out-of-the-blue exhibition must have been a shock." Gill surmised that Megan knew nothing of Aetherial intrigues. She must, however, be at least partly aware of Juliana's dire financial straits.

"Absolutely, but I knew she hadn't been idle all these years. I knew she'd make a triumphant reappearance when she was ready."

"Thank you for not calling it swansong," Juliana said in a wry tone.

"What?" Megan looked genuinely shocked. "I should hope not. This is the start of a new period, isn't it?"

For all their precautions against possible rain, the weather was perfect; a pure blue sky, a light breeze tempering the sun's warmth. The sea was a sheet of blue-green silk. The gates were due to open at one-thirty. At twelve— with the camera crews tapping their feet and Colin fussing that she was cutting it very fine—Juliana decreed that it was time to take off the covers.

Gill, Peta and Adam assisted, untying cords, pulling off layers of burlap and padding which Ned folded and removed to the foundry. Colin aided Juliana, moving a stepladder for her so she could polish traces of fiber or dust from each shape in turn. Adam was quiet, assisting without complaint as if he knew that this must happen and there was nothing to do but get on with it. Juliana worked quickly. All her fussing had been done the day before, so every piece was positioned precisely as she wanted it.

Then they were ready.

Midsummer Night was as timeless as a stone circle—albeit a surreal one. The polished surfaces of marble, bronze and glass glistened. Each piece stood monumental and silent against sea, sky and forest; nothing stirred, no strange energies gathered, no enraged Aetherials appeared. Standing beside Gill, Juliana expelled a long breath of gathered tension.

"Are you all right, Aunt J?" Gill said softly, putting her hand through Juliana's elbow. It was a spontaneous gesture, done before she could think twice about it. "It looks magnificent. So do you. It will all be fine."

"Thank you, dear." Juliana patted her hand, returning her small show of affection before turning away to issue a string of last-minute instructions. "The leaflets, who's got them? Do you all know where you're meant to be? Colin on the main gate, Ned on car park duty. Gill to help Megan to meet and greet; Peta in the Camellia House, directing people to the tent where I will be waiting with Adam. Once everyone's here, Colin will take charge of the entrance hall while the rest of you come down to the tent and help Adam to circulate with nibbles and champagne. Keep it flowing. Curtain up!"

Ned's sour warning that no one would come at such short notice proved groundless. When Colin opened Cairndonan's gates, car after car came sweeping along the drive. Each slotted into a parking space at Ned's direction and disgorged its load of journalists, art collectors and old friends. Megan seemed to know most of them, and ticked them off on a list; all Gill had to do was hand out leaflets—which had been hurriedly prepared and printed on Juliana's creaky old computer—and to send people in the right direction. They were strangers to her, but she played a quiet game of guessing who was who. This man, with the dark suit, bow tie and greasy grey comb-over: an art critic, possibly. This woman, in her chic little black dress with bright red tights; a gallery owner? Or this one, in a brown pants suit and severe-looking glasses: a museum curator, perhaps. There was a neat, smiling Japanese couple, a man of Middle Eastern appearance in a dark suit: collectors, for certain.

Later, when all the guests were there, Gill and Peta walked together down the covered path to the tent. Gill had dressed for her role in the plain, dark skirt and jacket she'd first arrived in: her old office clothes. "I wonder where Theo is?" asked Gill.

Peta shrugged dismissively. "I've no idea."

"It struck me that if he came across Rufus and captured him in the meantime, he wouldn't have any real reason to be here."

"If that's the case, he should have let us know," Peta said thinly. "Unless we're not important enough in his great schemes."

"No. I trust Theo. He won't abandon us, I'm sure."

In the tent, the atmosphere was already close and warm, electric with anticipation. Megan stood ready to introduce the event. Juliana looked imposing in a long skirt and fitted jacket of pearl-grey silk, her hair tied back with a jaunty silver headscarf. The look, Gill thought, was something like a peasant in a Soviet propaganda poster; part bohemian goddess, part warrior. Perfect.

Gill saw the brief look of trepidation, if not panic, in her aunt's eyes. Then her professional mask of poise came down, and it was as if Gill and the others ceased to exist. There was only Dame Juliana Flagg and her long-denied, eager public.

"Now we know our place," Peta muttered from the side of her mouth. "Waitresses!"

"Oh, well, she's like a grand diva taking the stage," Gill whispered back. "Good assistants are invisible assistants."

"It's been a pleasure and absolute privilege to know Dame Juliana for over twenty-five years now," Megan was saying. "A genius, a living legend who needs no introduction, I give you Dame Juliana Flagg and her new work, *Midsummer Night*."

There was wild applause, a scatter of well-mannered cheers. The crowd swelled towards the open end of the tent, their excitement filling the air with physical heat, a miasma of deodorized and perfumed bodies. Juliana held up her hands in response.

"What you are about to see is a work of complete insanity. It's too big, too long in the creation, too much of everything. But all I can say is welcome, thank you for making this long, long journey to share in my madness. Enjoy!"

Outside, Juliana made her way along the path, shreds of bark crunching beneath her feet and a lively sea breeze cooling her face. She felt exposed and insecure, like an actor stepping on stage after a long absence. A few folk were already there among the statues, unable to wait. When they saw the mass of guests following Juliana, they self-consciously mingled with the crowd as if embarrassed at being caught taking a sneak preview. She smiled at their eagerness.

She was nervous for all of five minutes; then she forgot her nerves and got into her stride. She'd forgotten how good it felt, all this attention, adulation, the heady pleasure of talking freely about the ideas she had kept bottled up inside for so long. She would have been happy to let them wander, but it seemed she was expected to give an official introduction. A reasonable request. It felt appropriate.

So she began a brief tour of *Midsummer Night*, surrounded by a stream of excited visitors and by the TV crews wielding their heavy cameras and large, fluffy microphones on poles. One of the interviewers tried to give instructions, "Dame Juliana, could you stand closer . . ." There was almost a scuffle, indignant guests displaced by the ruthless media.

"Please," Juliana called out. "Don't crowd each other. There is ample time for everyone to look around and film to your heart's content. Would you please back off with the TV cameras? I'll do as many takes as you like later, but this introduction is primarily for my guests."

Mildly chastened, the crews dropped back.

"Incidentally, I hope you will film the sculptures themselves, and not just shots of me talking about them," she remarked as they reorganized themselves. "I can't bear 'talking heads' on documentaries. People will want to see what it is I'm describing, not my boring mug."

Everyone laughed. Wincing, she thought, *I bet they'll show that bit.* Still, it didn't matter. Once she was under way, she forgot the cameras were there. It was as if she began the journey into the underworld that *Midsummer Night* described. Emotion pressed her throat as she recalled the feverish process of creation, the guilt of the trapped Aetherials.

"Thank you all so much for coming. I don't want to tell you what to think of this work, but I understand that you'd like me to say something about it. I know I'll be asked many questions today, not least, 'What took you so long?' "

More laughter. "All I can say is that it wasn't ready before. Now it is."

The movement of a hand caught her eye. A man at the back of the crowd was sketching a clear dollar sign on the air with a pointed finger. *Charles.* No—he wasn't really there, it was only her tortured imagination again. Her face turned warm. He'd phoned a couple of weeks ago to drawl, "My offer still stands, old girl. Don't forget," but she was surprised he had not turned up this afternoon or even phoned to make some languid, sarcastic insinuation. His silence was strange. The imaginary Charles smiled and raised his glass as he vanished.

"*Go Not into the Forest,*" she began. "This is the oldest piece in the group, which you may have seen, since it has been on loan to the Loch Tornan Sculpture Gardens. A child appears to be trapped, like a fish frozen in ice . . ." She cleared her throat, trying not to think of the creatures that had been lured into it; the gold-and-apricot girl, a beautiful brown-skinned youth with bright blue eyes like lamps in the darkness . . . "It is a . . . a warning, but more than that, it's a lament. Although it says, 'Don't go, for you may never come out again,' it also acknowledges that we have no choice. The seed that struggles to burst from the tree hints at potential."

She led the party on to the second piece, several narrow, curvy forms evoking pairs of trees leaning together to form a series of arches. The effect was that of a tunnel that drew people through it. Indeed, it had drawn someone in, one night many years ago; a tall pale female whose appearance had frightened Juliana almost more than any other Aetherial. She touched the silk-smooth curve of the first arch and imagined she felt something move under her hand, a flashing energy as bright as a koi carp slipping under the surface of a pool.

"*Pathway* is the simple title of this structure. It speaks for itself, really. You could see it as the mouth of the womb or the tomb; it's the way into the forest and if you are to exist at all, you can't avoid it. Does it lead in or out? Both, of course."

The gathered guests were silent, but for the clicking of camera shutters.

"You will have understood," she said, moving on to the third sculpture, "that the forest is a metaphor. It's a pretty simplistic one, I admit, but I can only work in a way that makes sense to me. And what makes sense is the immensity of nature and of natural forms; that, and the mystery of life. Here, *So Little Time* shows two figures clasping each other—or are they being torn apart?"

There were two Aetherials within this one, she recalled. They'd been the least human-looking; sinuous, like a pair of pale golden leopards; so barely seen, she thought perhaps she'd imagined them. "And this leads us on to one I simply call *Harvest*. This took me the longest of all to complete."

It was an exuberant tangle of figures, trying to escape the medium that held them, their forms smooth and indistinct within the honey-gold marble she'd used. "*Harvest*, because they are the progeny of the union we see in *So Little Time*. There's a sort of joy in their struggle to break free." The Aetherial ensnared here, Juliana recalled, had been a creature of extraordinary beauty in shades of blue and green, a soft watery being who looked incapable of harm. It had been wrong to capture her, wrong to capture any of them. "However . . ."

She moved to the fifth piece, which had three stately dancers; or the same figure, caught in three poses. "Number five in the catalogue is entitled *Let Them Steal Away*. They accept their state. They have completed the dance of life and now they are ready to reenter the underworld. We have to let them go." She shivered, remembering the graceful male with long black ringlets, whose essence gave the piece its power. He had looked all too human; unusual, a bit dissolute, like a character from a Restoration play, but more man than elemental. "And so that brings us to *Return* . . ."

Another series of arches like the first, these were made from black marble, their forms low and squat with half-seen hints of faces and limbs swelling from their trunks. Anyone drawn to explore these would have to bend double to pass beneath them. "It's hard to say precisely what is going through my mind when I'm working because it's such a visceral, unconscious process, but I believe I was trying to capture a sense of going down into the earth, into the roots of the forest. And so the cycle is complete. We emerge from the forest and we go back in, because the forest never quite lets us go."

Her fingertips found a cold electric tingle in the marble. The Aetherial within *Return* seemed to inhabit every inch of it. She'd been a dark woman, Juliana recalled, covered head to foot in black silk chiffon, a veiled creature who had somehow been a black cat at the same time . . . Juliana shuddered, remembering. A black widow, a goddess of death.

With difficulty she steadied her voice and went on, "We are all trapped within our lives, within our flesh, the spirit screaming to break free. But it's . . ." She swallowed, thoughts of Leon and Adam and Corah and John Montague crowding in on her. "Deeper than that, it is really about the difficulty of knowing that others are trapped, and feeling powerless to save them. People can be imprisoned by circumstance or by their own attitude. Some you can help, but this is about the ones you can't. Betrayed loved ones. Missing children."

Charles was there, again, in her mind's eye; this time his smile had vanished and he looked grey. That was what it would always come back to between them, the horror of which they dared not speak; that he'd betrayed her, and produced a child with another woman, and that the child had died. That was why he wanted Cairndonan, she was sure. To bury the memory, the guilt.

"What inspired the title, *Midsummer Night*?" called out one of the journalists.

"Well, Shakespeare's play, *A Midsummer Night's Dream*," she answered. "Where does it take place? In a forest, a magical place where the boundaries between the worlds break down. Earth and Otherworld become one. And it's not always pretty, but it is overwhelming. The image of the human spirit trying to burst free from the primeval forest is about fear and survival." She opened her hands, a gesture to show the tour was over. "Anyway, I don't seek to explain the mystery. Only to show it."

The waves curled and foamed below. The air was delicious, heady with ozone, the salt smell of the sea blending with pine, gorse and heather. The sunlight dappled the mountainous coastline with incredible colors, purple and green and russet, ever-changing. No one would guess, from her confident demeanor, that inside she was shivering with fear and exhilaration. She knew she'd unleashed something uncontrollable in the form of *Midsummer Night* and that it was bound to take its revenge. At the same time she thought, *Even if this turns out to be my last night on Earth, I don't care. This has been the most wonderful day, the fulfillment of everything.*

"Haven't you missed one out?" called someone.

She turned, looking up at the graceful white limestone figure that stood at the center of the group. "Yes. Pardon me. This is number seven in the catalogue, *Winter Came to the Wood*. I don't know that I've ever tried to articulate its meaning. It's about death, of course, and that period in nature when everything in nature is frozen iron-hard beneath snow and ice, when everything, to all appearances, is dead. It stands at the center. But it's also about . . . coiled potential. It's terrifying. Yet there is beauty in it." She stopped, her throat becoming solid as the impassive orbs of the eyes stared down at her . . . Finding her voice again, she went on, "It's about midwinter, the nadir from which we begin to circle outwards again. Yes, it is about the spiral of life, death and rebirth. And that, to me, is all quite scary. Anyway, that is my interpretation, but you may make up your own minds. Feel free to see something entirely different in these works. Indeed, I hope you do. Now circulate, ask questions, enjoy."

And all bugger off by six o'clock, she thought dryly. By seven, she wanted everyone gone, gates locked, no witnesses—except the few she could trust—to what might befall when the spirits of *Midsummer Night* broke free.

———

Gill felt a glow of satisfaction, watching the enthusiasm of the guests who'd journeyed so far to see this, Juliana's evident pleasure in the event. For two hours she obliged every whim of the TV crews, standing wherever they wanted her, repeating her commentary several times over while they got just the right shot. Gill watched the critics and the collectors weaving in and out of *Midsummer Night*, consulting their catalogues, pausing to examine the forms from every angle. The grouped sculptures cast their ineffable spell. The sun traveled its long arc, casting ever-changing light and shadow. That was when Gill realized that Juliana had even considered what kind of shadow shapes her works would cast as the sun moved.

It was the most extraordinary day.

"How are you?" she asked Adam, finding him beside her as they began to clear up.

"This is a strange age, everyone constantly asking each other how they are. So solicitous for each other's welfare." He smiled, not looking at her, sable hair falling over his forehead as he pulled the cork from yet another bottle of wine. "In my day, our parents never asked us how we were!"

"Didn't they?" She lined up glasses, passing them out as fast as he could pour.

"No, we were just expected to get on with things. Endure school, join the army. Never mind how exhausted, bored, frozen or full of bullet holes you are—you must never complain."

"That seems a bit sad. That they didn't ask, I mean."

"Not really. It was a different age, apparently, but it seems like yesterday to me." He added softly, "It stood me in good stead in Boundry. Rufus and his companions never asked me how I was, either. When people ask me here, it's strange, that's all."

"Feels strange to be cared about, does it? I know the feeling, Adam. My mother never asked me, either; mind you, she was a cast-iron cow. And when I came out of hospital, the one thing I hated was people asking me if I was okay! So I'm sorry. I withdraw the question. I assume you are enduring your suffering with the customary stiff upper lip."

He gave a soft laugh. "Since you asked, I'm quite well," he said, briefly meeting her eyes. "If Rufus comes, so what? I'm not afraid of him."

Perhaps it was bravado—yet he said it as if he believed it.

Gradually the afternoon wound down. The television crews were long gone, the last of the visitors making their farewells as Juliana graciously endured their gushing praise and air-kisses. Peta, Gill and Adam moved around the tent, gathering dirty glasses and plates, tidying up.

Megan came to Juliana, flushed with excitement. "We have serious interest already," she began, but Juliana cut her off.

"Don't tell me now. We'll discuss it tomorrow."

"Of course. You must be bushed. A raging success, though?"

"Yes, it has been. Wonderful. Thank you so much, Megan, but I can't bring myself to think about figures just yet," said Juliana, pulling the scarf out of her hair and shaking it loose. "I'll leave the details to you. Call me."

With Megan thus dismissed—the last to leave—Gill said, "What you said about your work—that it's only the elementals inside that give it its power? It's not true. You don't need them. Your work speaks for itself."

Juliana's eyes became moist. "Thank you, Gill. I know it, but I . . . lost confidence, somewhere along the way. I needed to hear someone say it."

"What now, Dame J?" said Peta. "The viewing is over. Nothing has happened. Will you put *Midsummer Night* back into storage until a buyer is ready to take delivery of it, and make it someone else's problem?"

Juliana sighed. Gill saw anxiety in the tired lines around her eyes. "Now," she said, "I am going to spend the night among my sculptures, and take whatever comes."

"Really, Dame J, are you sure?" said Peta.

"Please, I've had the most interminable argument with Ned and Colin about this—don't you start. I finally got them to agree that Colin will watch the house and Ned will patrol the grounds while I—and my trusty friends, I hope—will watch the sculpture itself."

Gill tried to say something but Juliana interrupted. "What choice is there? If something happens here, I don't want to miss it. We're probably as safe among my statues as in bed. I wouldn't miss it for the world, in fact, and so I'm off to keep my vigil."

She walked out of the tent, a lone figure dwindling as she headed towards her strange stone forest. Peta and Gill looked at each other.

"Not on your own, you're not," said Gill as they hurried after her.

It was the longest day of the year; here in the northwest of Scotland, it seemed the light would last forever, changing and softening but never completely fading.

They sat leaning against *Pathway*, looking out at the sea as the sunset turned it to mirrored gold. They'd taken turns to go back to the house and change into warm, casual clothes: jeans, sweaters and boots. Juliana had set Colin and Ned to patrol the estate. They'd also brought a supper of cold leftovers and flasks of strong coffee, hot chocolate and brandy, wrapped themselves in duvets brought from the house. It would have been the most magical experience, Gill thought, like staying up all night to watch the stars while on a camping trip, if not for the unknown threat of the elementals trapped all around them. It was magical anyway, despite being unutterably frightening.

"Nothing was ever going to happen with all those people here, of course," said Juliana. "It's when night falls. That's the time. And this is the shortest night of the year."

"There is something around," Peta said uneasily, hugging herself. "I ought to be able to see it, but I can't. I can feel the Dusklands prickling my skin but I just can't *see* what's there."

"None of us are warriors. We're defenseless," said Gill.

"True," said Juliana. "But such things can't be defeated by physical violence in any case." She rose to her feet and raised her hands, like a sorceress reciting an incantation. "All of you bound within my stone circle, I release you now in exchange for the lost child, Leon. Go freely, but let the boy come home!"

Nothing happened.

Sighing, Juliana sat down. "Well, I have stated my *intention* that they leave. I don't know what more I can do."

"Intention is the thing that matters," Peta said softly.

So far north, with no light pollution from the ground, twilight lingered on indefinitely, brushing the sky violet. Stars appeared, shining in multiple layers, as thick and bright as those seen in the Spiral. Gill felt herself falling asleep, a delicious heaviness dragging her down . . .

"What shall we do to stay awake?" said Peta. "It's traditional to sing songs, isn't it?"

"I trust you are joking," Juliana responded.

Gill said, "Juliana, do you have Corah's letter on you? I'd like to see it."

Juliana breathed out, part groan and part sigh. "No. It's safe in my bedroom. Even if I had it, I don't think this is quite the moment to read it. We'll tease it all out later, dear, I promise. And whatever it says, I'll tell everyone. No more secrets, eh?"

"Even me?" said Peta.

Juliana laughed. "Of course. You're practically part of the furniture!"

Gill raised the camera and quickly framed a shot; the artist sitting beneath the sleek flank of her creation, other sculptures positioned like timeless monoliths behind her. It was a powerful image. Hoping there was still enough light, she took a photograph of her aunt in this reflective moment, then studied it on the small screen.

Gill caught her breath. All around Juliana were eerie, blurred lights, like figures half-sketched in fog. The stone forest was full of them. "Oh my god," she whispered. "Look at this . . ."

Before Juliana could respond, Peta uttered a soft exclamation, and Adam a shout of warning. Gill wasn't sure what happened next; heaviness pulled her down, like a giant invisible hand pushing her under water. It was like falling asleep with her eyes open. She could see but everything was dark and surreal; she couldn't move a fingertip.

A man with long, rippling dark hair was looking down at her.

Rufus.

Her head was tilted at an angle that enabled her to see her companions. She could just move her eyes, enough to observe that Peta and Juliana and Adam lay on the grass around her, paralyzed as she was, their eyes shining, white-ringed. The moment was nightmarish. The night glowed violet, brushed with stars, rippling like the ocean, serene and terrifying.

"Well, this is interesting," said Rufus. Shadow shapes of *dysir* moved around him, like silent sniffer dogs. "Lovely exhibition, Juliana. Sorry I couldn't be here sooner. I wanted a private viewing."

First out of *Midsummer Night* came his *dysir*. Gill saw their shadows flowing from the roots of each sculpture, silently circling Rufus as if they'd been waiting for his call. A hound-pack greeting their master.

Gill strained to speak, but couldn't. *Where is Theo?* She thought desperately. *Or even Colin . . .* but she suspected that he and Ned, wherever they were, also lay under Rufus's heavy spell. She wanted to shift closer to Adam, to protect him, but her body lay snug to the ground as if made of lead.

"I tried to stay away, but I can't resist the lure of art."

Rufus bent down to Adam, put his hands on either side of Adam's face and kissed him on the mouth. "Now, are you ready to come home, my Leith?"

Gill saw Adam's breathing quicken. No sound came out of him but his eyes shone in the semidarkness with wild denial. Perhaps it was all part of the nightmare but it seemed to her that the sculptures themselves were moving, stone turning pliable, swelling, heaving as if struggling to give birth.

"Well, we'll see." Rufus stroked Adam's cheek and straightened up. He smiled but his eyes held a hard glitter. "So, they're all here, are they? All my missing friends, trapped in the matter of your creations? My god, Juliana, however did you do this? There's something more than human in you, isn't there? You're some kind of evil genius, to lure my friends inside your works of art and make them part of it. The Spiral always inspires great art, among those humans who have the eyes to see it. It tends to play havoc with the sanity, of course. Mad genius."

He wandered into the circle and began to move from one sculpture to the next. At each, he would stop and touch the surface, tracing the contours as if caressing a lover, looking over every inch, tilting his head as if listening. Gill saw the way Juliana watched him; her eyes flickering in her frozen face.

Pain began to throb through Gill's body from being unable to shift position. Flashbacks to the hospital, anaesthetic, Peta's mask lying wet and hot over her face . . . panic flooded her but there was nothing she could do to resist it. Rufus was the *Dunkelman*, thousands of years old . . . his power over them as casual as it was complete. *Dysir* sniffed around her; they were only shadows, but their breath smelled of smoke and she felt the hot kiss of their tongues.

Reality wavered. Gill saw the shimmer of another form around Peta and realized she was trying to escape by changing. Rufus glanced at her and shook his head. The crimson aura faded, and Peta still lay paralyzed.

"I can sense them inside," he said as he went from one group to the next. There was a catch in his voice. "Trying to guess who is in each . . . I think I understand now. You only held power over your creation while it was inside your workshop, the intersection of realms. Now you've brought them outside, your hold is broken. *Midsummer Night* is losing its power. That was a hellish risk to take, Dame Juliana. Alas, it didn't pay off."

A faint grunt came from Juliana. He turned his gaze on her, blue twilight highlighting all the cruel angular beauty of his face. "Do you have the power to release them? No. I always knew they would not escape until I called them myself. That's why I'm here."

He went to the nearest arch of *Pathway*, stood with his hands resting on it. Something stirred inside the fine-grained stone; Gill saw a faint golden light moving. Rufus whispered, "Copernica?"

The light seemed to focus under his hands and hang there, pulsing. He moved on, stroking *Go Not into the Forest* as he passed, frowning slightly. "Sylvynus?" Then to *So Little Time*, where he touched and jerked away as if with a static shock. He gasped, "Idro, Idrina."

Rufus was like a sleepwalker in a trance now. He went from *Harvest* to *Let Them Steal Away* whispering, "Vivienne? Nicolas? Oh, you old bastard, is it you?" and at the linked arches of *Return*, "Sweet Lady of Stars! Ekaterina?"

When Gill saw Rufus's face again, he was weeping. Tears streamed down his face and his mouth was open, uttering soundless sobs. He passed out of her sight as he moved towards *Winter Came to the Wood*, but she heard his voice, very faintly, "Nothing inside you, is there? Or something so cold and old, it's not sentient anymore."

Gill saw elusive shapes moving within each sculpture, pulsing with the rhythm of waves beating upon a rock. Solid stone writhed like living flesh, groaning . . . the air stirred into a slow whirlwind. A terrible noise grew, like some wounded monster groaning at a very great distance . . . the sound coming closer . . .

And then there was a mass of writhing light and shadow, amorphous energies, birthing themselves from the cold stone of their prisons. They

groaned with mindless, massed anguish, a noise that turned Gill's blood
to ice.

Juliana rose suddenly to her knees with a gasp. She found her feet, leaning against *Pathway* for support. Gill felt her own body burning with pins
and needles. Adam's hand suddenly grabbed her arm, making her cry out
with pain and shock.

The writhing mass was like a great swaying ball of fireflies. It was all
around them; Gill could see nothing but dancing light and shade and her
ears rang with its hideous moaning. Corporeal figures formed briefly, dispersed, reformed; A tall pale woman with red-gold hair, a pair of twins as
sinuous as lynxes, a veiled woman who seemed cut from the night, a pale
man with sleepy sardonic eyes and ebony ringlets, a blue-green water
nymph—Rufus stood with outstretched arms as they converged on him.

She wondered, through her daze, if they were glad to see him or ready
to kill him; if they even still knew who he was.

Triumphantly he greeted them as they went into his arms. "Copernica.
Sylvynus. Idro, Idrina. Ekaterina, Nicolas—you rogue—Vivienne—it's
been so, so long, but you are free again. I came for you."

They all looked feral, beautiful and mad, with staring eyes. They em-
braced Rufus and he hugged and stroked them, eyes spilling tears. Gill
managed to crawl a few inches towards Adam and they held each other,
silent and trembling like frightened children. There were others, too, insubstantial specters and *dysir*—but only these seven were strongly visible.

The pale, amber-haired woman, Copernica, turned slowly and pointed
at Juliana, who stood pressed against the stone flank of her work as if she
could barely stand. She spoke, her voice ghostly and raw, like the creak of
a rusted gate. "I know her. She is the one who imprisoned us. Chained us
like beasts in a cage."

"It's true, but she barely knew what she was doing," said Rufus, staring
levelly at Juliana. "Go gently on her."

"But she trapped us—sacred Aetherials, whose freedom is sacrosanct!
It's blasphemy."

"A grave crime," said the heavy-eyed man with black ringlets. "She should
die."

"Take her to Boundry." The voice emanated from the veiled woman,
Ekaterina. "Flay her."

"Take her hands, so she may not work anymore," said one of the lynx-
twins.

"Let her be crushed beneath her own great stones," said Copernica.
"That would be justice."

Gill saw Peta climbing unsteadily to her feet, her crimson Otherworld form shimmering weakly around her. She put herself in front of Juliana, saying fiercely, "Lay a finger on her and you'll all regret it."

Rufus laughed. "As you see, they are not happy." His tone was silky, but deathly serious. "They want revenge."

Juliana raised her chin, resting her head back against the stone. Her voice was rough. "Do what you will, then. The truth is, I acted in revenge for you taking Adam, and a small child named Leon, and others who vanished and came back insane. However, it seems it's one law for you and another for us. I was only protecting my domain. If you want a cycle of vengeance forever more—fine. Take me. There's nothing we can do to stop you, but don't hurt anyone else."

"Please, my friends, be merciful," said Rufus.

His followers ignored him. Flowing in an amorphous mass, they seized both Peta and Juliana, seeming almost to swallow them. Gill cried, "No!" Juliana stood unresisting between them, but Gill saw the suppressed terror in her face. Specters and *dysir* wove a mesmerizing dance around them.

"Leith," said Rufus, his gaze swiveling. "How much do you care for Juliana and your other new friends? I might persuade them to forgo revenge, if you will give up your ridiculous tantrum and come home."

Gill felt Adam stiffen. He sat upright, but she could still barely move. Peta called out, "I don't think they're listening to you, Rufus!"

"No," Juliana added. "Leith, don't even think about it."

And then the air above *Midsummer Night* shimmered, blurred, exploded with scores of white shapes.

Theodorus appeared with a host of Lashtorians, at least fifty of them, all white and grey and silver, bursting from the Dusklands to surround Rufus and his dazed followers. Rufus's chaotic power seemed to be instantly overwhelmed by the organized forces of Lashtor. What followed was a minor riot; dazed Aetherials lashing and clawing like cornered wild cats, the Lashtorian force piling in to subdue them. Gill saw a flurry of muscular wings, of short batons flashing white and silver.

Gill tried to rise, only to be shoved down again. The impact pushed all the breath out of her. Pain speared her thigh. Normal feeling returned to her body, followed by indignation and anger. One of the Lashtorians held her pinioned. Her hands were caught painfully behind her back and she was hauled upright—emitting an involuntary cry as the movement tugged her hip at a painful angle.

Nearby, Juliana, Peta and Adam were already being held by Theo's men and hustled to one side away from the chaos. All looked bewildered. As Gill was manhandled towards them, Theo turned. He was only a few feet from her and she caught his eye.

"Not us!" she cried. "What are you doing?"

She expected him to shout to his comrades that they were arresting the wrong people. Instead, he shook his head and said brusquely, "It's to keep you from harm's way. You agreed to come with us as witnesses. Cooperate as I asked and you won't be harmed."

Juliana pulled against her captor, who gave her arms a warning jerk. "Hey!" Gill shouted. "Be careful with my aunt. Can't you see she's—" Gill wasn't sure what word to use; "elderly" or "past her prime" sounded inappropriate, if not downright disrespectful. Juliana was not *old*, but she was of an age that demanded respect and dignity. Gill only meant to remind Theo of that—but Juliana silenced her with a glare.

"Don't you dare, Gill. We are cooperating, Theo, but your comrades seem a little . . . overzealous."

"I ask your patience," Theo said unrepentantly, turning away.

"Don't struggle," added a voice in Gill's ear from the slender Aelyr who was holding her. She recognized him from Lashtor; it was Fleorn, the one she'd talked to in the kitchen cave. "You're safe. Just go quietly with us."

"We get the message," said Peta.

In the center of *Midsummer Night*, the struggle was subsiding. Rufus's comrades were each held firm between two Lashtorians. It took six or more to hold Rufus himself. The captives were hauled to their feet, pushed into a straggling line, all of their strange, not-quite-human faces set with bewildered anger beneath tangles of hair.

As they were marched past the spot where Gill and the others stood, the only one to spare a glance for Juliana's group was Rufus himself. As he stumbled along in the grip of several tall Lashtorians, he turned his head and gave a horrible, furious smile.

It was a look of defiance Gill would have expected, yet still it turned her cold. Around them, the sculptures of *Midsummer Night* stood sentinel, devoid of life yet still disturbingly watchful. And in the center, the figure of *Winter Came to the Wood* stood as luminous and cold as snow, as if its spirit slumbered inside it like the earth itself waiting for spring.

"They're taking us towards the foundry," said Peta as they crossed the cliff tops. "Towards the Naamon portal."

19

Queen of Fire

They made an extraordinary sight; a mass of semi-lucent figures flowing along the paths towards the cliffs, like a host of angels from a medieval painting. It was a faerie procession such as John Montague could only have dreamed of capturing on film.

They crossed a corner of the garden, joining the natural ridge of rock beneath which, Gill realized, the service tunnel ran from the house to the foundry's secret door. Where they joined the ridge, there stood a small chunk of stone like a milestone. It had been unremarkable in daylight, but now she saw that it glowed blue and was carved with serpent designs. Somehow she knew that it was a marker, a place to join the *conlineos* that led to Naamon.

We're in the Dusklands, Gill realized. If only for one night, she was seeing everything with Aetherial eyes. *The serpent is a creature that slides in and out of the underworld with ease.*

Rufus and his seven cohorts were taken in the lead, with Juliana, Peta, Gill, and Adam following, each of them being marched along in the grip of a Lashtorian. More of Theo's comrades flowed on either side of the column, guarding it. The *dysir* and other spectral energies drifted with them as if drawn in a strong current, but the Lashtorians seemed concerned only with Rufus and his seven friends; the ringleaders. Gill now recognized some faces from Sibeyla. Berenis's touch on her was gentle, but Peta—held fast by Fleorn—was struggling.

"You're not supposed to be arresting *us*," she said indignantly.

"We're not," called Berenis. "Fleorn, be gentle. They're coming with us as witnesses, not prisoners."

"Are we?" said Peta. She shook her hands as Fleorn released her wrists, placing a shepherding hand on her back instead. "So why do I get the impression that if I made a break for it, I wouldn't get very far?"

"Do stop arguing and just go along with them," Juliana said tartly from in front of her. "We consented to this."

"I know, but I wasn't expecting us to be carted off like suspects! I'm wondering what we've let ourselves in for, by making this agreement with Mark. Theo, I mean."

"I really don't know," said Juliana. "He assured me that, as long as we went along and answered questions, he would protect me from any consequences regarding the creation of *Midsummer Night*. We have to trust him."

"And I would, if I still knew who he was," said Peta. "The Lashtorians must have been concealed in the Dusklands, waiting for their moment. So well hidden that I never sensed a thing!"

Fleorn remarked, "It's said that living on Earth deadens Vaethyr senses. Evidently it's true."

"Can't you be content with wrongful arrest," she retorted, "without insulting me into the bargain?"

Gill stayed quiet, letting Peta do the protesting. Ahead, she could hear Rufus's companions arguing with their captors, demanding to know what was happening; it didn't sound as if they were given any answers. When she stumbled on the uneven path, uttering a grunt of pain as she jarred her hip, Berenis steadied her and spoke in a low voice over her shoulder. "I'm sorry. This situation displeases me as much as it does you. Please bear with us awhile; it will soon be over."

"Where are you taking us?" asked Adam behind her. His voice was calm, if slightly shaky.

"Not far," said Berenis as they came to a small door that brought them into the tunnel's end and the trapdoor. "You will see."

Inside the foundry, the space that had held *Midsummer Night* was empty now. There were no walls or ceiling to be seen, only a black, misty cavern, backlit by the red glow of Naamon.

A thrill of alarm passed through Gill. She remembered what lay beyond, so vividly that she could sense it, taste it; the steep treacherous slopes, shifting plates of rock riddled with streams of magma. She recalled Peta and Juliana trapped on the ledge, the horror of their fall, Theodorus lying insensible . . . fear rose inside her.

It was Adam she was most worried about. Hadn't he suffered enough at the hands of Aetherials without going through this, too? Theodorus was at the head of the column with Rufus and the others, so she couldn't even speak to him.

Peta said, "I should warn you, the Naamon side of the portal is falling to pieces. It's dangerous."

"We know," said Berenis.

"You need to watch your step, because if anyone falls off the downhill side, it's a hellish long way down."

"We know," he repeated. "We will not let you fall."

"Are you taking us all the way to Asru?"

"No. You'll see, soon enough."

There was a pause as the group bunched in the mouth of the portal. Gill turned dizzy as the atmosphere changed, hitting them like a hot wind. Her eyes stung with sulfur and smoke as she saw the long black tilt of Mount Khafet framed in the doorway, the sky red above it. Theo's comrades were silhouetted against the glow. Then they began to move again, slowly now as Lashtorians stood ready to help each prisoner in turn to climb from the broken step onto the uphill side of the flank. Gill heard her aunt breathing heavily, gasping a little despite steadying hands. Gill's own heart filled her throat as she stepped off the broken step and felt loose rock sliding beneath her boots. Berenis held her firm. They were outside the soot-dark gatehouse in the realm of Naamon. No one fell. Juliana shook her head and brushed down her skirts, as if to show she'd not been nervous in the slightest.

"Everyone all right?" she asked softly. "Good."

The procession began to snake its way upwards, with jet-black rock underfoot, the huge basalt sweep of the dormant cone above them and the branching yellow-hot seams of lava flowing below. Another realm. The Spiral!

The acrid air made Gill cough as they climbed. Her hip protested, but she could bear it as long as they kept moving. Some twenty minutes later, they crested a rise and she saw the vast ruined bulk of the citadel above them; the edifice that she had first seen with Theodorus. It had looked impressive enough from the air; from the ground, it was monumental. It appeared desolate and forbidding, like a gigantic charred skull that had crashed to earth and fossilised beneath the caldera of the summit.

Peta whistled. Juliana said, "What is that?"

None of the Lashtorians answered her. Gill spoke, her voice croaky. "Theo and I saw it from above. It's a fortress, a citadel almost. Some queen . . ."

"It's extraordinary." Juliana paused to cough. "The scale of it! Oh, goodness, it puts anything I've ever tried to create firmly in proportion. It's as much sculpture as architecture."

"We couldn't see anything inside," said Gill. "It looked like a shell."

The crooked ridge brought them towards the edifice, its great bulk towering higher with every step they took. They processed through a vast open gateway and between a series of great walls, stumbling on shale as they ascended from one terraced level to the next. At last they crossed a huge courtyard—the host of Lashtorians snowy against the dark rock—and entered the stronghold proper.

They passed through a series of cavernous rooms with soaring pillars, walls pierced by windows like rounded, red-glowing eyes. Gill noticed symbols carved around the pillars and, in her heightened state, she felt that she understood their message. The symbols spoke of the dance of the fire of creation, about power, a great ruler controlling all the realms as the head controls the branching body . . . a primal, twinned being of fire and darkness . . . she couldn't put any of it into words, but the message left her awestruck.

By now, she was thirsty and sweaty, her clothes abrading her skin. The trek ended as Theodorus brought everyone all into a circular space somewhat like a temple. It was a well of darkness, illuminated by a faint red blush filtering through four high embrasures.

Here the column broke up into a milling mass. Theodorus departed, taking some of the Lashtorians with him, leaving the rest to stand guard. Rufus and his fellow prisoners were herded away from Juliana's group so that they were standing apart, yet close enough to exchange words if they raised their voices. Gill glanced across at the watchful, feral faces of Rufus's companions, their shining eyes. Adam stared too. There was no emotion in his face. It disturbed her to see his expression so blank and numb, as if he were facing a firing squad.

"What's happening?" she whispered.

"Theodorus has gone to meet Vaidre Daima and other representatives of the Spiral Court," Berenis answered. "Until he comes back, we wait."

The Aetherials stared icily at the humans, no kindness in their expressions. They were like cats in their mixture of appealing beauty and utter disdain. Their eyes chilled her.

Rufus himself looked the least alien of them. His eyes were dark, narrow, on fire with silent fury. The Lashtorians were pale flames in the gloom, while Rufus and his seven friends were dim yet colorful jewels.

"Do you recognize them?" Peta said softly to Adam.

He nodded, but didn't elaborate. Gill tried to recall how Rufus had addressed them. The tall, shapely woman with sunset-colored hair was Copernica. Idro and Idrina stood entwined like a pair of sinuous lynxes; even the Lashtorians had been unable to separate them physically. The heavy-eyed man with curly black hair, who looked like some dissolute eighteenth-century rake . . . that was Nicolas. The small dusky-skinned woman, Ekaterina, hard to see in the gloom since she was all in black . . . there was something gentle yet intensely disturbing about her, as if she were a midwife who came to ease you into death rather than birth. The beautiful young man with bright blue eyes, his skin as brown as an oak tree, what was his name? Sylvynus, that was it. He stood arm-in-arm with the undine woman, Vivienne. She had the look of a medieval portrait: a serene oval face, a long twist of brown hair over one shoulder. Seen from the corner of the eye, though, her whole form had a blue-green shimmer like the scales of a phantom fish . . . a mermaid or an undine. Vivienne of Melusiel, the realm of water.

Recalling the notes and sketches she'd found in Boundry—Rufus's joking plea for Copernica to leave Adam alone—Gill couldn't help imagining Adam naked with her, both loving and hating it, twisted by guilt . . . She felt a stab of protective anger. Jealousy, almost. These creatures had tormented Adam for decades and haunted him to the edge of insanity, all too willing to aid Rufus's dark designs.

It was hard to take in. She slid a protective hand through Adam's arm and put herself slightly in front, making herself his shield. She couldn't begin to guess what he felt. His arm against hers felt heavy and lifeless and his face stayed blank.

Copernica spoke, her voice low and rich. "I see that *he* is still the focus of your existence, Rufus." She glared at Adam with a slight smile on her mouth. The smile was not affectionate.

"Yes, and always will be," Rufus answered, pushing long skeins of hair out of his eyes. His perfect face was gaunt, gouged by shadows.

"So it's his fault we've come to this!" said Nicolas. "I always said Leith would betray you. Human, how could he help it? He led this mob of inquisitors to us, didn't he?"

"Quiet," said one of the Lashtorians. They ignored the command.

"He's been unwell," said Rufus. "It isn't possible to remake him without first breaking him. I think he realizes how foolish he's been." He spoke with soft menace, looking across at Adam.

"We must punish him," said Vivienne.

Adam retaliated, his voice hoarse. "Punish me, how? Have you anything left? What more can you do?"

Rufus's unblinking stare didn't waver. "You would be surprised—but it changes nothing. You will come back to me, Leith."

"Never."

"I'll make a wager with anyone that you'll come back of your own free will. You are bonded to me, Leith, my Mistangamesh, and you know it."

Copernica hissed, "Still an idiot, Rufus!"

His eyes flashed with anger. "You abandoned me, Copernica, sweetheart. You poisoned the others against me, and one by one you lured them all away. You all deserted me, so don't presume to tell me whom I may or may not love."

"And it's because of Leith that we left! You cared nothing for us. You lost your mind to your fixation with that *boy*," she soaked the word with contempt, "that mere human boy. You left us all scattered by the wayside.

Losing your heart, we forgive, but to utterly lose your wits . . . *that* was what we found unbearable, don't you understand?"

"So you all flounced out in a huff to make a point?"

"What was the point of staying? We knew no other way to make you *see*. We couldn't bear to watch you in the grip of this obsession."

The whites showed around his irises. "You may be right, but you know why Leith obsesses me. You know who he is!"

She hissed in derision. "Has anything changed? Has he awoken? It doesn't look so to me. He's still lovely to look at, I'll admit, but as human and as vacant as ever. An empty vessel, still."

"Refilling the vessel was bound to be a long and difficult process."

"But this difficult? All your years of devotion, and all he does is run away and betray you? When will you accept it? There is no vessel to refill! *He is not your brother.*"

All seven of them began talking at once, a tide of emotion directed at Rufus, Vivienne and Sylvynus clinging to him, Copenica's voice rising above the others until one of the guards snapped, "*Quiet!*"

"Think what you like," Rufus retorted as they subsided. "Have I lived all these thousands of years to give up after a mere century? I will never give up. And you have always known that, so why expect less of me? I thought you were loyal and would support me through anything. I was wrong! I despise your decision to walk out."

Nicolas said, "And where were you when we were lured into the stone forest? Did you try to free us? No. You cared only for Leith."

"You abandoned me, dear friend. If you became ensnared, it was your own fault. As things fell out, I couldn't come after you, since all the portals to Boundry were sealed for fourteen years. You were trapped, I was trapped. You left out of jealousy? How utterly childlike. How unworthy of semi-mortals. You should have understood that Leith's presence did not make me love you any the less."

Copernica laughed. "If you ever loved us."

"We know you only ever used us," said Vivienne. Despite her surly words, her eyes were liquid with adoration. "Yet we were happy to be used. I'm sure we would be again. But your fixation upon Leith changed you, Rufus. Don't you know that it broke our hearts?"

"We went *gladly* to slumber in the stone forest." It was Ekaterina who spoke, her voice quiet and velvet-rich. "We welcomed sleep as if it were death."

"Dear Lady of Stars, what drama!" Rufus exclaimed. "Don't you realize that we're about to be tried before the Spiral Court itself on who-knows-what spurious charges? Not me alone, but all of us! What will you do—testify against me, or stand with me?"

"Why should we stand with you?" Copernica lashed back. "We could denounce you for crimes of which the Spiral Court has not the faintest idea!"

"And why would you do that?"

"To punish you for loving Leith too much, and the rest of us too little."

Rufus folded his arms. His mouth twisted. "Have you grown to hate me so much that you will see me cast into the Abyss? Because I tell you now, if you denounce me, you denounce yourselves." His eyes were dark, full of pain and passion, so intense they might have melted a hole in the rock wall. Gill saw the hold he had over his followers, as powerful as it was effortless. She understood why Adam feared him. "You were complicit. You hid me. You joined me in every adventure. If you testify against me, you testify against yourselves, and we will all fall together."

Copernica blanched. They all stared, as if it had only just begun to sink in that they were in dire trouble. Even the strange twins, Idro and Idrina, looked fearful. These were not gullible mortals but seven charismatic Aetherials, all as strong and merciless as cobras, whose powers were unguessed—all of them in thrall to Rufus, regardless of how bitterly he'd wronged them.

"What charges?" asked Nicolas. "What will they accuse us of?"

"Oh, what will they *not* accuse us of?" Copernica exclaimed, shaking back her sunset fall of hair.

"Think on it," Rufus said thinly. "My only crime against you, my dear friends and lovers, is my steadfast belief that Leith there is my brother. You would revile me for being steadfast? I know you're so angry with me, *only* because you still love me. If you'd ceased to love me during your forest slumber, why would you care? Yet you do."

He folded himself against Copernica, who was nearest to him, and kissed her. Stiffly, she accepted the embrace. Then Rufus looked at his flock with the same raw emotion that Gill had seen in him when he pleaded to know Adam's whereabouts. It looked authentic, irresistible.

"Come, we knew the moment of reckoning would arrive. We've been fugitives from justice for three hundred years. We should be grateful that we've deferred it for so long, and had so very much fun in the meantime. Isn't that worth a word in my favor?" He looked at each of them in turn, his expression a warm and imploring half-smile. Tears glistened in his eyes. "If we defend each other, the Court might prove merciful."

This time, no one argued. They were silent, subdued. Rufus smiled.

"Of course we love you, Rufus," said Vivienne. "That is given." She leaned forward in her captor's grasp and kissed Rufus lingeringly on the mouth. "We would all follow you into the Abyss—and you know it."

Their conversation continued, but that was the turning-point. Gill saw that they were reconciled, comfortably under Rufus's spell again. He'd won them over without apparent effort because he seemed so genuine. After all, thought Gill, even the most monstrous people could inspire love, and even give it back.

And was Rufus a monster, or simply amoral? Was there a difference?

The Lashtorian escorts—standing with the patient dignity of monks—let the human party lean against a wall while they waited. Gill was aware of being thirsty, tired, gritty and hot. She ached all over. She raised her eyes to meet those of Peta and Juliana. They all exchanged grim smiles, even Adam, to affirm that they were bearing up.

"Where are we?" asked Juliana, after a while. "Is this the Spiral Court?"

"No," said Peta. "That's said to be in Asru, the realm of ether, at the very heart of the Spiral, where we go only . . . only in the most dire straits. I don't know what this is. Some incredibly ancient ruin."

Rufus, hearing her, raised his head and answered, "It was the stronghold of Queen Malikala."

Peta frowned. "Are you sure?"

Gill remembered Theo's words, as they had flown through smoke and mist with the fortress tilting below them. "That was the name. Malikala."

"Yes, I am sure," said Rufus. "Many thousands of years have passed since her demise, so of course it has fallen into ruin, scoured by volcanic fires and shaken by earthquakes. But remember, I saw it in its glory days."

The trace of a smile lingered on his face. Peta pursed her lips. "So you say, Rufus."

"You can believe me or not, darling. It's true, I witnessed the dominion of Naamon over all the other realms. I saw her in the flesh, the magnificent Malikala, who was as black as this rock, with hair and eyes of living flame. I bore witness to her defeat by the wondrous Queen Jeleel when she diverted the waters of Melusiel to flood Naamon."

"We all know that story," said Peta. "Anyone could claim that."

"Well, it doesn't matter if I was there or not. This ruin was Queen Malikala's palace, long abandoned and lost, but still a place of power." He turned his face up to the ceiling and murmured, as if speaking poetry, "*O Maliket of Fire . . .*"

"Ah," Peta said thoughtfully. "It's true, then—the *conlineos* across Cairndonan estate was a shortcut, from the heart of Sibeyla to Queen Malikala's doorstep?"

"Exactly," said Rufus. "A ceremonial route. It must have been busy, long before humans inhabited the Highlands. After Malikala was defeated, and Mount Khafet woke up, it fell into ruin and disuse, of course."

"How long ago?" Gill put in.

"Oh, before mankind appeared, or when only their rude ancestors were grunting their way across the steppes."

Her jaw dropped. "But if you're that old . . ."

"I'm not old," said Rufus. "If you don't age, you can't grow old."

"Or ever learn any sense, apparently," muttered Juliana.

"If you're still here," Gill persisted, "why isn't Malikala?"

"But she is." Rufus fixed her with a dark stare that sent electric currents through her. "All around us. In the walls, in the rock of Mount Khafet beneath our feet, and most of all in the fires of the volcano. Can't you feel her?"

In the trembling silence, they all felt her. The great walls around them, the hot shifting rock beneath, all was sentient. The red embrasures were her multiple eyes. The stirring air, pungent with heat and sulfur, was the ancient queen's breath . . .

Peta laughed nervously. "I bet you tell a marvelous ghost story."

"I'm only speaking the truth." Rufus's voice was a soft hiss. "I am still here because it's my curse. I have never died, never kissed the mirror pool, never slumbered away the centuries in a sacred tree or a borrowed body, never been reborn. I have never had a rest."

Peta hugged herself, fingers tapping at her upper arms. "By choice?"

He laughed. "Yes. By choice."

"Why?"

"Because I can't abide idleness." His grin widened. "Because I didn't want to miss anything."

There was movement in the doorway to the chamber. Theodorus swept in, a handful of Lashtorians with him. "You'll have a chance to rest soon, Ephenaestus," he said. "You'll have eternity."

His comrades flowed into the room, joining the guards already there to usher the prisoners out of the chamber. Rufus flung back his head defiantly as they laid hands on him, his hair flowing gloriously around his shoulders. His face was a rictus of indignation. Gill realized that, for all his bravado, he was terrified.

Whatever his alleged crimes, he was a vivid presence and it was disturbing to think of him brought low, imprisoned and punished. But that was how he deceived people, with his beauty and passion. She felt Adam's fingers pressing between her elbow and rib cage. She remembered how Rufus had abused him, and hardened her heart.

Copernica and the rest were marched out in Rufus's wake. Then Gill and her three companions were alone, with just a handful of guards in the doorway.

"What will they do with him?" she asked quietly. "What sort of punishment would the Spiral Court impose? Death sentence?"

Adam flinched. Peta said, "Possibly."

"What would be the point of that, if Rufus can't truly die?"

"Well, we can, in a sense. It would sever *this* existence," Peta looked uncomfortable. "Rufus's essence would carry on and recreate itself, in time . . . Perhaps he'd be reborn, cleansed and innocent. Or . . ."

"What?"

"Gill, I've only lived this one short humanish life so far. I don't know what lies beyond." She gave an apologetic grin. "I'm actually quite scared by the thought."

"Join the club," said Juliana.

"Or what?" Gill persisted.

"As Rufus himself said, they might sentence him to be thrown into the Abyss." Peta's shoulders rose. "We return to the Source, which means dissolution. That, so I understand, is rather final."

"And that's why he's afraid," whispered Gill.

A short time later, Theodorus returned, now in his winged Otherworld form. He brought Vaidre Daima with him, and two new faces. One was a tall male of striking looks, his hair and skin and feathered cloak as white as swan's wings. His face looked as if it had been carved from ivory, with astonishing, high cheekbones. The only color about him lay in his eyes and a jewel on his forehead, forming a triangle of bright cobalt blue.

"Dame Juliana, Peta, Adam, this is Vaidre Daima—Gill has met him before—who will be presiding over the hearing." Vaidre Daima, a large, shadowy presence, greeted them somberly. "This is Albin of Sibeyla," Theo indicated the swan-white Aelyr, "who will present the charges against Rufus. And this is Earta, who has been nominated to present the Court's judgment."

Earta was so darkly translucent that Gill could see right through her. There were hints of peacock colors outlining a tall female shape, nothing more. It was a disconcerting feeling.

Juliana said, "So you are the judge, Albin represents the prosecution and Earta is the foreman of the jury?"

"In an extremely loose sense, if it helps you to view it like that," said Vaidre Daima. His tone was friendly. "We wanted a quiet word with you before the hearing begins, just to acquaint ourselves with what's happened to you. Don't expect a trial as you would have on Vaeth. We have our own procedures. It is important you understand that you are not witnesses for the prosecution, as such. You will be making simple statements of fact."

"But everything you can tell us of Rufus will help, however trivial," Albin added. Glimmering with his own light, he was the coldest, least human creature Gill had ever seen, a statue carved from limestone and brought to life, given bright blue gems in place of eyes.

Peta said, "But are you taking us to the Spiral Court itself? To Asru? Mark—sorry, Theo—what's happening?"

"I apologize for the confusion," said Vaidre Daima. "Theodorus had no opportunity to tell you. Yes, the Spiral Court's home lies at the heart of Asru, but the title refers to the body of elders who convene there, not the place itself. The nominated of the Court have traveled here to Malikala's stronghold for the hearing. A great audience chamber is being prepared as we speak."

Adam asked, "Where have you taken Rufus?"

"He and his accomplices are being held in a separate chamber," answered Theo. "You've nothing to fear now, because they won't be allowed near you again. You'll see them once more at the trial, and after that—never again."

"What's going to happen?" asked Gill.

"All we ask is that you give a plain, accurate description of your encounters with Rufus," said Vaidre Daima.

She winced. "All of them?"

"Yes. Tell the truth, and all will be well."

"And then we can go home?"

"Yes," said Vaidre Daima. "Then you can go home."

They endured patiently as Albin and Vaidre Daima asked questions. Adam stumbled over his words, head drooping in shame as he told the story that he'd told Gill. She felt herself turn hot as she was forced to admit how she'd let Rufus seduce her, and what he'd done afterwards. Juliana spoke in clipped tones, describing the events of 1919 that had torn the Montague family apart; the rumored disappearances of other humans over the years. She told the plain facts of Rufus's harassment of Adam, his attempted invasion of her house, the fight with Theo and his attack on them at *Midsummer Night*.

Peta said, "I haven't much to add. Rufus didn't really get a chance to start on me; he was all smiles and charm. Perhaps he meant to get me on his side, as if to say, *We're Aetherials together.*"

"And did he get you on his side?" asked Albin, his gaze as quick and piercing as a hawk's.

"No! Not at all. Maybe he meant to divide me from my friends—but he couldn't. I've witnessed most of what they've told you. I can vouch for the truth of it."

"Good," said Vaidre Daima. "Don't be afraid. You are not on trial, your words will not be twisted against you. All you need to do is present the plain facts."

"In any case, their statements are but a drop in the ocean of evidence that stands against Rufus," Albin stated.

Gill thought despairingly, *It's going to be a long day.*

20

The Spiral Court

Lamps lit their way, each one casting a small pool of light that dazzled their dilated eyes and rendered the darkness beyond even more profound. Perhaps Aetherials could see perfectly in these conditions, but Gill was struggling. They were brought into the audience chamber, a huge space with great vaults and arches like a cathedral built of jet-black basalt. She could well imagine an ancient queen holding court here, but now it felt unutterably desolate, abandoned.

Everything seemed designed to overwhelm.

Lamps of blue glass had been hung from each pillar, and placed in a half-circle on the opposite side of a sunken central area. The light was cold and eerie, bright enough to obscure what lay behind. Squinting, Gill made out rows of tiered seating, like stone benches curving around an amphitheater—the sort of place spectators might sit to look down at the arena below. An audience, members of a senate, or a judge and jury . . . All was thick black shadow behind the semicircle of blue lamps, but she saw figures moving up there.

She felt fingertips digging into her arm. Peta's eyes were bright, holding tiny lamps in miniature. "The Spiral Court," she whispered. "They're here!"

Berenis brought them to sit on a low bench at the rear of the chamber, just on the lip of the sunken area. Gill had Peta on her left, Adam on her right with Juliana on his right. Across the arena, they faced the barely seen court. The bench was rough and cold to the touch; if ever it had been topped with a polished wooden seat, such furniture was long gone. Berenis, Fleorn and other Lashtorians stood behind them and all around the sides, clearly visible in their white garments—in contrast to the unseen members of the Spiral Court.

To their right, Rufus and his seven followers stood in a curved row, closely guarded by Theodorus and his comrades. Accused criminals in the dock, thought Gill. She felt exposed, vulnerable. It was as if they were in the spotlights while their interrogators hid in the shadows.

Peta had told her something of the Spiral Court, not least that it was a mystery, even to most Aetherials. It was not a fixed body; its members shifted and changed all the time. They might serve for a few years, or only a few months, as time was measured on Earth. They were called to service, rather like a jury, from the ranks of the oldest Aetherials still in corporeal form. When Gill had asked how they were summoned, Peta was vague. "I'm not sure of the process," she'd answered, "but it's said that the oldest Aetherials of all, ancients who have dispersed into the fabric of the Spiral itself, summon them. The constant flux of members means that it's somewhat democratic. Less likely to turn into a dictatorship, you see."

"Dispersed into the fabric . . . ?" Gill had said, caught on that point.

"Yes. The fabric of the Spiral itself is sentient." Peta smiled. "So they say."

Gill was dwelling on her words as the Court assembled. She saw the graceful ice-white figure of Albin, just inside the arc of lamps, and beside him the winged form of Theodorus. This strange audience chamber, inside a gigantic soot-black shell poised over a volcano—she could easily believe it was alive, inhabited by the restless spirit of an ancient Aetherial tyrant.

Directly ahead of her, the darkness shaped itself into an imposing male figure: Vaidre Daima. She had an impression of dark skin highlighted with the merest sheen of blue; a headdress and a great cloak of feathers—was it a costume, or a winged form, or simply an aura that made him appear larger than life? Her head ached from trying to see him clearly. His eyes were narrow and golden, like slits in a mask.

"I call this assembly of the Spiral Court to order." His voice was low but penetrating. "I am Vaidre Daima, nominated by the Court to conduct this hearing of the allegations against Rufus Dionys Ephenaestus and those who shielded him. It is our duty, the sixty members of the Spiral Court here present, to determine the identity of the accused, the gravity of their crimes and their fitness to receive the sentence already pronounced upon them."

Something brushed past Gill, making her jump. Suddenly the chamber was full of translucent shifting figures—she grabbed Peta's hand in pure shock. Half-seen Aetherials were moving all around them—around witnesses, Lashtorians and the accused alike—as if to examine them, to absorb information by touch or scent. It was like being surrounded by tangible ghosts. Now and then she caught a glimpse of a highlight on a cheekbone, the flash of a golden eye, or a plait of silken hair. When the Aelyr brushed past, Gill could feel the texture of clothing, the press of fingertips or the brush of feathers. At the uninvited touch violent shivers ran through her.

Juliana bore the intrusion without flinching, her face bearing a slight frown. Adam closed his eyes; Gill put her hand through his arm to reassure him. She and Peta exchanged a look. This was something a jury at home would never do—wander around the courtroom examining everyone, like guests strolling around Juliana's exhibition? It was unutterably disturbing. The half-seen Aelyr put Gill in mind of wind and water, fire, even light itself—you couldn't hold them, yet they were real, and their physical power was profound. These beings seemed to be a different form of matter, of a different plane.

After a few minutes, the Aelyr seemed satisfied, and returned to the darkness of their seats. Vaidre Daima spoke again.

"Who brings the accused before us?"

"We bring them," said the tall ice-white male. "I, Albin of the House of Sibeyla, and Theodorus of Lashtor, aided by his brothers of the pure essence of air. Alone among the Aelyr, when others have long fallen by wayside, Theodorus and the brotherhood of Lashtor have held true to an ancient vow, to pursue and bring Rufus Dionys Ephenaestus to justice before the Spiral Court."

"This is a kangaroo court!" Rufus shouted suddenly. He struggled, briefly, against the two Lashtorians who held him. "Where is my defense lawyer?"

"Silence," said Vaidre Daima. "You are not on Vaeth. You must understand that the Spiral Court passed sentence upon you in eons past, and it cannot be revoked. This hearing is to confirm the rightness of that sentence. You will have a chance to defend yourself in due course."

"Damn right I will."

Gill saw the frosty, imperious look Albin gave Rufus, as if his presence was a mere formality, an irritation. "I wish him luck in his defense of the indefensible," he said in a scalpel-thin tone.

"I would ask you, Albin, to refrain from making personal remarks," said Vaidre Daima. His imposing presence, like a great silhouette, dwarfed even Albin. "All that concerns us today are facts. Are you Rufus Dionys Ephenaestus?"

Rufus rolled his eyes. "That's for you to decide, since you've made up your minds about everything else," he said.

"Answer yes or no!"

"Yes. I am a Rufus Dionys Ephenaestus, at least."

"Albin has presented an impressive list of charges, which I now invite him to put to the accused."

"They are the charges of the Spiral Court itself. Theodorus and I have merely enacted its will." Albin's voice rang out like metal striking stone. "Rufus Ephenaestus, the main charges against you are as follows. That you brought about the downfall of Aetherial civilization upon Vaeth by extreme treason. That you made repeated attempts to intervene in human affairs and history—charges under this category are too numerous to list. That you abducted one Vivienne Talovaros of Melusiel, causing great grief and distress to her house. That you repeatedly abducted and abused human beings, in contravention of laws forbidding us to harm humans. That you slew your own brother, Mistangamesh Ephenaestus."

"Not true!" Rufus gasped.

"Silence, or you will be removed!" barked Vaidre Daima.

Albin continued, "Further, you are charged that with your seven accomplices, you did form an eightfold web in order to deform the fabric of the Spiral, a malicious and illicit act deserving of the severest punishment."

"Oh," whispered Peta. "So that's how they made Boundry!"

Gill wanted to ask what she meant, but Albin spoke on. "Furthermore, you are charged that when summoned to the Spiral Court to answer questions, you resisted all attempts of the Spiral Court's lawful agents to detain you, and that instead you lived in hiding in order to evade justice while continuing your crimes. Deception, kidnap, enslavement, malicious damage to the Spiral. Treason, murder, genocide. Any one of these charges is enough to earn the sentence passed upon you in your absence."

"What sentence?" Copernica called out.

Vaidre Daima answered, "The sentence being that the perpetrator of any or all of these crimes, together with his accomplices, be cast into the Abyss."

"*What?*" A soft murmuring of shock came from Copernica and the others.

There was a horrified pause. Rufus had apparently guessed what would happen when he was caught; he'd even spoken casually about it, yet it still seemed to ambush him. He looked stricken, furious and terrified.

"Sentence first, verdict later!" he yelled. "What is this, *Alice's Adventures in Wonderland*? You're just a pack of cards!"

"Enough," said Vaidre Daima. "The detailed charges have been studied by all members of the Spiral Court prior to the hearing. It is only necessary to summarize them here. The accused may answer the charges point by point, if you will. That you betrayed the civilization of the Felynx upon Vaeth . . ."

"You can't prove it," Rufus said simply.

"Genocide, as a result of your betrayal."

"You have no evidence. Not a shred. There's no blood on my hands."

"That you caused mischief among humans?"

"No. I offered them choices, that's all. It's not my fault if they chose wrongly."

"That you abducted Vivienne Talovaros from her family in Melusiel."

"She is standing beside me. Ask her."

"I'm asking you."

"Then I answer that her family *chose* to believe she was abducted because they could not accept that she preferred a fiery life with me to a dull, watery little existence with them."

"That you kidnapped and imprisoned various humans . . ."

"Oh, come on, I'm hardly the first Aetherial to play with mortals! Since when has that been a capital crime? Most came more than willingly, and I use the term *came* with precision. We killed no one. When they bored us, we threw them back!"

"That you formed an illegal eightfold web."

"Aelyr have always played with the fabric of the Spiral. Since when do we need a license? The charge is nonsensical."

"That you murdered your brother, Mistangamesh."

At that, Rufus began to breathe hard, sweat dewing his face. He looked on the verge of collapse. "No. No. No. I did not kill him."

"Would you care to outline the circumstances of his death?"

"We were living in Europe, in seventeen-something. It was a quarrel over a woman. But it was a jealous husband who killed him, not me. Not me!" Rufus pointed at Adam, who looked back blankly, as he had in the foundry. "You see that man there? That is him. Any of you who saw him in those days, tell me that is not his image in the very flesh! He was mistakenly reborn in human form, but I found him. Now it's my fraternal duty and heart's desire to reawaken him. Until he wakes up and admits he is Mist, I call him Leith. We are Aetherial, which means that if we die, we come back. I have devoted every moment of my time for the past ninety years, as measured on Vaeth, to reawakening that man, my brother. To accuse me of killing him is a complete travesty!"

"Why would you want to bring him back to life?" Albin said levelly. "To expunge your crime?"

"Because I love him, of course."

"Not for some other reason?"

"No."

"Because you love him."

"Yes."

"And yet, in life, you were bitter enemies. Could you wish to bring him back for any reason, except to resume your feud?"

Rufus was speechless, at least for a moment. Vaidre Daima lifted his hands. "You've said enough. Let the man in question speak." He beckoned to Adam, who looked bewildered. Berenis and Fleorn drew him to his feet. Gill stood too, as did Peta and Juliana, to show solidarity. "Are you Rufus's brother, Mistangamesh?"

"No, I'm not. He's mistaken me for someone else."

Gill could almost have wept, to see Adam standing straight and proud as he answered Albin's questions. It plainly caused him anguish to speak of his experiences. He frequently faltered, but her heart went out to him for his dignity.

Then, with shock, Gill heard her own name being called.

She stood, rigid, staring up at the dark tiers mounting in unfathomable darkness, the burning blue circle of lamps below and the forbidding mask of Vaidre Daima staring down at her. Albin watched her like some ice demon. She felt Rufus's hostility like heat.

Abruptly, she made her statement. The plain truth. How she'd first met Rufus in Boundry; how Adam had fled terrified to her doorstep, and how Rufus had viciously restored her pain after their night together. Rufus listened with a chilling smile. After she'd finished, he put in, "When we first met, you say I did no worse than ease your painful leg? And the sex that later took place between us . . . you admit it was consensual?"

"Yes." Gill was horribly uncomfortable, aware of Adam's eyes on her. "But . . ."

"Is it not possible that the sudden recurrence of your pain was a coincidence?"

"It's possible, yes," Gill said through clenched teeth, "but it wasn't. He did it deliberately, when I wouldn't cooperate and refused to tell him where Adam was."

"No more questions," he said.

Then it was Juliana's turn. She had a lot to say. By the time she sat down again, she looked exhausted; Gill reached over to clasp her arm in fellowship. Juliana put her own hand over Gill's, nodding. Rufus remarked sneeringly, "A shame you can't produce your aunt Corah to testify to the events you describe."

"Of course I can't," Juliana snapped in disdain. "She's dead, my mother and my great-uncle John are dead—all of them prematurely, thanks to Rufus. The damage he did to my family is incalculable."

"Secondhand evidence!" Rufus exclaimed. "Hearsay and opinion! Let the Court hear what *you've* done, Juliana."

"Silence," said Vaidre Daima. "No one is on trial here but Rufus and his accomplices. Would anyone else care to speak?"

"I would." Vivienne stepped forward. "Rufus is correct to say that he did not abduct me. I went with him because I love him. I did not need or ask my cousin there, Theo Talovaros, to launch some vendetta on my family's behalf. Rufus acts out of love. If you had seen the anguished devotion with which he's tried to bring back his brother, you'd know I speak the truth!"

"We might equally deduce," said Albin, "that you have been the victim of coercion, indoctrination or delusion."

"Hey, what about free will?" Rufus cried. "All these folk I'm said to have seduced—doesn't it occur to you that they allowed it because they *wanted* it?"

"We are not talking of mere "seduction" but of kidnap, torture and murder," said Albin. "The brave testimony of Adam Montague holds more weight than all other accusations put together. Hold his plain anguish in your mind. Think on the fact that even Rufus has not denied it. Then consider whether all of his dishonest, self-justifying outbursts hold the slightest weight."

There was a somber, telling hush.

"Questions?" asked Vaidre Daima.

"I think Albin's prejudice speaks for itself," said Rufus.

The arguments went on for hours, it seemed. Finally a brief recess was called; enough to stretch aching limbs and take a drink, to find an outlying cave where they could relieve themselves. By then, Gill's head was whirling with tiredness and anxiety. All she wanted was for it to be over, never to see Rufus or any of them again. Just to go home with Peta, Adam and her aunt.

Home? she thought, catching herself.

Presently they were called back for the summing up.

Albin began, "The long pursuit of a devious criminal and traitor to all Aetherial kind ends here today. To claim insufficient evidence or doubt over identity is disingenuous. Every one of you knows who Rufus is. Each one of you here *knows* who he is and what he has done. Sweep aside all of these mendacious niceties and what is left? A traitor devoid of conscience. Sadist. Murderer. Traitor. Genocide."

Vivienne called out, "And if any of it's true, who cares? Rufus is the fire and passion of life, and he has never wavered. If he causes mischief, so what? He has brought laughter and change. We're all with him of our own free will, because we find him worthy of love. Is that wrong?"

Rufus groaned. "Valiant try, Vivienne. Thanks for writing "guilty" across my forehead."

Vaidre Daima said, "So, Rufus, have you any final words in your own defense?"

"Yes, I have," said Rufus, straining slightly against the guards who held him. He was a defiant figure, his hair streaming in a magnificent tangle down his back. There was something sad and desperate in his defiance. Gill saw sweat on his brow. He looked vulnerably human amid the semi-mortals who surrounded him. "This trial is a pantomime. I do not recognize the authority of the Spiral Court to try me. You have not one shred of evidence to prove that I am the traitor who destroyed whole civilizations. I call myself by his name, yes, but you cannot prove he and I are one and the same person. Great Lady of Stars, I'd have to be over twenty thousand years old!"

"Do you deny the charges?" said Vaidre Daima, sounding unutterably weary.

"Yes, I deny them."

"Do you deny that you are Rufus Ephenaestus?"

"I challenge you to prove it." His eyes shone manically. "I challenge you to prove any of this before you destroy eight innocent Aelyr souls."

"Do not think to mock the Spiral Court," Vaidre Daima said in a heavy, dangerous tone. "It is up to them to decide your fate. They will weigh what proof is required."

"I'm sure you've already made up your minds." Rufus stood square and poised, like a dancer. "Let these be my last words, then. You are complacent, all of you. Complacent, from the beginning of time. Let's be perfect Aetherials! Ancient Estalyr, bestriding the Earth and weaving the Spiral. Adaptable Aelyr, ruling the Earth and partaking lavishly of its various forms of life. And oh, then, humankind gets too troublesome, so let us surrender and retreat to our safe little Spiral, pull up the drawbridge behind us. Well I say fuck it! Let us go into the human world, let's seduce and exploit and turn it all upside down and bring some passion into their tiny lives! Challenge them, screw them over, take them for every penny! What are we for, if not to shake them up? Even the sacred Felynx Empire itself— in fact, who better to shake to their foundations in their wretched smug complacency? I bring ecstasy and disaster to mortals in order to bring change! So some of them died. So what? People always die, with or without my intervention. Without me, their tiny little lives would never be anything at all! It's called passion, you staid self-appointed drones of the Spiral Court! Life and passion!"

Gill flinched, swapping eloquent looks with Peta and Juliana.

"Your remarks are noted," Vaidre Daima said coldly. "I call upon the court to give due consideration to all they have heard today. Perhaps they will reflect that it is high time your 'passion' was checked. Earta, will you weigh the vote?"

"I will, my lord." The peacock-hued Aetherial dipped her head in assent.

"The court will adjourn until the sun of Naamon rises again. Then the decision of the Spiral Court will be heard."

Rufus, taken away in the grip of his guards, had turned ashen grey.

———

"I thought he might have completed that self-destructive rant by walking out and flinging himself into the nearest fissure," said Juliana as they were taken back to their side chamber.

"That would be too easy," said Theo. "Try to sleep if you can. Berenis and others will be posted outside your doorway, so you'll have as much privacy as possible. I fear you won't be very comfortable, for which I can only apologize, but it will soon be over."

As he made to leave, Peta caught his arm. "Theodorus," she said firmly as he turned to face her, a head taller than her. "Do you know that woman, Vivienne?"

"No, I don't know her. Why?"

"Because she has the same name as you. Talovaros."

He bit his lower lip. "We are of the same *eretru*, family, yes, but I'd never met her before. She was born long before me. I heard of her disappearance while I was in Melusiel, but it was only one of many factors that convinced me to hunt Rufus. Why do you ask?"

"Your mission to arrest him . . . I wondered if you were simply carrying out orders, or if you had some personal interest in taking him down?"

He glanced at the open doorway, where Berenis and Fleorn stood guard, like two faint flames in the dark passageway beyond. "What made you think that? The fact that Vivienne is a distant relative of mine?"

"Well, Aetherials are not always very good at recognizing authority. I wasn't aware that the Spiral Court had a sort of police force in the form of you and your brotherhood. So, are you dedicated to upholding the Spiral Court's laws from a sense of duty, or do you have some agenda of your own?"

He was silent. His mouth a flat line, he made to turn away, but Peta snapped "Mark!" and he turned to her again.

"If I could ask one kindness of you, do not call me that. I am Theodorus here. Show me that much respect at least."

Peta drew back, crossing her arms over her waist. "All right. I apologize. Theodorus it is. Please answer my question."

"I uphold the policy of the Spiral Court," he said stiffly. "I took vows to do so."

"But this policy must accord with your own beliefs, or you wouldn't do it." Peta leaned closer to him. "Come on! I know you. Even at sixteen, you were full of principles. You'd never do anything you didn't agree with. I simply don't believe you are 'just following orders.'"

"Why does this concern you?"

"Because I want to know where my Mark went! What is it you believe, to have devoted years to this . . . crusade?"

Theo seemed to struggle with himself. Eventually he said, "I believe that beings such as Rufus, who violate the natural separation between the Aetherial and mortal realms, are an abomination and must be stopped. We must not harm humans, nor each other. That is the Spiral Court's founding principle."

Peta gazed at him, digesting his words. "Sounds reasonable enough."

"Thank you," he said dryly.

"But natural separation?" She blinked. "Is there a natural separation? I was led to believe that Earth and Spiral are both spun from the same fabric, the same original star-stuff. We're privileged to see into other layers and travel deeper than humans—and to play with creation a bit—but that's all. I know there's a barrier standing between the two, but it's artificial. The Otherworld spills into Vaeth in all sorts of ways. Wouldn't you say?"

She was watching Theo's face intently as she spoke. Gill watched both of them, wondering at the meaning behind Peta's probing gaze and Theo's tightening expression. "Mark—sorry, *Theo*," Peta added. "Tell me, what's changed since I last saw you? You weren't like this before."

Muscles moved at the corners of his jaw. "I've come to realize that it's best for Aetherials if Spiral and Earth exist in total separation."

Peta's expression changed minimally, taking on a subtle cast of wariness. "Oh, do you? Why?"

Suppressed passion entered his voice. "In Sibeyla, in Lashtor, I found purity. Aetherial perfection, that allows us to be completely ourselves. Pure Aelyr. By trying to live on Earth as Vaethyr we are muddied and contaminated. Human blood runs in our veins and we become caught up in mortal affairs and lose our real selves. It is no way for us to live!"

"Oh my god," she said under her breath.

He opened his hands. "See? You even invoke their gods, instead of our Lady of Stars."

"Just a turn of phrase."

He suddenly caught her shoulders, drawing her up towards him. "I wish I could make you see and feel it, Peta! I wish you'd join us."

"How? You're an all-male community, so I've been told. I'm female, as you seem to have forgotten."

"I didn't mean come to Lashtor itself; I meant, live in the Spiral, become fully Aelyr. Find your pure essence and burn out all the human contamination."

Gill saw her catch a quick breath and stand rigid as Theo let her go. "I can't. I don't see it as contamination. I love Vaeth and I'd never turn my back on it. And I'm sad—no, horrified—that you have."

"When the Great Gates stood sealed, it was as if the Spiral could breathe again," he said. "There was no coming and going across the borders, no leaking of Vaethyr into the Aelyr realm, nor of Aelyr being tempted away. No conflict of interest. It was a good time."

"Not on Earth, it wasn't."

"Then you should have been *here*. The reopening of the Gates was devastating. If I had my way, the Gates would be sealed for all time. If first the Vaethyr could all be gathered in and purified, so much the better—but if they insist on staying on Vaeth, that's their choice."

"Purity, what is that?" Peta exclaimed.

"Experiencing our pure Aelyr-Estalyr essence."

"Well, if we were on Earth, I'd say it sounds like you've caught a dose of religion. Which is fine, as long as you don't inflict it on the rest of us."

"Not religion, Peta," he said with veiled impatience. "We don't worship gods."

"I know that. It's still a belief, an ideology."

"It's an ideal; what's wrong with that? It's the truth, that's all, the pure truth."

"All believers think that," she retorted. "Oh, Mark, what have you turned into? A Puritan crusader, who wants to sever the Earth from the Otherworld?"

"Don't mock me, Peta."

"I'm not mocking you. You're terrifying me. You can't tell me that *that* is Spiral Court policy?"

"It could be, as the nominated members flow and change. There's a current in that direction."

"What has it got to do with Rufus, anyway?"

His eyes swam with dangerous light as he gazed at her. "Rufus is a criminal traitor who has caused immeasurable harm to Aelyr civilization. Aside from that, his debauchery and cruelty and wanton mingling with mortals—it's everything I despise! And you should, too. He must be punished, as a warning to others. It's the first major strike towards separation."

Peta stepped away from him, looking shaken. She said, "The Mark I knew—he's quite gone, then?"

"He's standing here before you," said Theodorus. "This is who I am, now."

Some of his Lashtorian brothers came in, carrying quilts like the one Gill had had in Lashtor. Theo made that his cue to escape.

His fellows brought food, too; a salad of grains mixed with nuts and herbs, dried fruits, heavy moist bread, and a sweet-sharp cordial to wash it down. It wasn't a warming meal, so they were glad of the volcanic heat seeping through the rock. Without it, they might have been frozen by now. The Lashtorians had even found a place for them to relieve themselves and wash, a sort of cave with its floor split by deep rifts, and hot cloud-blue water bubbling from an underground source.

So the night passed and they tried to sleep, using the quilts to cushion themselves on the rock floor as best they could. Every time Gill dozed off, the ache of her hip brought her awake again, until she gave up and sat against the wall instead. Peta was already there. Soundlessly, she was crying.

She'd never seen Peta in tears before; she wasn't emotional like that. Passionate, yes, but not tearful.

"Hey, what's up?" Gill moved beside her, sitting like Peta with her knees drawn up and the quilt wrapped around her. "Is it Mark?"

Peta pressed the heels of her hands to her face, taking a few moments to answer. Then she let her hands fall and rest loose on her raised knees. "Not exactly. He started me thinking, I suppose, but it's not about him. I'd heard about these extreme Aelyr purists, even met one or two, but I never expected Mark to become one. The thing about them, the purists, is that they're so clear and polished, they're like rock crystal. It's like looking into a mirror—like the time you looked into the mirror with the mask on? Only here, it's all about stripping the masks away . . ."

"What on earth are you talking about?"

"I did something dreadful, Gill. Cruel, horrible, unforgivable."

"You?"

"You sound surprised. That's sweet."

"Peta, you can be quite annoying, but you're basically a gentle, decent person."

"How d'you know?"

"Anyone can see it."

"Don't start arguing with me before you even know what I did. There was this man in my home village, Cloudcroft . . . an Aetherial. Lawrence Wilder. He had an incredibly important duty towards his fellow Aetherials but he was refusing to carry it out. It's a long story . . . to keep it short, the situation brewed for years and many of us got angry and decided to end it by force." She shuddered, her body tense in every line. "I thought it was the right thing to do at the time. You get caught up in a crusading fervor. You're convinced it's correct to compel someone to do what *you* think is right, because you tell yourself it serves the greater good."

"What did you do?" Gill breathed.

"We conspired against him. A vast gang of us carried out a horrible ritual of public humiliation and brutally forced him to carry out the duty he'd refused. The result was very nearly utter catastrophe, which was narrowly avoided only by Lawrence's own bravery—his willingness actually to *die* for what we'd made him do. Oh yes, we got what we wanted, but at what cost?

If you'd seen his eyes, his face that night . . . I'll never forget it." Her voice was a painful whisper. "We thought we were valiant warriors, reclaiming Aetherial rights. But what were we, actually? A bunch of vile playground bullies, that's what. A lynch mob."

Shocked, Gill didn't know how to respond. "What about the others? Did they regret it afterwards?"

Peta gave a grunt, not quite a laugh. "We never really discussed it. I suppose many did, but people hate to feel ashamed, don't they? So they justify their behavior. Or they find someone or something else to blame, as if to say, 'That wasn't really me, I'm not like that.' But I *am* like that, Gill. I can't justify it. I won't even try."

"You're very honest."

"It's taken until now. Mark's innocent of all that, and I can't sully him with what I did, even if he wanted to be with me again, because now, every time I close my eyes, I see Lawrence's face as we turned on him. And I have to live with it."

Gill didn't know what to say. She had no reassurance to offer, since she knew nothing of the situation. She simply asked, "Can you?"

Peta's bony shoulders rose and fell with her breath. "Thank you for not trying to comfort me. I don't know. We'll see."

Presently she fell asleep, her head on Gill's knee; but Gill stayed awake, absently stroking Peta's hair as she waited for the long night to end.

Morning on Mount Khafet was little different to the night. Reddish light sifted into the chamber, but Gill couldn't tell if it was dawn or volcano fire. There was a stirring in the doorway, the voices of Lashtorians calling them to rise. She felt thick-headed from lack of sleep, but she dragged her locked skeleton to the bathing cave and revived herself in the volcano-heated spring. It helped, as did a small breakfast of Lashtorian bread and cheese and sharp cordial.

No one spoke; there seemed little to say. One by one they washed and breakfasted, and then there was nothing to do but wait for Theo to summon them. Juliana was grim-faced and stoic, Peta tense, restless and bright-eyed. Adam's complexion was colorless.

At last Theodorus came, and led them to the audience chamber. "It's time to hear the verdict," he said. "Don't look so worried! It's almost over, and then you can go home. Both Spiral and Earth itself will have cause to be grateful for the help you've given us."

He looked bright-faced and excited. For him, it was the culmination of a quest. In the chamber, the court members and the host of Lashtorians were gathered as before, surrounding Rufus and the other prisoners. Al-

bin's pearl-white face was serene with fulfilment. Gill felt an anxious
swoop in the pit of her stomach. Juliana and Peta looked tense, somber;
Adam's face was bone-white. They all knew that Rufus had reached the
end of a long road. He couldn't be too surprised. Most probably he should
be grateful to have had such a long reprieve before the powers of justice
caught up with him. Still, to think of him condemned to the Abyss, however wicked his crimes . . . it was astonishingly difficult. The image of a
long plunge into death made her heart contract with denial.

Gill felt Adam's hand closing around hers, so tight it hurt. She came of
a culture where the death sentence was no longer passed, considered too
barbaric even for the worst of criminals. For Adam it was different. In his
time, murderers had been routinely hanged on the gallows. He had seen
fellow soldiers killed around him; perhaps he'd even seen them shot by firing squads for desertion. Did that make it easier or harder for him to think
of Rufus being executed?

She wondered if Juliana was thinking about Corah's letter. Gill couldn't
think about what it had said. It was too much.

She thought, *If Rufus were some brutish dictator standing there, surrounded
by thugs, wouldn't we just think "good riddance"? But we let his beauty and
charm take us in, and we're still doing it even now. We have to be hard. Beauty
means nothing if the soul is rotten. When he's gone, Adam will be safe.*

The court chamber settled and at last Vaidre Daima spoke the words.
"Have you weighed the vote, Earta?"

Earta rose, bright and visible as if a beam of light had been turned upon
her. She looked like a goddess fused with a strange bird; coppery green
skin, a halo of sharp, peacock-hued feathers framing her face and cascading down her back. She held a small scroll in a hand that sported pointed
green fingernails of astonishing length. "I have, my lord Vaidre Daima."

"Is the verdict unanimous?"

"No, my lord."

"Then the Court will abide by the majority decision."

"We have been unable to reach a clear majority decision, my lord."

Gill glanced at Rufus. His face was like porcelain, so pale it seemed lit
from within. It looked like a death mask. His eyes were wide, dark as blood,
glittering with absolute, glacial terror.

"How then does the vote stand?"

Earta paused, tapping her prodigious fingernails against the scroll. "After our best and repeated efforts to gain a majority—those against sentence
being carried out, twenty-nine. Those in favor of sentence being carried
out, thirty."

Rufus groaned audibly. Gill pressed closer to Adam, hardly noticing the
pain as his hand crushed hers.

Vaidre Daima let out a long breath. In his quiet, controlled way, he looked angry—or at least, deeply disapproving. After a moment he spoke, his voice low, measured and clear. "In that case, the outcome being unclear, it falls to me to make the decision. As magistrate of these proceedings, my verdict is not permitted to be based upon personal views, but only upon the fair and impartial balancing of evidence. This judgment also must be informed by the will of the ancients who, although they no longer walk among us, are yet all around us, part of us. Rufus Dionys Ephenaestus, there is indeed a powerful consensus that you are the perpetrator of the many serious crimes with which you stand charged—but consensus is not proof. Moreover, there is a clear and powerful undercurrent of doubt over the validity of the case. Weighing these concerns, these very serious concerns . . ."

"*Doubt?*" someone gasped; Gill thought it was Albin. Murmurs rose, but Vaidre Daima held up a stern hand, fury plain in his stern, cold expression. A complete hush fell. He spoke gravely into the silence.

"Rufus Dionys Ephenaestus, I find no case to answer. You are free to go."

21

Return

Pandemonium filled the chamber.

Rufus was grinning and dancing as he turned to hug his comrades, all their differences seemingly forgotten. They spun in gleeful circles, laughing. Theodorus and the Lashtorian party appeared stunned at first, too shocked to express anger; then a tide of protest began. There were shouts, curses; the strange, echoing voices of the unseen court were raised in cries both of approval and dismay. The whole chamber roiled. Gill and the others turned to stare at each other in bewilderment. Adam's face was bone-white.

Over the commotion, Vaidre Daima was still speaking, his words drowned. Gill heard Theo's voice rising in anguish, "No. No! All it's taken us to find him—everyone acknowledges his guilt—how is this possible?" Albin's strident tone rang out like a steel bell: "This is an outrage. A travesty!"

"Silence before the Spiral Court!"

Vaidre Daima's voice sliced through the noise. The chamber grumbled into restless silence.

"Rufus Dionys Ephenaestus, it is my ruling that the case against you is deeply flawed. There is insufficient support upon the Council for your guilt to be determined one way or the other, still less for sentence to be carried out. Therefore I have no option but to dismiss the case. Your unauthorised *dysir* have been confiscated and you are prohibited from attempting to procure any more. On condition that you stay away from these folk of Vaeth," he indicated Juliana and her companions, "and make no further attempt to communicate with or harass them in any way, and on condition that you never again attempt to form an eight-fold web—you are free to go. Anyone who tries to detain you will be in breach of the Spiral Court's ruling and subject to punishment."

"Free," Rufus echoed, his voice bouncing clearly from the vaults of the chamber. "Thank you, my lords and ladies of the Spiral Court. Wisdom and justice are sovereign here today." With his hair rippling around his shoulders as he turned, he executed an extravagant, mocking bow. "Did you hear that, brother Theodorus of Lashtor and my lord Albin of Sibeyla? No case to answer. Free. Free!"

"On the conditions I have stated," Vaidre Daima said sharply. "Do you accept them?"

"Yes, my lord," said Rufus, with a sudden show of respect—or a good imitation of it, at least. "We all accept it. We'll depart and live in peace. Thank you."

"I demand a retrial," said Albin. His tone was icy, spiked with fury.

Vaidre Daima's reply was grave and reproving. "There will be no retrial, Albin. You have had your chance."

"We thought you supported us," Albin persisted. "We kept you informed at each stage of our hunt for the defendant. Why did you smile approvingly upon our actions, only to reach this incomprehensible decision?"

"I believe you know precisely why." There was an edge to Vaidre Daima's voice. Murmurs rose, and again he held up his hands for quiet. "Of course you are anxious for an explanation and you deserve one, but you only need to look inside yourself. Yes, you have supporters on the Council, but plainly not enough. Many members saw straight to the heart of your game. This was not about bringing an ancient villain to justice. It was about making an example of him in order to further your cause of separation. However, despite your best efforts to load the council in your favor, Albin, the strategy has failed."

In a sibilant tone, Albin said, "Your judgment is a betrayal."

"I regret that you see it so, but I trust you will come to understand it. The council had a free vote and could not reach a consensus, so I must. I cannot and will not allow you to use someone such as Rufus, guilty or not, for your own political gain. As great as the distaste for his past behavior may be, there is far greater distaste for the alternative: the curbing of Aetherial freedom and our relationship with Vaeth."

Albin said nothing, apparently deciding that silence was more eloquent than an undignified argument. There was no expression on his lime-white face, and his eyes and the gem on his brow made a demonic blue triangle. Goose bumps flared on Gill's skin as if the temperature had dropped. Albin, she suspected, would make a terrifying enemy. Rufus seemed benign in comparison.

"Now I call an end to these proceedings," said Vaidre Daima. "Stand back, let Rufus Ephenaestus and the other defendants pass. Court dismissed!"

The Lashtorians obeyed without question, standing out of the way with bowed heads and clasped hands. The faces of Theo and Albin were stiff with disbelief, but there was nothing they could do. With measured, showy grace, as if leading a parade, Rufus led his companions out of the chamber. He grinned around him, as he went, flourishing a hand in the direction of Juliana and the others. Copernica and the rest followed him with quiet hauteur, slight smiles touching their lips. None of them made any attempt to approach Adam.

Gill and Peta, Juliana and Adam stood rooted where they were, confused and wondering what to do. The Lashtorians were beginning to leave, and the Spiral Court itself breaking up, its barely seen members dispersing into the shadows. It seemed everyone had forgotten about them.

"What the hell happened?" asked Gill. "I thought it was a foregone conclusion!"

"Obviously not," said Peta.

"Well, that's bloody wonderful, that is," said Juliana. "So Rufus is still on the loose. What the hell will he do next? It's all right, Adam, you'll stay with us. We won't let him near you."

"Thank you," Adam said faintly. He looked resigned and rigid, like a man about to be led to his execution. His plain fear, more than anything, filled Gill with foreboding. It had been disturbing to think of Rufus being put to death . . . but it would have been a tidy ending, a new start for Adam. Now nothing was certain.

As they hesitated, wondering whether they could simply leave, Theodorus came to them, shouldering his way through the departing crowd. In his self-contained manner, he looked devastated. Berenis followed him, a few yards behind.

"This is unbelievable," Theo said. "After all our work, and a virtual damning confession from his own mouth—!"

"Obviously it wasn't enough," said Peta.

"They know," he pointed in the direction of Vaidre Daima and the seating tiers, where shadowy figures were melting away in the darkness. "Every member of the Spiral Court knows full well who Rufus is and what he's done! They should not have needed more. What were they thinking? Damn it, the humans' evidence wasn't as powerful as I'd hoped . . ."

As he spoke, Gill saw a member of the Spiral Court coming towards them; it was the green-bronze woman, Earta, who'd given the court's verdict. Berenis hovered in the background, looking somehow embarrassed, even sheepish. Gill had already formed the impression he'd supported Theo out of loyalty, not conviction.

"I hope you're not blaming us for this, Mark," Peta said, looking squarely into his eyes. "We told the truth, as we agreed. You didn't ask us for dramatic embellishment! This is not our fault."

"No," Theo said tightly, running his hands over his burnished scalp. "No, of course it's not. You were the least of it. With or without you, they should have convicted him, because they *know* he is guilty. This is a bitter blow. Earta?" He turned to her as she reached them.

Even at close quarters, the Aelyr woman had a disturbing translucency. Her skin and clothes were dark, her cheekbones sheened like silk where the light caught, but in shadow her contours were like the night sky, blackness filled with distant stars. The shimmering stand of feathers sprouting from her hair and her long fingernails caught dancing emerald lights. "Theodorus," she said. "I'm sorry. I know this is not what you and Albin expected."

"It's not a matter of what we expected, but of what is *right*," he retorted. "You say you are sorry, but which way did you vote?"

She dipped her head, long feathers swaying. "The vote is confidential."

"Against the sentence, I assume."

"I understand why you brought him before the court, but it was not a simple matter. I voted for fairness, as was my duty. To be frank, I didn't expect the vote to be so perfectly split, but . . ."

"So what happened? We were carrying out the Spiral Court's will in bringing him before them! Has some corruption entered their ranks, what?"

She raised a pacifying hand. Peta slipped a hand through Gill's arm as they listened. Earta's manner was warm, sensible, measured. There was no obvious hint that she was a secret supporter of Rufus. Something else had compelled them to let him go.

"There have been recent changes of personnel upon the inner council," Earta said. "The majority may well have been in favor of Albin's point of view a short time ago, but there's been a shift of policy. The separatist faction has declined, and those who favor free interaction with Vaeth are in the ascendant."

Peta laughed. "That's always been my stance. The less we have of gates and barriers the better. Easy come, easy go. Do as you will, as long as you harm no one; that's my philosophy. I can't be doing with Puritans like Albin either—but anarchists like Rufus only add fuel to the purists' fire, don't they?"

"*Harm no one*," Juliana echoed. "I thought it was Aetherial law not to cause harm, either to each other or to humans. What happened to that principle?"

"The laws we have are more by 'gentleman's agreement' than anything," said Earta with a rueful smile. "They change and shift with the will of the ancients."

"Anyway, controlling Aetherials is like herding cats," Peta put in.

The peacock-green woman laughed. "Still, we try."

"Dame Juliana is correct, though' Theo said bitterly. "Say one-third of the Spiral Court supports separation from Earth, and one-third supports benign interaction, and the last third supports anarchy and destruction—still by a two-thirds majority they should have enforced the sentence!"

"In theory," Earta sighed, "but reality's another matter. The shift of Spiral Court policy is towards upholding the basic right of Aetherials to keep the Great Gates open, in order to come and go as they please. That may change, with every new influx of courtiers; but that's how it stands today. And you, Theodorus, knew it had been moving in that direction for some time, but you've refused to acknowledge it."

He set his jaw. "Albin believed that the balance was in our favor."

"A short while ago, he was right. Albin spent a good deal of energy whispering in people's ears, swaying them to his cause. He might have succeeded, but other currents of opinion proved stronger. His efforts served to galvanise many against him, in fact."

Gill saw Albin a few yards away, speaking to a small knot of Lashtorians. The chamber was otherwise nearly empty. The lamps were cold blue moons flickering in an immense blackness. As Albin spoke, his gaze turned to fix on Theo's group. Gill felt cold with fear.

"He claimed he had them in his palm," said Theo. "Evidently he was wrong."

"I tried to tell you that," put in Berenis.

"Quite," said Earta. "We would all rest easier, wouldn't we, if Rufus and his cohorts were now on their way to the Abyss? But the problem was that the whole case was political in nature, designed by Albin and by you, Theodorus, to promote separation between the Spiral and Vaeth. The case against Rufus looked like propaganda."

"A showcase trial," said Juliana.

"But it wasn't *just* propaganda," said Gill. "I've seen him in action. He's like some god of chaos, Loki or someone, who goes around causing havoc then pretending it's all a joke. But it isn't. He's dangerous. It looks to me as if letting him go was just as political as trying him in the first place. And no one gives a damn about the humans stuck in the middle! About Adam."

Earta inclined her head, a gesture of agreement. "It's all about the balance of power on the Spiral Court. It's true that for long ages past, their policy was to capture Rufus and punish him. But as time went on, as Rufus continued to evade capture, the mood of the Spiral Court changed—it changes like the seasons, as members come and go—so interest in catching Rufus began to wane. Albin and the brothers of Lashtor were among the last to take up the age-old vendetta against him, but they did so for idealistic reasons. Yes, they were carrying out the Spiral Court's orders from eons ago—but Aelyr outlook has changed in the meantime. You misjudged the mood of the Court, Theodorus. Policy has shifted. The inclination now is to let the Great Gates stand open and allow free passage of Aetherials in

354 Freda Warrington

and out of the human world. I condemn Rufus's activities, but that doesn't justify curtailing the rights of all Aetherials."

"Rights entail responsibilities, in some circles," Juliana said under her breath.

Earta gave an almost-human shrug. "Yes, Rufus should have been found guilty, but the Spiral Court could not allow Albin's faction to use the hearing for political reasons. He made a bid to do so, but half the court and Vaidre Daima saw through it."

"So, convicting Rufus would have been a breach of his Aetherial rights?" Juliana said dryly. "It's political correctness gone mad."

Earta looked blankly at her, but Peta and Gill exchanged a wry grimace. Gill said, "What about the treachery of bringing down an Aetherial empire?"

She shrugged. "It's no good *knowing* someone is guilty, if there's no actual proof. It was so long ago, it's no longer relevant to most. There are younger Aetherials upon the Spiral Court now who don't care what happened in history. Rufus is a hero to some."

"You don't say," whispered Peta.

Gill saw Albin advancing towards them, his narrow white form glowing.

"Walk away from him," Berenis said urgently, catching Theo's arm. "Don't let him engage you in endless recriminations about whose fault it was! It is not the purpose of Lashtor to attach ourselves to such causes! Our purpose is only to contemplate the Spiral, not act as an army for those who would change everything! I'll tell you now, if Rufus is to be retried for some breach of his conditions, it will not involve us. They'll have to find some new force to arrest him."

"We will never agree about this," Theo said, pulling himself free of Berenis' grip.

"You can't claim to enact the will of the Spiral Court when they plainly can't agree about anything. Or if you do, you now have to enact their will to stay joined to Earth!"

"Which I can't. If I'm in the wrong, if all of Lashtor turns its back and pretends this never happened, what am I? Outcast?"

Albin stopped, gazing at Theodorus. The look in his eyes was hard. Gill didn't see how he could blame Theo for their failure, but still, she wouldn't put it past him. All he said was, "This is not over."

"Yes it is," Theo responded grimly. "It is over, Albin."

Albin watched him for a few seconds, his blue gaze deadly. He said nothing else. Then, without emotion, he turned away and made his way out of the chamber, swiftly vanishing into the blackness.

"Thank you," said Berenis, releasing a breath.

"For what?" Theodorus said bleakly. "This is a disaster. Ephenaestus walks off laughing. Albin's plans lie in ruins, and we have nothing to say to each other. The Spiral Court and Lashtor simply melt away as if it's no concern of theirs!"

"What else?" said Berenis. "The decision is made."

"And what about us?" asked Juliana. "What if Rufus comes after Adam yet again? I suppose you don't have such a concept as witness protection?"

Theodorus didn't answer, apparently lost in his own thoughts. Belatedly he reacted, realizing she'd spoken. "I'll see you home," he said. "Vaidre Daima imposed conditions on him to keep away from you."

"But who will protect us?" asked Gill. "Like Berenis said, it won't be the Lashtorians who come to detain him next time."

Theo had no answer to that. He said quietly, "I trust his sport with you is over, but I'll come to make sure you reach home safely."

They trod the sepulchral corridors of Malikala's fortress in a desultory fashion, aching with tiredness. Around them, the red-washed blackness felt stifling. Juliana could not wait to escape. She felt a rising fear that they might not find the portal again, and be trapped in Naamon forever. She felt almost sorry for Theo, who carried himself with a kind of broken dignity, as if his whole life's work had been destroyed.

"The trial was an utter shambles," said Juliana. The tension released by the end of the trial left her seething. "The 'jury' was hardly impartial."

"I know it seemed that way," said Peta, "but you're comparing it to how trials are conducted at home. Aetherials do things differently."

"And don't care about the consequences, obviously." As she spoke, she saw a familiar shape moving across their path, barely visible amid the thick curves and folds of the passageway. Without pausing, Juliana strode forward and called out, "Vaidre Daima! Wait."

He stopped and turned, a large and impassive figure in the shadows. Gill made a small noise of dismay, and Juliana thought that perhaps it was not such a good idea to have attracted his attention. Too late now.

"Yes, Dame Juliana?" he said calmly.

"I'm not an idiot, and I believe I understand your reasons for letting Rufus go, but really, hasn't it crossed your mind that your decision has left us all, especially Adam, in worse danger than we were in before? The proceedings in there were an absolute disaster!"

The narrow golden eyes vanished and reappeared as he blinked. She realized then that he knew, but didn't care; or if he cared even a little, he was not going to do anything about it.

"You heard the conditions I imposed upon him. He would not dare break them."

"Oh, wouldn't he? Who is going to punish him if he does? Just Theo, on his own? It seems to me that your conditions were more a suggestion than a restriction!"

Vaidre Daima moved closer to her. She hadn't realized how tall he was until now and his eyes were alien, as cold as Albin's. "I gave all the safeguards I could, but the fact is, freedom is freedom. My obligation was to serve the most important principle of all, that of Aetherial autonomy. It has been whispered on the Spiral Court, however, that your unusual powers should come under further investigation."

"Oh," Juliana gasped. "So now you're threatening me, for daring to argue with you?"

"No, but certain factions are demanding that questions be asked."

"Who? Albin? Is he demanding my scalp in place of Rufus's?"

Vaidre Daima's silence was telling. "Aelyr of all factions. Whatever their different views, one factor that unites us is unacceptability of humans displaying Aetherial-like powers. In all honesty, since you've presented yourself to me, I must ask those questions."

Peta broke in, "Hold on—we were told that as long as Dame Juliana cooperated with the trial, there would be no recriminations about her sculptures!"

Vaidre Daima was unmoved. "Questions are not recriminations. Still, I must insist." He spoke quietly, "All I ask is the truth."

"It's all right," said Juliana, raising a hand to pacify the others. "I've nothing to hide. A child vanished, and shortly afterwards I had a vision of an Aetherial who thanked me for this offering and offered me prodigious artistic gifts in return. Ever since then I feel I've been atoning for this wicked bargain . . . but that's all I can tell you. I don't understand it myself."

He said nothing. Instead, he placed his large, long-fingered right hand on her forehead. The touch was strangely soothing. Juliana closed her eyes, letting him learn whatever it was he needed from her. A night breeze blew gently through her and she saw visions; a child wandering into a forest, lost to sight . . . a pale Aetherial standing before her, thanking her for the gift of the child and offering unlimited inspiration and in return, the power to capture magic in her sculptures.

The touch ceased. Juliana jerked, as if shocked out of a deep sleep.

"Strange," said Vaidre Daima. "No such child was ever received in the Spiral. No such Aetherial exists. It seems you imagined or dreamed him, nothing more. Yet your power is real. It comes from within you."

"Does it?" She was dazed. She felt she'd always known it.

"Yes. You have an ability to deform reality, to create small portals. It's an Aetherial power, and yet you are human . . . it's something I've never encountered before. It means you have a certain undefined power *over* Aetherials."

"Meaning what?"

"That many upon the Spiral Court might consider you too dangerous to be allowed to leave."

"What?" Gill exclaimed. "How did this happen? One minute Rufus is the one in the dock—now he walks free and we're under suspicion instead? Dame J's done nothing wrong!"

Vaidre Daima ignored her outburst. For those moments as he stood in thought, Juliana stood entirely at his mercy. She was aware of Gill and Peta tensing ready for battle, but she endured calmly and waited for his decision.

"Do you have anything to say?" he asked. Still neutral, ready to listen to all sides before delivering judgment.

"I never intended to misuse the power," she said. "I always acted to protect my domain from the predations of those called the *Dubh Sidhe* or the *Dunkelmen*, whom we now realize were Rufus and his happy band. The very people whom you've just released to carry on as if nothing had happened!"

"They will not defy my ruling," Vaidre Daima repeated firmly. "If you are still worried, I will send some Aelyr to stand guard until you are certain of your safety . . ."

Juliana bristled at his apparently condescending tone. "No, keep your protection. We don't need it. We've managed without it until now and no doubt we'll manage again."

Vaidre Daima gave a nod. He stepped aside, opening one hand to indicate the way out of Malikala's stronghold. "Our agreement stands; those you captured were suspects, and you helped at the hearing, so I will not detain you. However, I suggest you make haste, before someone less tolerant than me chooses to probe your unexplained talents."

Albin? Gill wondered, hardly daring to believe he'd let them go. As they hurried on their way, Vaidre Daima called enigmatically after them, "If Rufus does come back, you can be sure he will regret it."

They found the portal and stepped back into the foundry with a profound sense of relief. In the surface world, it was late afternoon. They found the world peaceful, the house quiet, as if nothing had happened. Gill felt she'd gone beyond exhaustion and was now oddly wide-awake and energetic.

There was a huge fuss from Colin, who had found them missing—what the hell happened, where had they been, didn't they realize he'd spent hours searching? Juliana calmed him as best she could. "Colin, desist. I'll explain it all later. For now, we need lots of tea and coffee, food, and then sleep, hours and hours of wonderful sleep."

"I'm on the case."

"Where's Ned?"

Colin bit his lip, blinked; his eyes had a wild look, emphasised by pouchy shadows beneath them. His hair was a mess, his chin rough with stubble. "He was out on the estate searching for you and he said that there's a big white horse wandering around. Rufus's horse. He's trying to catch it."

"God," Juliana sighed. "If you see him, tell him to leave it be. Rufus may or may not come back but, to be quite honest, I'm too tired to care. If he shows up, tell him to take his horse and bugger off!"

"That would be my pleasure. I'm just so glad to see you back."

Adam excused himself, saying he wanted a bath before he fell asleep where he stood. The rest ate soup, toast and apple pie, and then withdrew to the sitting room where they'd held their meeting about the exhibition . . . it seemed weeks ago. Juliana ushered Peta, Gill and Theo in there with matter-of-fact brusqueness, "There you are, sit down and rest for a while, take stock of things, get drunk, whatever. Quite frankly, I'm past caring what happens. I'm off to bed." She paused. "One thing I know is that Adam is a grown man and, try as I might, I cannot be a full-time bodyguard to him. He will have to learn to protect himself."

"I think he knows that, Dame J," said Peta.

Juliana nodded and withdrew with a tired wave. "Good night. We'll see what the morning brings. I cannot think about *anything* until I've had some rest."

Corah's letter, Gill thought. *The exhibition. Rufus . . .*

Theodorus moved as if in a dream, his eyes unfocused, his expression flickering with something close to pain, or perhaps self-doubt. He retained his usual dignity, but the crusading zeal had gone out of him. It was hard to see him like that, shaken, disillusioned. Gill wondered if he was now more like the young man Peta had loved and lost.

"You were going to explain what an eightfold web is," she said to Peta, "and why it's bad."

"Oh, that—god, yes, I'd forgotten." Peta leaned on the mantelpiece, yawning. "Aelyr can change the fabric of the Spiral. If they want some more space, they can create it, but they can't do it alone. You have to have a certain number of people, with the right abilities, to create a sort of web of energy which can then be stretched . . . I'm not explaining this very well. I've never seen it in action, so that's all I can tell you, really."

"Your description is a fair one," said Theo. "It's meant to be done with the agreement of the clan or community that it affects. Rufus and his friends were outlaws. They formed an eightfold web without agreement from anyone, and used it to create a hiding place, Boundry . . ." He trailed off and sat down in a chair, looking into the unlit fireplace.

With a groan, Peta sat on the chair-arm beside him. "Mark, anyone can see you're devastated. I'm so sorry this has gone wrong."

He didn't answer at first. At last he said carefully, "It's difficult to comprehend. It's my fault."

"How so?"

"I was too fixated upon that goal. Demonstrating that crimes like Rufus's would be stopped and punished, and that those crimes were the result of unfettered interaction with Vaeth. I thought people would *see* the rightness of separation. I never stopped to consider that the tide might go another way. So blind."

"No, don't blame yourself," said Peta. "You know, it happens on Earth, too; if the penalty for a certain crime seems just *too* harsh and drastic, juries have been known to find the accused person innocent, even if everyone knows they're as guilty as hell."

"That's not quite what happened."

"It was a factor. Obviously many Aelyr feel that they *should* have total freedom to make merry on Earth, as a matter of principle, regardless of the rights and wrongs of it."

"Then Albin and I misread the mood."

"He made a play for power and lost. He was using you, Mark."

Gill noticed that he didn't object to her use of his old name. His gaze roved to the gilt-framed paintings on the walls. He shook his head. "We shared a belief."

"No, no, no," said Peta. "You have nothing in common with that cold old devil. You're kind, straight and true. Albin is bent. There's something devious and malevolent in him, you can see it in his eyes!"

"If you're right, again, I was blind to it."

Cautiously, Peta stroked his shoulder. Gill wondered whether to leave the room, but couldn't do so without it being obvious. "Mark," Peta said gently. "You know, if you don't want to return to Lashtor, you're welcome to stay here. I use the term *here* loosely, since this isn't my house. I expect I'll go back to Cloudcroft, at least until I decide what to do next. I'm just saying, if you want to come with me, you'd be more than welcome. Your family would like to see you. Don't you think?"

She gave a small, impish smile. He smiled too, and put his hand on hers. "Ah, Peta. You think any good can come of this?"

"Well . . . yes. I had a horrible feeling all along that your quest was doomed, but I don't think any less of you for it. You believed in something. Now it's not there anymore, that must be hard to bear . . . but I'm still here. You're not on your own. We could get to know each other again."

He nodded. His head was lowered, his gaze on the carpet. "That's a wonderful prospect."

"Yes." Her smile broadened, pinched at the corners with threatening tears. "Rediscover where you really belong after all."

He stood up. Peta rose too, looking at him with her head on one side. He touched her cheek, kissed her on the mouth, stood looking into her face. "I can't turn aside at the first setback. I belong in Lashtor."

"Do you?"

"Nothing's changed, Peta. It's been good to see you again, but I have traveled too far. You can't turn me back into Mark."

She frowned, her mouth forming a protest that didn't come.

"I have to leave now. I'm sorry. I'll keep a lookout for Rufus as I go, but I doubt that he'll dare to trouble you again. I'm sorry for everything you've been through. I'm forever grateful for your help."

"But," Peta stalled. "Don't go. Mark, wait. I thought . . ."

He stepped away with a slight bow, a graceful gesture of parting. "This has only made me more determined to continue the fight. I remain dedicated to the cause of purity and separation, even if I must pursue it entirely alone."

"Mark," said Peta, raising a cautious fingertip to touch his blank, ravaged face. He looked away from her. Her hand fell.

"Those were my vows, Peta. I can never put them aside. Perhaps one day you'll feel the same; until then, I wish you well in all that you do."

After Theo had gone, as hard as she tried to hide it, it was plain that Peta was devastated. She tried to laugh it off, but her face had the paralyzed look of someone desperately fighting tears. She excused herself, saying that she was going to have a bath and fall into bed.

"Let me stay with you," said Gill. "You shouldn't be on your own."

"I'm fine!" Peta snapped. "Really, Gill, I'm okay. An old boyfriend decides to be an arse; it's no big deal. I just want some peace and quiet. I need time to think."

Gill let her go. She wondered if she should have argued more, but her inclination was to take people at their word. If Peta said she wanted to be alone, Gill assumed she meant it. She decided, at that moment, that what she most wanted was the solitude of Robin Cottage.

As she stepped outside, she realized there was someone following her, a soft-moving shadow. She turned. It was Adam. He was in clean clothes, his black hair was tousled and damp from his bath, his eyes soft, wary, but fully self-aware and calm. "Gill, can I come with you?"

"Oh," she said, startled. "Yes, if you like."

He read the puzzlement in her face and added, "I don't want to be in the house anymore. I felt safe in the cottage. I'd like to talk to you."

Gill closed the front door and switched on a light. It felt strange to be back here, after all that had happened at Cairndonan and Naamon. The cottage felt small, bleak and chilly. Untenanted.

"Have a seat," she said to Adam, and set briskly about transforming the atmosphere. She drew all the curtains, lit a fire, switched off the overhead light in favor of table lamps and candles. She poured two glasses of white wine and sat beside him, hardly knowing what to say. "Thank you," he said, taking the glass she offered.

"This will help take our minds off things." They sat next to each other, a foot of space between them; not completely at ease, but close to it. Gill noticed that Adam had brought his ivy-leaf mask and placed it in the vase with hers: two strange faces nestling together. She was aware of slight discomfort in her thigh; it would be good to get her clothes off . . . she found herself blushing at the unwitting implication . . . strip everything off and take a shower . . . "We could watch TV, if there's any reception."

Adam shook his head. "Sitting here with you is all I want. You've made the room beautiful."

"Amazing what you can do with a few candles. I was thinking of the time you first arrived. It's good to see you, er . . ."

"Less mad?" Adam gave a quiet laugh.

"I wasn't going to say that, but as you mention it . . ." She studied his strong, clean profile and thought that he was physically as beautiful as Rufus, in his way; more so, in fact, because Adam had a sweetness about him that Rufus—as old and cold as stone—lacked. "Look, you make yourself comfortable. Help yourself if you want something to eat. I need to shower, wash off the ash of Naamon."

Once she'd finished drenching herself in suds and delicious hot water, she toweled her hair, then wrapped herself in a thick dressing gown, trying to look as frumpy as possible so that Adam would not . . . well, she wasn't sure what either of them were hoping in secret.

"I was thinking about my sister's scrapbook," he said, as she sat beside him again. "So strange, to read what happened to them after I'd gone. I heard that Ned Badger gave the missing letter to Juliana . . . have you seen it?"

"No," said Gill. "Juliana said she couldn't bring herself to read it herself, yet. She just told me a bit of what was in it, namely that my mother wasn't Melody's natural child. She was adopted."

"So you were right," said Adam. "Thank god!"

She looked at him, shocked. "I beg your pardon?"

"Forgive me." He colored, and at the same time smiled so mischievously that she turned warm inside, like honey. "I couldn't come to terms with the idea that you were somehow my great-niece. It always felt as if we were friends, not blood relatives. Now I know why."

"Yes. Fair point."

"Were you upset to hear it?"

Gill shrugged. "It feels so distant, it's neither here nor there. I'm still me."

"It doesn't matter," said Adam. "Hearts matter, not blood."

She poured more wine. "Still, I would like to know what the rest of Corah's letter said. Wouldn't you?"

"I'm not sure I would," Adam said pensively. "She said quite enough in her scrapbook. She always enjoyed shocking people. It was . . . like listening to her voice. That's why I got upset. Because she was talking to us, yet she wasn't there."

"She sounded like quite a woman, your sister," Gill said, smiling. "Ironic, that while you were desperate to escape Rufus, she was driving herself mad trying to find him again."

He met her eyes; his were so beautiful, like crystal, containing such a bright soul. She was sure he knew or guessed far more than he'd yet admitted. "But why?" he said.

"To find you."

"No. There was a great gap in her account. I know the effect Rufus has on people. He is like a drug. People seek him out, drive themselves mad trying to find him, even though he is poison! So yes, I can guess what's in the letter and I don't want to hear it."

"Do you forgive her?"

"Forgive?"

"I know you found it all a bit . . . disturbing. About the men and the drinking."

"Oh, there's nothing to forgive. Corah would still wind me around her little finger, if she were here. But would she forgive *me*, for not protecting her that night? I was the one who failed."

She took his hand. "Not your fault. You were overwhelmed."

They were sitting close now, their clasped hands resting on his thigh. It was the most natural thing she'd ever felt, as if they'd always known each other. "Overwhelmed, not just at that moment, but always. I think Rufus will have me back in the end."

"No!" she said firmly. "No. What on earth makes you think such a thing?"

He answered calmly, "Before I joined the army, I was a spoiled, good-for-nothing brat. The things I saw in France . . . You can't endure such things—or be held prisoner in the Otherworld, and live far beyond your time—and not be unhinged by it. I could never be 'normal' as the world might see it. I really don't belong anywhere now, except with him. Anyway, I wish I'd been strong and found a way to outwit Rufus, or at the very least not to submit to him as I did. Wish I'd been a better person, that is all."

"Don't we all," said Gill. "You're not that bad, Adam. If you didn't have a sense of decency, you wouldn't be tormenting yourself about what you should or shouldn't have done."

He smiled, his eyes downcast. "It's all right. I'm not scared of Rufus anymore."

"Good, but please tell me you won't just give up and go back to him, after all we've been through!" Denial pushed so strongly through her that she couldn't find words to express it. "You can't!"

"Of course I won't." Then there was a spark in his eyes, a more calculating intelligence than she'd given him credit for. "It's the only ace in my hand."

"What does that mean?"

He didn't answer, only laughed softly. "Never mind." The long black curve of lashes fell against his cheeks, swept up again as he looked at her.

Gill turned warm, her heart beating too fast. "I suppose, if you lived in the surface world again, you'd begin to age again, like a normal human, would you? We'd be the same age as each other, more or less."

"I suppose so," he said. "That would be fine by me. I never wanted to stay the same age for ninety years, like some strange specimen pickled in formaldehyde. I'm ready to grow old with dignity now. However, I'm not sure I'm ready for whatever strange new world is out there."

"Don't say that. There's so much to discover."

"Really, after all I've seen and done, I would be a fish out of water." He sipped his wine, pensive for a moment. A shadow brushed her; she saw then that it would actually be easy for him to go back to Rufus; back to the devil he knew. He asked, "What about you, Gill? What will you do?"

"I don't know. I don't recognize the person I was when I came here. I've stopped moping and being scared of my own shadow, so that's a good start, isn't it? I've come to terms with the fact I'm never going to be an Olympic runner. I keep thinking about photography, feeling excited about capturing magic of some kind in an image. Like your uncle John. I understand him. I can't explain, but it's so good to feel *excited* about something, I can't tell you. Anyway, I can't think beyond tonight. There is only *now*."

Adam raised his glass. "Here's to now."

"Cheers," Gill responded, letting her wine-glass touch his with a faint bell-like *chink*. They drank, looking at each other over the rims. Then

Adam put his glass down and produced a small, folded bit of paper from a pocket.

"For all I've said," he murmured, "I've done something very, very wicked."

"Wicked, you? What?"

"I've done what Corah asked, and written down what I think it says in her letter." He gave a one-sided smile.

Gill put down her own glass and said, "Then what you're holding there is a sort of . . . scurrilous betting slip?"

"I suppose it is. Doubly wicked, then. I told you I was a sinner, Gill."

"Show me!" She made a grab for the square of paper, but he lifted it high above his head, out of her reach, teasing. She stretched for it, so that her body was involuntarily pressed against his from thigh to shoulder. They hung there for a moment, panting and laughing. *Sod it*, Gill thought, and kissed him. The folded paper fell down behind the sofa, lost.

What else were they to do? She buried her hands in the thick black silk of his hair and drew him to her. Adam's lips folded gently and eagerly between hers, his hands moving over her shoulders, downwards. The tender pressure and warmth of his hands through her clothes and the sweetness of the kiss spilled streams of fire through her.

She'd been in denial all this time, pretending his beauty stirred nothing in her, never dreaming he might feel the same. Yet she shouldn't have been surprised. It had been smouldering for a long time. His lips moved over her cheeks, her jawline and down her neck, returning to the warmth of her mouth again.

Gill took his hand and led him upstairs.

It was slow and tender, a warm and almost hesitant worship of each other as their clothes were shed. It was nothing like the time with Rufus; no fevered violence. The sheer earthy simplicity of it was miraculous. She marveled at the feel of Adam's slender, firmly muscled flesh beneath her as she slid her hands over him, dwelling on the scar she found in his side; the bullet hole that had nearly killed him. He kissed her scarred thigh with the same tenderness. He had other marks, too, his pale skin marred by welts on his ribs and back. Scars left by the battle field, or by Rufus? She didn't ask, only tasted the salt of her own tears as she kissed her way along the wounds.

Adam was so sweet, so gentle. She knew he wasn't inexperienced— since Copernica and the others had used him for their pleasure over the years—and yet it felt pure; truly the first time either of them had ever done this in simple love and innocence.

There were no boundaries between them, only this long, delicious journey, a sensual flow that went on until weariness stole over them. Finally, they lay spent across her bed, loosely tangled together. He looked like a young god, flawed yet as strong and graceful as a stag.

I'm not in love with you, Adam, I'm not, she told herself firmly. *I don't do love. Not yet, anyway; I'm not ready. This is just . . . I don't know what it is, but gods . . .* "You're beautiful," she said out loud.

He lay gazing at her from beneath heavy lids, laughing softly, his eyes languid and hazed with joy. "So are you."

Oh, I know what this is, Gill thought. *Of course. Healing.*

Smiling still, he bent his head to touch hers and rested there, their faces close together. "Now I know," he whispered. "After this, nothing out there can ever frighten or hurt us again. That's what you've shown me. Whatever else happens to us, we had this."

"Yes," said Gill. "Yes."

Alone in her bedroom, Juliana at last took the creased letter from her pocket and began to read it from the beginning. It was the first time she'd allowed herself to read it properly, to accept what Corah was saying instead of pushing it away.

Not quite alone; Corah materialized on the far side of the room, and sat against the pillows on her bed, legs folded beneath her. She watched, smiling, as Juliana read again that Melody and Robert, the people she'd always assumed to be her natural parents, had adopted her sister, Christina.

You're having the obvious suspicions. No natural children came along for Melody and Robert. You, too, were adopted, Juliana.

To explain, I must go back to that night, the night of the Dunkelmen. *In the middle of the onslaught—menacing laughter, thrashing trees, elusive lights—someone seized me. Everything went still. The darkness rushed on without me as I looked up into a face of such beauty that the world simply stopped. The face shone like ivory, as if the radiance of a thousand candle flames glowed softly from it. Don't ask me to describe his clothes, his hair; it all blended into shadow. All I remember was the dark arch of his eyebrows, the glow of his eyes and that soft, wicked smile. I knew what it was to be spellbound. I allowed him to kiss me—my dear, a nun would have allowed it—and I draw a veil over the other liberties he took—only let me say that I didn't merely allow, I* craved. *Even now I tremble to recall. It was as if he'd opened a door to heaven, not Melody's idea of a chilly, virtuous heaven, but a paradise full of rich colour and overpowering sensation. He opened the door just a crack to let the golden light spill through, and then he slammed it shut again.*

Then it seemed to Juliana that she was not reading after all. Instead her eyes were unfocused and she was listening as Corah's smoky voice narrated the tale. With every word, Juliana saw a series of vivid images.

That's what happened to me that night. That's what I was doing while Uncle John died, and Melody was terrified out of her wits, and Adam vanished.

I came round cold and disheveled, as if I'd been ravished and left for dead, which really, I had, and I was horrified at it all, of course. But afterwards, where Melody armoured herself with Puritan outrage and penance, I went on craving. And Melody knew, or guessed—I was left seemingly unable to hide my thoughts or desires—and she was quite, quite disgusted with me. The Dunkelman *had torn our lives apart and yet he left me feverish with longing. Thus, when we went searching for Adam—all around Cairndonan at first, and later, in pure desperation, seeking the answer from a parade of self-styled psychics and charlatans— in truth I was searching for something more than Adam. I sought the* Dunkelman *himself.*

I found him.

It was in 1938 that we went to see a performer called Erich Harani. He was quite famous in the day as a stage hypnotist, an escapologist, a medium, with every kind of trickery at his command. He was reputed to hold the audience in his hand like a blob of warm honeycomb. Melody and I went in one more vain, desperate attempt to find some kind of answer about Adam.

The moment this young man exploded onto the stage—literally, in a flash of smoke and fire—as vibrant in his masculine beauty as some Russian dancer—I knew him.

Melody did not recognize him. Or, if she did, she denied it to herself. I could write for pages about his hold upon the audience and the miraculous illusions he wrought—suffice it to say that he held us all, molten and swooning, like five hundred puppets swaying to his command. For part of the show he became a medium, telling members of the audience extraordinary things about their lost loved ones that he could not possibly have known. The place was awash with tears and sighs. He said nothing to us about a lost brother—but he looked at me, straight at me. Then I knew for sure it was him.

We tried to go backstage, but there was a crowd and we were turned away. Somehow I got rid of Melody—persuaded her home and to bed—and I went back to the theater alone. This time I was let in and there he was, the Dunkelman, *languid amid oceans of flowers and all the mirrors, costumes and chaos of his dressing room. There were at least seven other worshippers in there with him—but when I came, he sent them all away.*

Did I find out anything about Adam? No, I did not. I tried, but he deflected my questions and anyway, conversation did not last long. He had me, I had him, again and again—he took me to a hotel and there was champagne, delirium, the heat of that honey-sweet wicked paradise enveloping me.

I woke up alone and—as I was soon to discover—pregnant.

I was unmarried, and our parents still alive but frail; the potential for upset was huge. Melody was aghast. We had to avoid scandal and distressing the parents; and, to be frank, I wanted no child, whereas Melody's own fruitless state was an equal burden to her. So I went away, had the baby, and Melody took it as her own. Took you.

Is that what you wrote on your betting slip, Juliana? If so, you can claim your winnings now.

Truly, I thought Melody would make a better mother than me. Well, I don't think she was any worse—that would have been hard, indeed. Neither of us had much affection to give and rather a 'just get on with it' mentality. And, you know, our obsession with finding Adam—mine with finding the Dunkelman *again—never abated. It became an end in itself, a form of insanity, an illness.*

Because I went on seeking, you know. I went to other stage shows, only to find that 'Erich Harani' had been replaced by a different performer. He was good, but he was not the same man—not the Dunkelman *I craved. I never gave up hope, but I never found him again.*

Our search fizzled out in the end. I came here to hold debauched house parties and shorten my life with drink and cigarettes. Melody desiccated. Really, she sank into ennui, turning ever more austere, thin and holy.

So here, in place of the love and honesty you failed to receive, is a bloody great house and grounds for you to look after!

Who knows who we might have been, Adam and Melody and I, if we hadn't drawn the Dunkelmen *down upon us with our ignorant mockery? That one night destroyed everything. I have lived every day since with those awful images seared into me; dear Uncle John, grey-faced in death. Melody, shivering and witless. Adam, simply gone. And I, despite all that, infected forever by that angelic face, the feel of the* Dunkelman's *lips on mine and his body against me, the scent of rotting leaves and peat rising up all around, so that I would search in a fever of madness for the rest of my days. A wicked, lascivious, sinning, damned and restless soul.*

It seemed to Juliana then that her eyes had refocused on the words; that she was reading the end of the letter, and that Corah was behind her, reading

out loud over her shoulder. So close and real, yet untouchable. Juliana felt
tears pressing at her throat, her eyes. Exhausted as she was, she had a feeling that sleep would be elusive tonight.

> *Can you find it in your heart to forgive us all? I still cannot feel like a
> mother to you, but nonetheless, I am very, very fond of you. Please don't
> live here in bitterness, but create, and enjoy, and play. Oh, and if ever
> you find Adam—give him my dear love's kiss and welcome him home as
> I would have done.*
>   *Your affectionate Aunt (Mother),*
>   *Corah.*

22

So Little Time

Next morning, Juliana made her way down to *Midsummer Night* on the cliff tops near Cairndonan Point. The sky was cloudy and there was a light wind off the sea, carrying spots of rain. It appeared the contractors had been back in her absence; the tent and the canvas roofing over the pathway had been removed. There was no shelter if it decided to pour down, but she didn't care. The exhibit stood as she'd left it, and yet she saw it suddenly with new eyes. Heavy, curving shapes of stone, so very pleasing to the gaze. It worked as a whole. The group did everything she'd intended, describing the mysterious journey in and out of the forest of life.

Although its inhabitants were gone, her creation still had an indefinable power. She realized then that Gill was right. The magic lay in what she'd created, not in its Aetherial hostages. As Vaidre Daima had suggested, each sculpture acted as a small portal. She could see it clearly now. Not that the work contained literal holes, but it had a magnetic quality that drew you in, layers that would absorb you like water into gossamer. The portals led nowhere, except into the sculpture itself, yet they created an unearthly effect—even for humans.

Yet she had to make them safe and suddenly she knew how. Her intention had created the portals and now her *intention* was what would close them. She passed between the forms, touching each in turn as if giving a blessing; simply bidding them to seal. It was done. All their magic lay in their remarkable shapes and the story they told, but the danger was gone—unless she chose otherwise.

While she was thus occupied, she noticed Rufus's white horse some yards away, framed against the trees. Her heart contracted with alarm, until she saw Ned, not Rufus, with the animal. Next to the glossy white expanse of Chamberlain, he looked darker and more spindly than ever

"Ned!" she called, walking along the bark path and across the grass towards him. He was holding the horse by its forelock, stroking its nose as if to reassure it. She'd never even realized he liked horses; it seemed there was much she'd never troubled herself to find out about him. As she approached, he gave a furtive sideways glance that made her controlled anger boil close to the surface. "I see you caught him."

"I have no quarrel with the horse, Dame J," Ned said thinly.

"Has anyone told you what happened?"

He paused. His eyes were red-rimmed. "Enough. So, for all your efforts, Theodorus and his friends let us down. I told you they didn't care and that they'd betray us."

"There was a little more to it than that, but yes, Rufus is still on the loose." She moved forward to stroke Chamberlain's glossy neck. The horse blew into her hair, nostrils flaring. In everything—his behaviour and warm, grassy scent—he was like any normal horse, and yet somehow he was larger than life; not unlike Rufus himself.

"They are all as bad as each other, the *Dubh Sidhe*," Ned said bitterly. "Not one of them is to be trusted."

"He's been warned not to come back here."

"You think he'll listen? Who will stop him?"

She scratched Chamberlain's forelock and didn't answer. She said quietly, "Ned, I read the letter."

He shook his head, teeth bared in disapproval. "I should have destroyed it."

"You had no right to keep it from me."

"Oh, had I not? You tell me how it's benefited you, knowing all the foul things that Miss Corah wrote?"

"That's not the point! You were never meant to read it!"

"I was trying to protect you!"

"No. You were trying to protect yourself. *You* were the one who didn't want to believe it. You thought if you concealed Corah's story, it wouldn't be true anymore."

"No." Sweat sheened his narrow face. "All I've ever done is strive to protect you from these evil, wretched beings that have plagued Cairndonan for centuries. Wasn't it better for you to think you were born of decent stock, of Melody and Robert Flagg, than to carry the burden of this awful taint, knowing you descended from these creatures of vile depravity?"

"Do you include Corah in that description?"

"Yes," he said fiercely. "I do."

They glared at each other in mutual rage. "You had no business, Ned. How dare you take our private lives into your own hands like that? Who asked you to do that? *Who asked you?*"

"To keep you free of their clutches, so that you didn't end up like—like Corah, or like my own mother. To protect you from all of it."

"Don't talk to me of 'protection.' How dare you assume this knowledge was going to break me! I'm not some wilting flower."

"I know that."

"Yes, it's distasteful, but we all have to deal with such difficulties at some point! How dare you keep the truth from me? You had no right to make that decision! What you did is indefensible." She stopped, took a breath, trying to stem the rant before she began screaming at him. "Indefensible. I can't speak to you. I don't know you."

"In that case, there is nothing more I can say," Ned answered tightly. "I offer you my resignation."

"What?"

"I made a mistake, Dame J. I wronged you. Therefore I resign."

"Good," she snapped. "Accepted. Find somewhere safe to put the horse, then you can pack your things and get out."

Rain planted cold drops on her head as she stormed away from him. As her temper cooled, she realized that there were questions she must still ask him before he left. About Leon. She had to know the truth of the sinister hint he'd dropped, that he knew the child's fate. Her heart sank. Ned was right, in a way; it would have been easier not to know. She'd barely begun to assimilate Corah's story. Could Corah be trusted not to weave some wild fabrication? Juliana remembered her as being almost too honest and outspoken; she enjoyed games, but she was not one to lie. And if it was true that Corah was her mother . . . was it possible to believe that *Rufus* of all people was her father?

No. She was not even close to wrapping her mind around it.

As she entered the Camellia House, Colin was there in the doorway to the main house, calling her. "Dame J! There you are. Your agent's on the phone. Will you speak to her?"

"Yes, of course. Tell her I'm on my way."

It was an effort to drag her mind back to the surface world. In every quiet moment she seemed to be back in Naamon, her surroundings all dramatic black rock painted by red fire, or full of half-visible figures drifting behind a wash of cold blue lamp-light . . . Sudden reminders of telephones and agents and money seemed unreal, even bizarre.

"Megs, I have to start working again," she said as she picked up the receiver in the office. "So many ideas!"

"Juliana," said her agent, sounding startled. "That's fantastic news, but if I can pull you back to the matter of *Midsummer Night* . . ."

"Oh, yes. Sorry. I am really away with the faeries this morning."

"Well, the response to the viewing has been staggering. We already have four offers averaging around eighteen million U.S. dollars. They're amazing, but they've been simply blown out of the water by this one—are you ready? A billionaire based in Dubai has offered fifty-two point five million dollars for the group. That would make it, as records stand, the most expensive sculpture ever sold! However, I think we can negotiate him up a bit. Juliana? Are you still there?"

Juliana let go of the breath she'd been holding. "That's fantastic, Megan, but don't let's get too excited. I can almost guarantee that at least two of those offers are fakes."

"Oh?" The cautious note in Megan's tone suggested she knew more than she'd let on so far—which was good. It was what agents were paid to do.

"The top one will be a fake offer set up by my estranged husband, Charles, designed so that when—as he expects—I snatch the bidder's hand off, he can have a damn good laugh at my greed. However, I think you'll find that one or even two of the lower offers have also been set up by Charles through intermediaries."

"Why would he do that?"

"So that once the sale is complete, he can have the pleasure of revealing that I've inadvertently sold the work to him. He wants to gloat, to be able to remind me for the rest of my days that he saved my financial skin. It would be insufferable!"

There was a long, ominous hesitation at the other end. Eventually Megan said, "Dame J, I will of course thoroughly investigate the provenance of any offer before we begin negotiations, but . . ."

"Well, do, because he's very clever, very slippery."

"Um, I can well believe Charles is capable of it, but I hardly think any of his offers will stand, in view of his . . . situation."

"What?" She gripped the receiver more tightly. "What situation?"

"His, er . . . political, um . . . difficulties."

"Sorry, Megan, I know nothing about it. I've been rather out of touch."

"Oh," Megan sounded embarrassed. "It's been all over the news for two days. You haven't heard?"

"No. No, I was in no position to watch TV or even listen to the radio yesterday."

Another pause at the other end. "I had no idea you wouldn't know. Look, can I suggest you watch the news? Then you'll understand. I really thought he might have called you himself . . . but he probably didn't have the chance, or was too ashamed."

"*Ashamed?*" A smile tugged at her lips. "This I have to see. Thank you, Megs, I'll call you back, okay?"

Upstairs in her private sitting room, Juliana switched on the television and made herself a pot of tea as she waited for the next bulletin. She had only a few terrestrial stations, no rolling news channel, and so she had ten minutes to wait. She looked at her watch. Perhaps she could send Colin down to the village for a newspaper . . . probably all the village knew about it already, whatever it was.

There was a knock on her door, but she'd left it open and Peta walked in. She looked tired, her pale skin almost translucent and her unruly hair in more of a mess than usual. "Can I come in?"

"Of course, my dear." Juliana put the teapot on a tray with milk and two cups, and carried it to a small table. "Just waiting for the news, apparently my ex-husband's been up to something . . . you don't know about it, do you?"

Peta looked blank. "No, sorry. I was awake half the night thinking, and then I fell asleep and couldn't wake up."

"Are you all right? Where's Theo?"

Peta gave an offhand shrug. "He went back to Lashtor."

"I suspected he might. Did you—how can I put it—manage to resolve things between you?"

"Oh, yes." Peta gave a tired smile. "I rather foolishly hoped he might give up his crusade, after things went wrong in Naamon. I thought he might lose his faith, so to speak, and revert to the Mark I used to know. But no, that was like expecting a monk to give up his vocation after one setback. Stupid."

"Come along, sit beside me." Juliana patted the sofa. "I can see you're upset."

Peta raised a hand, fingers spread in denial. "No, I'm fine, truly. Not heartbroken, or anything. Just sad. It was never really about us getting back together. It was about understanding what had happened to him. Which I do, I think. I'm not very happy about it, but it's okay." She growled. "Oh, what a stupid, stupid waste of a lovely man! But it's his decision. At least I know." She accepted a cup of tea from Juliana. "How about you, Dame J?"

"Hmph." Juliana picked up Corah's letter from a side table and shoved it into her hand. "Read that."

"Are you sure?"

"Yes! I have to break the spell of secrecy!"

Peta read quickly, her mouth dropping open.

Meanwhile, Juliana paced around, keeping half an eye on the television. She waited until Peta had finished it, and made the inevitable expressions of surprise. Then Juliana said, "Is it possible to be certain that Corah truly met Rufus a second time? She may simply have slept with some stage entertainer who looked a bit like him, and constructed an elaborate fantasy around the experience. She said herself that when she went to see this Erich Harani a second time, it was a different man . . . I can't even think about it. What do you make of it?"

"Honestly, I don't know. Everything Corah says is sort of comical . . .

or would be if it were about someone else, and not about you and your family. Have you shown it to Adam? Where is he?"

"Another sensitive topic! He . . ." Juliana took the letter from her and put it back in the dining room, on top of the scrapbook. Returning, she sat down again, heavily. "Let's just say he didn't sleep in his room last night."

"Oh? Should we be worried?"

"I'm always worried about him. It's worse than having a child to look after! But . . . according to Colin, he was seen heading towards Robin Cottage with Gill."

"Ahhh," Peta whispered. "I always had a feeling about those two . . ."

"Well, who can blame them? Two attractive young people who've been through a horribly stressful time . . . and of course, discovering that they are not actually blood relatives after all. Perhaps that took the brakes off. What else? Had a ghastly argument with Ned about the letter and he insists he's leaving. Oh, and I've had an offer of fifty-two point five million dollars for *Midsummer Night*, from a billionaire in Dubai."

Peta spluttered on her tea, nearly choking. "But that's fantastic. Isn't it? Solves all your financial worries—even after tax?"

Juliana huffed. "Except it's not real. It's got Charles written all over it. I accept the offer, it all goes horribly wrong and there is Charles laughing his oily laugh and dangling a check in front of me that I have to accept. So he thinks, at any rate."

Whirling graphics announced the news. Juliana sat forward and pointed the remote to increase the volume. "Here we go. Bloody hell, there he is."

Footage played, showing Charles being escorted from his London house by two uniformed police officers. Camera flashes strobed his face; journalists shouted questions to which he retorted grimly, "No comment, no comment."

"Senior government minister Charles Sandford-Barnes has been released after his arrest yesterday, during which he was questioned for nine hours over alleged corruption charges stretching back eleven years," the female newsreader was saying. "Our correspondent is outside his London home. Michael, what can you tell us?"

A man in a beige overcoat appeared, standing in a rainy street with a microphone in his hand. "Yes, it's believed that Charles Sandford-Barnes was released on police bail in the early hours of this morning but his whereabouts are currently unknown. What we know so far is that he faces three serious charges of corruption."

The newsreader asked, "Politicians have often been subject to such allegations over the years, but often they are perceived as being allowed to get away with it. Isn't it quite unusual for anyone to be charged with an actual offense?"

"Yes, indeed, but commentators are suggesting that Sandford-Barnes has been used as a scapegoat by a government eager to dissociate itself from what some see as endemic corruption. A government spokesman made the following statement earlier . . ."

A piece of film ran, showing a short, red-haired woman outside 10 Downing Street, half a dozen microphones around her. "Mr. Sandford-Barnes's resignation and the subsequent police investigation make plain our intent to root out corruption at all levels. This is all part of a continuing drive towards transparent government."

"What utter bollocks!" Juliana exclaimed.

Over a shot of a disgruntled Charles being eased into the back of a police car, the correspondent continued, "Charles Sandford-Barnes has resigned from his position and his bank accounts have been frozen. Although free for the time being, he is expected to be questioned again and further charges may follow."

There was more talk; the news presenter turned to a commentator in the studio, who spoke of bribery, of great wedges of money slipping into back pockets in exchange for peerages and political influence, or for industries to have controversial planning permissions nodded through, of illegal party funding. He spoke of unknown whistle-blowers. He spoke of a change in mood within the ranks of government, a new policy of disassociating themselves from all such immorality in time for the next general election. "However, sources are suggesting that this has all come too late, that Charles Sandford-Barnes is seen as the tip of a large and murky iceberg and that, as further revelations come out, the prime minister may well be left with no choice but to call a general election."

The item ended. Juliana pressed the off button and sat gaping at the screen. "Fucking bloody hell," she said.

Peta eyed her warily, as if trying to judge whether this news was welcome or not. "Did you know this was happening?"

"No, I absolutely did not. Correction—I knew Charles was right up to his tits in bribery, blackmail and backhanders, and always has been. But I thought he was unassailable. He led me to believe that, regardless of what people knew about him, he knew something even worse about them. He gave the impression that he was too powerful ever to be found out." Juliana laughed out loud. "Turns out he was wrong!"

Peta raised one eyebrow. "Are you pleased?"

"Of course not. That would be inappropriate."

"So what they're saying is that everyone is at it, but because they can't get away with it any longer, someone must be sacrificed?"

"And Charles is it. Oh my god, he's ruined. No wonder he didn't come to the exhibition."

Juliana laughed, but inside she was shocked. Not jubilant. However rotten it was at the heart, there had been something oddly magnificent about Charles's sinister power.

"As in the Spiral, so in the outer world," said Peta. "A change of political mood means that Rufus goes free, while Mr. Sandford-Barnes pays for his fun."

"I wonder who turned him in?" Juliana said thoughtfully.

The phone rang as she spoke. Juliana answered and was taken aback to hear Charles on the other end. His dark, velvety voice sounded ragged. The line crackled, and she could hear a car engine droning in the background.

"I've been trying to call you," he said. "I suppose you know."

"Charles? I've literally, just this minute seen the news. What's happening?"

"I'm on my way. I need to see you."

"*What?* No, Charles, don't come here! Not now."

"I have to."

"But aren't you—aren't you supposed to stay where the police can find you?"

He gave a short laugh. "Damn the police! They should answer to me, not the other way round! I have to see you, Jules."

"No, no. Turn around, go back to London before they realize you've gone."

"I'm on my way," he repeated flatly. "I need answers."

"Where are you?" The line went dead. She put the receiver back on its cradle with some force. "That's all I need! Why's he coming here? What does he think I can do for him?"

Peta shrugged. "Hide him?"

"In his dreams. If he shows up, I'll call the police myself. He is not dragging me into this."

"Well, get Colin to make sure the main gates are locked."

"Oh, there's no point in trying to lock him out." She groaned. "If he turns up, I'll see him, of course. If he wants someone to commiserate with his ill-fortune, though, he is out of luck. Poor bastard."

Juliana went to the window and looked out. There was no sign of any activity outside; Charles might still be miles away. The sky was darkening, a strong wind blowing. "Looks like a bit of a squall out there," she said. "I think there's a storm coming. Peta, could you switch a light on? It's suddenly like midnight in here."

As she spoke, her eyesight went dim and foggy, making her wonder if she was about to pass out, or have a stroke. No; not her eyes. Reality itself had warped. Peta didn't answer; instead she heard Ned's voice calling her name, coming gradually closer from a great distance. Everything felt slow and dark and echoey. She tried to turn round and it seemed to take a century. When she managed it, she found herself looking at a nightmarish transformation.

The room was as black as Naamon and its walls writhed gently in the edge of her vision. The only light was a dull red glow, enough to see that Peta was on her feet, looking horrified, and that Ned was crawling in through the doorway on hands and knees—the twisted ivory horn clasped in one hand—as if battling a powerful river current.

Rufus was standing in the center of the space, holding a familiar envelope in one hand. He shone as if bathed in a beam of moonlight. "Poor old Charles, eh?" he said. "He had it coming."

"What have you done to my house?" Juliana gasped. "How long have you been here?"

"Oh, a fair while. Reality has shifted a little way into Dumannios, that's all." Rufus laughed, brandishing the letter. "Corah was quite a girl, wasn't she? Fascinating."

A tidal wave of emotions went through Juliana, all of them horrible. "You were not meant to read that! Is nothing sacred to you?"

"Not really, no."

Peta attempted to grab the letter, but he gave a light push and she fell back onto the sofa as if he'd thrown her. "Hm. So, according to this, I had her again and again backstage at some seedy theater until she went home pregnant with you?"

Juliana stared at him. She was almost beyond speech. Rufus was the only person in the world who could answer the question. "Is it true?"

"Well, let's examine her claim. It seems to me that this illusionist she seduced could have been anyone. You said it yourself, hardly twenty minutes ago. It's a pitiful tale, isn't it? To think she was so very desperate for a second taste of my charms that she cast my glamour over some second-rate stage magician and carried away his seed thinking it was mine? Should I be flattered? It's a sordid episode all round."

"Shut up," Ned hissed weakly from the doorway.

Juliana could not respond. She was mortified. The knowledge that Rufus had read about Corah's obsessive pursuit of him and now stood there laughing about it was vile. His mocking dismissal of Corah's claim was worse. It pierced her like a poison-soaked spear. It was a betrayal, a violation, both of Corah and of Juliana herself.

"I don't care," she whispered at last. "I would rather anyone had fathered me but you. I wish you had been thrown in the Abyss."

"This is why," Ned's faint, agonized voice came from the doorway. "*This* is why I wanted to protect you, Dame J. I'd have done anything to spare you this."

Silently she cursed Vaidre Daima for letting Rufus go free. Now he'd come for revenge, and she cursed herself for letting him render her so completely powerless. She had to steel herself against his taunting, or go mad. There was an unseen force in the air, holding them like flies in tar. Around the room, cloudy shapes appeared, resolving into masked Aetherial specters. Seven of them . . . his followers.

Rufus tutted. "This is a poor attitude towards your possible father. After I brought poor Charles to his knees for your benefit, too. A storm on the way, you think?" He grinned. "You could say that."

Gill had slipped into sleep with Adam's arm around her, her head resting on his chest, one hand curled limply on his hip. When she woke, a strange crimson light glowed through the window, and Adam had gone.

For a moment she was confused. Then she sat up in a panic. "Adam?"

The clock said one-thirty. But was it afternoon or night? The cottage shook as if from an earth tremor. She leaped out of bed and crossed to the window. The world looked wrong, wrapped in purplish twilight, trees on the far side of the stream silhouetted against a fiery glow. She could hear a soft, tearing roar . . . the sound made by the rivers of magma in Naamon.

"Adam!"

She got dressed as she searched the cottage, awkwardly pulling on jeans and sweatshirt, hopping as she forced her feet into walking boots. He was not in the bathroom, nor downstairs, but the front door stood wide open. Outside, the whole landscape seemed wrapped in the strange atmosphere of the Dusklands—no. Dumannios. The ground was as black as obsidian . . . Everything was different, distances greater. The stream had gone and the trees were vanishing as she watched, blowing away like plumes of smoke. Instead there was a slope ridged with solid lava in front of her, transected by a split that boiled with yellow, molten rock.

On the far side, climbing towards the house, she saw Adam.

The ground was tearing apart in front of her, the magma stream widening even as she approached it. She was running full out now. Soon the chasm that lay across her path would cut her off from Adam and the house. In a split second she judged that if she slowed down now, the tilt of the ground would take her slithering straight into the chasm. Instead she accelerated.

With a yell she flung herself off the lip, felt the roasting heat enveloping her body, acrid fumes in her throat. Thick yellow-hot liquid flashed below her. Then she hit the other side, rocks burning her hands like red-hot coals, one foot skidding into thin air and almost taking her into the cauldron below. She scrambled up, grunting with pain, and ran on.

She ran as if her accident had never happened—no, hardly that. Pure adrenaline masked the pain. Her gait was uneven, she would never regain the speed she'd lost—but at that moment, she could still do it. She flew.

"Adam," she shouted. "Wait!"

He looked calmly over his shoulder at her, not even breaking his stride. "I'm going to the house," he said. "Rufus is there."

Unnatural darkness had fallen, but every window blazed with light. Gill tried to gather her scattered thoughts. Juliana, Peta, Ned Badger and Colin . . . presumably they were all inside. She caught up with Adam at the front lobby, but while he went straight towards the stairs—as if sleepwalking—Gill paused and looked around. The house felt strange, pulled out of shape in some indefinable way. She heard voices and soft laughter. Music was playing; she recognized it as the light classical music that Juliana had piped into the dining room at mealtimes.

The entrance hall was empty, but as she glanced into the big dining room, she saw all of Peta's mannequins brought to life. Shock froze her for a second. Seven elegant figures, in masks and costumes as colorful as a field of flowers, stood raising champagne flutes to each other. A moment later, they vanished. The dining room was dark again.

Stifling a gasp, Gill backed away.

"Colin?" she called out softly, retreating. "Ned?"

She found Colin in the office behind the front desk—lying on the floor, bound and gagged. His face bore swollen red bruises and he was semiconscious, groaning and restless as if drugged. Gill dropped to her knees, fumbling to untie the tightly-knotted gag, shocked by his injuries. "Colin, wake up!" His eyes came half-open, swiveling.

"Gill." His voice was hoarse. "Got to find Dame J."

"What happened to you?"

His eyes were red with anger and confusion. "Don't know, thought a storm was coming—everything went black and weird and they just *appeared*. Bastards. Tried to make 'em leave but . . . I dunno. They do something without touching you, feels like you've been knocked down by a lead weight. Tried to fight 'em but they just laughed, dragged me in here, roughed me up a bit . . ." He tried to stand but stumbled back to the floor. "Fuck, I can't wake up."

"Try," said Gill, hauling on his arm. "If it's Rufus and his friends, we can't defeat them with physical violence."

"Like hell," said Colin. "Give me another crack at them. No long-haired fairy gets the better of me."

"Is Juliana upstairs?"

"Yeah, I think so."

"Have you seen Rufus?"

"No. Come on, let's get going," Colin urged, then leaned on the desk, groaning. "Shit, I think they broke my ribs." Gill couldn't wait for him to recover. She ran out of the office and took the stairs two at a time.

Upstairs, all the lights were on and yet the light looked dim and treacly, the walls wavering, the air full of flickering shadow. "Adam?" she called. Terror and foreboding filled her, thick as sand, so heavy she wanted to sink to the floor and close her eyes just to escape. Still she forced herself on. The open door to Juliana's apartment seemed a tiny black slit at the top of a steep hill.

Gill reached it, struggled through the hallway and into the sitting room as if swimming through tar. Ned was crouching on the floor just inside the doorway; he looked like a terrified sentry who refused to leave his post. Rufus's power lay heavy and seductive on the place, telling her that if only she succumbed to sleep, she would wake in her own bed and everything would be normal again. With all her strength, she fought it. Adam was just inside. She touched his arm, but he stood like a statue and didn't react.

The room appeared twice its normal size, dim yet full of strange lights, the walls moving with many-layered veils. The seven masked beings that she'd glimpsed downstairs were now spaced around the boundary, their forms shining and shifting.

They stared from feathered and jeweled alien faces—they were wearing Peta's costumes, Gill saw in disbelief, but she recognized other attributes; Copernica's pale red locks, Ekaterina's darkness, Vivienne's green-blue aura . . . Juliana and Peta were close together in the middle of the room, nervous and defiant; and there was Rufus facing them, as sleek as a panther, his hands on hips and his hair a luxuriant, tangled cascade. His *Dunkelman* form shimmered around him as a translucent crimson sheath.

"What are you doing?" cried Gill.

"Whatever the hell I like," said Rufus. He looked at her, grinning. "We are celebrating. You look deliciously sweaty, Gill. Perhaps you would care to join me in a celebratory tumble for old times' sake?" He seemed to be the only one who could walk around freely, as if he moved in air, while the rest of them struggled in quicksand. He came towards her and reached out, one hand brushing her shoulder before she jerked away. "Oh, come on. Join the fun. I intend to have everybody in the house before the night is out."

"It's time for you to leave." Gill tried to sound forceful, failing miserably. "Go on, get out, and take all your friends with you!"

"No," said Rufus, his eyes narrowing. "We like it here. We plan to stay."

"Like hell," Colin growled behind Gill.

He charged at Rufus, head down. Rufus put out a hand and Colin stopped as if he'd hit a concrete post. He jerked, stumbled backwards then hit the floorboards with force. Yet he hadn't come within ten feet of Rufus.

"Don't!" cried Juliana. "Is he all right?"

"Yeah, I'm just great," Colin rasped, coughing. Ned crawled a little further into the room, fighting the enchantment that weighed him down. Copernica and her six companions stood motionless, resembling Peta's mannequins but for the snake eyes glowing in the eye slits.

"They've even stolen my fucking costumes!" Peta exclaimed. "Unbelievable!"

"Take it as a compliment," said Rufus. "You make them for Aetherial use, don't you?"

"What do you want?" asked Gill.

"You aided Theodorus and Albin in trying to bring a death sentence upon us. However—not guilty." Rufus spoke tauntingly, pointing at himself. "Not guilty, not guilty, not guilty. I am a free man. Juliana's house pleases me and I am minded to make it our new home. Who is going to stop me?"

"I'm calling the bloody police," Colin gasped.

"Oh, try it. Call them out a dozen times; they will never find us here. We'll vanish into the Dusklands, and how many times can you cry wolf before they charge you with wasting police time?"

The space around them settled, but it was all wrong. It was Cairndonan House on a greater scale, its faded colors darker and more vivid, containing all the brooding power of the fortress. There were monumental black walls standing behind the veils that held Juliana's paintings and ornaments. The space held two worlds at once. Gill thought she could smell sulfur, and sense the ancient queen's brooding presence. Naamon, Mount Khafet.

"What have you done to my house?" Juliana asked quietly. "Am I imagining this?"

"No," said Peta. "It's the eightfold web. Rufus and his friends are doing this . . . they each hold a separate node of the space they want to change and pull everything into a different shape. Or place. Or something."

"Actually, that's not a bad explanation," said Rufus. "Couldn't have put it better myself. We each hold a point in space and stretch it as we please. It's how the Aelyr have always expanded the Spiral."

"Which was the other thing you were forbidden to do," said Peta.

"Oh, screw that," said Rufus. "You know my feelings about authority. All along the *conlineos* from Boundry to Naamon, the membrane between Earth and Spiral is thin. If you tear it away, you will find Queen Malikala's fortress and Juliana's house in the same space. So that is what we're doing, breaking down the barrier that keeps them apart."

"What's this in aid of, revenge?" snapped Juliana. "You don't give a damn for the promise you made Vaidre Daima, you just walk into my house—"

"My house now, I believe," said Rufus. "I don't want revenge. I'm just being practical. Where better to situate my new stronghold? Malikala's fortress and your magnificent house, fused as one."

Juliana blanched. "This is my home. These are my friends and family. You can't do this to us."

"You know," said Rufus, "if you really were my daughter, Dame Juliana, you would have some cunning way to defeat me—a portal right under our feet ready to swallow us, perhaps? Still—you have power, without question. You imprisoned my friends for a good few years. I respect that. Perhaps you are mine, a chip off the old block, indeed. Half Aetherial and half Corah! No wonder you're special. Why don't you stay here, share in it?"

"How *dare* you invite me to stay in my own home!" she exploded. "So you violated my aunt. That doesn't make you any kind of father, Rufus."

"There was no violation, I assure you. Her own words made that *very* obvious."

"Stop it!" For the first time, Juliana sounded close to breaking. "Enough. It's all wrong, you look young enough to be my grandson!"

"And you, dear daughter, look much younger than we know you to be. You are so ungrateful for the gifts of longevity, beauty and creativity I've given you."

"And you know that any supposed relationship between us is nothing but a source of malevolent amusement to you. So let's leave it aside."

"If you say so," Rufus agreed mildly.

"So you're requisitioning Cairndonan, and we can't stop you."

"Not even the Spiral Court can stop me now. I'm innocent, don't you know? We're no longer fugitives. With this as our new power base, other Aetherials will be drawn here. In time, we could take over the Spiral, banish the Spiral Court, cause Earth and Otherworld to slide one into another, all barriers gone. It would be a new Aetherial anarchy!"

"It sounds like a nightmare," said Peta.

"Mmm." Rufus smiled. "As if the world had turned into one gigantic Hieronymus Bosch painting. And I will be King of Pleasure, King of Pain."

"Maybe Theo and Albin had a point, after all," said Peta.

Rufus laughed. "Certainly Vaidre Daima is a bit of a liberal idiot."

Now was the moment for some great act of heroism, thought Gill. Juliana should weave a portal to suck Rufus into oblivion. Ned should rush in and stab him with the unicorn horn, or Peta reveal some secret that would destroy him where he stood. It was not going to happen, though. How could you fight beings who were able to tear apart reality itself? It was anguish to witness Juliana's despair, her stoic bravery. The strange house trembled around them and Gill wondered if there was anything resembling the real world still outside.

She realized that Rufus was waiting for something.

"What do you expect me to do?" Juliana asked. "Hand you the keys and say fine, enjoy the house, don't forget to pay the gas bill?"

"I can give you money," said Rufus. Amusement played around his predatory eyes. "Or you could stay here, daughter, become our tame artist. We can use your talents to lure in Aetherials, or indeed to trap any who come with unfriendly intent. That would work, wouldn't it? And what of you, Peta? You could make our masks and clothes for our ceremonies, solstices and ancestors' nights and all the rest, even the Night of the Summer Stars itself." His gaze on Peta became languid. "You're tempted, aren't you? I've seen the way you look at me—trying to hate me, but not succeeding. Wondering." Peta flushed scarlet as he continued, "Why not join us, become your true Aetherial self again?"

Her chin rose in defiance. "I am my true Aetherial self, regardless of what you or Mark or anyone says. No one bullies me."

"Well said," murmured Juliana.

"So there it is," said Rufus, outstretching his palms as if to encompass the house, the stronghold, everything. "I don't want to hurt anyone; only as a last resort. What are you going to do? You can run away if you want. Or put up a fight—that could get nasty, though. I don't recommend it. Stay and be welcome. My house, my kingdom, my rules."

Adam spoke for the first time. "What is your price?"

Rufus blinked at him. "Price, Leith?"

"What would you take in exchange—to give this up and walk away?" He took a few slow steps towards Rufus with no obvious sign of fear. His voice shook slightly, nothing more.

"You couldn't pay it," Rufus said with a sneer. "You've made it repeatedly plain that you won't pay it. It doesn't matter, Leith; you made your choice to leave me and I accept it. Never mind. Look at this beautiful house and palace and power base I've acquired instead!"

"Name it," Adam said simply.

Gill followed him and clasped his arm, but he pressed her hand as if to say, *It's all right*. She let go and stepped back, understanding that he must do this, that he'd been preparing for it all night and longer; perhaps since the moment in the foundry.

Rufus shook his head, affecting skepticism. "You'd make me say it, and be humiliated again?"

"Put all back as it was, walk away, never trouble this household again. Those are my conditions. What do you want in exchange?"

"You know what I want." Rufus's luminous gaze rested on Adam, unblinking. "You."

There was a soft stirring among the Aelyr. As soon as Adam spoke, and Rufus looked back at him with that sly mixture of profound relief and victory, Gill knew that this was what Rufus's staged manipulation had been all about. *It's the only ace in my hand*, Adam had said.

"If you keep the promise, I'll come with you."

"But it must be of your own free will," said Rufus. "No imprisonment, no drugs, no coercion this time, I swear. Come because you choose it freely."

Adam nodded. "Of my own free will."

There were a couple of stifled gasps; Gill wasn't sure who'd uttered them. Then silence, a host of shining eyes focused intently upon Rufus and Adam. Few of those eyes looked friendly. Rufus went on looking at Adam, his head tilted. He reached out to caress Adam's cheek. As hard as he tried to hide it, Gill saw the suppressed, triumphant joy roiling beneath the surface. She felt ill.

Juliana said gravely, "You know, don't you, Adam, that you're agreeing to go back to him for good?"

"Of course," Adam said without expression. "That's what I'm offering."

"I can't ask you to do this," she said.

"You haven't asked. It's my choice." Adam spoke steadily, and there was a self-possession about him and a fierce light in his eyes that Gill had never seen before. The balance had shifted; he was suddenly the stronger one. Rufus's need for him had always been his weakness. "Let me do this one thing, Juliana."

"Rufus!" exclaimed Vivienne. He ignored her, all his attention concentrated on Adam.

"Do you swear it?" Adam gazed back unflinching. "That if I come back, you'll close this rift, leave Cairndonan for good and never trouble the people here again?"

"Yes," Rufus answered. "If you place your willing self in my hands, I swear it on my blood, I swear it by the Lady of Stars herself."

Gill noticed a stirring among his followers. One of them—Nicolas, she thought—cursed under his breath. She felt a curl of panic in her chest. She was desperate to stop Adam from sacrificing himself—but how? It was done, the bargain made. With an enigmatic smile Rufus stepped back and gestured to his companions. "Release the web."

They didn't move. Around them, the house with its soaring dark walls trembled softly. Their anger was palpable, lending the air its own dark heartbeat.

"Rufus!" exclaimed Vivienne. "You made promises to *us*! We'll be together again and create our own heart of power, you said. What about that? This is Queen Malikala's fortress in our hands and you'd give it all up for him?"

"Of course he would!" snapped Copernica. She pulled off her mask, her eyes blazing. "Nothing's more important than his precious Leith. Since the moment Rufus saw him, Leith's always been set above the rest of us, and always will be. All of this was aimed at Leith, and never about our wishes at all!"

Rufus reached out and caught Copernica's chin, looking into her defiant eyes. "And you know why. Leith is the channel for Mistangamesh to return. That's my one true aim and I've never made a secret of it, never deviated. You're damned right, I've achieved my heart's desire to defeat the Spiral Court and seize a power base to rival theirs—and yes, I'd give it all up, just to have my brother Mist back. And that's exactly what I'm doing. If only you bear with me, all will be well again. I'll make amends."

"It's too late."

His fingers tightened on her pointed chin. "Release the web. Don't make me force you."

Nicolas said, "If you make us do this, you'll never see any of us again."

Rufus laughed through his teeth. "You love me. Whatever I ask of you, you'll follow me regardless. Posture all you like; one peep on a dog whistle and you'll come bounding back to your master. All of you."

"Not this time," said Copernica, jerking free of his grip. Her face, unmasked, was more terrifying by far; white and scaled like that of a snake, the eyes slanting green slits. "You've made your choice. You've chosen Leith above us. Go, and go to hell, Rufus. This is the last task ever we do for you."

Gill shot an anxious glance at Juliana. Her aunt looked pale. If Rufus couldn't control his followers, his bargain with Adam would be for nothing.

"Fine, have your tantrum. Your views are noted. Just release the web."

"What if we refuse?" said the voice behind Vivienne's mask.

"Then I'll unravel it for you!" Rufus turned on her, losing his temper. "I am part of it and it only takes one of us to cut the thread."

"Ekaterina is holding your place," said Copernica. "We can make or break the web with seven, Rufus."

"I doubt it," he snarled.

"Do you?" Her voice had a cold, smooth timbre, like gold. None of the seven looked close to human any more; costumes and masks had transformed to flesh and scales and feathers, wrapped in tall auras of fire. "You forget that we're adepts; that's why you brought us together. Of course we can make a sevenfold web. Look." The masked ones raised their hands and

Gill saw faint lines of light gleaming in the air, joining each of the seven to all the others. Rufus, standing with Adam, looked small and human in their midst. He was not part of it. For the first time, he began to look alarmed as well as angry.

"Stop this."

"With or without you, we mean to claim this place of power," said Copernica.

"No, no, no," said Rufus, his eyes manic. "I trusted you!"

"And we trusted you," she replied. "Now we discard you. This at least will be some recompense for our troubles. From you, and—" She pointed at Juliana. "From her."

"Can't you do something?" Juliana exclaimed. Her voice was gritty with fear and outrage.

Rufus's only answer was to open his hands, a gesture of helplessness.

The seven Aelyr stood rock-still with only their pale hands in motion on the darkness, forming a series of eerie gestures; crossed over the heart, uncrossed, palms facing out then lowered, turned, crossed again. As they played this sinuous cat's cradle, the web glowed green and so bright it made Gill's eyes hurt. Juliana's face was grim, like steel. Even Peta looked frightened now. The three women drew instinctively close together, clasping each other's hands for strength.

Tension formed, straining the air, making her eardrums ache until she thought they might burst. The room bulged and trembled. Gill closed her eyes—dizzy with terror as if about to plunge from a great height—waiting for Naamon to erupt and the world to end . . .

Something hit her boot. A voice was wheezing words she couldn't quite hear. She looked down and saw the alicorn at her feet, realized that Ned had thrown it. "Use it," he was saying on the last of his breath. "Work together!"

Gill bent to grab the alicorn with no idea of what he meant. As she did so, Juliana and Peta each clasped it as if it were a bit of driftwood in the ocean. Perhaps it was Peta who initiated it, or Juliana; it began spontaneously, and Gill was simply carried along as energy began to flow from each of them. She *saw* it. A shimmering red haze from Peta, silver-white fire from Juliana. It took her by surprise, flinging her hands off the staff like an electric charge.

"Gill!" Peta said fiercely.

She got a new, firmer grip, hung on as if caught in a gale. It hurt like hell. No clear thoughts at all. Never in her life had she considered that she had any power of her own, yet it was there, a tingling rush up her spine, pouring down her arms. Her power was blue-black and it welled from somewhere so deep she didn't recognize it, from far back in her own ancestral past, from some ancient Hindu deity, from Kali herself . . .

"Now what?" cried Juliana.

"I don't know," said Peta. "Sculpt something!"

A cone of light was beginning to form around them, spinning faster and faster. They held up the alicorn vertically between them, so that it formed the apex of the cone. Thicker and stronger whirled the cone, forming a bright barrier. And then they used it to push against the web.

Their cone was as solid as armor, forcing back the hostile energies, reclaiming their own space. Force and counterforce felt like a vast increase in gravity. Gill groaned, hardly able to stand, certain they would be crushed. She couldn't see Rufus and Adam anymore; saw nothing but whirls of black, white and red. Gradually they began to establish their own territory, to protect it and to push out its boundaries. Slowly the lines of the web were forced out of shape. The cat's cradle stretched, distorted, and began to break.

She heard Rufus shouting. In that moment, it seemed even he was powerless.

There was a *whoosh* of air, a violent jolt, the crash of a vase falling. Pain ceased, pressure released. Naamon lost its hold; in her mind's eye she sensed the *conlineos* sealed, the Naamon portal shut tight . . . The black, shimmering walls vanished like smoke sucked out of the air by a vacuum—and Rufus's companions vanished with them. Gill collapsed to her knees; Peta stumbled on top of her, flailed briefly and then helped her up, Juliana seizing both their arms to steady them.

Peta's masks and garments lay pooled on the carpet, empty. The face of each mask was a white blank.

Rufus was still there, hanging onto Adam as if they'd both been caught in a storm. It had never before occurred to Gill how much of his power was drawn from his followers, his eight-fold web. Without them—at least for these few moments—he was impotent.

Gill looked up in dazed disbelief to see the room restored to its normal dimensions. All was in its usual sepia and dark red tones, furniture, windows showing squares of windswept grey sky—everything as it should be. Juliana was turning around in amazement, taking in everything. Then she shook herself, rushed to help first Colin and then Ned to their feet.

Both men were dazed, punch-drunk almost. She made them sit down and silenced their self-recriminations with a few acerbic words. Peta gave Gill a long, heartfelt hug.

In the midst of it all, Rufus stood looking humanly bewildered. Such was his ego, his followers' rebellion had plainly come as a complete shock. Now he looked so hurt, even vulnerable, that Gill felt almost sorry for him. Almost. He managed to compose himself but his eyes were wild, his mouth a manic grimace.

"There," he said shakily, "You see. You three always had the power to stand up and fight me, instead of just stoically taking it. Marvelous! I'm impressed. I am also fucking furious and pissed off to hell with those idiots, my so-called faithful—but, Lady of Stars, you three were good. I'd take my hat off, if I had one."

"What happened?" said Gill. "Where did Copernica and the others go?"

"Drawn into Naamon when the realms separated," said Rufus. "The web was weaker without me, of course."

"Well, that was something." Juliana exhaled loudly, swept her hair out of her face. "Sculpting with light, with energy! I never dreamed it was possible!"

"Reclaiming your territory, as any matriarch should," said Peta. "It was you against Queen Malikala."

"Is it too much to hope that you'll walk away now and cease harassing us, Rufus?" said Juliana. There was a vicious edge in her voice.

He looked calmly at her. "If Leith is ready, we'll be on our way."

"What do you mean?" said Gill. She paused to cough; her throat was parched. "Your bargain is null and void, surely? Isn't it?"

Adam shook his head. Her heart dropped in sharp dismay. "No, it isn't. I gave my word. Rufus kept the bargain; it was Copernica, not him, who tried to break it. The promise stands."

"Adam!"

His only response to her protest was to turn away from her. "I have to go. It's the price for Rufus to leave you alone."

"We can deal with Rufus!" Juliana said in exasperation, but Adam only smiled sadly.

"That isn't the point. I made a vow. I must keep it."

Rufus emitted a fervent sigh of triumph. "Such a sense of honor, my brother. Oh, well. We didn't need the others, anyway." He reached out and touched Adam's shoulders, caressed his hair and cheeks. Adam didn't resist the touch; he looked tranquil, expressionless. Rufus went on, "All the suffering you went through in Boundry was never meant to cause you pain—but you know that, don't you? It was only to break down *Adam*, because he was a block to you becoming your true self again. And don't forget there was pleasure, too. A surfeit of pleasure, wouldn't you say? Yet you even let yourself be tortured by guilt over that! I couldn't win. It was all for the higher cause of unlocking my beloved brother, but, all right, I admit my tactics failed. From now on things will be different. No pressure, no coercion, none of that. We will simply walk side by side and talk until you remember. Boundry is changing, all its ways in and out unblocked. We don't have to hide there anymore. We're free to go anywhere we like. Look—why not take a few minutes alone to say your farewells to your friends. I'll meet you when you're ready. That will show our newfound trust, won't it? Name the place."

Adam paused, considering. "On top of Cairndonan Point, near *Midsummer Night*."

"Perfect," said Rufus. "The boundary between land and ocean, between realms. I'll be waiting." Gill saw the shine of tears in Rufus's eyes. She thought grimly, *He loves Adam. However twisted and destructive, it's real.* "Perhaps we should have reached this understanding long ago. It might have spared us oceans of pain."

Then Adam stepped forward, and went into Rufus's arms.

"There," said Rufus. "That was simple, wasn't it?"

When they'd gone—followed by Gill and Peta, who couldn't let Adam go so easily—Juliana remained rooted in the center of the room, trying to master herself. She and Adam had barely found any words for each other; he'd given a stiff bow and a gracious murmur of thanks, while all she'd done was nod in wordless acknowledgment. It was a hopelessly inadequate way to part, but what was there to say?

Now she stood there, hardly daring to believe her surroundings were real. Blissful normality had never seemed so precious, or so bitter . . . She was dimly aware of Colin and Ned muttering in the background, arguing about who should have done what. The truth was, they had both done their best, but there had been a tide of Otherworld forces against them that they couldn't fight.

She should stir herself to make sure they were all right, but she seemed to be paralyzed, stunned by all that had happened. A familiar noise brought her back to life; the deep rumbling growl of an engine, fat tires plowing through gravel. Colin went to the window, then turned his bruised, dazed face to her. "Er, Dame J . . . visitor."

She joined him, looked outside and swore. A sleek bright red Lamborghini was pulling up on the front drive and Charles was getting out of it. He could hardly have chosen a worse moment to arrive. His dark overcoat swung as he slammed the door and marched towards the front door, a large bunch of keys in one hand. Leaving Colin and Ned where they were, Juliana hurried along the landing and went downstairs to meet him.

In the lobby, Charles came towards her and pushed straight past as if she wasn't even there. His face was the color of rice paper, his pale eyes frenzied. "Where is he?" Charles growled.

"Who?"

"I know he's here!" She stood aghast as he strode off down a corridor towards the rear of the house, coat flaring.

"Charles!" Juliana called, following him. Her voice rang out, imperious, enough to make him glance round. The whites of his eyes were bloodshot, a map of red veins. He looked utterly demented. Her heart shrank to a cold stone of dread. "Charles, wait!"

"I know he's here, that bastard!" He was plunging in and out of rooms as if searching for something, muttering ferociously under his breath. "This damned house! Should've bulldozed it by now, destroyed it!" As he came out of her downstairs drawing room, she put her arms across the doorway and tried to block him. He shoved past her with such force that she fell, catching her head on the corner of a picture frame.

Her ears rang and she saw stars. By the time she'd picked herself up, Charles had vanished.

"Colin!" she yelled, not knowing if he could hear her.

For several minutes she walked the corridors past the art studios, searching. She was alarmed but oddly clear-headed; surely this crisis could be no worse than the weirdness of the eightfold web. Finally, as she reached the far wing of the house, she saw a door standing open that was always, always locked.

The gun room.

He was at the gun cupboard, his back to her. She heard the ominous crunch of bullets going into chambers, mechanisms locking into place. She knew he'd kept a set of keys, but never dreamed he'd use them. Too angry to think she might be in danger, she marched up to him. "Charles, stop it! What the hell are you going to do, shoot me?"

At that, he became still. The hand holding the rifle fell loosely to his side and he uttered a groan. He moved to the window and stood gazing out at the rear gardens. He shuddered. A couple of tears fell from his eyes.

Cautiously Juliana went to his side and said more calmly, "What the bloody hell are you playing at?"

"Have to withdraw my offer on the house, old girl." He gave a raw laugh. "Lost it all, lost everything. Bastards. I'm going to prison."

"I know. We saw the news," she said.

"I hate this damned house."

"Why the hell did you want to buy it, then?"

He gave a cadaverous laugh. "To demolish it, of course. Erase everything."

She tried to keep her voice level. "You wanted to see me ruined, the house destroyed. Why?"

"Because of the boy," said Charles, putting one hand over his eyes.

"Who?"

"My . . . the child."

"Leon." She understood, and knew she'd been right about his motives after all. "Guilt, is it? You wanted to snatch the house from under me and demolish it, not just to punish me, but to sweep your guilt away?"

"He's dead. I always knew he was dead."

"And I knew it too. We pretended otherwise because we daren't face the truth, but there it is. We let a little boy die, Charles. Your son. Our self-ishness and negligence killed him. You can raze Cairndonan House to the ground but the guilt will always be there."

"I know," he groaned. "Don't I know it!"

"Honestly, Charles, you always knew your activities might unravel one day—that was the risk you took—but why take it out on me? I really thought you'd handle it with more dignity than this. How about we unload the gun, put it away and have a drink?"

As he raised his head, she realized that he was far from seeing reason. His eyes swam with psychotic rage. Quietly he asked, "Do you know a man who calls himself Rufus Hart?"

Juliana paused, full of foreboding. "I've met someone by that name, yes."

"Done more than met him," he said savagely. "It was him, that Rufus, who unraveled it all. I don't even know how he did it. You sent him, I know you did; he told me."

"He was lying," she said, aghast. "I didn't send him!"

"Why else did he come? Happy, are you, with what you've done to me? Got your revenge, Jules? You know what Confucius said—if you go seek-ing revenge, be sure to dig two graves."

"I don't know what you're talking about! I was happy to let you go your own dark way. You were the one who wouldn't stop plaguing me!" Until that moment, she hadn't believed Rufus's assertion that he had caused Charles's downfall. The knowledge that his claim might be true filled her with unspeakable dread.

"Is he here, that slithering toad of a boy toy of yours?"

"I can assure you, he's not my boy toy."

"Is Rufus here?" Charles raised the rifle and held it two-handed. She jerked back, shocked. "Don't lie to me!"

"He was here. He's gone now."

"How long ago?" Charles seemed to take her hesitation as the answer he wanted—that Rufus was still somewhere on the premises. "Where is he?"

"Not in the house. He's gone. Charles, please—"

He froze, focusing on something outside the window. It gave a view right across the gardens to the cliffs and, as she glanced out, she saw what had caught his attention—the tiny figures of Rufus and Adam, Gill and Peta, windblown in the distance on Cairndonan Point.

"There he is!" he rasped.

"Charles, please. Calm down. Let me get you a drink, and we can—"

"There he is! That bastard." He turned, his face contorted, the red-veined eyes almost bursting from the sockets. "I knew it!"

"No!" She tried to block him, but he simply shouldered past her, heading for the door.

Juliana pushed herself off the wall she'd collided with, groaning in shock and despair. The damned gun cupboard! He'd deliberately brought the keys with him, which meant he must have intended violence before he even left London. Terror swept away her self-possession. She began to pursue him.

He was outside and striding across the garden now. Juliana couldn't keep up. He was possessed. She shouted, but a strong wind off the sea carried her words the wrong way, made her feel she was battling a river current.

"Dame J!" Colin's voice was faint behind her. She kept going, thorns catching at her sleeves as she hurried down the pathways. By the time she reached the cliffs, she was panting for breath and her throat was raw, a stitch cramping her ribs. She saw Rufus on the cliff top, his hair rippling on the wind. Gill and Peta were a few yards away, talking to Adam while Rufus simply waited, looking out to sea. The waves were ferocious. They were all exposed and vulnerable, unaware of Charles bearing down upon them, and no matter how loudly Juliana yelled in warning, she could not make them hear.

Rufus and Adam had left the house quietly, like a pair of brothers or lovers departing after a pleasant family visit. Everything seemed so quiet and peaceful, normal even, as if the preceding drama had never happened. Rufus went to wait on the cliffs, but Adam followed almost at once, apparently deciding there was no need to linger in the house after all. He was dignified, calm.

Gill walked through the garden with him—with Peta a few yards behind at a discreet distance—only to realize that, after all, there was hardly anything to say. They'd said it all last night.

"I almost get the feeling that you *want* this to happen," Gill murmured. "Do you?"

"No, but perhaps it's where I belong after all. As I said, there's no place for me in this new world."

"You haven't even tried! After all your struggles to escape, you're giving up? Look, Rufus's power base has deserted him. If you ran away now, how could he stop you?"

"He'd find someone else to help him plague Juliana. I can't take that risk. Anyway, that's not the point. I made a promise."

"He manipulated you into it."

"I know. Don't you think I manipulated him, too?"

"But you're not his brother!"

Adam shrugged. "As long as he believes I am, I can keep him from harming anyone else." He looked back at the house, the half-wild garden with its rugged rocks and gorse. "I realize now that I said goodbye to all this long ago. No point in lingering. Will you walk all the way with me, you and Peta?"

"Yes, of course. I wish it hadn't come to this."

He smiled. "Because of last night, I can go with a glad heart, Gill. It's not some unknown horror I'm going into. It's only Rufus."

"Perhaps we'll meet again." She shrugged, determined not to start crying. "Who knows?"

Out on Cairndonan Point, a fierce wind was blowing. Gill turned her head, inviting Peta to catch up to them , and the three of them walked slowly together over the rough grass. They glanced at the curving forms of *Midsummer Night* as they passed, Gill half-hoping that Rufus had been drawn in and consumed by Juliana's power—but no. He was already there on the cliff edge, framed against the restless silver of the sea, his hair blowing around him like a banner.

Waiting for Adam.

It was trying to rain, and the tide was high, the swell strong as if the disturbances between Earth and Otherworld had churned it to fury. Seagulls hung on the wind currents. As soon as Adam drew ahead, he was gone from them; such a simple, subtle departure, no goodbyes. Gill watched him and Rufus meet on the edge of the cliff. They must both keep their vows now and there was nothing she could do to change Adam's mind. She wasn't sure she even wanted to. *It's the only ace left in my hand*, he'd said. His decision, his sacrifice, his destiny.

Peta stood arm in arm with her, murmuring about Juliana's husband Charles, how he'd been disgraced, how the news was full of it; Gill tried to listen, but her mind was elsewhere. At some point, either Rufus would take Adam towards the Boundry portal, or she and Peta must accept that it was over and walk away. So, so hard to do it. It felt like abandoning a friend.

A man appeared as if from nowhere, shouting as he bore down on them.

Because of the wind direction, he was only yards behind them before they heard his yells or even noticed his approach. "You! Rufus Hart!" he screamed.

Gill and Peta glanced round. Peta breathed "Oh god, he's here!" Gill recognized Juliana's estranged husband at once from the photos she'd seen: a tall, grey-haired alpha male in an expensive-looking dark overcoat . . . face contorted in snarling fury, and a heavy-duty rifle in his hands.

White panic sheeted her mind. She looked at Rufus and Adam, saw them both turning with startled faces. Rufus began to smile, his expression a characteristic mixture of surprise, recognition, and amusement.

Charles lowered the rifle and fired.

Two shots rang out, deafening. It looked as if he was aiming into thin air but he'd been aiming at Rufus, compensating for the wind; Gill only realized it because, even as he pulled the trigger, Adam stepped in front and took both bullets. He reeled back into Rufus, who clutched wildly at him as the momentum took both men off the cliff edge. Gill screamed. The wind blew through the grass and white gulls continued to wheel and shriek over the cliffs; but the landscape was abruptly empty.

She was sobbing for breath as she reached the cliff edge. She saw Adam on the rocks far below; arms splayed, motionless, broken, surf pounding over him, turning red as it washed away. The wind stole her cries. Rufus lay near him, almost submerged.

Dimly she was aware of shouts behind her, some kind of struggle. It never crossed her mind that she, too, might take a stray bullet. The only thing that mattered was Adam. She had to find a way down . . . but there were hands on her shoulders. Peta was gripping her, physically restraining her from stumbling towards the precarious cliff paths. Below, the sea was throwing itself furiously at the rocks where Adam lay.

Rufus had survived the fall and he was dragging himself over the rough, tilted rocks, seawater pouring from his clothes and hair. She heard his howl of anguish as he reached Adam. And then his voice ran on in an unintelligible babble, fragments of it reaching their ears—imploring Adam to return to life, telling him that he could not, *could not* be dead.

Gill went on struggling against Peta until her strength went and she sank to her knees, staring down at the scene below; Rufus, drenched, spray crashing furiously around him, his hair dripping around him in ropes. He was wrestling now with the body, trying to keep it from slipping out of his arms as the waves fought him for possession.

His raw grief ripped her to pieces.

She felt Peta's arm around her, anchoring her as if to keep her from falling after Adam. Rufus's anguish was unbearable to witness. Who could decree that he deserved it? *No one*, thought Gill, *no one*.

A giant wave burst over the rocks, exploding in foam and tons of surging seawater; and when it subsided, Rufus was still clinging there, but Adam was gone.

23

Winter Came to the Wood

There was nothing they could do. It all happened so fast in the fierce maw of the tide.

Juliana heard the gun go off. She saw Adam jerking backwards into Rufus, both of them falling . . . an incoherent cry came from her throat. She couldn't take in the horror of what she was seeing. Gill and Peta were on the cliff edge, both still in the firing line—then Colin reached Charles and wrested the rifle from him. Charles stumbled backwards and fell as if his strings had been cut.

As Juliana reached him, he was lying propped on one elbow on the grass. She meant to run straight past, but when she saw him, she stopped. Charles's face was blue-grey and ridged with pain, his right fist gripping his left shoulder. Tears oozed from his swollen eyes. "Colin," she called out, "keep that damned gun out of harm's way! Go and see what's happened—" She pointed to the cliff edge. It was all she could do to speak. "Then call an ambulance. I think he's having a heart attack."

"I'm on it," Colin said grimly. After that, she left everything to him.

"Ambulance will be too late," Charles gasped.

"What have you done?" she cried. "You've just killed two people! Why?"

He struggled to speak, his face taut with pain. "Only aiming at him, that bastard, Rufus Hart. He ruined everything. The other one, I didn't mean . . . Mistake. Who was it?"

"It could have been Leon, for all you knew."

"No."

Juliana couldn't even try to explain. "You've shot two people for nothing." She swept away the tears that were soaking her face. "You could have killed us all! How does that help relieve your guilt? Dear god, Charles!"

"Forgive me," he gasped. "The billionaire . . . the one from Dubai, wanted to buy *Midsummer Night*? Not real. Friend of mine, put him up to it."

"I know that, too," she sighed. "I guessed. I'm not as stupid as you think I am, Charles. Never have been."

He gave a weak smile. "Well, now the joke is on me. My will—my solicitors will contact you."

"You're not dead yet." Juliana tried to swallow the painful ache in her throat.

"I'm sorry, Jules. I always loved you, old girl." His forehead was clammy, his face a rictus of pain. "I'm so terribly sorry."

She looked at his distraught face and felt a tug of pity that was slow to fade. "Too late, my dear. You wanted to ruin me and destroy my house! So you got found out and had to fall on your sword, Charles? And now you take the easy way out by dying? Lucky you. No trial for fraud or murder, no prison, no more guilt over a lost child."

"Not just guilt," he said in a thick whisper. "Grief."

The ambulance came surprisingly fast, considering the distance it had had to travel. Charles was unconscious by then, slipping away. Juliana watched as the paramedics worked urgently on him, lifted him into the back of the vehicle with an oxygen mask on his face. When they asked if she wanted to go with him, it came as a shock. She murmured some excuse, that she was no longer his next-of-kin . . . She felt dreadful, letting him go alone, not even holding his hand for that final journey, but how could she leave Cairndonan now? Metal doors slammed and the ambulance sped away, blue lights flashing. Peta and Gill were at her side by then, both shattered yet still as protective as daughters.

Colin had called the coast guard too. He'd simply lied, pretending to be a member of the public who'd seen an unknown man falling from the cliffs. Later, they would hear the drone of the helicopter fading in and out along the coast for hours, but nothing would be found.

To Juliana, he'd told the truth of what happened on Cairndonan Point; that Adam's body had been swept away into the sea, while Rufus had survived. Juliana felt numb, switching into brusque, coping mode because she hardly knew what to feel, how to react. It was too much to bear. They all agreed to say nothing about Adam or Rufus to the police; the rifle had been disarmed and locked away. There was nothing for the authorities or media to know, except that a disgraced government minister had collapsed while visiting his ex-wife . . .

Later, she would receive a call from the hospital to say that Charles had been dead on arrival.

Adam and Charles, both gone. Juliana had developed a healthy loathing for her ex-husband and had barely known Adam at all; she couldn't claim unconditional love for either of them. Yet they had both been part of her.

Strange, Charles had spent years trying to destroy her. Now she was already missing his sharp, cunning wit and their jousting matches. It was hard to imagine a world without his adamantine, amoral power shining in it.

One act of undeserved mercy she performed: as soon as the tide abated, she had Colin and Peta bring the broken survivor, Rufus, up to the house.

"Adam can't have planned what he did," said Gill. She sat shaking under a blanket at the kitchen table. "But the way he stepped out—without a second thought—it was as if he'd rehearsed it, like he'd been waiting for that moment all his life."

"I wish to god I understood why Adam would bother to save Rufus's life after everything he did to him!" said Juliana. "Of all the pointless sacrifices!"

Colin, in a businesslike manner, was making mugs of hot chocolate. He slammed one down in front of Rufus, who was sitting at the far end of the table with a pool of seawater gathering beneath his chair. His face was white under the soaked tangle of hair. He'd let them bring him back to the house but so far he had not uttered a word.

"Adam was so calm last night, so at peace," said Gill. "Happy. I'd never seen him happy before. There was no sign he was likely to do such a thing. Unless that *was* the sign. I don't know."

"Perhaps he decided that the only way to escape Rufus was to die," Peta said bluntly.

"No!" said Gill. "He would never have tried to take his own life. He gave his word to Rufus and he meant to keep it."

Juliana placed a hand over hers. "I suspect Peta's right; he knew no other way to end this. It makes a ghastly kind of sense. He didn't deliberately set out to end his own life, but when the chance presented itself, he took it. Perhaps he meant to take Rufus with him."

"No," said Gill, "he wouldn't do that!"

"Maybe it was because he'd made peace with himself that he decided it was time," Peta said firmly.

"I don't know," said Gill. She felt Rufus's ravaged, dead-fish stare on her as she spoke. "You could be right, but there was more to it than that. He said something last night. Told me he felt he had truly died when he was wounded in the trenches in the First World War, and that he's just been walking around like a ghost ever since. He said he didn't feel part of the world anymore. He stepped into the line of fire because he's brave. He saved Rufus without thinking twice. It was just what he had to do."

"Finishing what he believed should have finished ninety-odd years ago?" asked Juliana.

"Yes." Gill was suddenly arrested by the memory of Adam's serene expression, the limpid gleam of his eyes, every look, every word he'd said taking on new significance. His insistence that this new, unfamiliar world held no future for him . . . Still she wished with all her heart and soul that it hadn't happened. "Who could blame him?"

"I blame him," Rufus murmured under his breath. "Self-pitying idiot!"

"Don't call him that!" Gill said, shocked.

"I do call him an idiot! There was no need for him to martyr himself for me. Chances are those bullets would have passed straight through me and I would have laughed in Charles's arrogant face. But no, he has to be the hero. I don't know who was the greater fool, Leith or Mistangamesh himself; both as stubborn as hell. Not that anyone in this room can understand."

"I still say you had a case of mistaken identity," said Gill, "and tormented an innocent young man into madness."

"You don't understand," Rufus whispered.

Juliana turned on him and said, "What did you do to my husband, Rufus?"

"Exactly what I said I could," he hissed, a poisonous light in his eyes. "A shame you failed to warn me that Charles was a gun-toting maniac. Excuse me if I can't commiserate with your loss. Oh, how lucky for him to drop dead! If he'd lived, the very pits of Naamon would have been too good for him. He slew my Leith."

Then Rufus's brief flare of energy failed. His face the color of dust, he swayed where he sat, and dropped his head into his hands.

After a brief silence, Peta asked, "Are you going to speak to the police, Dame J?"

"And say what?" Juliana released a heavy breath. "A young man who hasn't been seen for ninety years has been shot dead and vanished over a cliff? If the coast guard find nothing, they'll think it's a hoax and I'll make a large, anonymous donation to their funds. But I cannot face the police just yet."

"No no no," Colin put in. "No police. That's the last thing we need."

Juliana continued, "When the tide brings his body to shore, it may be many miles from here . . . when it happens, then we'll decide. If we lay claim to him, we'll find ourselves facing a great many questions . . . but then, at least, we can give him the sendoff he deserves."

"Unless the ocean has claimed him for itself," Rufus said, his voice husky.

"Rufus," Juliana said coolly, "It goes without saying that I don't want you here. However, my conscience won't let me throw you out in this miserable condition. You can stay here—"

"Dame J!" Colin began in horror, but she waved down his protest.

"*Just* until you've decided where to take your wretched self—but let me tell you it had better not be within five hundred miles of here or Boundry."

"You know how deep it cuts, don't you?" said Rufus with a grim laugh. "Being offered kindness by your enemies?"

"Are we enemies?" asked Juliana. "Family, surely. Colin, take him to one of the guest rooms. Dry him and put him to bed."

Rufus's head drooped and he swayed, close to collapse. When she signaled Colin to help him up, he didn't protest, but let himself be guided out of the kitchen. Gill went with them, obscurely worried that either man might launch an attack on the other. Nothing happened, though; Colin simply looked pained, and Rufus staggered like a drunk in his grasp.

In the hallway, at the foot of the stairs, Rufus halted and stared up at the great stained glass window. The masculine forms of two finely built young men, as graceful as angels, were skilfully delineated by lead-lines; the bowman with his red-tinged hair and bowed head; the slain victim lying prostrate, dark hair spilling around him. "That was not exactly how it happened," he whispered, "but close. Very close."

After her conversation with Megan, Juliana put down the phone. It was done. A benefactor was to buy *Midsummer Night* and place it on permanent public display at a sculpture garden in the north of England. It was not the highest of the genuine offers she had received, but it was the most sound, and more than enough to pay off all her creditors and to begin to live again. She'd saved herself on the precipice. Cairndonan's future was secure—for her, and one day, if she wanted it, for Gill.

Some days had passed and Rufus remained in one of her guest rooms, refusing to eat, a pallid doppelganger of his former self. No one could help him, it seemed. Who would dream that he could be so felled by grief, after all he'd done? She didn't want to pity him, but it was impossible not to. The loss of Adam had devastated everyone.

Ned Badger hadn't yet carried out his decision to leave, and she'd let the matter rest for the time being. On the fourth evening, she worked up the nerve to ask him exactly what he had meant about Leon's fate.

She'd been putting off the moment, fearing that it might lead to another argument, more recriminations; dreading the truth. Instead, it seemed their anger had burned out and they were calm, even cordial. Grim-faced, Ned simply nodded and suggested that she put on a coat and sturdy boots. Then he led her through tangled woodland to the center of the old ruined watermill.

In his right hand he held the alicorn that Gill had relinquished to him.

He was also carrying a flashlight, and a canvas bag folded flat under his left arm. The sight of it chilled her. Juliana found the ruins unspeakably desolate, with the looming, overgrown walls like some desecrated abbey. The doorway opposite hung like a surreal painting: an oblong of green, framing an albino horse that stood on the far bank of the river. It was Chamberlain, standing patiently in the meadow opposite as if waiting for Rufus to return.

Ned carefully picked his way over the rubble, giving Juliana a hand where the going was precarious. It would have been easy to step into a weed-covered gap and break an ankle. He brought her to a millstone that lay tilted against a wall, partly shrouded in ivy and brambles.

"This is where I found the child," he said, his eyes white-ringed in the gloom. "Beside this stone."

"What happened?" She could barely keep her voice steady.

Then at last she saw his composure dissolving. He began to tremble. "Flora said he'd had a fever. Perhaps he was delirious when he left the house, dreaming that the *Dubh Sidhe* were calling him . . . we can't know. He must have tripped and taken a blow to the head; he was dead when I found him, poor bairn." His voice became ragged, while Juliana listened in growing horror. "I let the millstone become his tomb. I pushed his body beneath it."

She shuddered at the image. "Why didn't you tell anyone?"

"I meant to!" The words were a snarl of pain. "But I panicked. I thought if I told anyone, the telling would make his death real. But if I kept it secret—then I could believe it was only some bad dream. I could believe that the *Dubh Sidhe* might still come and take him, that he'd live again in the Otherworld. Later I put the alicorn across the doorway to protect him. That's why it was there. To show them where to find him."

"Oh, my god, Ned. Were you out of your mind?"

"Of course! Weren't we all? But wasn't it better for us to believe he'd been stolen by the dark ones?"

"No! The hope was false!"

"Yet the hope kept Flora alive," he said darkly. "Maybe I did wrong, but at the time it made sense. I only meant to protect us all. I feared, too, that if the body was discovered, they'd suspect Flora or me of killing him."

"And did you?" she whispered.

"No. It happened as I'm telling you."

"Ned!"

Tears dripped down the pinched face. "What do you wish to hear, that Flora or I suffocated him? They used to put out unwanted children to die, did they not?" His voice was anguished, barely audible. "The existence of that boy caused you such agony! Flora loved the child in her way, but you've no idea how bitterly she hated the way your husband used her to bear a son. She was ill enough that I worried people might suspect her. But she was innocent. Or guilty of nothing more than leaving a door unlocked. If *that* was done on purpose, I can't say." He stopped, clearly drained.

"Then I take you at your word." Juliana fell silent, listening to the sounds of the wood: branches creaking, birdsong. "I don't blame Flora. She was unwell, as you say, and we were all to blame for not taking better care, Charles and myself most of all. But I still can't believe you left poor Leon out here alone."

"No more alone than he was in the rest of his short life," he said roughly. "I can't excuse what I did. But it still seems to me the only thing I could have done at the time."

Then Ned knelt down beside the millstone and began pulling ropes of ivy away from the gap beneath it. Juliana helped, feeling complicit in the act as if caught in a horror film. Blood dripped where they caught themselves on brambles. At last the gap was clear and he shone the flashlight in, revealing . . . more heaped rubble, a dusty layer of leaf mold and cobwebs. She stared, waves of dread rising horribly through her. Nothing.

Then she saw a dull gleam, like a knurl of burnished wood.

Ned scooped away the thick debris, and there lay the skeleton. She almost hadn't believed him until she saw for herself. The tiny bones had turned yellowish-brown with exposure. The rounded skull looked so small.

Juliana turned away and wept.

They were both quiet for a time, heads bowed, tears falling. Eventually, Juliana sighed and murmured, "He should have a proper burial."

"Yes. A proper grave, marked with stones, and the ivory horn at its head to guard him."

"But we'll do it privately," she added. "I am not involving the authorities. It would be grotesque."

Saying nothing, Ned gathered up the bones of the skeleton one by one and placed them into the canvas bag, the skull last. He did so with all the reverence of an undertaker . . . indeed, he had always so resembled an undertaker that Juliana felt a morbid smile pulling at her mouth. "What are you going to do?" she asked.

"I am going to take him with me." He rose, his head bowed.

"Where? Ned, you don't have to resign. I'm aghast at what you did and yet I can see you acted out of some mistaken idea of 'protecting' us, not out of malice. I can't be angry any more. Stay with me. I need you."

He raised his head, looking squarely at her. "Thank you, Dame Juliana, but it's time for me to go. Chamberlain is waiting. I need to see what lies beyond."

He pointed at the horse and at the green meadow beyond, where the path to Boundry lay. "Why?" she asked.

"I've feared the Otherworld for too long. Perhaps I feared it because I always knew it would claim me."

She let him go, observing as he walked across the planks over the mill-race and vaulted onto Chamberlain's back, then carefully positioned the bag containing Leon's tiny skeleton before him on the horse's withers, the bone staff held across it. Juliana watched, realizing that for all the time she'd lived here, she had never entered Boundry.

"Ned, wait," she called, hurrying towards him. "Is there room up there for an extra passenger?"

The horse needed no guidance to find his way home. Placidly he trod the route along the meadow's edge and across the stone circle. A drowsy light dusted their way, and Juliana noticed the bluish shimmer of the stones. They passed along a tunnel of greenery and between two black sentinels half-hidden in the long grass.

Juliana rode behind Ned, sitting sideways with one hand on his waist to steady herself. The horse's rump was warm, broad and safe beneath her. An image of herself as Queen of Elfland fleeted through her mind, making her smile. At this moment, that was how she felt.

This place was Naamon's opposite, with no boiling lava or terrifying chasms. Instead the landscape lay serene under the molten light of the sun. They rode through orchards where the lacy foliage glowed spring green and each fruit shone like a jewel. The dwellings were the same honey color as the astonishing sun. White mountains floated along a strange horizon that seemed to curve the wrong way, fraying into the deep blue sky as if melting into other, unseen dimensions. She saw the violet-blue lake, as Gill had described. Two long-legged grey herons skimmed the lake's surface. Nothing else stirred.

With tears running down her face, Juliana watched all this beauty taking shape around them.

"This was always here, and we never knew?" she whispered.

"We knew," Ned said quietly, "but how to find a way in, until your niece came? And would we have dared?"

"Where shall we lay the bones to rest?"

"A long way farther in yet," said Ned. "I'll know the place when I see it."

How far? Juliana wondered with a pang. It would be so easy and mesmerizing to continue this soporific ride onwards forever into the heart of the Spiral, she thought. But wouldn't there come a moment when they or the horse grew tired? Then they must dismount, find food and a place to rest—and all the concerns of everyday life would kick in again. Then what?

The alternative—that they could ride forever without fatigue or hunger—would mean that this was a kind of dream. Or even that it was an actual afterlife.

Too strange.

"Ned, stop!" she exclaimed.

She saw, to their right, a broad green rise with a house of mellow ochre stone along one side—and at the top, a gigantic angel of indigo-black stone. "Look at that! Take me closer."

Ever obedient, Ned turned Chamberlain and brought them to the statue. Juliana slid to the ground and stood gazing upward. Gill had described the creation, but its reality was breathtaking. Juliana walked all around its base, sliding her hand over its glassy contours, staring at the serene, featureless face far above. Ned sat patiently with one hand holding the bag and the staff on Chamberlain's withers, waiting for her.

"This dwarfs anything I've attempted," she said at last. "How did they create such a thing, and how did they transport it here?" She rested her hands on the cool surface. The stars glinting inside the inky surface made her feel she was looking into another universe. "It's like a kind of obsidian. Or like the night sky made solid. Perhaps the Aelyr don't need crude tools and materials to create such objects. They must manipulate reality through sheer willpower. Everything human artists try to create is a primitive imitation." She laughed. "I'm an ape, imitating angels!"

Yet her fingers were itching to hold a chisel and hammer poised over a raw block of limestone. The urge to create never left her.

She fell to her knees, head bent in quiet tribute to those who were gone. She reached out with a finger to inscribe their names on the base, one below the other, like the names of the war dead. A schoolgirl gesture, she thought, like writing on a steamy mirror. Leon. Adam-Leith. Cora. Melody. Flora. Charles.

Yes, even Charles.

Where she'd expected to see faint oil-smears from her fingertip, the names appeared as if they'd been engraved deep into the stone.

Then she rose, brushing down her skirts, and looked up at Ned Badger. "You will take care of Leon?"

"Yes." He inclined his head, the loyal manservant again. "It's my last duty."

"Thank you," she said, resting one hand on Chamberlain's neck. "We must part company here. I'm going back now."

He looked steadily at her, as if he'd been expecting this. Disappointed, but not surprised. "Great wonders may lie deeper in."

"Yours, not mine."

"I doubt this chance will come again." She realized his words weren't meant to persuade, but to warn. "The portal won't stay open indefinitely. Aetherials will come and close it against humans. If you go back, Dame Juliana, there may never be another chance."

"I know that. But the wonders are for you, my dear Ned, not for me. My life is on the surface world, and I have work to do."

He acknowledged her decision with a formal inclination of his head. That was all; they'd already said their real goodbyes in the mill. She watched for a few minutes as Chamberlain's big pale form dwindled towards the lake's edge; all the time she was wondering who Ned Badger really was. Then she took a last look at the statue, and began to retrace her steps towards Cairndonan.

Juliana took a slow walk back through the woods, cutting towards the clifftops where *Midsummer Night* stood. The sculpture-forest was luminous in the gloom. Soon it would be gone, painstakingly wrapped, removed by crane and transported by truck to its new home. It would be so strange to live without it—like having her heart torn out. It was time, though. It was the end of an era, the beginning of a new phase.

Juliana approached the statue at the center, *Winter Came to the Wood*. This figure was the most human of the group, the hardest of all to part with. None of Rufus's followers had been trapped within it, and yet there was *something* inside, some ill-defined spirit or essence. She reached up to stroke the high white cheekbone, icy marble under her fingertips. "Who are you, what do you want with me?"

Suddenly a wind was whirling around her. The world tilted. An immense weight was bearing down . . . the statue itself was falling, all its mass crushing her, trapping her like Leon beneath the millstone . . .

She lost consciousness for a moment; either that, or pure shock lifted her into a trance state in which she entered another plane, an Aetheric plane. She saw the truth then. So many delusions.

No Aetherial had taken little Leon, nor given her arcane powers in return. The child had simply wandered away and died. Misadventure. There had been no evil bargain; it had been a dream, a symbolic interpretation of her own guilt. The statue did not represent her dream lover; the essence that dwelt within it was a wild, untamed thing, barely even aware of her existence. It raged around her, pulling itself out of the statue, gone.

She came back to reality, finding herself on her knees on the bark path. *Winter* had not fallen. With its blank marble eyes, it stood watching serenely from the heart of her petrified wood, changeless and eternal.

Rufus kept himself to the room Juliana had given him, emerging now and then to wander the corridors as if in a trance. His presence was unutterably disturbing, yet Gill couldn't help but feel sorry for him. However wickedly he'd behaved, it was hard to see anyone so broken. It wasn't in her to rejoice at his downfall.

She was spending most of the time with Peta, idling about, eating, strolling, taking photographs and talking. Recovering. There was no question of leaving Juliana alone while Rufus was still here, but they'd begun to talk about what they might do next. "Treat this place as your home," Juliana had said. "You'll probably get the bloody place in my will, anyway."

The thought scared Gill a little.

"I've always had this idle fantasy about going back to India," she told Peta. "I'd love to see my grandfather again, if he's still alive."

"Why not do it, then?" said Peta. "We could both go, if you fancy some company?"

A thrill of hope stirred in Gill. It would be a new start. It felt unexpectedly warming to think that her friendship with Peta might be permanent. She'd never had a truly close female friend before. She smiled and said, "As long as I can still borrow your camera?"

And so she began to think of packing and leaving Robin Cottage. It was Peta, helping her to tidy up, who found a scrap of paper discarded behind the sofa. "Don't throw that away!" Gill cried, spotting her about to drop it into a waste paper bin. "What does it say?"

Peta unfolded it. "It's an equation."

"What?" Gill took it from her and saw that Adam had written, "R+C=J." She laughed, tears springing into her eyes. "It's Adam's betting slip."

"Eh? You've lost me."

"Corah's letter. Her invitation to take a guess at what the letter would say?"

"Oh," said Peta, catching onto what she meant. "Ah, I *see*. The initials of the main players. He got it!"

"Yes, but he was too tactful to write anything blatant so this was the most he dared suggest. Don't tell Juliana."

"That's too funny," said Peta. "All the same, I really don't think Corah would have paid out winnings on the strength of it. I think Adam had quite a wicked sense of humor, underneath everything."

"He did," Gill agreed. "Oh, he looked like a choir boy but he really wasn't."

"Gill, you hadn't . . . fallen for him, had you?"

"No," she sighed. "No. I got right to the brink of it, but I couldn't let myself go over. And I didn't. It felt right that we . . . had that time together, but I knew it wasn't meant to last. It was about us helping each other to heal. And I liked him so much. He was so gentle, such a *gentleman*, and so beautiful . . ."

She couldn't go on.

"They don't make 'em like that anymore," Peta said sadly. "That's a fact."

Last of all, Gill plucked two masks from their place in the vase: her own, and the one Peta had made for Adam, that he'd left behind. "Peta," Gill said lightly, "Have you made some changes to these?"

"Haven't touched them since I gave them to you," Peta answered. "Why?"

The stark black goggles were gone from Adam's mask; instead it showed gentle eyes peering through a veil of ivy. On Gill's, the red crystals now appeared as exotic decoration rather than bloody tears. The expression was serene, the mouth parted in a slight smile. "It's just that . . . never mind."

"Oh, that," Peta said with a soft laugh. "It happens, with no help from me."

Later, they walked along the beach together, the shoreline a broad flat curve of liquid gold. Gill dropped her head back and drew in breaths of pungent, salty air. The sky above was pure blue. The cliffs of Cairndonan Point and the tall grey walls of the islands out to sea were timeless; she imagined their roots reaching deep into the Otherworld.

Taking the camera from her pocket, she captured a shot of Peta with scarf and red hair flying, half-turning with the beach behind her. Out to sea, Gill saw the black dot of a seal swimming through the waves. It was hard for her to be on the beach without thinking of Adam; every time she saw a sleek dark head on the tide she would wonder, *Could it be . . . ?*

She would hold this place, full of pain and wonder, inside her forever.

Their walk brought them up the cliff path, through the gardens and around the house to the front drive, where Colin and Juliana stood, waving to a retreating black Mercedes. Charles's red Lamborghini was still parked crookedly with its top down, just as he'd abandoned it.

"That was Charles's solicitor," Juliana said, indicating the departing car as she saw Gill and Peta. "Just keeping me informed regarding legal things; decent of him to make the journey, really."

"Will you be going to Charles's funeral?" Gill asked.

Juliana grimaced. "I suppose I shall. Apparently he left everything to me in his will. Which amounts to precisely nothing, thanks to the massive question mark over his personal fortune. His estate's been seized by the court. Even his pulling wagon belongs to them now. That's all right; I never wanted money from him. Certainly don't need it."

There were soft footfalls on the gravel drive behind them. They turned to see Rufus emerging from the house with his usual easy grace, a long brown raincoat flaring like a cloak around his legs as he approached. It looked like a garment Charles might have left behind, years ago, and yet it suited him. He seemed different; his face was pale yet radiant, the rat's-tail hair now silky smooth again, his eyes soft and grave.

Colin started towards him, braced for a confrontation, but Juliana put out a hand to stop him.

"Rufus," she said delicately. "I hope this means you're ready to, ah, move on?"

His perfectly-shaped mouth curved into a smile. "Isn't this what you desired?" He gestured in the direction the solicitor had taken. "The beast slain?"

Juliana's color rose. "I never intended any harm to Charles! It was idle talk, Rufus. We made no bargain. I never meant you to . . ."

"But when you deal with the faerie folk, my daughter, you have to take very great care indeed." His eyebrows rose, teasing and sinister. "You can't trust us. We may decide to take 'maybe' as 'yes.' I told you I could bring down governments, Juliana. After all, I've had thousands of years of practice. It's what I do. Aren't you going to thank me?"

They all stared speechless at him.

Rufus sighed, pushed his hands into his coat pockets and shook back his hair, looking at the sky. Without effort, he held their attention. There was an unfailing glory in his dishevelled beauty. "You also can't say I haven't been punished," he said. "It was always going to burn me, one day. There's no pleasure, no purpose in anything without Leith. We *still* have unfinished business, Mist, my brother."

Tears ran down his upturned face. Gill felt her own eyes stinging, despite herself. Rufus went on. "Everything I fought for . . . none of it has meaning anymore." He breathed softly in and out. His expression was composed, his skin the color of old ivory, translucent, calm, empty. "It's a little late for me to become a reformed character, I fear. So, I'll go away, find some high place like Lashtor to be alone, meditate upon the folly of my entire existence until I fade into the Spiral itself. Perhaps Mistangamesh will be waiting for me there."

He lowered his head, looking at them from sad, sober eyes. "All things come to an end. The game with Charles was my last. I don't ask forgiveness, but I hope you derived a little entertainment from it, so that it wasn't all for nothing. But now, like him, I'm finished. All games are over."

"Seriously?" said Gill.

"No," said Rufus, a manic grin breaking across his face. "Just kidding."

With that, he ran and vaulted into Charles's car, landing in the driver's seat. The engine woke with an enormous roar. Then the Lamborghini lurched forward, scattering them all as it gouged a deep parabola in the gravel. It shook and throbbed, the tailpipe blowing out fumes like Mount Khafet. The tail swayed as Rufus completed the turn, grinning at them over the steering wheel as he gunned the vehicle onto the straight of the driveway. His hand shot into the air as he rocketed past them, calling out, "Farewell, losers!" as he went.

"Bloody hell!" cried Juliana. "Why didn't someone take the ruddy keys out of the ignition?"

"Can he even drive?" Peta exclaimed. "Ohh . . . if not, he's a fast learner."

Colin actually ran a few hopeless steps after him, only to be sprayed with gravel and exhaust fumes as the vehicle roared away. He skidded to a halt, cursing.

Juliana called, "Colin, is the main gate still open?"

"Yeah, course it is! I opened it for the bloody solicitor!"

"Oh," she said. The Lamborghini vanished from sight, its jubilant roar dwindling into the distance. There on the driveway, Juliana sank down into a crouch, put her head in her hands, and laughed until she cried.

Later, she sat at her dressing table with a glass of red wine at her elbow. In front of her lay the last item Ned had left for her; the large black-and-white photograph that John Montague had taken on the Night of the *Dunkelmen*. That last, telling image.

Except it told her very little. Ned's attached note explained that the plate had not been developed until some years later, by which time the negative was badly degraded. The print made from it showed hints of a ghostly forest, overexposed by the magnesium flash and full of blurred movement. A blotchy grey fog of age and damage veiled everything. Hopeless.

Yet if Juliana half-closed her eyes, she fancied she could make out Corah's wide-eyed expression in the shadow of her hood—and Rufus's face beside hers, staring straight at the camera lens. She could have sworn he was winking.

When she fully opened her eyes again, there was nothing to see but grainy swirls. She sighed.

Ned had also brought to light some dusty boxes: a whole archive of John's work that she assumed had been lost years ago. Later she would en-joy examining those images, trying to piece together his story—to discover whether he had truly caught the *Dunkelmen* in action. For now, though, that pleasure could wait.

"Sculpting beauty from stone is all very well," she said, looking into the dressing table mirror as she picked up her glass of wine. "but I need someone of flesh and blood."

"Don't we all," said Corah's soft, smoky voice behind her.

"I don't know if you're the best or the worst person to advise me," Juliana responded with a laugh. "Dare I give Colin a chance? He's so much younger than me . . ."

"So?" Corah smiled. Her mouth was almost black against the powder-white face. "I highly recommend a younger man, if you need someone who can keep up with you. Look at you, so beautiful: human, and yet glowing with all that Aetherial blood."

"It was Rufus, wasn't it? The stage performer you met just before the war, according to your letter? It was really him."

"Would I lie to you, darling? I know everyone thinks I'm mad, but I've never been dishonest, with you or with myself. What happened, happened. Of course you should give your Colin a go. He worships you! Take a risk, Juliana. Live."

Softly she asked, "What about Adam? Is he there with you?"

"Adam is fine, darling," the apparition said enigmatically. "He is always with me."

When Corah faded, it felt like a parting. Juliana drew and released her breath. No more tears; it was a time for plans, contemplation, a new start. *I'm going to do it,* she thought. *Open Cairndonan to any and all students who wish to come here. Open my frozen old heart to Colin and test his ardor. Unleash my inner Corah!*

She raised her glass and said out loud, "Here's to you, my crazy mother and my devil of an impossibly old, impossibly ageless father. This is what you made between you. This grey-haired, mad artist. And I'll tell you now, I'm not finished yet."

The reflection in the mirror had a golden glow, eyes alight with passion, her hair glittering softly silver. Not young, never that again, but ageless, even a little glamorous.

"Not bad," Juliana told her reflection. "Not bad at all for your age, you old tart."

Epilogue

The ocean rolled him in its murky deeps. Like flotsam he sank among driftwood and tangles of sea-wrack, amid discarded bottles and the empty shells of sea urchins and clams. At the tide's mercy, he ebbed and flowed with the sliding sands of the sea-bed.

The current could wash up his bloated corpse somewhere along the coast, or it could lose him forever in the deep trenches of the Atlantic. The story ended here, in peace. And it didn't seem strange that he was somehow still *aware* of it.

At the same time, he was within a statue at the heart of a pale stone forest. He had dwelled here forever, timeless.

Another aspect of him, his shadow-self, existed in a high, stony realm in another plane, watching and waiting.

It felt natural to be in several places at once. The resting soul-essence of each Aelyr spread through all points of space and eternity. A multitude of lives flickered around him, like the rippling heat haze above a burning city. He observed it all without emotion.

Then came the wrench.

From somewhere deep in the Spiral his *fylgia* shrilled a warning and his soul-essence woke, bursting from his wintry stone cocoon like a storm. The scattered parts of his being all rushed towards each other.

In a blinding moment like the birth of a star, spirit and body fused.

Then he felt the weight of the ocean on him, the intense cold. Water roared in his ears as he pushed up through the surging foam. Air hit his lungs and he coughed, exploding into a world of violent sensation and pain. At that moment, there was nothing in his mind except the pure knowledge of who he was; that he was reborn and had no choice but to survive.

Mistangamesh first relearned how to breathe. Then he began to swim.

A long time later, the calm sea broke into a mosaic of light as a head emerged. As sleek as a seal, the swimmer approached the shore along the golden path made by the setting sun. When his feet met firm sand, he staggered upright and began to wade through the waves, water rolling from his sodden black hair, seaweed trailing from him.

The wide shining flats of sand were empty. No one saw him. The beach on which he'd washed up might be the one he'd left, or it might be on the other side of the world; he couldn't tell.

Mistangamesh stood at the edge of the tide, his long reflection suspended in the wet sand. He looked up at a wall of cliffs, at seabirds wheeling against the golden sky. He was exhausted, but he was Aelyr once more, clear-sighted, powerful.

Washed clean by the sea.

Memories had surfaced during his long swim. They were grainy, like a silent film projected onto fog—lives lived by someone else—yet he could call on them if needed. He remembered everything. Adam . . . Juliana . . . Gill . . . everyone.

Rufus.

The thought of his brother struck him like a hard, bright light. So vivid, the cruel, beautiful face that had teased and tormented him down the ages. Their endless feud. Their failure to go their separate ways, Mist because he felt responsibility to protect human innocents from his brother, Rufus because his greatest delight was to control and torment Mist.

Obsession, tangled in coils of love and loathing.

So many images of pain and betrayal . . . until Rufus's mischief had spilled into tragedy, and caused both Mist and the human woman whom Mist had loved, to be violently slain.

Wracked with grief and guilt, Rufus had spent the intervening years trying to bring his brother back to life. Mist, however, could not forgive him. He refused to be found.

He remembered shock, blood and grief . . . blackness as his soul-essence fled into the heart of the Spiral . . . and then a decision to stay in elemental form forever. Rufus would never torment him again. The game was over.

And yet here he was: alive once more, in the form that had belonged to the hapless, innocent Adam. He could remember being Adam . . . but Adam, or Leith, was not *him*. Mist groaned, put his hands to his eyes then pushed back the soaking mass of his hair. Water fell from him in drops of molten gold.

Mist couldn't explain how he'd been reborn in human shape as Adam, with no Aelyr awareness. He had no idea how his Aetherial soul-essence had drifted to Cairndonan and seeped into the statue, *Winter Came to the Wood*. It was as if he'd been drawn towards Rufus against his will. Nor could he explain how Rufus had found Adam and recognized him as his brother in slumbering form.

There was no excuse for Rufus's brutal treatment of Adam, except for his sheer desperation to shock Mist "awake." For Rufus, that was motive enough. And he had, after all, been right all along.

Yet there was something that Rufus had never understood.

For all his cunning, he'd never worked out that Mistangamesh could not reawaken until Adam actually *died*. He'd been blind to the fact that Mist's essence was hidden inside *Winter*. And more—it had never crossed his mind that Mist could not resurface until Rufus had relinquished his claim.

Mist realized then that he had finally, completely escaped from Rufus.

He was free to walk away into a new and different life.

"No, not free," he said to the sky. "As long as Rufus is out in the world, it's still my duty to find him and stop him. It was my last promise to our father . . . but wouldn't Father release me from the promise, after all this time? Haven't I tried enough? This time I could walk away."

One thing was new. He had never had the choice before.

Mistangamesh had been in limbo too long. It felt so good to be alive. Relishing every sensation—even the damp cling of his clothes, and the feel of a sea-breeze drying the salt on his skin—he stood poised on the threshold between land and sea, between surface world and Spiral, life and death.

He turned, and began to walk along the shore.

About the Author

Freda Warrington grew up in Leicestershire, England. She spent her first years out of school as a graphic designer and illustrator and eventually became a full-time writer. She began writing short stories at a very early age, and by nineteen she had her first novel well under way. She has written nineteen novels, including the Jewelfire trilogy and the Blood Wine sequence, all of which have been published in the United Kingdom *Midsummer Night* is the second of her Aetherial Tales novels, and her second book to be published in the United States. The first of the Aetherial Tales, *Elfand*, won the Romantic Times Best Fantasy Award. Learn more at www.fredawarrington.com.